THE
CAMBRIDGE EDITION
THE LETTERS AND
D. H. LAWRENCE

THE WORKS OF D. H. LAWRENCE

GENERAL EDITORS
James T. Boulton
† Warren Roberts

SONS AND LOVERS
Part I

D. H. LAWRENCE

EDITED BY

HELEN BARON

AND

CARL BARON

CAMBRIDGE
UNIVERSITY PRESS

PUBLISHED BY THE PRESS SYNDICATE OF THE UNIVERSITY OF CAMBRIDGE
The Pitt Building, Trumpington Street, Cambridge, United Kingdom

CAMBRIDGE UNIVERSITY PRESS
The Edinburgh Building, Cambridge CB2 2RU, UK
40 West 20th Street, New York NY 10011–4211, USA
10 Stamford Road, Oakleigh, VIC 3166, Australia
Ruiz de Alarcón 13, 28014 Madrid, Spain
Dock House, The Waterfront, Cape Town 8001, South Africa

http://www.cambridge.org

This, the Cambridge Edition of the text of *Sons and Lovers* now correctly established from the original sources and first published in 1992, © the Estate of Frieda Lawrence Ravagli 1992. Introduction and notes © Cambridge University Press 1992. Permission to reproduce this text entire or in part, or to quote from it, can be granted only by the Literary Executor of the Estate, Laurence Pollinger Ltd, 18 Maddox Street, Mayfair, London W1R 0EU. Permission to reproduce the introduction and notes entire or in part should be requested from Cambridge University Press. Acknowledgement is made to William Heinemann Ltd in the UK and the Viking Press in the USA, who hold the exclusive book publication rights for the work as published (copyright 1913) in their respective territories, for the authorisation granted to Cambridge University Press through the Frieda Lawrence Ravagli Estate for use of the work as published in preparing the new scholarly text.

Reprinted 1993
First published in paperback 2002

A catalogue record for this book is available from the British Library

Library of Congress cataloguing in publication data
Lawrence, D. H. (David Herbert), 1885–1930.
Sons and lovers / D. H. Lawrence: edited by
Helen Baron and Carl Baron
p.   cm. – (The Cambridge edition of the letters and works of D. H. Lawrence)
ISBN 0-521-24276-2
I. Baron, Helen. II. Baron, Carl. III. Title.
IV. Series: Lawrence, D. H. (David Herbert), 1885–1930. Works. 1979.
PR6023.A93S6   1992   823′.912 – dc20   91-12669 CIP

ISBN 0 521 24276 2 hardback
ISBN 0 521 00718 6 paperback (in 2 parts)

Part 1 of a 2 part set. Not sold separately

CONTENTS

General editors' preface   *page* vii

Acknowledgements   ix

Chronology   xi

Cue-titles   xvi

Introduction   xix

    The composition of *Sons and Lovers*: origins   xxi

    'Paul Morel' (first version, October to November or

        December 1910)   xxiv

    'Paul Morel' (second version, *c.* 13 March to mid-July 1911)   xxviii

    'Paul Morel' (third version, 3–15 November 1911,

        February–April 1912, revised May–June 1912)   xxxi

    Sons and Lovers (fourth version, July–November 1912)   xxxix

    Edward Garnett's editing of the novel   xlix

    Lawrence's 'Foreword'   l

    The period of printing and proof revision (January–April 1913)   liii

    Ernest Collings and the design of the dust-jacket   lv

    The contract   lvi

    Jessie Chambers's novel   lvii

    The first edition   lix

    The American edition   lx

    Reception   lxiii

Contents

Text | lxxi

  The surviving manuscripts | lxxi
  The galley proofs | lxxii
  The page proofs | lxxviii
  The Cambridge edition | lxxviii

SONS AND LOVERS | 1

Appendixes

  I Foreword to *Sons and Lovers* | 465
  II Locations | 475

Explanatory notes | 507

Glossary | 581

Textual apparatus | 589

  Line-end hyphenation | 674

A note on pounds, shillings and pence | 675

GENERAL EDITORS' PREFACE

D. H. Lawrence is one of the great writers of the twentieth century – yet the texts of his writings, whether published during his lifetime or since, are, for the most part, textually corrupt. The extent of the corruption is remarkable; it can derive from every stage of composition and publication. We know from study of his MSS that Lawrence was a careful writer, though not rigidly consistent in matters of minor convention. We know also that he revised at every possible stage. Yet he rarely if ever compared one stage with the previous one, and overlooked the errors of typists or copyists. He was forced to accept, as most authors are, the often stringent house-styling of his printers, which overrode his punctuation and even his sentence-structure and paragraphing. He sometimes overlooked plausible printing errors. More important, as a professional author living by his pen, he had to accept, with more or less good will, stringent editing by a publisher's reader in his early days, and at all times the results of his publishers' timidity. So the fear of Grundyish disapproval, or actual legal action, led to bowdlerisation or censorship from the very beginning of his career. Threats of libel suits produced other changes. Sometimes a publisher made more changes than he admitted to Lawrence. On a number of occasions in dealing with American and British publishers Lawrence produced texts for both which were not identical. Then there were extraordinary lapses like the occasion when a typist turned over two pages of MS at once, and the result happened to make sense. This whole story can be reconstructed from the introductions to the volumes in this edition; cumulatively they will form a history of Lawrence's writing career.

The Cambridge edition aims to provide texts which are as close as can now be determined to those he would have wished to see printed. They have been established by a rigorous collation of extant manuscripts and typescripts, proofs and early printed versions; they restore the words, sentences, even whole pages omitted or falsified by editors or compositors; they are freed from printing-house conventions which were imposed on Lawrence's style; and interference on the part of frightened publishers has been eliminated. Far from doing violence to the texts Lawrence would have wished to see published, editorial intervention is essential to recover them. Though we have to accept that some cannot now be recovered in their entirety because early states have not survived, we must be glad that so much evidence remains. Paradoxical as it may seem, the outcome of this recension will be texts which differ, often radically and certainly frequently, from those seen by the author himself.

Editors have adopted the principle that the most authoritative form of the text is to be followed, even if this leads sometimes to a 'spoken' or a 'manuscript' rather than a 'printed' style. We have not wanted to strip off one house-styling in order to impose another. Editorial discretion may be allowed in order to regularise Lawrence's sometimes wayward spelling and punctuation in accordance with his most frequent practice in a particular text. A detailed record of these and other decisions on textual matters, together with the evidence on which they are based, will be found in the textual apparatus which records variant readings in manuscripts, typescripts and proofs; and printed variants in forms of the text published in Lawrence's lifetime. We do not record posthumous corruptions, except where first publication was posthumous. Significant deleted MS readings may be found in the occasional explanatory note.

In each volume, the editor's introduction relates the contents to Lawrence's life and to his other writings; it gives the history of composition of the text in some detail, for its intrinsic interest, and because this history is essential to the statement of editorial principles followed. It provides an account of publication and reception which will be found to contain a good deal of hitherto unknown information. Where appropriate, appendixes make available extended draft manuscript readings of significance, or important material, sometimes unpublished, associated with a particular work.

Though Lawrence is a twentieth-century writer and in many respects remains our contemporary, the idiom of his day is not invariably intelligible now, especially to the many readers who are not native speakers of British English. His use of dialect is another difficulty, and further barriers to full understanding are created by now obscure literary, historical, political or other references and allusions. On these occasions explanatory notes or a dialect glossary is supplied by the editor; it is assumed that the reader has access to a good general dictionary and that the editor need not gloss words or expressions that may be found in it. Where Lawrence's letters are quoted in editorial matter, the reader should assume that his manuscript is alone the source of eccentricities of phrase or spelling. An edition of the letters is still in course of publication: for this reason only the date and recipient of a letter will be given if it has not so far been printed in the Cambridge edition.

ACKNOWLEDGEMENTS

The first debt of gratitude, which we gladly acknowledge, is to Warren Roberts for his support and advice: we esteem him not only as a friend but also as the one who set the standard for serious modern scholarship on D. H. Lawrence.

We are indebted also to the rest of the editorial board, Michael Black, James Boulton, Lindeth Vasey and John Worthen, who have fulfilled their function over and above the call of duty. We gratefully acknowledge hospitality and guidance from David and Carole Farmer, Elizabeth Mansfield and Pat Roberts. The work could not have been done without the help of many academic institutions: the Bancroft Library at the University of California at Berkeley; the Harry Ransom Humanities Research Center at the University of Texas at Austin; Cambridge University Library, especially its map room; Nottingham University Library; Nottingham County Libraries; the Library and the Department of Metalwork at the Victoria and Albert Museum; Laurence Pollinger Limited; the Records Department of Liberty Retail Limited; New York Public Library; the Newspaper Department of the British Library; the Department of Special Collections at the University of California at Los Angeles; the Manuscripts Department at the University of Indiana.

We have been much encouraged along the way by help towards publishing some of the research material, from Fredson Bowers, Andrew Cooper and Dieter Mehl.

We have also been grateful to be able to approach a number of experts for information and corrections: George Lazarus, George Hardy, Alan Griffin, Keith Sagar, Philip Gaskell, Barry Supple, Marie and Richard Axton, David Newmarch, David Kelley, Mara Kalnins, Anthony Rota, Andrew Robertson, Guy Collings, Paul Eggert, Andrew Brown.

Finally, one of the pleasures of engaging in this overlong enterprise has been to draw on the knowledge and generosity of spirit of family and friends: Edward Baron, Joy and Eric Worstead, John Woolford, Sylvia Adamson, Julien Wynne, Desanka Rowell-Ozim, Harriet Crawford, Simonetta de Filippis, Christopher Ricks, Hans Schwarze, James

Worstead, Mark Kinkead-Weekes, Stephen Parkin, Patrizia Fusella, Dorothy Armstrong, Angela Brewer, Annick and Michel Degrez, David Johnson-Davies, Allison Melville, Mary McCarthy.

January 1991   H. B.
                                                  C. B.

CHRONOLOGY

11 September 1885	Born in Eastwood, Nottinghamshire
1891/2	Aged 6 moved from 57 The Breach to 3 Walker Street
September 1898–July 1901	Pupil at Nottingham High School
c. October–December 1901	Clerk at J. H. Haywood Ltd for c. three months
11 October 1901	Death of his brother William Ernest
Winter 1901–2	First attack of pneumonia
April 1902	A month's convalescence at Skegness
October 1902–1908	Pupil teacher; student at University College, Nottingham
August 1906	Lawrence family and friends on two-week holiday in Mablethorpe
7 December 1907	First publication: 'A Prelude', in *Nottinghamshire Guardian*
October 1908	Appointed as teacher at Davidson Road School, Croydon
November 1909	Publishes five poems in *English Review*
before July 1910	Writes and abandons 'Matilda'
18 October 1910	Decides not to publish 'The Saga of Siegmund'; 'Paul Morel' 'plotted out'
c. October–November/ December 1910	'Paul Morel' I – only 100 pages written
3 December 1910	Becomes engaged to Louie Burrows
9 December 1910	Death of his mother, Lydia Lawrence
19 January 1911	*The White Peacock* published in New York (20 January in London)
c. 13 March–mid-July 1911	'Paul Morel' II – abandoned after c. 355 pages
4 October 1911	Meets Edward Garnett
5, 20 October 1911	Meetings with Heinemann
7 October 1911	Renews contact with Jessie Chambers; soon after sends her 'Paul Morel' II

3–15 November 1911   Receives Jessie Chambers's advice and
                              begins 'Paul Morel' III – writes 7 pages,
                              begins again and writes 74 pages
19 November 1911   Ill with pneumonia in Croydon
6 January–3 February 1912   In Bournemouth for convalescence,
                              rewrites 'The Saga of Siegmund' as *The
                              Trespasser*
by 12 January 1912   Invited to Germany by relatives, Hannah
                              and Karl Krenkow
4 February 1912   Ends engagement to Louie Burrows
9 February 1912   To Eastwood
14 February 1912   Has decided to go to Germany in May
mid-February 1912   Collects Jessie Chambers's notes, takes up
                              'Paul Morel' III again and delivers
                              completed pages to Jessie
28 February 1912   Resigns from teaching post
early March 1912   Meets Frieda Weekley
3–8 March 1912   Visits Alice and Henry Dax in Shirebrook
6 March 1912   Has written 'two thirds or more' of 'Paul
                              Morel' III
25–31 March 1912   Delivers last pages of 'Paul Morel' III to
                              Jessie Chambers before visit to G. H.
                              Neville in Bradnop
1 April 1912   Jessie Chambers hands 'Paul Morel' III
                              back with 'notes'
11 April 1912   Offers 'Paul Morel' III to Walter de la
                              Mare but 'parts I want to change'
3 May 1912   To Metz with Frieda Weekley
11–24 May 1912   Stays with Krenkows in Waldbröl, near
                              Cologne
by 16 May 1912   Begins revising 'Paul Morel' III
23 May 1912   *The Trespasser*
1 June–5 August 1912   With Frieda Weekley in Icking, near
                              Munich
9 June 1912   Sends 'Paul Morel' III to Heinemann
3 July 1912   Receives Heinemann's rejection
4 July 1912   Sends 'Paul Morel' III to Garnett at his
                              request
by 18 July 1912   Receives Garnett's notes on 'Paul Morel'
                              III

4 August 1912	Has decided to rewrite 'Paul Morel' III; has probably revised pp. 1–85
5 August–*c.* 5 September 1912	Walks to Riva, Italy
11 September 1912	'working like Hell' at 'Paul Morel'
17 September 1912–30 March 1913	At Villa di Gargnano, Lago di Garda, Italy
15 October 1912	Renames novel *Sons and Lovers*, has written three-fifths
30 October 1912	Has written 400 pages: '*heaps* better' but 'I funk' the last 100 pages
18 November 1912	Sends *Sons and Lovers* MS to Duckworth
1 December 1912	Learns Garnett will shorten the novel
20 January 1913	Sends Garnett 'Foreword' to *Sons and Lovers*
February 1913	*Love Poems and Others*
5 February–3 March 1913	Revises galley proofs of *Sons and Lovers*
3 March 1913	'coming to the end of my cash'
11 March 1913	'don't mind if Duckworth crosses out a hundred shady pages'
22 March 1913	Receives contract for *Sons and Lovers* and £50 advance
22 March–by 10 April 1913	Revises page proofs of *Sons and Lovers*
19 April–17 June 1913	At Irschenhausen, near Munich
mid-May 1913	Reads Jessie Chambers's novel
29 May 1913	*Sons and Lovers* published in London by Gerald Duckworth
19 June–6 August 1913	In England
7 August 1913–June 1914	In Germany, Switzerland and Italy
17 September 1913	*Sons and Lovers* published in USA by Mitchell Kennerley
1 April 1914	*The Widowing of Mrs. Holroyd* (New York)
before May 1914	Receives faulty £10 cheque from Kennerley 'making up *Sons and Lovers* accounts'
July 1914–December 1915	In London, Buckinghamshire and Sussex
13 July 1914	Marries Frieda Weekley in London
26 November 1914	*The Prussian Officer and Other Stories*
December 1914	Learns Kennerley refuses to pay outstanding *Sons and Lovers* royalties

30 September 1915	*The Rainbow*, suppressed by court order on 13 November
June 1916	*Twilight in Italy*
July 1916	*Amores*
15 October 1917	After twenty-one months' residence in Cornwall, ordered to leave by military authorities
October 1917–November 1919	In London, Berkshire and Derbyshire
26 November 1917	*Look! We Have Come Through!*
October 1918	*New Poems*
November 1919–February 1922	To Italy, then Capri and Sicily
20 November 1919	*Bay*
May 1920	*Touch and Go*
9 November 1920	Private publication of *Women in Love* (New York)
25 November 1920	*The Lost Girl*
10 May 1921	*Psychoanalysis and the Unconscious* (New York)
12 December 1921	*Sea and Sardinia* (New York)
March–August 1922	In Ceylon and Australia
14 April 1922	*Aaron's Rod* (New York)
September 1922–March 1923	In New Mexico
23 October 1922	*Fantasia of the Unconscious* (New York)
24 October 1922	*England, My England* (New York)
February 1923	Begins lawsuit against Kennerley
March 1923	*The Ladybird, The Fox, The Captain's Doll*
March–November 1923	In Mexico and USA
April 1923	Kennerley yields rights and plates of *Sons and Lovers*
27 August 1923	*Studies in Classic American Literature* (New York)
September 1923	*Kangaroo*
9 October 1923	*Birds, Beasts and Flowers* (New York)
December 1923–March 1924	In England, France and Germany
March 1924–September 1925	In New Mexico and Mexico

August 1924	*The Boy in the Bush* (with Mollie Skinner)
10 September 1924	Death of his father, John Arthur Lawrence
14 May 1925	*St. Mawr together with The Princess*
September 1925–June 1928	In England and, mainly, in Italy
7 December 1925	*Reflections on the Death of a Porcupine* (Philadelphia)
21 January 1926	*The Plumed Serpent*
25 March 1926	*David*
June 1927	*Mornings in Mexico*
24 May 1928	*The Woman Who Rode Away and Other Stories*
June 1928–March 1930	In Switzerland and, principally, in France
July 1928	*Lady Chatterley's Lover* privately published (Florence)
September 1928	*Collected Poems*
July 1929	Exhibition of paintings in London raided by police; *Pansies* (manuscript earlier seized in the mail)
September 1929	*The Escaped Cock* (Paris)
2 March 1930	Dies at Vence, Alpes Maritimes, France

CUE-TITLES

A. Manuscript locations

ColU   Columbia University
NYPL   New York Public Library
UCB   University of California at Berkeley
UN   University of Nottingham
UT   University of Texas at Austin

B. Printed works

(The place of publication, here and throughout, is London unless otherwise stated.)

Delavenay   Emile Delavenay. *D. H. Lawrence: L'Homme et la Genèse de son Œuvre*. 2 volumes. Paris: Librairie C. Klincksieck, 1969.

E.T.   E. T. [Jessie Wood]. *D. H. Lawrence: A Personal Record*. Jonathan Cape, 1935; reprinted Cambridge: Cambridge University Press, 1980.

Griffin   A. R. Griffin. *Mining in the East Midlands 1550–1947*. Frank Cass, 1971.

ILFL   Richard Garnett, ed. *The International Library of Famous Literature*. 20 volumes. Edward Lloyd, 1899.

Letters, i.   James T. Boulton, ed. *The Letters of D. H. Lawrence*. Volume I. Cambridge: Cambridge University Press, 1979.

Letters, ii.   George J. Zytaruk and James T. Boulton, eds. *The Letters of D. H. Lawrence*. Volume II. Cambridge: Cambridge University Press, 1982.

Letters, iii.   James T. Boulton and Andrew Robertson, eds. *The Letters of D. H. Lawrence*. Volume III. Cambridge: Cambridge University Press, 1984.

Letters, iv.   Warren Roberts, James T. Boulton and Elizabeth Mansfield, eds. *The Letters of D. H. Lawrence*. Volume IV. Cambridge: Cambridge University Press, 1987.

OED   Sir James A. H. Murray and others, eds. *A New English Dictionary on Historical Principles*. 10 volumes. Oxford: Oxford University Press, 1884–1928.

OED *Supplement*   R. W. Burchfield, ed. *A Supplement to the Oxford English Dictionary*. Oxford: Oxford University Press, 1972.

Roberts   Warren Roberts. *A Bibliography of D. H. Lawrence*. 2nd edn. Cambridge: Cambridge University Press, 1982.

INTRODUCTION

INTRODUCTION

The composition of *Sons and Lovers*: origins

Sons and Lovers, D. H. Lawrence's most widely read novel, has achieved a reputation for being at one and the same time a fictionalised account of his own personal history and a classic depiction of the mother–son relationship comparable in status with that of Sophocles' play *Oedipus Tyrannus*. Lawrence himself spoke of the novel both as 'autobiography' and as 'the tragedy of thousands of young men in England'.[1] In order to create a work which he felt was 'as art, a fairly complete truth' (ii. 665) Lawrence inextricably intermingled fiction and autobiography,[2] but the origins of the novel were rooted in his preoccupation with his mother's life.

'What ever I wrote, it could not be so awful as to write a biography of my mother. But after this – which is enough – I am going to write romance – when I have finished Paul Morel, which belongs to this' (i. 195). So Lawrence wrote on 6 December 1910 as his mother lay dying. He was twenty-five and about to publish his first novel, *The White Peacock*. He had already drafted a second, and 'Paul Morel' was to be the third, eventually published as *Sons and Lovers* in May 1913, after he had written it four times. He called it 'Paul Morel' for the first two years, but in October 1912 decided upon a new title (i. 462), whose words, 'sons' and 'lovers', present in the manner of a conundrum the central role of the mother in the novel.

Lawrence had sketched an outline of his mother's life on 3 December 1910, showing the ways in which he felt it to be fundamental to any account of his own:

My mother was a clever, ironical delicately moulded woman, of good, old burgher descent. She married below her. My father was dark, ruddy, with a fine laugh. He is a coal miner. He was one of the sanguine temperament, warm and hearty, but

---

[1] *Letters*, i. 490, 477. Subsequent references to *Letters* will be given by volume and page number in brackets in the text. Cf. also *Letters*, i. 576 and 'The Theatre' in *Twilight in Italy*.
[2] See E. T. 110.

unstable: he lacked principle, as my mother would have said. He deceived her and lied to her. She despised him – he drank.

Their marriage life has been one carnal, bloody fight. I was born hating my father: as early as ever I can remember, I shivered with horror when he touched me. He was very bad before I was born.

This has been a kind of bond between me and my mother. We have loved each other, almost with a husband and wife love, as well as filial and maternal. We knew each other by instinct. She said to my aunt – about me:

'But it has been different with him. He has seemed to be part of me.' – and that is the real case. We have been like one, so sensitive to each other that we never needed words. It has been rather terrible, and has made me, in some respects, abnormal.

I think this peculiar fusion of soul (don't think me high-falutin) never comes twice in a life-time – it doesn't seem natural. When it comes it seems to distribute one's consciousness far abroad from oneself, and one 'understands'. I think no one has got 'Understanding' except through love. Now my mother is nearly dead, and I don't quite know how I am. (i. 190)

It was reflections such as these on her marriage and its consequences that Lawrence developed into a novel during the next two years, while at the same time grappling with the personal problems he intimates here. However, in his earliest attempts to put together a core of maternal biography Lawrence appears not to have been preoccupied with the embattled marriage but with a romantic relationship which preceded it. In the course of the protracted evolution of *The White Peacock* he 'crossed out nearly three pages of heavily revised text' containing 'two complete versions of Mrs Beardsall's life before marriage', which were probably written at some time between October 1908 and March 1910, and included the following:

"How old are you, mother?" asked Lettie, who had continued to contemplate my mother.

"Fifty, nearly fifty one," replied my mother, in tones which said "Yes—I'm creeping on—you'd better beware."

"Do you feel very old, Little Woman?"

"Eh no. I am an elderly woman ... It's not a question of years; it's merely being different people all in a lifetime."

"You were lovely when you were a girl, I know. Long brown ringlets, hadn't you, Dearie? And were you bright and witty? I know you were. Why didn't you have your portrait painted?"

"I did once."

"Then where is it?"

My mother shook her head, then said:

"I was eighteen, when we lived in Kent. He began several sketches. I can remember the scent of the vines. He finished one, but he kept it."

"Who was he, mother?"

"He was artistic; he used to tell me verses, hiding behind his easel."

"Did you like him, mother?"

"Of course. I was a girl then. Now I am a woman rather more than middle-aged—another person."

"What became of him?"

"We left Tonbridge. He was only a tutor. I am a middle aged woman."

"You are tantalising, dearie. But there isn't one man, is there?"

"Several, for most people," replied mother calmly.

Lettie was sitting on the hearthrug, leaning against my mother's knee, watching the fire.

"And you choose the best all round?" queried Lettie.

"If you have the chance," was the cool reply: "But," continued mother, suddenly becoming serious "You have to determine whether you'll marry a husband, or the father of your children. I married the father of my children; a husband might eternally reproach me for it."[3]

Lawrence may have had a number of reasons for taking this discussion out of *The White Peacock*, but its similarity to Gertrude Morel's fondly preserved, if more bitter, memory of John Field in *Sons and Lovers* retrospectively gives his removal of it the character of a postponed obligation to treat the subject more fully. He appears to have made his first extended attempt to explore it in fictional form some time before July 1910. For there survives an unfinished, unpublished manuscript relating the early life of a 'Matilda Wootton', whose characteristics, family relationships and main experiences are closely echoed by those of the young Gertrude Coppard in *Sons and Lovers*; and both seem to derive from the same fund of maternal material.[4] The opening chapter introduces Matilda as a ten-year-old in 1860, and describes her family and forebears. In chapter two she is shown at the age of eighteen, employed as a teacher's assistant, and beginning to form a romantic attachment to a young man whom she meets on her morning walk to school.

The 'Matilda' manuscript consists of a forty-page opening chapter in three sections, and eight pages of a second chapter: structural signposts which indicate it was to be a novel, as does the leisurely pace of the writing. But Lawrence broke it off and explained on 24 July 1910 to his

---

3 *The White Peacock*, ed. Andrew Robertson (Cambridge, 1982), pp. 369–71.

4 Roberts E392, located together with two carbon typescripts at UCB; further typescripts at UT. The untitled manuscript begins 'There is a small cottage off the Addiscombe Road ...' (It will be published as an appendix to 'Paul Morel'.) The name 'Matilda' may have arisen from play on 'Mater', Mother, DHL's predilection for which is evident from 'Mater', 'Mutterchen', 'Mutter', 'Ma', 'Matoushka' in Act I of *A Collier's Friday Night* (*The Complete Plays of D. H. Lawrence*, 1965).

friend, Louie Burrows: 'As to "Matilda" – when I looked at her I found her rather foolish: I'll write her again when I've a bit of time' (i. 172).

'Paul Morel' (first version, October to November or December 1910)

The unfinished novel 'Matilda' was an abandoned precursor of *Sons and Lovers*, but not an early version of it, for by the autumn of 1910 Lawrence had set his third novel on an overtly different course. He named it 'Paul Morel'. A shift of emphasis from the maternal to the filial had been precipitated by his mother's illness, which began in mid-August. Whether or not Lawrence realised at once that it would prove fatal, it must immediately have intensified his artistic preoccupation with her life – but in a new form, because he was now confronted with the problem of his future without her.

At about the same time he found himself under obligation to write a new novel. On signing the contract for *The White Peacock* in June 1910 he had undertaken to send Heinemann his second novel by the end of August 1910 (i. 161, 182). He was keeping to this schedule and by 4 August had finished 'The Saga of Siegmund' (the first draft of *The Trespasser*). He sent it to Ford Madox Hueffer for comment; but the severity of the criticisms he received from Hueffer in early September made Lawrence reluctant to publish the novel and therefore he needed another with which to meet his contract (i. 175, 178). Hueffer forwarded 'The Saga of Siegmund' to Heinemann's office in October 1910 where it remained until December 1911. This left Lawrence free to work on 'Paul Morel', which he mentioned for the first time on 18 October 1910, when writing to the firm (i. 184):

> I am not anxious to publish ['The Saga of Siegmund'], and if you are of like mind, we can let the thing stay, and I will give you – with no intermediary this time – my third novel, Paul Morel, which is plotted out very interestingly (to me), and about one-eighth of which is written. Paul Morel will be a novel – not a florid prose poem, or a decorated idyll running to seed in realism: but a restrained, somewhat impersonal novel. It interests me very much. I wish I were not so agitated just now, and could do more.

A chapter plan has survived in one of Lawrence's college notebooks[5] which illuminates his expression 'plotted out':

[5] Roberts E320.1; Clarke (microfilm at UN: MS LaP 25 p. 4v). (Angled brackets indicate deletions: the transcription is facsimile, except the first 'Floss' and 'Flossie' where DHL's revision covered the original 'Je' and 'J'.) The notebook contains plans for some chapters of 'Laetitia' (see *The White Peacock*, ed. Robertson, p. xviii).

I.

I. Introduction – he pushes her out of the house before the birth of their son.

Aunt Ada
II. Tears without cause – watching the engines on Engine Lane – young sister ⌡

        playing in Breach –
          house   Sunday school – super.Cullen⌡ Newcome lives there
          long lane
III. Sent to school – young brother –⌐Miss Wright – visit to Cullens⌐ <Je>Floss

Miss Wright ⌡
IV. Move from Breach – Mrs Limb – Father hospital ⌐ making toffee in evening.

V. Return of Father – walks with Mabel – filling straws – visit to Aunt Ada

VI. Band of Hope – Fred strikes father – father blacks eye – Miss Wright –
Fred in office – horse manuring – Mabel – painting

VII. Fred dancing – quarrels with father – Gertie teacher –
Wm. learns from her – <J>Flossie friends – Mabel jealous – Wm.
    at
<with> Mr Bate's school – painting .– visit Aunt Ada

VIII. <Death of Fred> Death of Fred – Wm. ill – Mabel – death
of Walter Morel<.>– Aunt Ada superintends

II.

Wm.
I. <Fred> begins at Haywoods.

II. Goes to Miss Wright for painting – meets Flossie much
& Newcome⌐
   ⌐ – reads & learns – neglects Mabel – she becomes engaged.

III. Advance at Haywoods – Miss Haywood & painting (red-haired
Pauline) – Newcome very jealous

IV. Flossie passes high – renewed attention of Wm. – great
friendship after painting in Castle – death of Miss Wright

V. Flossie in College – death of Miss Wright

Since few such plans have survived, little is known about Lawrence's practice in this respect, and it is impossible to tell whether this plan was one of many or precisely the plotting out that he referred to in his letter. It does not match any surviving draft of the novel, and there is no firm evidence of its date, but the fact that the father's name is already established as Walter Morel, while the character who later became Paul is as yet called William, points to *c.* September 1910, after Lawrence had sent off 'The Saga of Siegmund' sometime after 4 August and before he announced the novel as 'Paul Morel' on 18 October.

Several episodes in the second manuscript, 'Paul Morel', correspond with items listed in the chapter plan, particularly under Part I. Some were retained as Lawrence rewrote the novel and occur in *Sons and Lovers*: notably 'he pushes her out of the house before the birth of their son', 'tears without cause', 'move from Breach', 'Father hospital', 'filling straws' and 'W[illia]m. begins at Haywoods'. These parallels with the second and fourth manuscripts indicate that the presence of the mother-figure is silently assumed throughout the chapter plan. Despite being mentioned only in the opening chapter, and indeed only as 'her', she is essential to 'young sister' and 'young brother' in chapters II and III and must thereafter be present since her death or departure would occasion comment.

Several names in the plan are the same as those of people who are known to have been acquaintances of Lawrence in his youth. But the fiction that he intended to create out of this material cannot now be known. His Eastwood friend and contemporary, Flossie Cullen, was the nurse who attended Mrs Lawrence in her illness; her father was a superintendent at the local Sunday School. But since she was not a college girl, it seems possible that Lawrence took external characteristics from her but otherwise based the character on Louie Burrows, whom he met at University College, Nottingham, and described as '"my girl"' in Coll' (i. 193). Flossie Cullen's governess, Miss Wright, taught Lawrence French, and appears to be the model for the Miss Wright who teaches Paul to paint in the chapter plan, and for the Miss May who does so in the second manuscript.[6] 'Aunt Ada' and 'Mrs Limb' were both the names of people whom Lawrence knew, but no character in the second manuscript appears to be based on either of them. Mrs Limb's daughter Mabel was a friend of Lawrence from childhood until her death in 1909, and it is possible that 'Mabel' may have been intended to have external characteristics of Mabel Limb. But the main features of William's relationship with Mabel in the

[6] Having been removed from *Sons and Lovers* the Cullen material found its way into *The Lost Girl* (ed. John Worthen, Cambridge, 1981, pp. xx–xxi).

chapter plan, 'walks' and 'neglect', are salient features of the relationship between Paul Morel and Miriam in both the second and the final manuscript. This suggests that 'Mabel' may also have been a forerunner of the character later called Miriam who was based in large part on Lawrence's childhood friend, Jessie Chambers. But it seems likely that Lawrence intended to make very complex use of these elements, for in chapter III of the plan Lawrence wrote 'Floss' over at least 'Je', possibly 'Jess'; and in the second manuscript the character called Miriam belonged to a family modelled on the Cullen household.

However, as this is a plan, possibly incomplete, of a novel that was never written to this shape, its chief interest lies in revealing the general direction of Lawrence's thoughts. They were moving towards dealing principally with the life and relationships of William (later, Paul) Morel, and away from sustained overt focus on the mother. They appear to have reached the point either of ending with, or being stuck at, the death of an evidently important character, Miss Wright.

Clearly, a crucial shift in Lawrence's approach to his maternal material had begun during the latter half of 1910. The salience of the mother's youthful romance, and the leisurely exploration of her formative years in a context of stern mid-Victorian religion, were being replaced by an emphasis on the years of suffering caused by mismarriage. As in *The White Peacock*, it is the father-figure who dies. But Lawrence's inclusion of the 'death of Miss Wright', and his difficulty in placing it, may indicate the beginnings of an awareness that if he continued his novelistic exploration of family material he would face a choice. He could either emphasise the fictional, and permit himself to dispose of the father-figure, or he could allow the biographical reality to determine the shape of his plot – which would require the mother-figure to die. Some time was to elapse before he could bring himself to make this choice.

Lawrence had probably left off writing the new novel before his mother died on 9 December 1910, and his intense grief disabled him from taking it up again during the bleak period that followed: 'The third novel "Paul Morel", sticks where I left it four or five months ago, at the hundredth page' – he reported to his publisher on 11 February 1911 – 'I've no heart to tackle a serious work just now' (i. 230). None of the hundred pages has survived: this first draft of *Sons and Lovers* remained 'stuck', and he abandoned it in favour of a fresh start.

'Paul Morel' (second version, *c.* 13 March to mid-July 1911)

The fresh start came a month later, and was much more successful: he wrote about 355 pages between 13 March and mid-July before again abandoning it, perhaps unable to devise an ending. The bulk of this second manuscript has survived,[7] revealing a plot similar in places to the above plan and very different from the final novel. The main features of the Morel family are already established, but the college boy Arthur has a larger role and the older brother William a smaller one than in *Sons and Lovers*. Miriam is placed in the refined Staynes household, but her relationship with Paul develops along similar lines to that of the finished novel. Again it is the father-figure who dies – of remorse in prison. At the climax of the story, Morel is roused to uncontrollable anger by an abusive tirade from his younger son, Arthur, and throws a steel at him which kills him. The incident was based on a similar manslaughter committed by the brother of Lawrence's father, which had been reported in the local newspaper.[8] In the chapter that follows Walter Morel's death, a precursor of Clara Dawes named Frances Radford is introduced just as the surviving manuscript comes to a halt. It is not clear precisely where Lawrence abandoned this writing, because he later transferred some of the last pages into the next draft.

From the first Lawrence was convinced that it would be an important work. 'I have begun Paul Morel again', he announced on 13 March 1911 to Louie Burrows, now his fiancée. 'I am afraid it will be a terrible novel. But, if I can keep it to my idea and feeling, it will be a great one' (i. 237). The next day he told Helen Corke, an intimate friend with whom he had collaborated on 'The Saga of Siegmund': 'I have begun "Paul Morel" again – glory, you should see it. The British public will stone me if ever it catches sight' (i. 239). And a day after this he brought Frederick Atkinson, Heinemann's reader, up to date: 'I've begun again "Paul Morel". I swear it'll be a fine novel: no balderdash' (i. 240).

His use of 'terrible' echoes the letter of 3 December 1910 about his relationship with his mother, and points to the tragic implications which he was eventually able to bring to the fore. But a month later, his pride in the new work's potential was battling with his reluctance to write: 'I have

---

[7] For the numerical identification given in Roberts of all the surviving manuscripts of *Sons and Lovers*, and their locations, see the section below entitled 'Text'. For the dates established by comparison with the paper DHL used for his correspondence, see Helen Baron, '*Sons and Lovers*: The Surviving Manuscripts from Three Drafts Dated by Paper Analysis', *Studies in Bibliography*, xxxviii (1985), 289–328.

[8] *Eastwood and Kimberley Advertiser*, 30 March 1900.

just done one folio, a dozen MSS pages, of Paul Morel. That great, terrible but unwritten novel, I am afraid it will die a mere conception' (i. 258). And after the Easter school holiday (14–24 April), his regular progress reports to Louie Burrows show that he was relying on her encouragement to urge himself forwards.[9] By 26 May he could predict that the first two hundred pages would be ready to show her during the Whitsun holiday, 3–10 June (i. 272); but suddenly on 29 May he posted her a 'mass', saying: 'I'm afraid it's heterogeneous; since I have never read it through, very blemishy. Correct it and collect it will you, and tell me what you think. This is a quarter of the book.'[10] Lawrence apparently envisaged a total of 800 manuscript pages, which seems very long, but in fact the paper was too small for more than two hundred words per page.[11] The surviving pages contain about a dozen alterations in Louie Burrows's hand.

Were it not for the fact that pages 72 to 353 of this draft survive, it would be easy to conclude from Lawrence's letters that he lost interest in it after writing the first quarter. Although on 12 June he claimed to Martin Secker, a recently established publisher who had offered to take a volume of stories, 'I am in the midst of a novel, and bejungled in work . . . ' (i. 275), his progress reports to Louie show him working reluctantly or not at all and slowly grinding to a halt by mid-July.[12]

The tone of Lawrence's letters suggests that he produced the second draft of 'Paul Morel' solely by effort of will: there is scarcely a hint of the pleasure in creative writing that he often voiced at other times. On the one hand, he knew that to succeed as a writer, he must publish another novel while the public still remembered *The White Peacock* (i. 276). On the other hand, virtually the only ambition which seems to have motivated him was the desire to publish a novel which would make enough money for him to marry Louie. Paradoxically, however, his letters to Louie during 1911 reveal the inexorable waning of whatever love he had felt for her.

Lawrence's dilemmas crystallised in early October, when in rapid succession he had an uncomfortable meeting with his publisher (5 October); he renewed contact with Jessie Chambers (7 October); and he announced to Louie, 'I haven't done a stroke of Paul for months – don't want to touch it' (10 October; i. 310). Lawrence was evidently reluctant to let Louie know that he had arranged to see Jessie Chambers, to whom he

---

[9] See *Letters*, i. 260, 262, 264, 265, 266, 269.
[10] See ibid., i. 263: DHL dated this letter '29 April' by mistake.
[11] The final manuscript of *The White Peacock* was 802 similar-sized pages (Roberts E430d).
[12] See *Letters*, i. 275, 279, 281, 289.

had been unofficially engaged for six years before proposing to Louie in December 1910, and whose role in nursing his first novel into existence he had valued highly.[13] Yet his relations with Jessie had become so strained that he had to contrive a meeting with the help of Helen Corke. On 7 October he took his brother George, who was visiting him for the weekend, to the Savoy Theatre – this he told Louie (i. 310) – and to the same performance Helen Corke took her weekend guest, Jessie Chambers. All four travelled back to Croydon together before Jessie and George returned by train to Nottingham.[14] Jessie Chambers wrote a memoir of Lawrence twenty years later, which was published in 1935 under the title *D. H. Lawrence: A Personal Record*, by E[unice] T[emple]. In it she did not recall that Lawrence talked to her about his current novel writing, but the outcome of their meeting was that he sent his unfinished manuscript to her for comment.[15] Lawrence must have made these arrangements days or weeks before the interview with his publisher.

Heinemann had remained silent even though Lawrence's proposed novel was more than a year overdue. Since August 1911, however, Lawrence had been in correspondence with Edward Garnett, who was literary adviser to the publishing firm Duckworth, and who had offered to secure magazine publication for some of his stories. When Lawrence and Garnett had their first meeting over lunch on Wednesday 4 October, by chance Frederick Atkinson, general editor for Heinemann, visited the same restaurant. Probably fearing that Lawrence was about to be enticed away by a rival firm, Atkinson pressed him to a meeting the next day, at which Lawrence was made to feel he had 'offended Heinemann's people mortally' by not finishing 'Paul Morel' (i. 310). A pleasanter meeting followed on 20 October. Heinemann tried to woo him back from Duckworth, first by offering to publish the volume of poems which Lawrence had promised (and in part already delivered) to Edward Garnett, and second by proposing an early date for the contracted novel, as Lawrence reported at once to Garnett: 'he wants me definitely to promise the next novel – the one that is half done – for March' (i. 317).

He could not begin work on it until Jessie Chambers returned his second draft with her comments. She was probably predisposed against this manuscript because she had been replaced by Louie Burrows in the role of confidante during the writing of it. The description of it which she later wrote for her memoir is largely disparaging, and has for a long time

---

[13] E. T. 189.　　[14] E. T. 186.
[15] It arrived 'some time' after their 7 October meeting (E. T. 190), 'October (or it might have been November)' (Delavenay 670), but she had returned it by 3 November.

been the only available account of this early version of the novel, but when compared with the surviving manuscript it is found to have certain limitations. She omitted from her summary of the plot almost everything which did not deal with Paul, Mrs Morel and Miriam Staynes (a character whom she perceived to be based on herself). She offered quotations which turn out to record the gist but not the actual words of the original. And her general criticism that: 'It was extremely tired writing. I was sure that Lawrence had had to force himself to do it',[16] despite matching the tone of his reflections as he wrote it, overlooks the fact that this draft abounds in Lawrence's characteristic vitality.

Notwithstanding these qualifications, her retrospective critique conveys not only her insights but probably also the conviction with which she articulated them to Lawrence at the time. Her chief recommendation was that 'what had really happened was much more poignant and interesting than the situations he had invented. In particular I was surprised that he had omitted the story of Ernest, which seemed to me vital enough to be worth telling as it actually happened. Finally I suggested that he should write the whole story again, and keep it true to life.'[17] The comments she sent Lawrence must have struck home, for they enabled him not merely to start again, but entirely to recast his novel towards the shape it was eventually to have when published. The effect was to put the novel in a different fictional genre. As Lawrence rewrote it, it became both more personal and more general. It left behind the genre of naturalistic romance and moved into the less well charted borderland between tragedy, realism and psychological exploration.[18]

'Paul Morel' (third version, 3–15 November 1911, February–April 1912, revised May–June 1912)

Jessie Chambers had sent the manuscript back with her comments by 3 November 1911, when Lawrence wrote to Louie Burrows: 'Tonight I am going to begin Paul Morel again, for the third and last time. I shall need all your prayers if I'm to get it done. It is a book the thought of which weighs heavily upon me. Say a Misericordia ... I really dread setting the pen to paper, to write the first word of Paul – which I'm going to do when I've written the last word of this' (i. 321–2).

---

[16] E. T. 190.   [17] E. T. 192.
[18] This is partially illustrated by an examination of the differences between the second and fourth manuscript versions of one episode in Helen Baron, 'Mrs Morel Ironing', *Journal of the D. H. Lawrence Society* (1984), 2–12.

An abandoned opening to the novel has survived, written on seven unnumbered pages of the same poor-quality lined paper as this letter to Louie Burrows. It begins: '"The Breach" took the place of Hell Row. It was a natural succession. Hell Row was a block of some half-dozen thatched, collapsing cottages ...' and ends 150 lines later, nearly half-way down the seventh page, with Gertrude Morel's discovery that the young man she had loved at twenty, 'a school teacher who was a good Latin scholar', had subsequently 'married his landlady, a woman of forty odd years, who had money'. This proved to be an abortive start, but when Lawrence copied it out again, expanding it, he was launched on his third manuscript. This time he wrote on a strong good-quality paper, water-marked 'Court Royal', which he also used for letters from Wednesday 15 November. That seems to be the last date at which he worked on the novel at this time, for thereafter his free time was filled with engagements until 19 November when he fell seriously ill with pneumonia. He had reached page 74.

Lawrence remained ill at his lodgings in Croydon until 4 January 1912 when he left for convalescence in Bournemouth. During this period, helped by Edward Garnett's encouragement and detailed criticisms as well as by the prospect of publication by Duckworth, Lawrence took up 'The Saga of Siegmund' again and largely rewrote it as *The Trespasser*. So he did not return to 'Paul Morel' for some months.

While confined to bed in Croydon, Lawrence had used up his supply of 'Court Royal' paper on correspondence between 21 November and 13 December. Thus it is certain that the surviving pages of the novel written on that distinctive paper, numbered 1–74 but now dispersed between the fourth manuscript and accompanying 'fragments' (sequences of discarded pages), are the first 74 pages of the third manuscript written in November 1911. Page 74 describes Walter Morel recovering from 'inflammation of the brain' and receiving a bedside visit from his friend Jerry. This is the scene found on the first surviving page (72) of the now-truncated second manuscript. The correlation between them explains why the beginning of the second manuscript is now lost: Lawrence had been writing his third draft with the second open before him, copying from and improving on it. He then discarded the first 71 pages of the earlier version, which he had already revised.

When Lawrence arrived in Eastwood on 9 February 1912 after the crisis of his severe illness, his life was in the process of radical change. He had ended his engagement to Louie Burrows on 4 February (i. 361), and on 28 February he resigned from his teaching post (i. 369). He would make an attempt to live by his pen. 'At the bottom I am rather miserable', he had told Edward Garnett on 29 January, just before he left Bournemouth (i. 358–9); once back in Eastwood his descriptions of his social life as 'jolly', 'howling good fun' and 'awfully fast' bespeak a façade of brittle flippancy (i. 368–9). Jessie Chambers remembered him as 'spasmodic and restless, resentful of the need to be careful of his health'; he maintained in company a 'jaunty exterior, but below the surface was a hopelessness hardly to be distinguished from despair'.[19] By 14 February he had decided that he would go abroad in May for the first time in his life, to visit some German relatives who had written in January inviting him (i. 350, 366). His primary motive seems to have been to get away from England for a while, and to try earning his living in the first instance by writing travel sketches.

The choice of early May as the date for his departure entailed an obligation to send 'Paul Morel' to Heinemann first (i. 371), at the end of April, a month after it was originally promised. For more than three months the seed of Jessie Chambers's advice to keep the novel 'true to life' had been left to germinate in Lawrence's mind, while he concentrated on *The Trespasser*. Now, having just completed his full-scale revision of that novel in six weeks, he settled down to rewrite 'Paul Morel' in under seven. He worked single-mindedly, turning away almost all other offers of publication, but he made time for two trips to visit friends who had left Eastwood, and took his novel away with him to continue writing it.

He resumed his third manuscript of 'Paul Morel' with the same kind of assistance and support from Jessie Chambers that he had sought from Louie Burrows while writing the previous version; but his relationship with Jessie also was soon to be at an end. None of his surviving correspondence of this period refers to her, and therefore her reminiscences are the sole source for some information about the writing of this draft. When in November 1911 Lawrence had received her criticisms and advice he had asked her to set down, for his use, some 'notes' on 'what I could remember of our early days'. He collected them from her in February, 'early in the week'[20] and took up the new draft at page 74, where he had left off in November, part way through the scene at Walter Morel's bedside. By 23 February he was able to report to Arthur McLeod, a former colleague at his Croydon school: '"Paul Morel" is going pretty well, now I have once more tackled it' (i. 367). He delivered the pages of manuscript to Jessie

---

[19] E. T. 199.
[20] E. T. 193, 195; either *c.* Monday–Tuesday 12/13 or 19/20 February.

Chambers as he wrote them, presumably so that she could 'correct it and collect it' for him, and give her opinion.[21]

When she received chapter IX, 'First Love' (later rewritten as chapter VII, 'Lad-and-Girl Love', in *Sons and Lovers*) in which, following her own injunction to keep the plot 'true to life', Lawrence now placed Miriam in the context of the Leivers family at the farm, she read it as history rather than fiction and took exception to a great deal of it, writing her objections freely over the pages of Lawrence's manuscript. She also summarised her criticisms of this chapter on four separate pages which she later gave to Lawrence.[22] In her memoir Jessie complained that once he had reached the 'treatment of Mrs. Morel and Miriam' he posted the pages of manuscript to her rather than bring them in person, because: 'he burked the real issue. It was his old inability to face his problem squarely. His mother had to be supreme, and for the sake of that supremacy every disloyalty was permissible.'[23] But she may have been mistaken about his motive for posting the ensuing pages to her, for between 3 and 8 March Lawrence took the first of his two week-long trips away from Eastwood. It included a visit to Shirebrook to see Alice Dax and her husband: Lawrence's intimate friendship with her was a source for many of the elements in the character 'Clara'.

On 6 March Lawrence wrote to Edward Garnett from Shirebrook that he was 'very busy indeed at the colliery novel' of which he had written 'two thirds or more', and suggested Garnett might like to see it before it went to Heinemann (i. 371–2). Two coincidences make it possible to deduce which parts of the third manuscript he wrote in Shirebrook: he finished one block of writing-paper and began another, while continuing his practice of using the same paper for correspondence; and then he later transferred two sections of the novel written on these two blocks of paper into the final manuscript, where they have survived. The first section describes Paul's quarrel and reconciliation with Mrs Morel which end chapter VIII in the published novel. It was written on paper also used by Lawrence for letters on 1 March from Eastwood and 4 March from Shirebrook (i. 370–1, nos. 396–7). The second section contains Paul's twenty-first-birthday letter to Miriam, in which he called her a nun. This

---

[21] E. T. 197; cf. *Letters*, i. 263.

[22] Jessie Chambers headed her critique 'Chapter IX'. It is one of five surviving documents which she wrote in relation to drafts of *Sons and Lovers* (Roberts E373c), now at UT. For a description and chronology, see Helen Baron, 'Jessie Chambers' Plea for Justice to "Miriam"', *Archiv*, cxxxvii (1985), 63–84 (reprinted in *Journal of the D. H. Lawrence Society*, iv, 1987–8, 7–24).

[23] E. T. 201.

became the end of chapter IX in the final manuscript, and Lawrence wrote it on paper which he also used for letters of 6 March from Shirebrook and 8 March from Eastwood (i. 371–4, nos. 399–400). On one of these pages Jessie Chambers added in pencil a different description of how Miriam reacted to Paul's letter.[24]

At some point during this period Lawrence met and fell in love with Frieda Weekley, whom he was later to marry. In preparation for his planned stay in Germany, he had written to his former college Professor of Modern Languages, Ernest Weekley, for advice 'about a lectureship at a German University'.[25] He was invited to lunch on a Sunday early in March and while waiting for the professor to return home, engaged his German wife Frieda in conversation. She recalled in her memoir twenty years later that Lawrence talked of the disillusionment his series of failed relationships with women had brought him; this led to a discussion of Oedipus in which 'understanding leaped through our words'; and later she received a note from Lawrence, saying: 'You are the most wonderful woman in all England.'[26] He must soon thereafter have realised that if his trip to Germany coincided with Frieda's forthcoming visit to her family in Metz, he and she would have more freedom to let their new relationship develop – their hectically arranged departure on 3 May was not at the time conceived of as an elopement (i. 386, 391), although it was only a matter of days before Lawrence began to insist that the situation be made known to Frieda's husband (i. 392).

Lawrence had been busy at the third manuscript of 'Paul Morel' for about a month when on 13 March he wrote to Walter de la Mare, the successor to Frederick Atkinson as Heinemann's reader, 'this novel – it won't be a *great* success, – wrong sort – should be finished in a month' (i. 375). This suggests he expected to finish it in mid-April. But on 25 March he went to Bradnop in Staffordshire to stay with his old school-friend George Henry Neville until 31 March and according to Jessie Chambers he delivered the last pages of the manuscript to her before leaving for Bradnop. It seems likely that Lawrence's estimate of mid-April was to allow for final revisions after collecting the manuscript on his return from Bradnop, rather than that Jessie had misremembered the date or was mistaken in her belief that the manuscript was complete.[27] For she asserts

---

[24] See Explanatory note on 293:15.
[25] Frieda Lawrence, *"Not I, But the Wind..."* (Santa Fe, 1934), p. 22.
[26] Ibid.
[27] E. T. 205. This chronology is further supported by Jessie Chambers's statement that 'The book was written in about six weeks' (E. T. 204). Neville's problematic claim that while staying in Bradnop DHL was 'busy with the final bringing into shape of *The*

categorically that she read the novel's ending at the time, and her narrative is particularly full at this juncture, because she saw the novel almost exclusively as autobiographical writing and it was the outcome that mattered supremely to her. She hoped that as he wrote Lawrence would achieve such profound understanding of his mother's possessiveness and domination that he would be bound to liberate himself from them; and that this in turn would naturally free him to acknowledge his love for herself.[28] But she wrote of her bitter disappointment at Lawrence's betrayal of her in this draft of the novel, not least in its indecisive ending: 'Having utterly failed to come to grips with his problem in real life, he created the imaginary Clara as a compensation. Even in the novel the compensation is unreal and illusory, for at the end Paul Morel calmly hands her back to her husband, and remains suspended over the abyss of his despair.'[29]

She recorded in her memoir that she returned the manuscript to Lawrence on the Monday after his return (1 April), but refused to discuss it with him on the grounds that she still felt hurt and he seemed defensive. Instead she gave him 'some notes on minor points'.[30] A few documents in her handwriting have survived which may be the 'notes' to which she referred. As well as the marginalia to chapter IX 'First Love' and the associated critical commentary described above, there are some pages in which Jessie tried to drive her points home to Lawrence by the different tactic of writing out three short narratives. One of these, which she entitled 'Easter Monday', was certainly her rewritten version of an episode in Lawrence's third manuscript for she appended a note to her own version, explaining: 'Pages 284–294 really do Paul an injustice. The brutality was not true of that period. If it had been so, subsequent events must have been different. These pages merely suggest something nearer to the actual spirit of the time.' The other two scenes are untitled, but correspond to scenes that occur in the published novel immediately after

Rainbow' and that they quarrelled over 'the bedroom scene' which later caused the novel to 'fall' (see *A Memoir of D. H. Lawrence: The Betrayal*, by G. H. Neville, ed. Carl Baron, Cambridge, 1981, pp. 44–5 and Appendix A, pp. 167–71) has led Mark Kinkead-Weekes to conclude that the scene in question was 'the bedroom scene in *Sons and Lovers*'. This hypothesis runs counter to the evidence that DHL had already completed the current draft of the novel; and it must be invalidated by the fact that *Sons and Lovers* did not 'fall' and that Neville, who shows himself well acquainted with *Sons and Lovers*, is unlikely to have made the statement about a scene he had read there. Since DHL later claimed to have begun *The Rainbow* at about this time (*Letters*, ii. 327) Neville may refer to material which DHL wrote out in Bradnop and later drew into *The Rainbow* when expanding Ursula's early experiences (see *The Rainbow*, ed. Mark Kinkead-Weekes, Cambridge, 1989, pp. xxii n. 11, xxv).

[28] E. T. 193.   [29] E. T. 202.   [30] E. T. 205, 209–11.

the description of the Easter Monday hikes, which in the third manuscript had ended chapter IX.[31] The two untitled scenes may therefore have been new material provided by Jessie at this time, or perhaps, like 'Easter Monday', her revision of Lawrence's text – in which case they would originally have been episodes in a later chapter of the third manuscript, now lost. The 'points' addressed by these three scenes could be described as 'minor' in comparison with Jessie's more radical judgement that: 'the entire structure of the story rested upon the attitude he had adopted. To do any kind of justice to our relationship would involve a change in his attitude towards his mother's influence, and of that I was now convinced he was incapable.'[32]

Lawrence's decision to pass the pages of manuscript on to Jessie Chambers as they were written meant that he had not yet surveyed the whole work and it is reasonable to assume that he now took the opportunity to read and check it. On 3 April he wrote to Garnett: 'I shall finish my Colliery novel this week – the first draft. It'll want a bit of revising. It's by far the best thing I've done' (i. 381). But on the evening of 4 April the first batch of proofs of *The Trespasser* arrived for correction, and Lawrence decided he must 'wage war on my adjectives' (i. 381). He seems to have made these proofs his priority during the next few days, for when some proofs of poems arrived from Walter de la Mare, who had placed them in the *Saturday Westminster Gazette*, Lawrence checked and returned them on 11 April, but excused himself from attending to them very closely 'because I am correcting just now the proofs of the Duckworth novel, and my mind is full of prose'. At the same time he took the opportunity to inform de la Mare: 'I have finished in its first form the colliery novel. Now I want to leave it for a month, when I shall go over it again. There are parts I want to change. Shall I send it to you for your opinion now at once, before I do any revising, or shall I pull it close together before you see it?' (i. 383)

It appears unlikely that Lawrence had done much work on 'Paul Morel' since 4 April, and he evidently no longer felt there was any urgency to deliver the novel to Heinemann. However, if he could contemplate sending it to de la Mare at once he must have written out afresh some or all of the pages of chapter IX which Jessie Chambers had severely defaced. For she had revised the text in handwriting which was sufficiently similar to Lawrence's to be mistaken in places for his; and she had not only deleted whole paragraphs, but added counter-arguments and objections in the margins, several of which accused Lawrence of falsehood. It

---

[31] See 207:9–209:8 and 210:12–211:10.   [32] E. T. 212.

therefore seems likely that after he had recovered the manuscript from Jessie on 1 April Lawrence spent 2–4 April not merely reading it through but deciding how much more work remained to be done, and making it provisionally presentable. His main conclusion appears to have been that it needed revising more extensively than he could undertake at once. He would therefore have to take it to Germany in May. Despite his intention not to work on the novel for a month, he took it with him on a visit to London 25–8 April, probably in order to show it to Edward Garnett when he and Frieda visited Garnett's home, The Cearne, on Saturday 27 April. For he wrote anxiously to recover part of it from Garnett's home: 'I believe Mrs Weekley after all left those first chapters of my Heinemann novel "Paul Morel" in your book-room' (i. 388). Garnett may therefore have had an opportunity to read at least part of the novel at this time; he returned it to Lawrence by 1 May (i. 389).

Lawrence's first week in Germany must have been one of the most extraordinary in his life, as he and Frieda began the process of bringing themselves – as well as her husband and her family – to terms with their new relationship. Garnett had called it 'making history' and Lawrence reiterated the phrase (i. 390, 395). Although he tried, he was in too great a state of emotional turmoil to work at his novel (i. 393), until he visited Hannah and Karl Krenkow (cousins of his mother's brother-in-law) in Waldbröl, leaving Frieda behind in Metz to decide about her future.

His stay in Waldbröl lasted only from 11 to 24 May, and by 16 May he had begun revising the third manuscript of 'Paul Morel', which he hoped to send to Heinemann within a fortnight (i. 405). He probably kept Jessie's 'notes', episodes and marginalia to chapter IX to refer to while making these revisions (which would explain why they have survived). Very little of the third manuscript can now be located, but fourteen pages which Lawrence later transferred into the final manuscript were of a distinctive blue paper which also crops up in letters written from Waldbröl. This suggests that some of the revisions he made to the third manuscript in Waldbröl were written out on these new pages, which later became parts of chapter XI, 'The Test on Miriam' in the published novel.[33] This was the time at which Jessie recalled hearing from him: 'I am going through *Paul Morel*. I'm sorry it turned out as it has. You'll have to go on forgiving me.'[34]

On 23 May, the day before he left Waldbröl to join Frieda permanently, Lawrence claimed that he had finished the novel 'all but 10 pages' (i. 411). After a short 'honeymoon', he and Frieda settled on 1 June in Icking near

[33] See Explanatory note on 328:40.   [34] E. T. 216.

Munich where they stayed for two months. There Lawrence probably looked over the whole manuscript again – and seems to have tinkered with the second chapter – before sending it off to Heinemann on 9 June.[35] He tried to enlist Walter de la Mare's support:

I sent that novel 'Paul Morel' off to William Heinemann yesterday. Now I know it's a good thing, even a bit great. It's different from your stuff ... It's not so strongly concentric as the fashionable folk under French influence – you see I suffered badly from Hueffer re Flaubert and perfection – want it. It may seem loose – and I may cut the childhood part – if you think better so – and perhaps you'll want me to spoil some of the good stuff. But it is rather great. Some Germans who really know a good thing when they see it speak in high praise. (i. 416–17)

But Heinemann rejected it at once, and wrote personally to Lawrence to explain: 'its want of reticence makes it unfit, I fear, altogether for publication in England as things are. The tyranny of the Libraries is such that a book far less out-spoken would certainly be damned (and there is practically no market for fiction outside of them).' He went on to tell Lawrence that the work contained parts which were as good as anything he had read by him; but that it 'lacks unity', it fails to enlist the reader's sympathy for any character including Paul Morel himself and 'in the early part, the degradation of his mother, supposed to be of gentler birth, is almost inconceivable' (i. 421 n. 4). This suggests that the social location of the novel alienated Heinemann. His phrase 'lacks unity' was elaborated by de la Mare, who wrote at the same time to Edward Garnett, 'It seems to me to need pulling together: it is not of a piece. But the real theme of the story is not arrived at till half way through' (i. 424 n. 1). The 'theme' of Paul's experience of conflict and failure in his love for Miriam and Clara was not 'of a piece' with his mother's life story.

Sons and Lovers (fourth version, July–November 1912)

Lawrence was infuriated by Heinemann's letter. He forwarded it immediately, on 3 July, to Edward Garnett and vented his feelings in a litany of

---

[35] *Letters*, i. 416. Some new pages inserted into the second chapter (*Sons and Lovers. A Facsimile of the Manuscript*, ed. Mark Schorer, Berkeley, 1977, Fragment 3, pp. 45, 46a–9a, Fragment 4, pp. 68–9, final manuscript p. 64) were of the same paper that DHL used for letters of 29 June, 3, 8, 18 July (i. 419–27), and for the short story 'Once—!', written between 2 and 29 June (Roberts E296; UT), in *Love Among the Haystacks and Other Stories* (ed. John Worthen, Cambridge, 1987, pp. 152–60).

curses (i. 422). His tirade ended in a resigned, even despairing postscript: 'And Heinemann, I can see, is quite right, as a business man.' But Garnett had already seized the opportunity to take up 'Paul Morel' on behalf of Duckworth. For not only did Garnett value Lawrence's potential as a working-class novelist, he had been undeterred when similar charges of formlessness and eroticism had been levelled at 'The Saga of Siegmund'. Their letters crossed, and Lawrence wrote again the next day, with relief: 'I have posted to you today the MS. of the Paul Morel novel. Anything that wants altering I will do. Your letter cheered me immensely' (i. 423). A few days later (8 July) he added: 'I will make what alterations you think advisable. It would be rather nice if you made a few notes again. I will squash the first part together – it is too long' (i. 423). Just as Garnett's notes on 'The Saga of Siegmund' had enabled Lawrence to return to it and convert it into *The Trespasser*, those he rapidly produced on 'Paul Morel' made Lawrence eager to rework that. The notes had arrived by 18 July and the manuscript by the 22nd: 'I got Paul Morel this morning, and the list of notes from Duckworth. The latter are awfully nice and detailed. What a Trojan of energy and conscientiousness you are! I'm going to slave like a Turk at the novel – see if I won't do you credit. I begin in earnest tomorrow – having spent the day in thought (?)' (i. 427).

Edward Garnett's notes on the third manuscript are now lost, but a list of preparatory jottings, scrawled almost illegibly in pencil and ink, have survived among Garnett's correspondence.[36] They are as follows (with undeciphered words and conjectured readings in square brackets, deletions in angled brackets):

331   "Fabian & Socialistic"
334   affected conversation rewrite [Immoralness] overdone i.e. too
          much [   ]
2<3>35   "The older Banville's "Le Baiser"[37]
341   talk is a little cheap

---

[36] On the back of a piece of paper bearing DHL's handwritten address in Germany, which DHL had probably put in with the manuscript when he sent it to Garnett; NYPL.

[37] Théodore de Banville (1823–91), highly esteemed for the technical perfection of his rhyming poems, also wrote plays of which 'Le Baiser' ('The Kiss') is a comedy (1887). Pierrot, who has never kissed a woman, is persuaded to give an old crone, Urgèle, a kiss, and when it transforms her into a beautiful fairy he demands 'tout', her 'all', in repayment. On the point of submission, she vanishes and Pierrot laments: 'je ne la verrai Plus jamais. *Nevermore.*' ('I shall never see her again'). Pierrot and 'Nevermore' occur in the novel, see 380:9, 271:23.)

348   "one of Circe's erect swine" *no*[38]

348   too literary

349   all this talk doesn't ring true

365   line / See l /

367   delete reference to Hibberts[39]

373   like a cynicism *lurid*

378   top half <part> cheap

379   Improve top of page

383   [these pages   no thankyou]

389   Improve

402   delete "I had rather—food [good]"—you are insensibly making Paul too much of a hero.

406   This seems cheap: you identify your sympathies too much with Paul's wrath.

Garnett's criticism of Lawrence for identifying with his hero seems to have prompted Lawrence to try to express to Garnett how much he felt he had changed during his life in Icking with Frieda: 'Here, in this tiny savage little place, F[rieda] and I have got awfully wild ... I want to rough it and scramble through, free, free ... I feel I've got a mate and I'll fight tooth and claw to keep her.' And he ended the letter: 'I *loathe* Paul Morel ... I'll do you credit with that novel, if I can' (i. 427).

He appears not to have written again to Garnett for two weeks, and then (4 August) on the eve of his departure with Frieda for a month's hike to Italy, he announced his decision: 'I am going to write Paul Morel over again – it'll take me 3 months' (i. 430–1). The paper evidence suggests that during those two weeks he had begun revising the novel, and had reduced the first 85 pages to 76. He deleted passages, and rewrote sequences of pages which he combined with sequences from the previous draft. The early pages from the third manuscript which he rejected at this rewriting have survived – probably because he left them behind in Icking when he sent the bulk of his and Frieda's other possessions ahead by train

[38] It is not known whether Lawrence read a complete translation of Homer's *Odyssey* before 1915 (ii. 253). However, an extract in *ILFL* from *Circe's Palace* by the American novelist Nathaniel Hawthorne (1804–64), first published in *Tanglewood Tales* (1852), relates how Circe transformed some of Ulysses' companions into swine but he compelled her to reverse her spell: 'She ... showed him the swine in their sty ... The comrades of Ulysses, however, had not quite lost the remembrance of having formerly stood erect' (*ILFL*, i. 255). Reference to Circe remains in *Sons and Lovers* only as the name of the Leivers' sow (267:8), but recurs in *The Rainbow* (ed. Kinkead-Weekes, 12:36), and *Studies in Classic American Literature* (chapter XI, where it is evident Lawrence read the whole of *Tanglewood Tales* including Hawthorne's Preface).

[39] *Hibbert Journal* (see Explanatory note on 467:2).

to Riva on the Lago di Garda. Three of the pages mentioned in Garnett's notes (331, 341, 373) were later revised in response to his criticisms and transferred to the final manuscript where they have survived;[40] the others are now lost along with nearly all of the third manuscript, which Lawrence rewrote on new paper in northern Italy.

While travelling, Lawrence received a letter from Hueffer informing him that the publisher Secker was 'anxious to make you an offer for a novel' (i. 433 n. 2), and Lawrence wrote immediately to Garnett suggesting Secker might have 'Paul Morel' on the grounds that 'I must get some money from somewhere, shortly' (i. 434). Perhaps he would have liked to avoid the labour of rewriting, but more probably he felt an antipathy behind Garnett's criticisms, as he indicated in another letter to him on the same day (13 August): 'Don't be cross with me about Secker. I know you don't care much for the Paul Morel novel, that's why I thought you'd perhaps be glad to be rid of it' (i. 439–40).

Once settled in northern Italy, however, his enthusiasm for rewriting it grew. He and Frieda arrived in Riva *c.* 5 September and collected their luggage, which must have included the bulk of his third manuscript of 'Paul Morel' together with the first 76 pages of the new draft begun in Icking. On 7 September Lawrence wrote to Garnett, 'I am glad to be settling down, to get at that novel. I am rather keen on it. I shall re-cast the first part altogether.' Frieda added: 'I think L. quite missed the point in "Paul Morel". He really loved his mother more than any body, even with his other women, real love, sort of Oedipus, his mother must have been adorable – he is writing P.M. again, reads bits to me and we fight like blazes over it, he is so often beside the point'.[41]

Since writing that third manuscript, Lawrence's life had changed dramatically. The atmosphere of misery and disillusionment which prevailed during its composition had now been resolutely left behind; Frieda's different cultural background and her outspokenness made her collaboration quite unlike that of Louie Burrows or Jessie Chambers; and because Frieda did not have independent personal knowledge of the participants in Lawrence's early life, she judged his fictional exploration of it in terms of literary and psychoanalytical qualities rather than historical accuracy. If Lawrence's major purpose had been to write directly and immediately from his life, he might have taken the opportunity to re-align

---

[40] See Explanatory notes on 306:34, 314:17, 341:28.

[41] *Letters*, i. 448–9. Cf. Frieda's comments on DHL's poem 'My Love, My Mother' ('The Virgin Mother') in Francis W. Roberts, 'D. H. Lawrence, the Second "Poetic Me": Some New Material', *Renaissance and Modern Studies*, xiv (1970), [4], 6; 'Corrigenda', xv (1971), 103.

his novel with the autobiographical reality: he could allow Frieda to, as it were, take over the character of Clara, and he could make the outcome a triumphantly successful and liberating relationship. However, what he did was to clarify the work he had already shaped, and this meant bringing out more fully its tragic nature.

On 11 September (his twenty-seventh birthday) he described himself as 'working like Hell at my novel' (i. 451), and with renewed confidence: 'Paul Morel is *better* than the *White Peacock* or *The Trespasser*. I'm inwardly very proud of it, though I haven't yet licked it into form – am still at that labour of love' (i. 455). In early October, when half-way through, he began to talk of changing the title (i. 458, 460) and suggested *Sons and Lovers* for the first time on 15 October 1912.[42] He had now completed three-fifths and felt he had improved it significantly, as he told Edward Garnett: 'I've got a heap of warmth and blood and tissue into that fuliginous novel of mine – F. says it's her – it would be' (i. 462).

What Lawrence meant by this claim cannot now be ascertained because very little of the third manuscript has survived for comparison: there are the remains of chapters I–III and IX; and a further sixty-three revised pages of the third manuscript are scattered among chapters VI, VIII, IX, X and XI of the final manuscript. However, it may be pertinent that at this fourth and final writing Lawrence introduced many dramatic exchanges in place of authorial commentary. For example, prior to Mr and Mrs Morel's quarrel in the first chapter Lawrence discarded sentences analysing their potential irritability, in favour of building a precarious tension into the scene: Mrs Morel, heavily pregnant and tired, is pouring hot liquid from a saucepan just as Mr Morel tipsily enters the kitchen. The description of the wakes holiday was now interrupted by a dialogue between Mrs Morel and William after he had burst into the house impatient to eat before the fair began. By introducing a series of such animated dialogues, Lawrence greatly elaborated the early years of William, the character based on his older brother, Ernest, whose life story Jessie Chambers had urged him to include. Again, before Mr Morel came home to find Paul had been born, Lawrence prepared his mood by showing him with his fellow-miners at work in the pit. The surviving pages of chapter IX 'First Love' in the third

---

[42] The phrase 'sons and lovers' occurs in the essay 'Experience' by Ralph Waldo Emerson (*Essays*, second series, 1844), but it is not certain whether this was among the essays by Emerson that DHL had read: 'The only thing grief has taught me, is to know how shallow it is. That, like all the rest, plays about the surface, and never introduces me into the reality, for contact with which, we would even pay the costly price of sons and lovers ... In the death of my son, now more than two years ago, I seem to have lost a beautiful estate – no more. I cannot get it nearer to me.'

manuscript provide evidence that when Lawrence rewrote them as chapter VII 'Lad-and-Girl Love' (181:40–207:5), he made far more intense his articulation of the inner emotional contours of the characters and their relationships; he also wrote at far greater length, expanding episodes and adding new ones until 575 manuscript lines had grown to 975.

Lawrence felt that the four hundred pages he had completed by 30 October had 'made the *book heaps* better – a million times'. But he had spent the last three days writing a comedy play (*The Fight for Barbara*) 'as a sort of interlude to Paul Morel. I've done all but the last hundred or so pages of that great work, and those I funk. But it'll be done easily in a fortnight' (i. 466). His calculation that a 'hundred or so' pages remained to be written must have been based on where he had reached in reading and rewriting the third manuscript. He slightly overshot his implied target of 500 or so pages for the final manuscript (hereafter MS) whose last page was numbered 540 and most of whose pages after 480 were large sheets covered with small handwriting. What he 'funked', therefore, was not only the last two chapters, but may have included one or both of chapters XII (MS, pp. 422–76) and XIII (477–506). It certainly included the death of Mrs Morel in chapter XIV. Frieda recalled: 'when he wrote his mother's death he was ill and his grief made me ill too'.[43] Perhaps paradoxically, the satisfying – 'wild' and 'free' – relationship with Frieda made the impact of reliving his mother's death doubly devastating, for he had chosen a 'mate' and uprooted himself from his mother's influence, and was now enabled to mourn fully not only her death and his part in it but its tragic implications for her whole life.[44]

Lawrence had completed the novel in under six weeks. He posted it to Duckworth on 18 November, and the next day sent Garnett an impassioned advocacy of its essential structure and meaning (i. 476–8). Frieda added a postscript to his letter (i. 479), and what they each said gives a glimpse of the way in which they had discussed and worked on the novel. It also indicates their anxiety that Garnett might renew the criticisms he had argued against the third manuscript, which must have centred on its lack of 'form'. Lawrence wrote:

I hasten to tell you I sent the MS. of the Paul Morel novel to Duckworth, registered, yesterday. And I want to defend it, quick. I wrote it again, pruning it and shaping it and filling it in. I tell you it has got form – *form*: haven't I made it

---

[43] *"Not I, But the Wind..."*, p. 74. DHL's stress is visible in his handwriting in chapter XIV, particularly MS, pp. 510–24 (see 428:8–444:22).

[44] See the poem 'The Mother of Sons' ('Monologue of a Mother') which Frieda included in her memoir, *"Not I, But the Wind..."*, pp. 76–7.

patiently, out of sweat as well as blood. It follows this idea: a woman of character and refinement goes into the lower class, and has no satisfaction in her own life. She has had a passion for her husband, so the children are born of passion, and have heaps of vitality. But as her sons grow up she selects them as lovers – first the eldest, then the second. These sons are *urged* into life by their reciprocal love of their mother – urged on and on. But when they come to manhood, they can't love, because their mother is the strongest power in their lives, and holds them. – It's rather like Goethe and his mother and Frau von Stein and Christiana –. As soon as the young men come into contact with women, there's a split. William gives his sex to a fribble, and his mother holds his soul. But the split kills him, because he doesn't know where he is. The next son gets a woman who fights for his soul – fights his mother. The son loves the mother – all the sons hate and are jealous of the father. The battle goes on between the mother and the girl, with the son as object. The mother gradually proves stronger, because of the tie of blood. The son decides to leave his soul in his mother's hands, and, like his elder brother, go for passion. He gets passion. Then the split begins to tell again. But, almost unconsciously, the mother realises what is the matter, and begins to die. The son casts off his mistress, attends to his mother dying. He is left in the end naked of everything, with the drift towards death.

It is a great tragedy, and I tell you I've written a great book. It's the tragedy of thousands of young men in England – it may even be Bunny's[45] tragedy. I think it was Ruskin's, and men like him. – Now tell me if I haven't worked out my theme, like life, but always my theme. Read my novel – it's a great novel. If *you* can't see the development – which is slow like growth – I can ...

I should like to dedicate the 'Paul Morel' to you – may I? But not unless you think it's really a good work. 'To Edward Garnett, in Gratitude.' But you can put it better ...

Have I made those naked scenes in Paul Morel tame enough. You cut them if you like. Yet they are so clean – and I *have* patiently and laboriously constructed that novel.

Frieda wrote:

I also feel as if I ought to say something about L.s formlessness. I dont think he has 'no form'; I used to. But now I think anybody must see in Paul Morel the hang of it. The mother is really the thread, the domineering note, I think the honesty, the vividness of a book suffers if you subject it to 'form'. I have heard so much about 'form' with Ernst, why are you English so keen on it, their own form wants smashing in almost any direction, but they cant come out of their snail house. I know it is so much safer. That's what I love Lawrence for, that he is so plucky and honest in his work, he dares to come out in the open and plants his stuff down bald and naked, really he is the only revolutionary worthy of the name, that I know, any new thing must find a new shape, then afterwards one can call it 'art'. I hate art, it seems like grammar, wants to make a language all grammar, language was first and then they abstracted a grammar; I quite firmly believe that L is quite great in spite

[45] Garnett's son David.

of his 'gaps'. Look at the vividness of his stuff, it knocks you down I think. It is perhaps too 'intimate' comes too close, but I believe that is youth and he has not done, not by long chalks! Dont think I am impudent to say all this, but I feel quite responsible for 'Paul'. I wrote little female bits[46] and lived it over in my own heart. I am sure he is a real artist, the way things pour out of him, *he* seems only the pen, and isnt that how it ought to be? We *all* go for things, look at them with preconceived notions, things must have a 'precedence'. We have lost the faculty of seeing things unprejudiced, live off our own bat, think off our own free mind.

Frieda's account reveals her perception of the fundamental structure of the novel: Lawrence had 'plant[ed] down' scenes and episodes so that by simple juxtaposition unexpected significances could come to light and familiar preconceptions could be resisted. This method broke with tradition – and with the still-prevailing taste for what Henry James called 'a controlling idea and a pointed intention'[47] – it was a new 'form', a new 'art'. Garnett was not convinced. By 1 December Lawrence had heard from him and wrote a postcard in reply:

I sit in sadness and grief after your letter, I daren't say anything. All right, take out what you think necessary – I suppose I shall see what you've done when the proofs come, at any rate. I'm sorry I've let you in for such a job – but don't scold me too hard, it makes me wither up.

D[uckworth]'s terms are quite gorgeous –

But I'm so afraid you'll repress me once more, I daren't say anything. Still another man wrote this morning that one of the most enterprising of the younger publishers wants the next novel I can let him have, at very satisfactory terms. – They comfort me after your wigging ...

[P.S.] Tell me anything considerable you are removing – (sounds like furniture). (i. 481–2)

The overture Lawrence had received was probably from Curtis Brown, the literary agent to whom he wrote in 1921: 'I wish I'd come to you ten years back: you wrote to me just too late' (i. 482 n. 2; iii. 701). If either Curtis Brown or Martin Secker had been able to take over the publication of *Sons and Lovers* they might have been sufficiently forward-looking to venture letting it appear as Lawrence wrote it. Garnett's judgement that the novel needed pruning before it could be published by Duckworth was based on twenty-five years' experience as a successful and effective editor of fiction. As his biographer explains, 'It could be argued that the reason for the cuts was primarily commercial. A seven and sixpenny novel usually

---

[46] No handwritten contributions by Frieda have survived.

[47] Henry James, 'The Younger Generation' first published in *The Times Literary Supplement*, 19 March and 2 April 1914 (Nos. 635, pp. 133–4, 637, pp. 157–8), revised and reprinted as 'The New Novel' in *Notes on Novelists* (1914).

ran to 120,000 words and *Sons and Lovers* in manuscript made 180,000 words.'[48] Inevitably Garnett's views about 'form' were influenced by decades of working within such conventions and perhaps he preferred to couch his reasons to Lawrence in terms of the novel's formlessness. But no counter-argument that Lawrence was creating a new tradition – that future generations of readers would accept Lawrence's different concept of how the parts of a novel relate to the whole – could have prevailed over Garnett's acquired knowledge of what the present market would support.

It was an ultimatum and Lawrence had no choice. He could not assert his own conception of himself as a potentially 'great' artist against the requirements of commercial realism (i. 422). He had not yet established his reputation or created his own audience. Worse, he was extremely short of money and was haunted by the fear that if he could not earn any by his art he would have to return to teaching or find some other way. He had Frieda to support, and the prospect of a divorce ahead (and the probability that damages would be awarded against himself as the guilty party). Having left his old life and barely begun to establish a new one, he had few friends and correspondents at this time, and was aware how few people were sympathetic to his cohabitation with Frieda and the outspoken novels he had published to date.

With one correspondent Lawrence allowed himself to voice a greater degree of impatience at the constraints of 'form' than he expressed to Garnett. Ernest Collings, an illustrator, had sent Lawrence a book of his drawings in autumn 1912, because he admired Lawrence's first two novels (i. 481) and was proud of the fact that 'several London booksellers refused to stock' his own book (i. 483). This initiated a regular correspondence which continued for a number of years. In the first letter that Lawrence sent Collings after receiving Garnett's 'wigging' about *Sons and Lovers*, he wrote: 'These damned old stagers want to train up a child in the way it should grow, whereas if it's destined to have a snub nose, it's sheer waste of time to harass the poor brat into Roman-nosedness. They want me to have form: that means, they want me to have *their* pernicious ossiferous skin-and-grief form, and I won't' (i. 492).

Garnett spent some weeks pruning and editing the manuscript, and then sent it on to the printer rather than back to Lawrence for checking. By 1 February 1913 Lawrence still had not received any proofs, but his correspondence with Garnett had become focused on the plays they were both writing, and some of his forcibly worded judgements suggest how he must also have felt about Garnett's criticism of his innovative novel:

[48] George Jefferson, *Edward Garnett: A Life in Literature* (1982), p. 150.

I'm sure we are sick of the rather bony, bloodless drama we get nowadays ... the
rule and measure mathematical folk. But you are of them and your sympathies are
with your own generation, not with mine. I think it is inevitable. You are about the
only man who is willing to let a new generation come in ... But I don't want to
write like Galsworthy nor Ibsen, nor Strindberg nor any of them, *not* even if I
could. We have to hate our immediate predecessors, to get free from their
authority. (i. 509)

   Lawrence may have sensed that his artistic purpose and future would be
difficult for Garnett to appreciate, and indeed their collaboration was soon
to be destroyed by the yet greater unorthodoxy of Lawrence's next novel,
The Rainbow. Although Garnett's insistence that *Sons and Lovers* should be
shorter received implicit support from several reviewers who commented
adversely on the length even of the pruned text, the reviews themselves
endorse Lawrence's longer perspective: nearly all the fiction reviewed in
the same columns as *Sons and Lovers* has now disappeared. Now that
Lawrence's reputation as a great and innovative writer is established, and
early twentieth-century preconditions as to form and length no longer
exist, there are no sound arguments for preferring Garnett's judgement to
Lawrence's. Nor does the survival of Garnett's edited version unchall-
enged for nearly eighty years give it anything other than a spurious
historical validity: eighty years is short in the life of a classic author and is
insignificant in comparison with the centuries it has taken to establish the
texts and even the canon of some earlier authors.
   But Lawrence could not be otherwise than grateful to Edward Garnett
for ensuring the publication of nine-tenths of *Sons and Lovers* however
much he would have preferred his manuscript to be published at once and
in full. He resigned himself to necessity: 'I don't much mind what you
squash out. I hope to goodness it'll do my reputation and my pocket good,
the book' (i. 496); and when he saw the results in the proofs, he expressed
his gratitude spiritedly, but with a growing uneasiness: 'It goes well, in
print, don't you think? Don't you think I get people into my grip? You did
the pruning jolly well, and I am grateful. I hope you'll live a long time, to
barber up my novels for me before they're published. I wish I weren't so
profuse – or prolix, or whatever it is. But I shall get better' (i. 517). 'I
admire my own work a good deal. You did well in the cutting – thanks
again' (i. 520). 'I finished and returned all the proofs of *Sons and Lovers* ...
It is rather a good novel – but if anything a bit difficult to grasp as a whole,
at first. Yet it *is* a unified whole, and I hate the dodge of putting a thick
black line round the figures to throw out the composition – Which shows
I'm a bit uneasy about it' (i. 522).

Edward Garnett's editing of the novel

Garnett's editorial marks on the manuscript can be clearly identified.[49] Although his main concern was to shorten considerably and to censor a little, it was inevitable that his choice of passages to delete would reflect his policy with regard to the novel's form; and accordingly they bulk large in the early chapters. Nearly all the reduction in length took place in chapters I to XI, and the censorship in chapters XI–XIII. There were no cuts in the last two chapters. In total he deleted eighty passages, varying from 2 to 185 lines, which shortened the manuscript by 2,050 lines, about a tenth. He worked systematically: there are two kinds of notation in the manuscript showing successive word counts; he marked passages for deletion provisionally in pencil and then confirmed them in ink, sometimes slightly differently.

In chapter I Garnett deleted just over a hundred lines out of eleven hundred, in thirteen short passages of between two and fifteen lines. Some are explanations of the miners' life, or generalisations about the Morel children's activities; and some are parts of dialogues, notably the quarrels between Walter and Gertrude Morel. The latter are constructed so that the actual words exchanged are the chief vehicle whereby mutual misunderstanding and latent anger are slowly but surely transmuted into overt hostility. Garnett's abbreviation of the exchanges meant that in the published novel the couple reached fever pitch more rapidly.

In chapter II he deleted about 250 out of approximately 900 lines. The ten excised passages are parts of episodes or conversations, nearly all twenty or more lines in length. But in chapter III, 'The Casting off of Morel, the Taking on of William', Garnett removed several whole episodes in a total reduction of approximately 320 out of 750 lines. These were mainly scenes in the life of William, which serve to diversify William's role as a precedent for Paul. They include William's bantering exchanges with his mother; his domineering reaction to her scorn of his girlfriends; his pride in his own physique; his amiable patronage of his younger brother; his impatience as a teacher. In addition some features of the portrait of Walter Morel were lost, as were some instances of Mrs Morel's wit and vigour of speech.

By contrast with chapter III, Garnett took only one passage of nine lines out of chapter IV. Many of the passages he deleted in chapters V to X were dialogue, some were whole conversations. Two of these underpin the topic of women's rights in the novel: Paul's discussion with his mother of

[49] They are marked in the Textual Apparatus '*Om. MS†*' and '*MS†*'.

Miriam's anger at the advantages men had over women in matters such as
education (chapter VII); and the conversation between Paul, Clara and the
Leivers family about equal pay for women (IX). Another exchange that was
lost contained Paul's disquisition to Miriam in chapter VIII on the relationships between the symmetrical roses of fabric design and theories of plant
structure. Here, Lawrence builds on Paul's hesitant theorising in chapter
VI of a connection between Impressionism in painting and protoplasm in
nature, to show him as a more experienced artist exploring the ideas that
were currently fashionable in art and biology. The longest sequence
Garnett cancelled was Lawrence's four-page description in chapter VIII of
the regular weekly rendezvous between Paul and Miriam at the Bestwood
library, which demonstrates their enjoyment of each other's company and
conversation, and thus validates the narrator's retrospective claim in
chapter IX: 'One Sunday evening they attained to their old, rare harmony.'[50]

Garnett's censorship was light. He removed six sentences from the
most explicit scene in chapter XII, 'Passion', one and a half from the
description of Clara preparing to swim in chapter XIII and a phrase from
chapter XI 'The Test on Miriam'. Otherwise he censored single words in
these chapters, altering for example 'hips' to 'body' (333:32), 'thighs' to
'limbs' (375:19) and deleting the word 'natural' in the phrase 'He could
smell her faint natural perfume' (375:30–1). But when checking the
proofs Garnett extended his censorship of the same scenes, chiefly in
chapter XII and a little in chapter XIII (see below).[51]

Lawrence's 'Foreword'

In January 1913 while Edward Garnett was pruning the manuscript of
Sons and Lovers and making it ready for the printers, Lawrence sent him a
seven-page essay (see Appendix I), saying: 'I was fearfully anxious to write
a Fore-word to *Sons and Lovers*, and this is what I did. I am a fool – but it
will amuse you' (i. 507). But he had not made sufficiently clear that it was
a private document, for on 1 February he hastened to assure Garnett: 'I
don't want neither a Foreword nor a Discriptive notice *publishing* to *Sons
and Lovers*. I wanted to *write* a Foreword, not to have one printed. You can
easily understand. I am fearfully satisfied with myself as it is, and I would
die of shame if that Foreword were printed.' Frieda added: 'We fought
over it' (i. 510).

This was the first instance of a process for which Lawrence offered a

[50] See 267:25.   [51] See Textual Apparatus 333:34, 383:23, 383:28, 401:32, 402:1.

theoretical explanation in the 'Foreword' to *Fantasia of the Unconscious* (written in 1921): 'The novels and poems come unwatched out of one's pen. And then the absolute need which one has for some sort of satisfactory mental attitude towards oneself and things in general makes one try to abstract some definite conclusions from one's experiences as a writer and as a man.'

Lawrence does not present his 'conclusions' in the 'Foreword' to *Sons and Lovers* as a set of explicit observations on the novel but as an attempt at a sustained account of the relationship between Man, Nature and God. Although this discussion has been thought to point forward to *The Rainbow* more evidently than back to *Sons and Lovers*, it has a strong affinity with Paul Morel's twin interest in Christian doctrine and in early twentieth-century scientific inquiries into the structure of the natural world, but the connection has been difficult to perceive because of Garnett's removal of certain passages from the novel. In the 'Foreword' Lawrence confronts these two interests and tries to sketch a new religious cosmology which would not conflict with scientific discoveries about the nature of matter.

But his purpose is hard to grasp immediately because he launches his argument in terms of the New Testament doctrine of the Incarnation of Christ: he takes the text 'The Word was made flesh'[52] and turns it on its head: the 'Flesh' gives rise to the 'Word'. His *tour de force* in subversion of biblical texts gives his essay the appearance of a purely theological discussion. But Lawrence was simultaneously doing two things: assimilating the post-Darwin understanding of Nature into a religious framework, while using the new science to challenge New Testament cosmology in its assertion of the primacy of spiritual and ethical values.

His argument appears to be: that which is primary, 'God', is that which makes life take shape; it is eternal, ever-active, indescribable, formless itself but giving rise to form. By conducting his argument entirely in terms of 'the Flesh' and 'the Word', etc., he avoids the hazards of definition, but his argument seems to equate God ('the Father', 'the Flesh') with – to risk a brief equivalent – the creative life energy of the universe, while the products of this creative life energy (nature, man, civilisation) he calls 'the Son' and 'the Word'. His argument becomes clearer when he develops a partly literal, partly poetic image of the life-cycle of the apple-tree and describes apple-blossom as 'God rippling through the Son till He breaks in a laugh' (470:38–9). They are a continuum but distinct: man glimpses

---

[52] John i. 14 (AV).

God, the life force, in action, through the beauty and transience of the natural world.

Lawrence's chief 'conclusion' seems to be that the creative life energy of the universe is independent of and more powerful than all the facets of man's existence on which man prides himself: consciousness; will; the production of laws, useful objects, works of art, and so on. Man cannot understand or control this creative life energy, which is essentially unknowable. He is aware of it in the spontaneous life of the body, but his tendency to believe that the human mind is powerful enough to control or enrich that life within himself is an illusion. Lawrence's second conclusion is that Woman has greater affinity with the creative life energy than Man has; and he disputes the Old Testament doctrine that Woman was born out of Man's body (Genesis ii.). He then argues that Man goes to Woman as to a source of life, for renewal, and away from her to the various activities in which he asserts his individual identity.

Some of the conclusions which follow from these arguments can be recognised in their relation to *Sons and Lovers* at the level of plot and action. One is that the 'unquestionable sincerity' of a man's profound attraction towards a particular woman cannot be dictated by his will or controlled by the law (468:27). Another is that if a husband does not respect his wife's greater affinity to the life principle and come to her for renewal, she will naturally reject him; and if they each fail to find another partner they will destroy themselves, by self-inflicted damage like alcoholism, by sickness, by meaningless activity or by fighting each other. Or the woman will seek a 'son-lover' – of whom the first example was Oedipus. However, a man who returns for renewal to his mother cannot achieve it complete.

At a deeper level, the 'Foreword' articulates the unspoken belief which underlies the novel: that the physical life of man and nature is far more important than the values of civilisation. Lawrence's stance was so unorthodox at the time that the 'Foreword' helps to explain why some reviewers of *Sons and Lovers* sensed its challenge to the traditional hegemony of spiritual values and called it 'morbid'. The ideas that Lawrence first propounded here he developed further in the 'Study of Thomas Hardy' (1914), whence they influenced the writing of *The Rainbow*. Similar lines of argument are found in 'The Crown' (1915), the revised pieces for *Twilight in Italy* (1916), 'The Reality of Peace' (1917) and the early versions of *Studies in Classic American Literature* (begun 1917). Lawrence later repeated some of the fundamental ideas of the 'Foreword' without the Christian terminology and with far greater clarity when writing *Psychoanalysis and the Unconscious* (1920), *Sketches of Etruscan Places* (1927) and *A Propos of "Lady Chatterley's Lover"* (1929).

The period of printing and proof revision (January–April 1913)

Sons and Lovers was typeset by Billing and Sons in Guildford, directly from the fourth manuscript. Work began on the galley proofs some days before 27 January and was completed on 21 February 1913.[53] The proofs were forwarded in batches as they were ready to Lawrence, in the small northern Italian town of Gargnano beside Lake Garda.[54] He had begun revising them by 5 February and had returned them all by 3 March (i. 512, 522). He sent them back in batches as he completed them, so he did not at this time have the entire novel in front of him in its printed form. Normal practice would have been for an author to receive the relevant pages of the manuscript with each batch of galley proofs, but it is not known whether that happened in this case.

As Lawrence sent back the corrected galley proofs, Billing and Sons ran off the revised text in page proofs. These were checked, dated and forwarded in batches to Lawrence, accompanied by the corresponding sheets of galley proofs, which were now cut so that the text on them began and ended at the same line as each signature of page proofs. The dates entered on the page proofs run from (Friday) 28 February to (Friday) 4 April, but Lawrence does not appear to have received any until Easter Saturday, 22 March (i. 529). He had probably dealt with them by 10 April (i. 538). A few corrected galley proofs and a complete but uncorrected set of page proofs have survived.[55] From the former it is evident that the

---

[53] The date '27.1' was entered by the compositors in the MS at pp. 196, 205 and 324. MS bears over eighty annotations of 'slip' and 'galley' numbers and compositors' names entered in the printing shop. The printers were working towards an octavo volume bound in signatures of sixteen pages, each page containing 44 lines of type. The first proofs were large sheets of paper on which four 88-line columns of type (designated 'slips') were printed side by side. As each column was two page-lengths, each sheet held eight pages of text, half a signature. The printers referred to these as 'galley' proofs, and the name is retained here, but the format was similar to the French *placard* proofs in use at this time. There were 209 slips, just over 52 sheets of galley proofs; and the finished volume was 26½ signatures.

[54] DHL was in Villa di Gargnano, 2 km. s. of Gargnano. The post normally took less than five days. The final batch was dated at Billing and Sons 21 February (Friday). It was probably forwarded to Duckworth to be checked by Garnett; DHL noted receiving it on (Tuesday) 25 February (i. 520).

[55] The galley proofs (Roberts E373f: listed by slip numbers), equivalent to pp. 353–68 and 401–23 of the first edition (parts of chapters XIII and XIV and the whole of chapter XV)

proofs were corrected and revised by the printer's reader at Billing and Sons, and then sent to Edward Garnett who further revised them before they were forwarded to Lawrence.

It was not the regular practice at this time to send the second proof to the author. For his first two novels Lawrence had only corrected one: galley proofs for *The White Peacock*, page proofs for *The Trespasser*. Therefore when he had finished correcting the galley proofs of *Sons and Lovers* he expected it to be published in about three weeks (i. 524). Duckworth's terms included an advance of one hundred pounds on the day of publication, and Lawrence told Edward Garnett on 3 March: 'I am coming to the end of my cash. Soon I shall have to ask Duckworth for something. I finished and returned all the proofs of *Sons and Lovers*' (i. 522). Lawrence was extremely short of money, and his financial anxieties, voiced in almost every letter to Garnett, were intensified by the arrival of Frieda's divorce notices on 4 March (i. 524).

But a second proof was evidently required because Duckworth had decided that the novel must be censored further, for on 11 March Lawrence impatiently consented: 'I don't mind if Duckworth crosses out a hundred shady pages in *Sons and Lovers*. It's got to sell, I've got to live.' It is not certain whether Garnett had indicated that proofs would be sent, or whether Lawrence was giving this blanket permission without expecting to see the results before publication. In the same letter he added, 'Ask Duckworth to send me £50, will you' (i. 526–7). His overriding concern was that the book should be on sale as soon as possible.

Having been unwell from 11 to 22 March, Lawrence appears to refer to the new round of proofs for the first time on 22 March,[56] in a sudden flurry of activity to do with the contract, an advance payment and the design of the dust-jacket, all of which gives the impression that he had just received a parcel and letter. The task of revising the page proofs was compressed by Lawrence's decision to travel. On 30 March, he and Frieda left Villa Igea in Villa di Gargnano where they had been since September 1912, and moved to nearby San Gaudenzio. Lawrence found, as he told David Garnett on 5 April, 'I'm so sick of the last lot of proofs of

belonged to the set DHL sent Ernest Collings. They were inherited by his son Guy Collings, and are now at UN. The page proofs (Roberts E373g) are at UT.

[56] DHL promised Collings on 22 March: 'I'll send you the first batch of proofs' (i. 529) and clarified on 28 March: 'Don't send back the proofs if you'd care to keep them – and I will send you the rest. They are the revised proofs, and not all have come yet' (i. 535). He sent Collings the set of galley proofs which he had revised and returned to the printers. It appears, therefore, that on 22 March he had begun receiving batches of page proofs with these accompanying galleys.

Sons and Lovers, that I have scarcely patience to correct them' (i. 536). He probably posted off the last batch before he and Frieda left San Gauden-zio on 11 April for Verona, from where they travelled on 14 April to Munich (i. 539). Lawrence was becoming impatient with Duckworth at the delay in publication, but optimistic that 'People *should* begin to take me seriously now' (i. 544).

Ernest Collings and the design of the dust-jacket

In the letter that Lawrence received on 22 March Garnett requested an illustration of collieries for the dust-jacket. But Lawrence could not draw them from memory and there were none to copy near Lake Garda, so he forwarded the request at once to Ernest Collings. He believed he himself would receive no payment from Duckworth for a design and was embar-rassed to ask this favour of Collings who was 'young and struggling' (i. 536). To give Collings an idea of the novel – and also perhaps as a return favour – Lawrence sent him all the revised galley proofs in batches as he finished checking each corresponding batch of page proofs. Duck-worth's specification for the cover was, Lawrence explained, 'something suggesting the collieries – headstocks ... One-third or so of the cover is to be picture, the rest a brief notice on the novel ... I enclose a draft of the size of the cover and spacing. They want this thing awfully soon too ... The thing is to be black and white' (i. 528–9).

Lawrence's draft design is preserved with his letter:[57] a slag heap to the left, a headstock and winch to the right, and four trucks across the front marked 'C W & Co'. Underneath in capitals he wrote 'SONS AND LOVERS' followed by: 'It is impossible that love really lie dormant. If it have that — —'. Rows of dashes fill the space below, indicating text. He wrote to Edward Garnett the same day: 'I have also written the brief notice for the wrapper. If it is wrong, tell me. Frieda insists on my enclosing her version also. Of course I think it not anywhere near it' (i. 529–30).

Lawrence praised the 'poetic quality' of the sketch he received within a week from Collings (i. 535), and he wrote both to Edward Garnett (i. 539) and his son David (i. 536) urging a favourable reception of his friend's work. Collings forwarded a finished design to Duckworth but received no acknowledgement, and eventually had to write to Garnett to recover it (i. 547 n. 3). On 13 May Lawrence apologised to him, saying he had just learnt that Duckworth now thought a colliery illustration 'unsuitable' (i.

---

[57] At UT; partially reproduced in Harry T. Moore and Warren Roberts, *D. H. Lawrence and His World* (1966), p. 37.

547). He begged Collings to blame Duckworth rather than himself, and two months later they met for the first time in London (ii. 53).

No illustration appeared on the dust-jacket of the first edition; nor did the announcement contain the words Lawrence had written on his draft design. Instead it read: 'Mr. D. H. Lawrence's new novel covers a wide field: life in a colliery, on a farm, in a manufacturing centre. It is concerned with the contrasted outlook on life of two generations. The title, "Sons and Lovers," indicates the conflicting claims of a young man's mother and sweetheart for predominance.'

The contract

Lawrence had learned of Duckworth's proposed payment for *Sons and Lovers* at the end of November 1912 and called it 'quite gorgeous' (i. 482), but he was offhand about publishers' terms: Heinemann appeared arbitrary, Duckworth was unbusinesslike,[58] and at this stage in his career Lawrence did not feel that royalties were his by right – he called himself a 'thief' (i. 482) and the money 'manna' (i. 511).

On 18 February 1913, in reply to queries from Garnett he said: 'No, I had no agreement for *Sons and Lovers* from Duckworth. As far as that goes I've never had an agreement for the *Trespasser*' (i. 518). A contract was eventually typed out on 19 March, and Lawrence received it three days later, together with a fifty-pound advance. In addition to the cash payment on the day of publication, the terms were: 15 per cent on the first 2,500 copies sold, calculated 'on the published price of twelve out of every thirteen copies sold' (the first edition cost six shillings), and 17½ per cent on all copies sold thereafter. The author was required to give the standard undertaking that the novel would contain nothing scandalous or libellous, and to offer the publisher his next work.[59]

[58] Heinemann's contract for *The White Peacock*, signed in June 1910, had agreed 15 per cent on sales (i. 161 n. 4), and no advance payment. Yet DHL had received a £15 advance on 8 September 1910 (i. 177 and n. 2), four months before publication in January 1911, which he may have requested to meet doctor's fees for his mother. He was surprised to learn in October 1911 that the contract provided for one annual payment, and the £40 owed him was not due until February 1912 (i. 310). He was even vaguer about Duckworth's terms for *The Trespasser*. When he received £50 in September 1912, four months after publication, he was surprised that Duckworth had paid him so soon (i. 448 and n. 1), but on 1 February 1913 he asked Garnett whether that was all *The Trespasser* would bring him (i. 511). See also below, p. lxii.

[59] Contract in Heinemann's files; see also *Letters*, i. 482 n. 1.

Jessie Chambers's novel

In May 1913, too late for it to influence the text of *Sons and Lovers*, Lawrence read the novel which Jessie Chambers had written as a rival fictional account of their relationship. She believed that: 'The Miriam part of [*Sons and Lovers*] is a slander, a fearful treachery. [Lawrence] has selected every point which sets off Miriam at a disadvantage, and he has interpreted her every word and action, and thought in the light of Mrs. Morel's hatred of her.' Therefore she wrote her novel in self-defence, both as a therapeutic exercise for herself and in the hope that Lawrence would eventually read it: 'I always intended that he should see it. I feel it a matter of honour.'[60]

It grew out of a short story of 1911, which she had also written to modify Lawrence's attitude, and which probably did have some influence on his novel:

It seemed to me that our long conflict had dated from the time when, as a boy of twenty, he had come to me and told me that 'he had looked into his heart and could not find that he loved me as a husband should love his wife'. So I recollected the incidents of that occasion with scrupulous care and sent them to him in the form of a short story some time in the spring of 1911.

... His answer came promptly: 'I have read your story but I don't think you'll get anyone to publish it with alacrity; it's too subtle ... ' Then his pose of detachment broke down: 'You say you died a death of me,' he wrote, 'but the death you died of me I must have died also, or you wouldn't have gone on caring about me ... They tore me from you, the love of my life ... It was the slaughter of the fœtus in the womb ... '[61]

Lawrence must have received this story just as he was embarking on his second manuscript. Versions of 'that occasion' occur in the second manuscript and the published novel. A version was also included in the third manuscript, and although it is now lost Jessie Chambers's revised transcript of it entitled 'Easter Monday', which she gave Lawrence in April 1912, survives (see above).

Jessie developed her short story into a novel, 'The Rathe Primrose',[62] in late 1911 but by February 1912 had decided to rewrite it. She sent it to

---

[60] The manuscript of this letter at UN (La M10), reads only 'March 1913', but from internal evidence J. T. Boulton establishes the date as 16 March (i. 527 n. 1) and not 23 March as in 'The Collected Letters of Jessie Chambers', ed. George J. Zytaruk, *D. H. Lawrence Review*, xii (1979), 27–8.

[61] E. T. 186.

[62] So titled in reference to Milton's 'Lycidas' (1638), 'the rathe primrose that forsaken dies' (l. 143).

Hueffer and Garnett, and during the winter of 1912–13 took Garnett's advice and turned it into a 'very simple' novel about herself.[63] In March 1913, she sent this to Garnett. On 15 March she received a set of galley proofs of *Sons and Lovers* from Lawrence with a request that she pass them on to his sister when she had read them; and she learned from his accompanying letter 'that Garnett had told him of my novel and had spoken praise of it, but thought it perhaps too quiet for the public. He wants to see it.'[64] Jessie later recalled: 'Garnett undertook to pass the novel on to Lawrence and I lost sight of the Ms for about six months, but I never heard whether Lawrence read it or not, although I am sure he did, from some bits in *The Rainbow*.'[65] She later destroyed her manuscript.

By the time Lawrence learned that he might see Jessie's novel, at the beginning of May 1913, he had become indignant in his own defence:

Will you send the MS of Miss Chambers here, please, at your leisure ... I see Frieda has written a defence of me against Miriam – or Jessie, whatever she shall be called. It's all very well for Miss Chambers to be spiritual – perhaps she can bring it off – I can't. She bottled me up till I was going to burst. – But as long as the cork sat tight (herself the cork) there was spiritual calm. When the cork was blown out, and Mr Lawrence foamed, Miriam said 'This yeastiness I disown: it was not so in my day.' God bless her, she always looked down on me – spiritually ... And look, she is bitterly ashamed of having had me – as if I dragged her spiritual plumage in the mud. Call that love! Ah well. (i. 545)

However, after reading her manuscript he reported his response in very altered tones to Garnett on 19 May: 'We got Miss Chambers novel. I should scarcely recognise her – she never used to *say* anything. But it isn't bad, and it made me so miserable I had hardly the energy to walk out of the house for two days' (i. 551). And Frieda, who had dismissed Jessie as 'white love, white of egg of my youth' (i. 532), now saw *Sons and Lovers* in a new light: 'Miriam's novel is very lovable, I think, and one does feel so sorry for her, but it's a faded photograph of *Sons and Lovers*, she has never understood anything out of herself, no inner activity, but she does make one ache! I only just realised the amazing brutality of *Sons and Lovers*' (i. 550).

This appears to chime exactly with the conclusion Jessie had drawn about *Sons and Lovers* in March when she received Lawrence's proofs: 'The story is painful, would be, I think, to a stranger even. It's rather a

[63] Delavenay 708–9.   [64] Zytaruk, 'Collected Letters of Jessie Chambers', 28.
[65] Delavenay 709.

hotch-potch; – at the end, one feels no further, only shocked and dismayed at the tragedy and the brutality of it all.'[66]

But Frieda interpreted her own sense of the brutality altogether differently: as a sign of life underneath the brittle crust of Christian civilisation. And Lawrence's emendations to Frieda's letter, designed to make it intelligible to Garnett, give the impression that Lawrence not only fully understood but also endorsed what Frieda was trying to articulate. She continued:

How that brutality [remains,] in spite of Christianity, of the two thousand years; it's better like that, than the civilised forms it takes! Its only a top plaster [(the civilisation)], and I'm sure brutality ought to develop into something finer, out of *itself*, not be suppressed, denied! Paul says to his mother, when she is dying 'If I'd got to die, I would be quick about it, I would *will* to die.'[67] Doesn't it seem awful! Yet, one *does* feel like that, but not only that after all! (i. 550)

The first edition

Having left Italy for Germany on 14 April, Lawrence and Frieda settled at Villa Jaffe, Irschenhausen, near Munich from 19 April until 17 June, and there on 19 May Lawrence received an advance copy of *Sons and Lovers* which was published in London by Duckworth on 29 May 1913.[68] Lawrence sent complimentary copies to his brother, his two sisters, his friend and former colleague in Croydon Arthur McLeod and his former landlady in Croydon Mrs Marie Jones.

During Lawrence's visit to England (19 June to 6 August 1913) it was evident that the novel was having 'quite a considerable success' (ii. 52), which led to a sudden expansion in his acquaintance among members of the literary world. But the book did not sell well. The libraries which had initially refused to take it soon consented (ii. 22); but by 22 July Lawrence was disappointed again: 'The damned prigs in the libraries and bookshops daren't handle me because they pretend they are delicate skinned and I am hot' (ii. 47). In September, a month after he had left England for Germany and Italy, he learned from Garnett that the sales had slowed down (ii. 67) and by 10 January 1914 he reported more in sorrow than

66 Zytaruk, 'Collected Letters of Jessie Chambers', 27; and cf. p. 117 where Jessie explained in 1935, 'D. H. L. proposed to me an association that we each regarded as binding and sacred. He said to me "*This* (i.e. our relationship) holds us together," and he was quite sincere. When, later on, he called it a "test" and pretended that the "test" had failed, he seemed to me inhuman.'

67 See 432:10. (DHL's emendations to Frieda's letter are given in square brackets.)

68 For the bibliographical problems associated with variant exemplars of the Duckworth first edition, see Roberts 14.

anger the insinuation of rival enterprises that Duckworth had not pro-
moted the book enough: 'The sales of *Sons and Lovers* are rather dis-
appointing. I am having letters from agents who say "that fine novel hasn't
had the success it deserved", and offering me £200 down for my next, on
the behalf of the best established publishers in England and America' (ii.
135). He continued loyally to offer his work through Garnett to Duckworth, but by 22 April 1914 he realised that sales had been very low, as he
wrote to Garnett, 'It was horrid to receive the accounts of *Sons and Lovers*,
and to see that Duckworth has lost a number of pounds on the book –
fifteen or so, was it. That is very unpleasant. Because I only had a hundred
pounds even then ... ' (ii. 165).

Duckworth reprinted the novel in 1916, 1922 and 1924. During the
summer of 1926 Secker, now Lawrence's British publisher, agreed to
produce a pocket edition of his works (for 3/6). He then negotiated the
titles away from Duckworth and issued *Sons and Lovers* in a pocket edition
of 2,500 copies in September 1927. Thereafter he produced cheap
editions in 1929 (4,220 copies), 1930 (5,000 copies), 1931 (4,100 copies),
1932 (5,500 copies) and 1933 (reset; 10,000 copies).

The American edition

The first American edition of *Sons and Lovers* was published in New
York on 17 September 1913 by Mitchell Kennerley, who had become
Lawrence's American publisher with *The Trespasser* in May 1912.
Kennerley printed from new plates, having reset the text of Duckworth's
edition using corrected page proofs sent to him by Duckworth.[69] But the
set sent to Kennerley had not quite reached the final state of correction,
for in chapter VI a short phrase is retained which had been removed
before the publication of Duckworth's edition (see Textual apparatus
entry for 145:34). Lawrence did not correct any proofs for this edition
(hereafter A1), although he would have liked to (ii. 67), and therefore its
other variants from the Duckworth edition (hereafter E1) consist of
American house-styling, the correction of errors and the introduction of
new ones.

In June 1913, Mitchell Kennerley wrote to Edward Garnett asking for
biographical information about Lawrence with which to publicise the
novel (ii. 26 and n. 3). Kennerley also arranged for part of chapter XV to

---

[69] Duckworth wrote to Mitchell Kennerley on Wednesday 23 April 1913 that he hoped to
send the corrected proof sheets of *Sons and Lovers* by Saturday's post; TMS NYPL.

be published as 'Derelict' in the September issue of *Forum*.[70] It appeared with the note: 'This remarkable sketch is taken from Mr. Lawrence's new novel, *Sons and Lovers* which will be published shortly.'

The dust-jacket did not repeat Duckworth's description of the novel but read:

This novel tells the story of two generations – men and women, boys and girls, and men and women again. It has the completeness and sincerity of a great novel, and it is written with the power and restraint of a great novelist. No book since "The Old Wives' Tale"[71] has presented a life-drama so convincingly, or built up living characters with such intimate detail of conduct or such vivid realization of conditions. Father and mother, sons and daughters, sons and lovers of women, they live their lives and go their several ways, in their strength and their weakness, with their passions and sorrows and triumphs. It is a book of contrasts, with the inevitability of destiny itself, and the appeal both of the simple and the strange.

Lawrence thanked Mitchell Kennerley in September for 'advertising *Sons and Lovers* so widely', adding, 'I do like the reviews',[72] but he did not receive a specimen of Kennerley's edition until October (ii. 82). Kennerley promised Lawrence two instalments of £25, but some time during the first quarter of 1914, after Lawrence had received the first £25, a cheque for £10 arrived[73] 'making up *Sons and Lovers* accounts', which turned out to be faulty and was rejected by Lawrence's bank in London (ii. 174). Although Lawrence returned it to him, Kennerley never honoured it. This so angered Lawrence that by January 1917 he had reversed the sums in his memory (iii. 74) and by 1920 he believed he had received nothing at all (iii. 576, 612, 651, 692).

---

[70] The text (pp. 343–52), beginning 'So the weeks' (456:37), was taken from A1. It shared with A1 two variants from E1, and introduced a further six minor variants. None is recorded in the Textual apparatus of this edition. *Forum*, which ran from March 1886 to June 1930 (and as *Forum and Century* until June 1940), was published by Mitchell Kennerley from 1910–16 in New York and London. In 1913 it was edited by Arthur Hooley (1910–15), and thereafter by Kennerley and others (1916–20). (It had published DHL's story 'The Soiled Rose', an early version of 'The Shades of Spring', in March 1913.)

[71] By Arnold Bennett (1908).

[72] *Letters*, ii. 77. His letter is conjecturally dated 25 September. Only one review has been found before this date, in the *New York Times Book Review*.

[73] Some time between the end of 1913 when he still had not heard from Kennerley (ii. 133) and April 1914 when DHL believed, erroneously as it turned out, he had now received £35 (ii. 165). The first cheque for £25 was acknowledged to have arrived, both by Frieda in December 1914 (ii. 245) and by DHL in February 1915 (ii. 279); and a letter from Edward Garnett to Kennerley acknowledging its receipt survives among the Kennerley papers at NYPL.

From late August to December 1914 Lawrence repeatedly urged Amy Lowell, the Imagist poet, to visit Kennerley on his behalf when she returned to New York, and in December he learned from her that Kennerley 'says he owes me only £10·· 7·· 6. But even that he won't pay me.' She also informed him that Kennerley's 'reputation is very bad', but she offered to put the matter into the hands of one of her lawyers, if Lawrence would send her his contract with Kennerley and a 'list of accounts'. However, Lawrence had to confess to J. B. Pinker (his agent from July 1914), 'I don't know what my agreement with Kennerley is. Duckworths did it' (ii. 246). In 1920 and 1921, when Lawrence tried to retrieve the contract, Duckworth at first claimed he could not find it (iii. 644), and then remembered that there had been no contract, but 'all arranged through letters – nothing definite – ' (iii. 651).

In October 1920 Lawrence instructed his agent in America, Robert Mountsier, to buy back the rights and the plates of the novel from Kennerley, who was continuing to issue reprints (iii. 612). In 1922 another New York publishing house, Boni and Liveright, issued a 'Modern Library' edition of the novel, without any authority from Lawrence (iv. 318–19) and in 1923 paid Mitchell Kennerley $800 for 10,000 copies. By February 1923 Mountsier had started a lawsuit against Kennerley which was expected to cost Lawrence $300–$500 (iv. 376). Thereafter the business was handled for Lawrence by Thomas Seltzer, who had become his American publisher. Kennerley yielded the rights and the plates in 1923, but no royalties on the sales he had made; and he immediately proceeded to advertise 'a new edition' which Lawrence believed to consist of his unsold stock (iv. 417–18). Seltzer published the first of his editions in 1923.

Considering the profitability of sales indicated by the large sum Boni and Liveright paid to Kennerley, Lawrence was hardly exaggerating when he wrote in 1924: 'America has had that, my most popular book, for nothing'.[74] But some time in 1924 Boni and Liveright paid his publisher, Seltzer, $112 for 1,400 copies, and in May 1926 Klopfer of the Random House publishing firm sent $400 to Seltzer for royalties on the 5,000 copies of the novel he was going to print. By autumn 1937

---

[74] 'The Bad Side of Books', introduction to *A Bibliography of the Writings of D. H. Lawrence* (Philadelphia, 1925), by Edward D. McDonald (reprinted in *Phoenix: The Posthumous Papers of D. H. Lawrence*, ed. McDonald, New York, 1936, p. 234). McDonald cites DHL's letter to Garnett of 22 April 1914 (ii. 165) as acknowledging the receipt of £35, but see preceding note.

a total of 82,400 copies had been printed in America and about 78,000 sold.[75]

Reception

'With his third novel Mr. D. H. Lawrence has come to full maturity as a writer', announced the first review, the day after publication (*Standard*, 30 May).[76] *Sons and Lovers* had at once attracted the highest accolade as a 'great' book containing 'the mark of genius'. Would it receive the general acclaim that Lawrence felt he had earned? By 10 June this was the only review he had seen and he told Garnett, 'I thought it was done by you, perhaps' (ii. 21), evidently suspecting a well-placed 'puff' designed to influence subsequent reviewers. Certainly Duckworth's advertisements quoted from it. And indeed the review endeavours to head off possible criticism of the novel's explicitness by asserting Lawrence's greatness: 'No other English novelist of our time has so great a power to translate passion into words'.

It was some weeks before anyone endorsed a valuation of this order. *The Sunday Times* (1 June, p. 6) 'cordially recommended' the book as 'undeniably one of the sincerest specimens of work which the current publishing season has produced'. For this reviewer the subject was Mrs Morel: she 'dominates the book, which sounds the note of tragedy at the start and keeps it up until the finish'. For Robert Lynd in the *Daily News and Leader* (7 June, p. 4), it was about 'the troubled life of the worker possessed by the artistic temper' and it revealed 'an individual attitude to life and an original sense of the vivid colours of the world, which are promising for the author's future'. The *Observer* reviewer (8 June, p. 6) thought the novel a hundred pages too long but commended it as 'a strong, sincere story', praising its 'photographic accuracy' and 'masterly ... grip of scenic actuality'.

'We finish Part I. with a strong feeling of admiration for the success of Mr. Lawrence's resolute reliance upon cumulative detail', declared *The Times Literary Supplement*'s reviewer (12 June, p. 256), who was the first to make a strong distinction between the novel's two parts. Approving its

---

[75] All information on royalty payments by Boni and Liveright and Random House are taken from the Random House files at ColU. The 'Modern Library' paid A. and C. Boni a total of $4,000 for 50,000 copies between 1926 and 1932. On 8 February 1933 the publishing firm Viking bought the rights, made new plates and took over publication of the novel in America (ColU).

[76] P. 5; reprinted in R. P. Draper, ed., *D. H. Lawrence: The Critical Heritage* (1970), pp. 58–9.

'sincerity' and 'long crescendo of realism' but objecting to its lack of 'reticence', this reviewer found Part II 'overwrought'. The *Westminster Gazette* (14 June) had reservations: 'in some respects [his] finest' novel but grudgingly conceded: 'this history of weakness is a remarkable piece of work. Charged with the beauty of atmosphere and observation, of which Mr. Lawrence is so complete a master ... a book to haunt and waylay the mind long after it has been laid aside.'[77] Howard Massingham was unreserved: it was 'far and away the best book [Lawrence] has yet written' (*Daily Chronicle*, 17 June).[78] W. L. Courtney regretted that few people would appreciate the novel because Lawrence defied 'certain conventions'; and yet his own praise increased when he came to Part II: 'it is here that the reader feels the remarkable power of the author' (*Daily Telegraph*, 18 June, p. 6).

'I liked the reviews of *Sons and Lovers*', Lawrence wrote to Edward Garnett on 21 June. He had arrived in England a few days earlier and had just received a long letter of congratulation from the novelist and journalist W. L. George (ii. 26).

Duckworth placed an advertisement, in the style of a brief review, in the *Nottingham Guardian Literary Supplement* (4 June) and *The Times Literary Supplement* (18 June) which drew attention to the question of Lawrence's stature: the book 'must secure for its author a position of distinction among modern novelists'. The bid for acclaim of this magnitude was only gradually answered. Acknowledgement came in the *Saturday Review* (21 June) that now that Lawrence had 'given us three' of his 'strange' novels, 'we should be able to make some estimate of his position among writers, yet there is about him something wilful which eludes judgment. Passages in "Sons and Lovers" tempt us to place him in a high class' for they reveal 'an author whose inspiration leaves behind the common artifices of the novelist'.[79] The *Athenæum* reviewer (21 June, p. 668), who was 'held captive from the first page to the last', thought parts of the book 'brilliant'. A long analytical review entitled 'The Brute and the Mystic' in the *Evening Standard and Pall Mall Gazette* by 'R. A. S. J.' (23 June)[80] opened: 'Such a novelist as Mr. Lawrence must be at once distinguished from one who is writing for the sake of a story or in order to exercise his pen. Nothing but intense eagerness about life itself and knowledge drawn from vivid experience lead men to write such books as "The White Peacock," "The Trespasser," and "Sons and Lovers".'

---

[77] P. 17; Draper, *Critical Heritage*, pp. 60–1.
[78] P. 3; Draper, *Critical Heritage*, pp. 62–4.
[79] Pp. 780–1; Draper, *Critical Heritage*, pp. 65–6.
[80] P. 3; probably the journalist and critic Rolfe Arnold Scott-James, see *Letters*, i. 318 n. 4.

But it was 'the cruelty of life' that Lawrence 'probes and searches and analyses in ruthless surgical fashion', according to the reviewer in the *Academy* (28 June, p. 218), who concluded that the novel was 'very depressing' and 'far from pleasant'. What the critic and poet Lascelles Abercrombie found unpleasant was Lawrence's 'constant juxtaposition of love and hatred' whereby 'whatever kind of love it may be, some kind of hate is mixed up in it'. His attack, centred on the 'epigram', 'Odi et amo', still rankled with Lawrence in May 1914: 'He talked of *Sons and Lovers* being all odi et amo. Well, I wish I could find the "Amo" in this poem of his. It is sheer Odi ...' (ii. 177). But the second half of Abercrombie's review showed that he was impressed against his inclination: 'You think you are reading through an unimportant scene; and then find that it has burnt itself on your mind'; and he concluded that Lawrence's 'understanding and vivid realizing of circumstance and his insight into character, and chiefly his power of lighting a train of ordinary events to blaze up into singular signficance, make "Sons and Lovers" stand out from the fiction of the day as an achievement of the first quality' (*Manchester Guardian*, 2 July).[81] 'A piece of fiction of the first water' repeated the *Glasgow Herald*'s enthusiastic reviewer (3 July),[82] who was surprised that 'so fine a work should have come, and come so soon, to justify' the promise of Lawrence's earlier publications. The reviewer in the *Irish Times* (4 July, p. 9) read the whole 'clever and enthralling story' at a sitting.

Hubert Bland opened a long appreciative review in the *New Statesman* (5 July): '*Sons and Lovers* is a very sincere and a very thorough piece of work, certainly the most thorough and the most sincere English novel that has come my way for many a long month.'[83] Although he was 'inclined to wish' that 'two or three of the incidents had been ... less photographically described' he did not reject Part II. But Hugh Walpole, the novelist, did. He praised the book as a 'courageous, honest, adventurous' work which 'in the first part of it at any rate, demands our most serious admiration' (*Blue Review*, July, pp. 190–3). Ethel Colburn Mayne, a writer of fiction and literary biographies, was as fierce in her denunciation of Part II as she was passionate in her praise of Part I: 'Mr Lawrence has hardly an equal' in his 'exquisite nature-pieces', and 'there are scenes which no word but the too lightly lavished "great" can justly characterize'. This was the

[81] P. 7; Draper, *Critical Heritage*, pp. 67–8.
[82] P. 4; Catherine Carswell reviewed *The White Peacock* and *The Rainbow* for the *Glasgow Herald*; but it is not known whether this piece was also by her. Her paper did not review *The Trespasser*, which was here referred to as *The Transgressor*.
[83] P. 408; on 28 July DHL asked the *New Statesman* to publish some of his sketches on the grounds that it had been 'kindly disposed' to *Sons and Lovers* (ii. 52).

longest of the reviews, published anonymously in the *Nation* (12 July).[84]
On 23 July a brief notice in the *Yorkshire Post* declared the book 'very
powerful indeed'.

The highest assessment both of the novel and its author came from an
anonymous reviewer in the *English Review* (August, pp. 157–8): 'This is
certainly a book which stands out far above the ordinary novel. It brings
the author's reputation very high. It makes one think that Mr. Lawrence is
going to be a great writer. As it is, of all the young writers he is quite the
most promising.' The book's 'outstanding quality' was so apparent to
Percival Gibbon that he could begin his review (*Bookman*, August, p. 213)
by pointing out the suitability of its publication by Duckworth, having
'naturally a place in a list which includes such authors as John Galsworthy,
Cunninghame Graham and Charles Doughty',[85] authors characterised by
their 'claiming acknowledgement and understanding from a limited circle
of readers rather than from that general public for whose accommodation
the circulating libraries have their being'. Similarly, under the heading
'Some recent notable novels' in the *Nineteenth Century* for October
(pp. 792–802), the last, chronologically, of these twenty-two reviews,
which are all the British and Irish reviews that have been found,[86] Darrel
Figgis placed *Sons and Lovers* alongside the work of esteemed contempo-
raries: H. G. Wells's *The Passionate Friends*, Hugh Walpole's *Fortitude* and
Miss May Sinclair's *The Combined Maze*,[87] as one of his four 'findings,
thus far, for this year'.

A number of earlier reviewers had invoked established writers. Lynd
objected that 'the men and women of the book are hardly real in the
intimate way of the characters, say, in "Jude the Obscure"'. The *Yorkshire
Post* reviewer found that 'There is a power in the book that often recalls
Mr. Thomas Hardy's "Tess"'. Massingham felt that though 'less of an
artist' than Arnold Bennett, Lawrence was 'indebted to Mr. Bennett's
method', which uses 'not the scalpel like Zola and Flaubert, but the
microscope'. However, 'where Mr. Bennett observes, Mr. Lawrence
analyses', and the second half of *Sons and Lovers* 'parts company from the
Bennett type', being 'infinitely more curious and more intense'. The

[84] Pp. 577–8; Draper, *Critical Heritage*, pp. 69–72.
[85] Robert Bontine Cunninghame Graham (1852–1936), writer of short stories and travel
sketches; Charles Montagu Doughty (1843–1926), travel writer and poet (cf. *Letters*, i.
95).
[86] *Birmingham Daily Post, Eastwood and Kimberley Advertiser, Nottingham Guardian, Sheffield
Daily Telegraph* and the *Scotsman* which had reviewed one or both of the earlier novels did
not review *Sons and Lovers*.
[87] May Sinclair, pseudonym for Mary Amelia St Clair (1863–1946), novelist.

reviewer in the *Irish Times* opined that Lawrence was 'an admirer of George Moore' since 'Paul's two love affairs ... are certainly diluted Moore'. The *Glasgow Herald*'s reviewer thought the 'tale' ranked 'as a story with Mr. Bennett's "Old Wives' Tale" and with Mr. Phillpotts' epic of maternal passion, "Demeter's Daughter."'[88] But it contains passages of description and talk which for touching, poignant beauty can be matched in neither of these books.'

'The pages that have to do with the early Morel history ... are finer than anything that the younger novelists have given us since George Douglas' "House with the Green Shutters"',[89] declared Walpole. But the 'zest' behind Lawrence's nature descriptions so reminded him of *Leaves of Grass* that he concluded: 'Walt Whitman's poetry is the only proper parallel' to the novel. This, however, was for the novelist Walpole a clue to Lawrence's failure: Lawrence was too much of a poet to fulfil the 'supreme duty' of the novelist, 'the creation of character'. For the poet Abercrombie, on the other hand, the fact that Lawrence 'is a poet, one of the most remarkable poets of the day' reduced the faults of his novel to insignificance.

More than individual predilection underlies their dialectically opposed use of 'poet', towards the end of a period of transition during which the historical pre-eminence of poetry as the crown of literature was being displaced by the novel. The poetry of Lawrence's novel was Mayne's retort to those who criticised it for lack of plot: 'How would a "plot" have torn through this fine web of poetry, realism, and shrewd or tender analysis!' The *Glasgow Herald* reviewer went further: 'He is a true poet and can stir to tears with the homeliest phrases ... And for this achievement what white-hot passion of feeling is needed only the poets know.' But in the *Standard*, despite praise for Lawrence's 'revelation of character', objection was made in terms that lend support to Walpole's argument (and echo Garnett's criticisms of the third manuscript): 'His weakness is that he is too often the lyrical poet making his creatures speak his thoughts, and this is a bad fault for a novelist.'

The dispute over Lawrence's success or failure in the creation of character centred on the character of Paul. There was near unanimous agreement that Paul's parents were 'vividly realised' (*Pall Mall Gazette*) – so much so that several reviewers found Gertrude Morel more shrewish

---

[88] 1911, by Eden Phillpotts (1862–1960), novelist and playwright.
[89] Pseudonym for George Douglas Brown (1869–1902), Scottish novelist, whose *The House with the Green Shutters* (1901) DHL had read and recommended to Louie Burrows in 1910 (i. 172).

and Walter Morel more attractive than they believed Lawrence intended them to. This reaction was 'a tribute to the strength of the illusion created' according to the reviewer in the *Athenæum*, who by that phrase explained his own ambivalent response to the characterisation of Miriam: 'Many men, and perhaps most women, will say to themselves as they read: "Yes, this is how Miriam seemed to Paul, but this is not what Miriam was."' *The Times Literary Supplement* reviewer protested at Paul and Mrs Morel's perception of Miriam as 'a spiritual vampire who would leave his soul no rest; but if we read her aright that is a most hapless obsession'. But the *Athenæum* reviewer took the argument beyond literary criticism with a speculation that hints at inside knowledge: 'We suspect ... that, if the girl's story had been written, we should have found her by no means so abnormal a person as represented, and her wayward lover considerably more comprehensible.' Since Hueffer had met Jessie Chambers[90] and had been the other recipient, with Garnett, of her autobiographical manuscript, it may be that he or Garnett influenced this reviewer, who also declared that the reader's incomprehension of Paul arose because 'the narrative reads like an autobiography'.

Massingham concurred that 'Paul is a projection of the writer's own personality' and therefore 'can never get far enough away from his creator to solidify'. Bland ruminated:

Paul is cleverly done. Upon his delineation – nay, upon his creation, one must say, for he is more than delineated – Mr. Lawrence has lavished all of art and all of craft that is his. Yet one feels that there is no Paul – no real man, that is, no substance in which all the multitudinous and warring qualities inhere. He is a complex of human relations rather than a human being that is related.

Percival Gibbon, in contrast, insisted that Paul was 'real', yet sought to explain why: 'he concludes by being extraordinarily ineffectual both as a lover and a man'. One reason was that 'With his diffidence and fastidiousness there goes a strain of the artist' and the other was 'the author's constancy to his artistic purpose, which never suffers him to see his people in a dramatic or spectacular light or on a level higher or lower than his own ... his business is to show them, dispassionately and accurately'.

Like Gibbon many reviewers endeavoured to engage at some depth with what they recognised as a serious work of art; and as a result they revealed underlying preoccupations and automatic assumptions which give a glimpse, for the modern reader, of the cultural environment into which Lawrence delivered his writings. The novel's 'unheroic hero'

90 E. T. 168–75.

prompted the *Westminster Gazette* reviewer to a disquisition on recent French influence, which had 'led Mr. Lawrence, in common with other novelists of great repute or promise, to place more emphasis on feeling than on action', and to take as his subject 'Man as he is rather than man has he ought to be', unlike 'all the great novelists, and the great tragedians' of the past. This was why the book was 'haunting in its very failure', according to Figgis, 'since its introspective knowledge is never accompanied by the wisdom that perceives the cause ... with the result that, like men, we may just blindly know and never, like gods, understand. That is not the great creative way, and its result is inevitably a strong morbidity.'

By denying the reader a seat in the gods, Lawrence provoked some reviewers to spell out their view of the inevitable alternative:

Mr. Lawrence strips everything naked ... Evidently he has found life a very bitter, ugly thing, with no joy in it, nor any warmth but the warmth of lust. His people are animals – highly developed, it is true – and very fine mentally, but throughout all the book there is no glimpse of spirit – Paul and the circle of people among whom he moves live by sense and sense alone. (*Academy*)

Lynd, who in 1915 became vehement about *The Rainbow*, was restrained here: 'Mr. Lawrence is an unusually able novelist with a curious eagerness for the beauty of words and an exaggerated sense of the physical side of love.' But Mayne articulated the same objection with passionate loathing: 'we revolt in weariness from the incessant scenes of sexual passion ... this morbid brooding on the flesh, this ... ever-hot and heavy lustfulness of Paul Morel. Did young man's figure ever more signally fail to move us to interest? We turn from him in fatigued repulsion – so futile he, so garrulous of his lust.'

Her review gave Lawrence a moment of self-doubt: 'Fussy old woman in the *Nation*! ... Do *you* think the second half of *Sons and Lovers* such a lapse from the first, or is it moralistic blarney?' he asked Edward Garnett on 16 July (ii. 40). But in a few days, when he had learned her identity, he wrote to Arthur McLeod, 'Thanks for the reviews – yes they are flattering. I saw the *Nation* ... it was an Irish spinster, a clever woman ... not old, for that matter' (ii. 47).

The word 'morbidity', used in three reviews – and in reviews of *The White Peacock*, *The Trespasser* and *The Rainbow* – draws attention to itself as having had at the time a salience and resonance which it no longer carries. The *Westminster Gazette* reviewer indicated part of its role when objecting to Lawrence's 'peculiar heavy morbidity which he mistakes for realism'. Like the other pair, 'sincerity' and 'lack of reticence', also found repeatedly in these reviews, 'realism' and 'morbidity' are positive and

negative aspects of the same kind of writing: realism was generally
welcomed but in its extreme form was felt to be unwholesome. Lawrence's
realism was judged 'brutal' and 'sordid' by some reviewers and when they
put their objections in terms of 'morbidity' they implied the criticism
mooted by Lynd: 'we miss the elation of the best imaginative writing'.[91]
The problem was Lawrence's rejection of the prevailing conviction that
the 'flesh' is rendered tolerable only if man remembers that he is primarily
a creature of the 'spirit'. Lawrence's assumption that the body is a source
of health independent of and in some respects greater than the spirit, was
felt to be 'morbid' in the sense of morally unhealthy – not in the modern
sense of 'preoccupied with death'.

Death, as an issue in *Sons and Lovers*, was hardly confronted by the
British reviewers, except obliquely when invoking 'tragedy'. But in the
Irish Times the 'fatal dose of morphia' administered by Paul, was noted as
'the last kindness he can do' for his mother. 'Whether or not it was right
for Paul to do the thing he did is an open question', was the only doubt
registered in a favourable review by the novelist Louise Maunsell Field, in
the *New York Times Book Review* (21 September).[92] The *Nation* (New
York, 11 December) was more caustic: 'her actual end is accomplished by
him by means of an overdose of morphia, intended, one must believe, not
only to relieve her anguish, but his own as well'. But whereas Field paid
tribute to the novel as 'plain spoken', but 'not in the least offensive',
'fearless' but 'never coarse', the reviewer in the *Nation* objected to the
implication that 'the free thinking and free living of a certain fashionable
London society' had penetrated 'to the lower classes'. Sinclair Lewis in a
cleverly non-committal review for the *St Louis (Morning) Republic* (25
October) which debated rival artistic evaluations of the book's realism,
presented Lawrence as about to make his first big reputation.[93]

In 1915 an American psychoanalyst, Alfred Kuttner, expounded *Sons
and Lovers* from a psychoanalytical point of view. Tackling head-on
something which had upset earlier reviewers, 'The very idea that an
excess of mother love should prove so disastrous to an individual's fate
seems monstrous', he explained that this aspect of the book met with
incomprehension because Freud's theories were not yet well known.
'Where Mr. Lawrence particularizes so passionately Freud generalizes.
Freud has proved beyond cavil that the parental influence regularly

[91] Cf. DHL's satire against 'uplift' in *Mr Noon*, ed. Lindeth Vasey (Cambridge, 1984),
pp. 156–7.
[92] P. 479; Draper, *Critical Heritage*, pp. 73–4.
[93] Reprinted in the *D. H. Lawrence Review*, xix (1987), 108. Two further reviews appeared in
New York: *Independent* (9 October) and *Outlook* (6 December).

determines the mating impulse.'[94] He expanded his analysis a year later having increased his estimate of the novel: 'It ranks high, very high as a piece of literature and at the same time it embodies a theory which it illustrates and exemplifies with a completeness that is nothing less than astonishing.'[95] Lawrence read the second article and hated it: ' "complexes" are vicious half-statements ... When you've said Mutter-complex, you've said nothing ... My poor book: it was, as art, a fairly complete truth: so they carve a half lie out of it, and say "Voilà". Swine!' (ii. 655).

Catherine Carswell described in her memoir of Lawrence[96] how reviewers and friends expected him to go on writing 'masterpieces' like *Sons and Lovers*. But as Lawrence made progress with his new novel, which was to become *The Rainbow*, he rapidly rejected *Sons and Lovers* despite having been pleased at its popularity. By the end of 1913 he looked back at it as written in a 'hard, violent style full of sensation and presentation' (ii. 132). Now, by contrast, 'I have no longer the joy in creating vivid scenes, that I had in *Sons and Lovers*. I don't care much more about accumulating objects in the powerful light of emotion, and making a scene of them' (ii. 142). Years later he was reported to have made a more radical criticism: 'I would write a different "Sons and Lovers" now; my mother was wrong, and I thought she was absolutely right.'[97]

Text

The Cambridge edition is based in principle on the text of the final manuscript as it left Lawrence's hands (MS), which is emended to incorporate Lawrence's proof revisions. In this section the fragmentary remains of the earlier manuscripts drafts are listed and the partial evidence provided by the surviving proofs is summarised, before the editorial principles are outlined.

The surviving manuscripts

The second manuscript (MS2) will be published in a separate volume in the Cambridge edition under the title *Paul Morel*. It survives in a truncated

---

[94] *New Republic*, 10 April 1915; Draper, *Critical Heritage*, p. 79. Kuttner had already (10 November 1914) written a destructive report for Kennerley on 'The Wedding Ring', an early draft of *The Rainbow* (ed. Kinkead-Weekes, pp. 483–5).

[95] *Psychoanalytic Review*, 10 June 1916; reprinted in E. W. Tedlock, *D. H. Lawrence and 'Sons and Lovers'* (1966), p. 77.

[96] *The Savage Pilgrimage: A Narrative of D. H. Lawrence*, (1932; reprinted Cambridge, 1981), pp. 34, 64, 67.

[97] Frieda Lawrence, *"Not I, But The Wind ..."*, p. 74.

state (pp. 72–353), the bulk of it as a continuous separate manuscript,[98] and 13 further pages incorporated in MS. It seems likely that Lawrence discarded pages 1–71 when leaving Croydon in January 1912, and that the rest survives because Lawrence left it with his sister Ada in Eastwood when he went to Germany in May 1912 (i. 411).

The abandoned seven-page start of the third manuscript is now located with MS2, probably because Lawrence also left these pages with Ada Lawrence. Of the third manuscript proper (MS3), 172 pages survive: 93 pages were transferred into MS;[99] and a further 79 pages survive outside MS. Of the latter, 56 pages were rejected from the opening chapters when Lawrence made a start on the fourth version at Icking in July 1912.[100] The other 23 are pp. 203–26 of chapter IX annotated by Jessie Chambers;[101] the chapter lacks its opening pages, but its number and title are known from Jessie's separate pages of comment (see footnote 22).

The fourth and final manuscript (MS)[102] consists of 530 pages, numbered 1–540. It was given by Frieda to Mabel Dodge Luhan in reciprocation for her gift of a ranch in New Mexico in 1924, and the following year she used it to pay Dr A. A. Brill for psychoanalysing a friend.[103] A photographic facsimile of the manuscript together with some fragments from early drafts has been published (see footnote 35).

The galley proofs

Of 52⅛ galley proofs 6 trimmed sheets are extant (G), equivalent to 39 of the first edition's 423 pages (395:39–411:32, 442:33–464:37). Fortunately, however, they belonged to the set Lawrence checked, and provide important evidence of the errors, corrections and revisions made at this stage.

The accuracy of the galley proofs

MS was not a difficult document to print from, being neat and legible even where heavily revised. The only certain evidence of the compositors'

---

[98] Roberts E373d; located at UT.

[99] This includes the thirteen pages previously transferred from MS2 to MS3, and fifteen which were not introduced into MS3 until the revision of May–June 1912.

[100] Roberts E373a, located at UCB; and published as six 'Fragments' in *Facsimile*, ed. Schorer (see footnote 35). Five pages (Fragment 3, pp. 45–9a) were not introduced until the May–June 1912 revision of MS3. There survive two additional pages (Fragment 4, pp. 68–9) which were unfinished pages of revision probably written in June 1912 but never incorporated into any version of the novel.

[101] Roberts E373b; UT.   [102] Roberts E373e; UCB.

[103] Letter from Mabel Dodge Luhan to Dr. A. A. Brill, 24 April 1925; UCB; see *The Letters of D. H. Lawrence*, ed. James T. Boulton and Lindeth Vasey (Cambridge, 1989), v. 65, 74.

verbal accuracy is provided by the few surviving G. They amount to 1,630 lines of type, or just under a tenth of the novel. In them the compositors made sixteen verbal changes from MS, and three corrections of pen-slips by Lawrence.[104]

But as the printers set the MS text in type, they repunctuated it, for Billing and Sons operated a house-style which was at variance with Lawrence's practice. In G the compositors made 437 changes of punctuation from MS; and in the whole book, out of a total of about 18,050 lines of type, the compositors changed Lawrence's punctuation (including paragraphing) between 4,000 and 5,000 times – 10 times a page on average, or once every 4 or 5 lines.

The revision of Lawrence's punctuation had a cumulative effect not merely on his style and rhythms but on his meaning, since Lawrence's meaning is peculiarly dependent on his punctuation. This is partly because he exploits punctuation to indicate tones of voice: for example by using dashes to indicate pauses, afterthoughts or changes of direction, and by deliberately ending a question with a full stop or a statement with a question mark. It is also because Lawrence wrote an unsubordinated prose – paratactic rather than syntactic – so that, for example, he sets arguments and people in apposition by a sequence of contrasting sentences beginning 'And' or 'But'. Among the changes introduced by the printers, question marks were added to questions and removed where the verb was merely 'said'; many commas were omitted, many exclamation marks added; frequently sentences beginning with 'And' or 'But' were joined to the preceding sentences; dashes were employed strictly for parenthesis.

In some passages the changes in punctuation altered Lawrence's meaning drastically. For example, he wrote:

Miriam pondered this. She saw what he was seeking: a sort of baptism of fire in passion, it seemed to her. She realised that he would never be satisfied till he had it. Perhaps it was essential to him—as to some men to sow wild oats. (362:20–3)

Lawrence's dash indicates that 'wild oats' are not the experience Paul wanted, but they became the same thing when the printers changed for commas: ' ... Perhaps it was essential to him, as to some men, to sow wild oats; ... '

In another example, Lawrence began a paragraph with 'And':

Yet she tried hard to scorn him, because he would not see in her the princess, but only the swinegirl.
And he scarcely observed her.

[104] For the verbal changes see next section. The corrections were 'One evening', 'always' and 'one' for DHL's errors 'One', 'alway' and 'on'.

Then he was so ill, and she felt he would be weak ... Then she could love him. (174:21–5)

As Lawrence wrote it, the one-sentence paragraph set Paul's point of view in apposition to Miriam's reflections. But the printers joined the sentence to the preceding paragraph, adding it to Miriam's thoughts so that it became a further reason why she should scorn Paul.

There are many places where a comma essential to the meaning is removed. For example Lawrence wrote: 'And she took him simply, because his need was bigger either than her or him' (397:38–9). The comma indicates that by 'simply' Lawrence meant 'in a simple manner'; but printed without the comma, 'simply because' became 'for the simple reason that'.

Tones of voice are affected throughout the novel. For example the tone of '"Clara?" he said, struggling.' is manifestly different with a comma instead of the MS question mark (397:22); and Paul's hesitation as he thinks out loud is turned to dismissive impatience in the repunctuation of; 'I don't know—I rather think he loves her—as much as he can. But he's a fool.' (361:33–4) as: 'I don't know. I rather think he loves her as much as he can, but he's a fool.' The present edition retains manuscript punctuation.

Lawrence's correction of the galley proofs

Of the sixteen verbal changes found in G, fourteen were printers' errors, and two were unnecessary corrections of Lawrence's text.[105] Only eight of the errors were corrected before publication: four on G and four later. It was Lawrence who corrected the four on G: one of them was self-evident in context, but the other three he alone knew were errors.[106] Of the four errors corrected later, two were self-evident in context, and two Lawrence alone could have identified as errors.[107]

One of the six errors which remained uncorrected was the misspelling of 'Colwick'. The other five are more important because they might be interpreted as revisions by Lawrence if these few G were also lost. They

---

[105] The printers set 'different from' where Lawrence had made a speaker say 'different to' (407:6); and inserted 'but' where DHL had written no conjunction – a recurrent feature of his style in this novel – 'He did not stir, sat gazing ...' (456:5). Lawrence left these as printed.

[106] These were 'marram', 'train' and 'Colwich' for MS 'marrain', 'tram' and 'Colwick'; but 'Colwich' appeared twice in the same paragraph and Lawrence corrected it only once (402:17, 411:22, 458:26, 29).

[107] These were 'her ... hair' for MS 'his ... hair' (453:4); 'saw far, far away' for MS 'saw, far away' (455:23)' Lawrence reduced the latter to 'saw', but MS reading is restored in this edition.

were: 'She felt them there' and 'would he not' for MS 'She left them there' (450:15) and 'would not he' (462:15); the omission of 'now' in two places (444:23, 463:1); and lastly the misreading of a revision which Lawrence made in very small writing on the last page of the MS. He deleted 'tiny speck', inserting 'almost nothing' in its place in the sentence 'On every side the immense dark silence seemed pressing him into extinction, and yet, tiny speck, he could not be extinct'; but he squeezed a version of the deleted words at the edge of the page: ' ... pressing him, so tiny a speck, into extinction ... ' (464:23). The compositor's error of 'spark' for 'speck' has never been corrected.

With regard to punctuation, Lawrence largely left the printers' changes in place. When faced with a similar degree of restyling in the proofs of his first novel, *The White Peacock*, he had tried to restore his own punctuation, but now he confined himself to a few corrections where the meaning or inflection of a sentence was affected. On the surviving G he added only 6 commas and 2 dashes, and all of them, except 1 comma, had been in MS. Given that the compositors had removed 117 commas from this portion of text, his reintroduction of 5 is minimal.

Revisions by the printer's reader on the galley proofs

The marks entered on the proofs before Lawrence received them influenced his proof-correcting. G shows that the printer's reader did not merely mark for later correction the still outstanding typographical errors: he also changed the punctuation twice, suggested improved readings in three places and queried a further seven passages. Of these seven, Lawrence refused to reconsider 'shapen' and 'realest' (396:4, 455:4), and deleted the queries; but the other five he altered.

He revised 'It' to 'impersonal' in response to a query in the margin against 'his experience had been It, and not Clara ... ' (399:16). A query against his description of Dawes as 'trying to get by unnoticed past every person he met,' led Lawrence to delete 'by' (406:7). In one paragraph two sentences were queried because Miriam first sat with her 'hands ... clasped over her knee', and then, 'suddenly took her finger from her mouth ... ' So Lawrence inserted: 'She put her finger between her lips' (461:3–4). A repetition was queried in the fourth paragraph from the end of the novel: 'a level fume of lights. Beyond the town the country, little fuming spots for more towns ... ' Lawrence not only changed 'fuming' to 'smouldering' here (464:1–2), but deleted 'the low fuming of' three sentences from the end of the book, which had read: 'Turning sharply, he walked towards the low fuming of the city's gold phosphorescence.'

Where the printer's reader entered revisions himself with a query, Lawrence deleted the query and let the change stand. In one instance, the compositor had omitted Lawrence's comma from the sentence, 'He wanted everything to stand still, so he could be with her again' (455:11–12). The reader inserted 'that' after 'so', and Lawrence accepted it, but also reinstated the comma. MS reading is retained in this edition. In another instance Lawrence had written: ' ... he took them out of the jar, dripping as they were, went quickly into the kitchen' (463:26–7). The omitted conjunction is a feature of his style in this novel, but Lawrence allowed the reader's inserted 'and' after 'were' to remain. However, the policy of this edition is that where there is evidence that the revision was made by someone other than Lawrence (even though he did not cancel it), MS should be preferred.

Another of the alterations Lawrence allowed to stand was the reversal of the words 'nights' and 'evenings', from order of importance to chronological order in his sentence. 'The days were often a misery to [Clara], but the nights and the evenings were usually a bliss to them both' (396:12–14). As noted above, the compositors had also changed Lawrence's word order from the less to the more usual, in the phrase 'would not he'. Lawrence himself did not reverse word order when revising: he substituted, added or deleted words. In the absence of any evidence that Lawrence initiated such changes, the present edition retains MS readings in these instances.

The printer's reader also altered the punctuation twice without adding a query.[108] In one case he was removing an ambiguity introduced by the compositor's change of punctuation. In the other, he changed Lawrence's 'Miriam.' to 'Miriam?' (456:27). Lawrence did not make any mark beside these changes. But he himself, when revising, did not substitute one kind of punctuation for another, he largely reinstated omitted MS punctuation (see above); therefore these substitutions by another hand are rejected and MS punctuation retained.

Revisions by Edward Garnett on the galley proofs

When Edward Garnett checked through G, he lightly abbreviated and censored the description of Clara and Paul's early morning swim in chapter XIII. Lawrence had written two similar sentences (401:22–3, 31):

---

[108] These revisions are easily distinguished from DHL's. The printer's reader wrote a long straight slash, but DHL accompanied punctuation changes, though not verbal revisions, with a slash that always had a large backward hook at the bottom.

"OO!" she said, hugging her breasts between her arms, "it's cold!"

and a short paragraph later:

She gathered her breasts between her arms, cringing, laughing:
"OO, it will be so cold!" she said.

Garnett deleted the first passage, and changed 'gathered' to 'hugged' in the second, apparently preferring an action in which Clara covered up her breasts to one that seemed to present them to Paul. Garnett had already censored the sentence which followed this second passage in MS, by changing Lawrence's:

He bent forward and kissed the two white, glistening globes she cradled.

to:

He bent forward and kissed her neck.

There are other instances where passages lightly censored by Garnett in MS had more sentences removed before publication; and despite the loss of the relevant proofs it seems likely that Garnett further censored the text, as here. In this passage Garnett's alteration was later revised in page proofs by Lawrence to read: 'He bent forward and kissed her, held her suddenly close, and kissed her again.' In such cases, the editors of the Cambridge edition assume that MS represents Lawrence's preferred reading more closely than the revisions he made in response to the cuts, alterations and errors he found in the proofs.

Revisions by Lawrence on the galley proofs

Lawrence revised this short section of the novel in over forty places, making many more changes on his own account than had been made or suggested by the printer's reader and Edward Garnett. By far the greater number of Lawrence's revisions in the surviving G were substitutions: he rewrote words and sentences in twenty-nine places, only two of which were in response to a query in the margin from the printer's reader. But he also made twelve deletions. Both revisions and deletions vary from one or two words to whole sentences. Additions are less frequent. Apart from the sentence about Miriam putting her finger between her lips, he only added three short phrases.

In the whole novel there are approximately 670 substantive differences between MS (as edited by Garnett) and page proofs, varying in length from one word to several sentences. This figure must include some alterations made by the printers and Garnett on lost G. In the absence of the rest of G the precise number cannot be known; but on the evidence of surviving G it must be a small proportion. The great majority must be revisions by Lawrence. The largest number occur in chapters VII and VIII followed by XII and XIII.

The page proofs

The accuracy of the page proofs

Comparison of G with the equivalent page proofs (PP) shows that Lawrence's revisions were nearly all printed correctly.[109] But in two places, where Lawrence had substituted a sentence ending with a full stop he had failed to delete the printed punctuation, which was therefore retained in PP with the new reading. In the first, he revised 'Had he been alone, after all?' to 'But he believed her too implicitly.' (407:18). The inappropriate question mark was removed before publication. In the second, he changed 'And not a place for him!' to 'And he had no place in it.' (464:2–3). The revision appeared with an exclamation mark in PP and thus it remained. The policy of this edition is to retain MS punctuation as much as possible. But where Lawrence evidently introduced complete new sentences on the other proofs which have not survived, the editors accept the punctuation which was printed with them in the first edition.

PP contained errors outstanding from G: ten identified in the small section of G discussed above, of which four were corrected on PP.

Lawrence's revisions on the page proofs

None of the revised sets of PP survives, but comparison between the unrevised set and the first English edition (E1) shows approximately 260 substantive changes (the largest number occur in chapter XII, followed by chapters VII and XIII). The great majority of these must have been revisions by Lawrence. In this edition substantive variants from MS found in PP and E1 are accepted, with the exception of reversals of word order, and any omission of the word 'now'.

The Cambridge Edition

The first decision an editor has to make is whether in principle to publish the whole text of Lawrence's final MS or Garnett's edited version of it.

The sole basis for making this decision is to answer the irreducibly

---

[109] His insertion 'She put her finger between her lips.' was written so small that 'fingers' was printed in error. He had changed 'never reached' to 'did not often reached' (408:22–3) but the printers corrected it.

hypothetical question: which text would Lawrence prefer to have published had he the choice? Evidence as to his wishes in the matter can now only be found in his letters of the period. Unfortunately this is partial evidence in the sense that not all his letters have survived and there are no transcripts of his private thoughts and conversations. Nonetheless an editor ought not select a few salient remarks from these documents as the basis for his decision but must weigh them all, considering as carefully as possible Lawrence's circumstances and attitudes.

This is a decision in principle which cannot have anything to do with the editor's opinion of the literary merit of the excised passages, whether they are essential to the novel as a whole work of art or whether they are examples of weak or redundant writing. The question at stake cannot be whether or not the editor believes that Garnett improved or damaged the novel by his trimming: these are critical questions which belong in a separate arena of debate from the editorial work. It is true that in weighing up the historical evidence of Lawrence's opinion, an editor is aware of a polemical clash on the question of literary form between Lawrence and Garnett, but in this matter, too, for an editor, the author must in principle have the benefit of the doubt.

We have set out our arguments above (p. xlviii) for concluding that Lawrence did not desire to have his MS modified by Garnett. He did desire to have it published; and it was the constraint of the market as perceived by the publisher to whom Lawrence had become committed which was deemed to necessitate a reduction of the novel's length and its sexual explicitness.

This is the crucial first decision for an editor. If an editor considers this question in the longer time-scale of the whole tradition of English literature, he or she may select Lawrence's final MS, as defended by him, regardless of contemporary commercial exigencies. If, however, an editor considers the question in historical terms strictly confined to the author's biography, then he or she may value more highly Lawrence's determination to have at least some version of the novel published in 1913, and may select the first edition as the simple fulfilment of that determination. The first edition may gain thereby some intrinsic merit, but it cannot achieve an overriding textual authority.

For the theoretical defence of the first edition as base-text is not straightforward. On the one hand there is the problem of defining and then accepting or rejecting those of Garnett's cuts which constitute censorship. On the other hand, as should be indisputably clear from the above examples, the extensive repunctuation of Lawrence's prose in the printing house pervasively altered his rhythm, nuance and meaning. If MS punctuation demonstrably conveys more faithfully Lawrence's meaning, an editor who preferred the first edition as base-text would be obliged to repunctuate it from MS (as well, as it goes without saying, as correcting observable transmission errors).

The Cambridge editors, having decided upon the complete MS together with its punctuation as base-text, are then faced with a second decision: whether to incorporate Lawrence's proof revisions. Again, the only sound basis for forming a judgement is to answer the question: what would Lawrence have preferred? It would be unacceptable for an editor to answer this question on the basis of personal literary–critical perceptions as to the meaning of the novel with or without the revisions. But there are no statements in Lawrence's letters to weigh and balance, apart from his protestations of weariness at the chore of proof-correcting. However, there is the evidence provided by collation of the manuscript with all the surviving printed states, which shows that he revised the proofs far more than he corrected errors in them. There is the further tangential evidence of Lawrence's normal practice. Not only did he have a highly individual method of writing and repeatedly rewriting his works, but it was characteristic of his publishing experience that he received proofs which inadequately represented his manuscript or typescript and then treated the task of proof-correction as a continuation of his creative activity on the work, making many more changes in the interest of revision than were needed to correct transmission errors.

From this the editors argue as follows: If Garnett had sent Lawrence's MS unaltered to the printers, Lawrence would still, when checking the proofs, have made a few corrections and a large number of revisions. His revisions, therefore, must represent his textual preferences. In the case of *Sons and Lovers* he did not enter revisions on the proofs solely because Garnett had pruned his MS. Indeed, in the majority of cases, by definition, he was revising text left unaltered by Garnett. However, it is evident in a minority of cases that a revision by Lawrence is prompted solely by the need to remedy some local effect produced by Garnett's deletion, and there, clearly, Lawrence's MS text is, in principle, to be preferred.

The Cambridge editors therefore consider that the MS text emended to incorporate Lawrence's proof revisions is the closest it is now possible to come to the text that Lawrence would have preferred to see in print. The fact that it is a construct is the inevitable result of the fact that Lawrence had as little control as he did over the publication of his work. Even the most rigorous adherence to a guiding principle (that of Lawrence's preferences) inevitably entails some less than ideal results: passages in MS are now published which Lawrence did not have the opportunity to revise in proof. Some readers may judge that Lawrence might well have revised some of these passages. But the decision in principle to reinstate Lawrence's MS must be implemented in full, not selectively. The novel which Lawrence laboured so intensely to create was, it must be said, different in many ways from the work with which the reading public has been familiar during the past eighty years, and that novel deserves to receive publication at last.

SONS AND LOVERS

Note on the text

The base-text for this edition is the manuscript (MS) which Lawrence completed in November 1912, and which was edited by Edward Garnett before being used as setting-copy for the first English edition (E1) published by Duckworth (29 May 1913).

The MS text is published complete, including the passages deleted by Garnett and not hitherto printed. MS has been edited to incorporate subsequent revisions made by Lawrence. The surviving documents containing evidence of his revisions are: six of the 52⅛ galley proofs (G), bearing corrections by the printer's reader (GCP), by Edward Garnett (GC†) and revisions by Lawrence (GR); a complete but unmarked set of page proofs (PP); and (E1).

The first American edition (A1) published by Mitchell Kennerley (17 September 1913) was reset in the USA from corrected PP whose text was almost identical with E1. Since Lawrence did not revise proofs, its variants have no authority but they are included in the apparatus, because A1 has been the text hitherto available in the USA.

Variants from MS readings found in these documents have been treated as follows:

—Punctuation variants have been rejected.

—In G only GR have been accepted.

—In PP and E1 substantive variants have been adopted with two exceptions. (i) Some can be argued to be further cuts for censorship purposes by Garnett, continuing those already made by him on the MS. (ii) Some G variants from MS and some GCP are solely changes of word order, which adjust DHL's use of Midlands dialect to forms more in line with standard English, or revise his reversal of the usual or logical order, and therefore where variants in PP and E1 appear to belong to this category, they have been rejected as changes probably made by a copy-editor or Garnett.

In the Textual apparatus MS passages deleted or altered by Garnett and now printed for the first time are recorded thus: *Om. MS†* or *MS†*. Any editorial changes to these passages are noted immediately after that entry.

The apparatus records all textual variants, except the categories listed below.

1 Manifest errors in MS accidentals, such as omitted apostrophes (e.g. 'o'clock'), spelling errors and uncompleted quotation marks have been silently corrected.

2 Minor inconsistencies in MS have been silently regularised as follows. Full stops occasionally used after chapter titles and personal titles (e.g. Mrs/Mrs.) have been silently omitted. Titles of books and magazines have been emended to italics,

and any quotation marks removed. Where double punctuation includes a redundant comma (e.g. ',?' and ',—'), the comma has been removed. When such readings occur in the apparatus as part of another variant, they are recorded. The separation of contractions (e.g. is n't) in MS (and A1) is not retained or recorded.

3 MS variation in the use of single and double quotation marks has not been regularised. DHL's variation in the use of hyphens has been printed as in MS, but where his omission of meaning-bearing hyphens introduces unintended ambiguity, they have been inserted and recorded in the apparatus, e.g. 'rocking-chair'.

4 Variants in the printed texts which consist of manifest typesetting errors are not listed in the apparatus. Variants in G or PP are not recorded if MS reading was restored before publication (E1), except where the correction was GR, all of which are recorded.

5 The following printers' regularisations of MS punctuation are not recorded: insertion of a hyphen in compound numbers; removal of quotation marks from pub names; alteration of all single quotation marks to double quotation marks (except where they occur within speech); italicisation of punctuation after an italicised word; removal of DHL's dash after the end of a sentence (e.g. '.—' and '?—', etc.); rendering DHL's short dash after unfinished speech as a double length dash.

6 The following printers' house-styling variants from MS are not recorded: the words 'bread-and-butter', 'connection', 'farther', 'half-past', 'H'm', 'labourer', 'on to', 'waggon', 'whisky' for DHL's 'bread and butter', 'connexion', 'further', 'half past', 'Hm', 'laborer', 'onto', 'wagon', 'whiskey'; and the forms 'good-night', 'to-day', 'œ' and '-iz-' for DHL's forms 'goodnight', 'today', 'oe' and '-is-'.

7 All chapter titles were printed in capital letters, but Lawrence mainly capitalised nouns: these differences are not recorded, but titles which first appear in PP or E1 have been edited according to DHL's practice, and the changes recorded.

TO
EDWARD GARNETT ✩

Contents

PART I

I	The early married Life of the Morels	9
II	The Birth of Paul, and another Battle	37
III	The Casting off of Morel, the Taking on of William	61
IV	The young Life of Paul	82
V	Paul Launches into Life	108
VI	Death in the Family	141

PART II

VII	Lad-and-Girl Love	173
VIII	Strife in Love	218
IX	Defeat of Miriam	255
X	Clara	295
XI	The Test on Miriam	322
XII	Passion	345
XIII	Baxter Dawes	386
XIV	The Release	423
XV	Derelict	454

PART I

Chapter I

The early married Life of the Morels*

"The Bottoms" succeeded to "Hell Row." Hell Row was a block of
thatched, bulging cottages that stood by the brook-side on Greenhill 5
Lane. There lived the colliers who worked in the little gin-pits two
fields away. The brook ran under the alder trees, scarcely soiled by
these small mines, whose coal was drawn to the surface by donkeys
that plodded wearily in a circle, round a gin. And all over the
countryside were these same pits, some of which had been worked 10
in the time of Charles II,* the few colliers and the donkeys burrow-
ing down like ants into the earth, making queer mounds and little
black places among the corn-fields and the meadows. And the
cottages of these coal-miners in blocks and pairs here and there,
together with odd farms and homes of the stockingers,* straying over 15
the parish, formed the village of Bestwood.

Then, some sixty years ago,* a sudden change took place. The
gin-pits were elbowed aside by the large mines of the financiers.
The coal and iron field of Nottinghamshire and Derbyshire was
discovered. Carston, Waite and Co. appeared.* Amid tremendous 20
excitement, Lord Palmerston formally opened the company's first
mine at Spinney Park,* on the edge of Sherwood Forest.

About this time the notorious Hell Row, which through growing
old had acquired an evil reputation, was burned down, and much
dirt was cleansed away. 25

Carston, Waite and Co. found they had struck on a good thing,
so, down the valleys of the brooks from Selby and Nuttall, new
mines were sunk, until soon there were six pits* working. From
Nuttall, high up on the sandstone among the woods, the railway ran,
past the ruined priory of the Carthusians and past Robin Hood's* 30
well, down to Spinney Park, then on to Minton, a large mine among
corn-fields, from Minton across the farm-lands of the valley side to
Bunker's Hill, branching off there, and running north to Beggarlee

9

and Selby, that looks over at Crich and the hills of Derbyshire; six
mines like black studs on the countryside, linked by a loop of fine
chain, the railway.*

5   To accommodate the regiments of miners, Carston, Waite and
Co. built the Squares, great quadrangles of dwellings on the hillside
of Bestwood, and then, in the brook valley, on the site of Hell Row,
they erected The Bottoms.

The Bottoms consisted of six blocks of miners' dwellings, two
rows of three, like the dots on a blank-six domino, and twelve houses
10 in a block. This double row of dwellings sat at the foot of the rather
sharp slope from Bestwood, and looked out, from the attic windows
at least, on the slow climb of the valley towards Selby.

The houses themselves were substantial and very decent. One
could walk all round, seeing little front gardens with auriculas and
15 saxifrage in the shadow of the bottom block, sweet williams and
pinks, in the sunny top-block; seeing neat front windows, little
porches, little privet hedges, and dormer windows for the attics. But
that was outside; that was the view onto the uninhabited parlours of
all the colliers' wives. The dwelling room, the kitchen, was at the
20 back of the house, facing inward between the blocks, looking at a
scrubby back-garden, and then at the ash-pits. And between the
rows, between the long lines of ash-pits, went the alley, where the
children played and the women gossiped and the men smoked. So,
the actual conditions of living in the Bottoms, that was so well built,
25 and that looked so nice, were quite unsavoury, because people must
live in the kitchen, and the kitchens opened onto that nasty alley of
ash-pits.

Mrs Morel* was not anxious to move into the Bottoms, which was
already twelve years old and on the downward path, when she
30 descended to it from Bestwood. But it was the best she could do.
Moreover, she had an end house in one of the top blocks, and thus
had only one neighbour, on the other side an extra strip of garden.
And, having an end house, she enjoyed a kind of aristocracy among
the other women of the 'between' houses, because her rent was five
35 shillings and sixpence instead of five shillings a week. But this
superiority in station was not much consolation to Mrs Morel.

She was thirty-one years old, and had been married eight years. A
rather small woman, of delicate mould but resolute bearing, she
shrank a little from the first contact with the Bottoms women. She
40 came down in the July, and in the September expected her third baby.*

Her husband was a miner. They had only been in their new home three weeks, when the wakes* or fair began. Morel, she knew, was sure to make a holiday of it. He went off early on the Monday morning, the day of the fair. The two children were highly excited. William, a boy of seven, fled off immediately after breakfast, to prowl round the wakes ground, leaving Annie, who was only five, to whine all morning to go also. Mrs Morel did her work. She scarcely knew her neighbours yet, and knew no-one with whom to trust the little girl. So she promised to take her to the wakes after dinner.

William appeared at half past twelve. He was a very active lad, fair haired, freckled, with a touch of the Dane or Norwegian about him.

"Can I have my dinner, mother?" he cried, rushing in with his cap on. " 'Cause it begins at half past one, the man says so."

"You can have your dinner as soon as it's done," replied the mother.

"Isn't it done?" he cried, his blue eyes staring at her in indignation. "Then I'm goin' be-out it."

"You'll do nothing of the sort. It will be done in five minutes. It is only half past twelve."

"They'll be beginnin'," the boy half cried, half shouted.

"You won't die if they do," said the mother. "Besides, it's only half past twelve, so you've a full hour."

The lad began hastily to lay the table, and directly the three sat down. They were eating batter pudding and jam, when the boy jumped off his chair and stood perfectly still. Some distance away could be heard the first small braying of a merry-go-round, and the tooting of a horn. His face quivered as he looked at his mother.

"I told you!" he said, running to the dresser for his cap.

"Take your pudding in your hand—and it's only five past one, so *you* were wrong—you haven't got your twopence," cried the mother in a breath.

The boy came back, bitterly disappointed, for his two-pence, then went off without a word.

"I want to go, I want to go," said Annie, beginning to cry.

"Well and you shall go, whining, wizzening little stick," said the mother. And later in the afternoon, she trudged up the hill under the tall hedge, with her child. The hay was gathered from the fields, and cattle were turned onto the eddish. It was warm, peaceful.

Mrs Morel did not like the wakes. There were two sets of horses, one going by steam, one pulled round by a pony; three organs were

grinding, and there came odd cracks of pistol shots, fearful scree-
ching of the cocoa-nut man's rattle, shouts of the Aunt Sally* man,
screams* from the Peep-show lady. The mother perceived her son
gazing enraptured outside the Lion Wallace booth, at the pictures of
5 this famous lion that had killed a negro and maimed for life two
white men. She left him alone, and went to get Annie a spin of
toffee. Presently the lad stood in front of her, wildly excited.

"You never said you was coming—isn't the' a lot of things?—that
lion's killed three men—I've spent my tuppence—an' look here—"
10 He pulled from his pocket two egg-cups with pink moss-roses on
them.

"I got these from that stall where y'ave ter get them marbles in
them holes—an' I got these two in two goes—'ae-penny a go—
they've got moss-roses on, look here. I wanted these."
15 She knew he wanted them for her.

"Hm!" she said, pleased. "They *are* pretty!"

"Shall you carry 'em, 'cause I'm frightened o' breakin' 'em?"

He was tip-ful of excitement now she had come, led her about the
ground, showed her everything. Then, at the peep-show, she
20 explained the pictures, in a sort of story, to which he listened as if
spell-bound. He would not leave her. All the time, he stuck close to
her, bristling with a small boy's pride of her. For no other woman
looked such a lady as she did, in her little black bonnet and her
cloak. She smiled when she saw women she knew.
25 When she was tired, she said to her son:

"Well, are you coming now, or later?"

"Are you goin' a'ready?" he cried, his face full of reproach.

"'Already?'—It is past four, *I* know."

"What are you goin' a'ready for?" he lamented.
30 "You needn't come if you don't want," she said.

And she went slowly away with her little girl, whilst her son stood
watching her, cut to the heart to let her go, and yet unable to leave
the wakes. As she crossed the open ground, in front of the Moon
and Stars,* she heard men shouting, and smelled the beer, and
35 hurried a little, thinking her husband was probably in the bar.

At about half past six her son came home, tired now, rather pale,
and somewhat wretched.

"Well!" she said, pretending to be a bit cross with him, "if you'd
been five minutes later, I should have cleared the things away.
40 Another time, you'd have been famishing hours ago—"

And she gave him his tea. He was miserable, though he did not know it, because he had let her go alone. Since she had gone, he had not enjoyed his wakes.

"Has my dad been?" he asked.

"No," said the mother. 5

"He's helping to wait at the Moon and Stars. I see'd him through that black tin stuff wi' holes in, on the window, wi' his sleeves rolled up—"

"Ha!" exclaimed the mother, shortly. "He'd got no money. An' he'll be satisfied if he gets his 'lowance, whether they give him more 10 or not."

The children were allowed to sit at the window of their mother's bedroom, and watch the folk coming home with toys from the bazaar, listen to the braying of the music, the shouting, the cracking of shots, the faint 'pang' of the thin iron target. Then at last they 15 were tired, and went to bed.

When the light was fading, and Mrs Morel could see no more to sew, she rose and went to the door. Everywhere was the sound of excitement, the restlessness of the holiday, that at last infected her. She went out into the side garden. Women were coming home from 20 the wakes, the children hugging a white lamb with green legs, or a wooden horse. Occasionally a man lurched past, almost as full as he could carry.* Sometimes a good husband came along with his family, peacefully. But usually the women and children were alone. The stay-at-home mothers stood gossiping at the corners of the 25 alley, as the twilight sank, folding their arms under their white aprons.

Mrs Morel was alone, but she was used to it. Her son and her little girl slept upstairs, so, it seemed, her home was there behind her, fixed and stable. But she felt wretched with the coming child. 30 The world seemed a dreary place, where nothing else would happen for her—at least until William grew up. But for herself, nothing but this dreary endurance—till the children grew up. And the children! She could not afford to have this third. She did not want it. The father was serving beer in a public house, swilling 35 himself drunk. She despised him, and was tied to him. This coming child was too much for her. If it were not for William and Annie, she was sick of it, the struggle with poverty and ugliness and meanness.

She went into the front garden, feeling too heavy to take herself 40

out, yet unable to stay indoors. The heat suffocated her. And
looking ahead, the prospect of her life made her feel as if she were
buried alive.

The front garden was a small square with a privet hedge. There
5 she stood, trying to soothe herself with the scent of flowers, and the
fading, beautiful evening. Opposite her small gate was the stile that
led uphill, under the tall hedge, between the burning glow of the cut
pastures. The sky overhead throbbed and pulsed with light. The
glow sank quickly off the field, the earth and the hedges smoked
10 dusk. As it grew dark, a ruddy glare came out on the hill top, and out
of the glare, the diminished commotion of the fair.

Sometimes, down the trough of darkness formed by the path
under the hedges, men came lurching home. One young man lapsed
into a run down the steep bit that ended the hill, and went with a
15 crash into the stile. Mrs Morel shuddered. He picked himself up,
swearing viciously, rather pathetically, as if he thought the stile had
wanted to hurt him.

She went indoors, wondering if things were never going to alter.
She was beginning by now to realise that they would not. She
20 seemed so far away from her girlhood, she wondered if it were the
same person walking heavily up the back garden at the Bottoms, as
had run so lightly on the breakwater at Sheerness, ten years before.

"What have *I* to do with it!" she said to herself. "What have I to
do with all this. Even the child I am going to have! It doesn't seem as
25 if *I* were taken into account."

Sometimes life takes hold of one, carries the body along, accom-
plishes one's history, and yet is not real, but leaves one's self as it
were slurred over.

"I wait," Mrs Morel said to herself. "I wait, and what I wait for
30 can never come."

Then she straightened the kitchen, lit the lamp, mended the fire,
looked out the washing for the next day, and put it to soak. After
which she sat down to her sewing. Through the long hours, her
needle flashed regularly through the stuff. Occasionally she sighed,
35 moving to relieve herself. And all the time, she was thinking, how to
make the most of what she had, for the children's sakes.

At half past eleven her husband came. His cheeks were very red
and very shiny above his black moustache. His head nodded slightly.
He was pleased with himself.

40   "Oh!—Oh!—waitin' for me lass? I've bin 'elpin' Anthony,* an'

what's think he's gen me? Nowt b'r a lousy hae'f-crown, an' that's ivry penny—"

"He thinks you've made the rest up in beer," she said shortly.

"An' I 'aven't—that I 'aven't—you b'lieve me, I've 'ad very little this day, I have an' all." His voice went tender. "Here, an' I browt thee a bit o' brandysnap, an' a coconut for th' children." He laid the gingerbread and the cocoanut,* a hairy object, on the table. "Nay, tha niver said thankyer for nowt i' thy life, did ter?"

As a compromise, she picked up the cocoa-nut and shook it, to see if it had any milk.

"It's a good 'un, you may back yer life o' that. I got it fra' Bill Hodgkisson. 'Bill,' I says, 'tha non wants them three nuts does ter?—arena ter for gi'ein' me one for my bit of a lad an' wench?' 'I ham, Walter, my lad,' 'e says, 'ta'e which on 'em ter's a mind.' An' so I took one, an' thanked 'im. I didn't like ter shake it afore 'is eyes, but 'e says 'Tha'd better ma'e sure it's a good un, Walt'—an' so, yer see, I knowed it was.—He's a nice chap, is Bill Hodgkisson, 'e's a nice chap!"

"A man will part with anything so long as he's drunk, and you're drunk along with him," said Mrs Morel.

"Eh tha mucky little 'ussy, who's drunk, I sh'd like ter know?" said Morel. He was extraordinarily pleased with himself, because of his day's helping to wait in the Moon and Stars. He chattered on.

Mrs Morel, very tired, and sick of his babble, went to bed as quickly as possible, while he raked* the fire.

Mrs Morel came of a good old burgher family, famous independents who had fought with Colonel Hutchinson,* and who remained stout Congregationalists.* Her grandfather had gone bankrupt in the lace-market* at a time when so many lace-manufacturers were ruined in Nottingham. Her father, George Coppard, was an engineer, a large, handsome, haughty man, proud of his fair skin and blue eyes, but more proud still of his integrity. Gertrude resembled her mother* in her small build. But her temper, proud and unyielding, she had from the Coppards.

George Coppard was bitterly galled by his own poverty. He became foreman of the engineers in the dockyard at Sheerness. Mrs Morel—Gertrude—was the second daughter. She favoured* her mother, loved her mother best of all: but she had the Coppards' clear, defiant blue eyes, and their broad brow. She remembered to have hated her father's overbearing manner towards her gentle,

humorous, kindly-souled mother. She remembered running over
the breakwater at Sheerness, and finding the boat. She remembered
to have been petted and flattered by all the men when she had gone
to the dockyard, for she was a delicate, rather proud child. She
remembered the funny old mistress, whose assistant she had
become, whom she had loved to help in the private school.* And she
still had the bible that John Field had given her. She used to walk
home from chapel with John Field, when she was nineteen. He was
the son of a well-to-do tradesman, had been to college in London,
and was to devote himself to business.

She could always recall in detail a September Sunday afternoon,
when they had sat under the vine at the back of her father's house.
The sun came through the chinks in the vine-leaves, and made
beautiful patterns, like a lace scarf falling on her and on him. Some
of the leaves were clean yellow, like yellow flat flowers.

"Now sit still," he had cried. "Now your hair, I don't know what it
is like! It's as bright as copper and gold, as red as burnt copper, and
it has gold threads, where the sun shines on it. Fancy their saying it's
brown. Your mother calls it mouse colour."

She had met his brilliant eyes, but her clear face scarcely showed
the elation which rose within her.

"But you say you don't like business," she pursued.

"I don't—I hate it," he cried hotly.

"And you would *like* to go into the ministry," she half implored.

"I should—I should love it, if I thought I could make a first-rate
preacher."

"Then why don't you—why *don't* you." Her voice rang with
defiance. "If *I* were a man, nothing would stop me."

She held her head erect—he was rather timid before her.

"But my father's so stiff necked.* He means to put me into the
business, and I know he'll do it."

"But if you're a *man*—!" she had cried.

"Being a man isn't everything," he replied, frowning with puzzled
helplessness.

Now, as she moved about her work at the Bottoms, with some
experience of what being a man meant, she knew that it was *not*
everything.

At twenty, owing to her health, she had left Sheerness. Her father
had retired home to Nottingham. John Field's father had been
ruined: the son had gone as a teacher in Norwood. She did not hear

of him until, two years later, she made determined inquiry. He had married his landlady, a woman of forty, a widow with property.

And still Mrs Morel preserved John Field's bible. She did not now believe him to be—well, she understood pretty well what he might or might not have been. So she preserved his bible, and kept 5 his memory intact in her heart, for her own sake. To her dying day, for thirty-five years, she did not speak of him.

When she was twenty three years old she met, at a christmas party, a young man from the Erewash Valley. Morel was then twenty-seven years old. He was well-set-up, erect and very smart. 10 He had wavy, black hair that shone again, and a vigorous black beard that had never been shaved. His cheeks were ruddy, and his red, moist mouth was noticeable because he laughed so often and so heartily. He had that rare thing, a rich, ringing laugh. Gertrude Coppard had watched him fascinated. He was so full of colour and 15 animation, his voice ran so easily into comic grotesque, he was so ready and so pleasant with everybody. Her own father had a rich fund of humour, but it was satiric. This man's was different: soft, non-intellectual, warm, a kind of gambolling.

She herself was opposite. She had a curious, receptive mind, 20 which found much pleasure and amusement in listening to other folk. She was clever in leading folk on to talk. She loved ideas, and was considered very intellectual. What she liked most of all was an argument on religion or philosophy or politics, with some educated man. This she did not often enjoy.* So she always had people tell her 25 about themselves, finding her pleasure so.

In her person, she was rather small and delicate, with a large brow, and dropping bunches of brown silk curls. Her blue eyes were very straight, honest and searching. She had the beautiful hands of the Coppards. Her dress was always subdued. She wore dark blue 30 silk, with a peculiar silver chain, of silver scallops. This, and a heavy brooch of twisted gold, was her only ornament. She was still perfectly intact, deeply religious, and full of beautiful candour.

Walter Morel seemed melted away before her. She was to the miner that thing of mystery and fascination, a lady. When she spoke 35 to him, it was with a southern pronunciation and a purity of English which thrilled him to hear. She watched him. He danced well, as if it were natural and joyous in him to dance. His grandfather was a French refugee who had married an English barmaid—if it had been a marriage. Gertrude Coppard watched the young miner as he 40

danced, a certain subtle exultation like glamour in his movement,
and his face the flower of his body, ruddy, with tumbled black hair,
and laughing alike whatever partner he bowed above. She thought
him rather wonderful, never having met anyone like him. Her father
5 was to her the type of all men. And George Coppard, proud in his
bearing, handsome, and rather bitter; who preferred theology in
reading, and who drew near in sympathy only to one man, the
Apostle Paul;* who was harsh in government, and in familiarity
ironic; who ignored all sensuous pleasure—he was very different
10 from the miner. Gertrude herself was rather contemptuous of
dancing: she had not the slightest inclination towards that accom-
plishment, and had never learned even a Roger de Coverley.* She
was a puritan, like her father, high-minded, and really stern. Therefore the dusky, golden softness of this man's sensuous flame of life,
15 that flowed from off his flesh like the flame from a candle, not
baffled and gripped into incandescence by thought and spirit as her
life was, seemed to her something wonderful, beyond her.

He came and bowed above her. A warmth radiated through her as
if she had drunk wine.

20 "Now do come and have this one wi' me," he said, caressively.
"It's easy, you know. I'm pining to see you dance."

She had told him before she could not dance. She glanced at his
humility, and smiled. Her smile was very beautiful. It moved the
man so that he forgot everything.

25 "No, I won't dance," she said softly. Her words came clean and
ringing.

Not knowing what he was doing—he often did the right thing, by
instinct—he sat beside her, inclining reverentially.

"But you mustn't miss your dance," she reproved.

30 "Nay, I don't want to dance that—it's not one as I care about."

"Yet you invited me to it."

He laughed very heartily at this.

"I never thought o' that. Tha'rt not long in taking the curl out of
me."

35 It was her turn to laugh quickly.

"You don't look as if you'd come much uncurled," she said.

"I'm like a pig's tail, I curl because I canna help it," he
laughed—rather boisterously.

"Aren't you having anythink to drink?" he asked.

40 "No thank you—I am not at all thirsty."

He hesitated—divined that she was a total abstainer—and felt a rebuff.

Then he pursued a number of quite polite, interested questions. She answered him brightly. He seemed quaint.

"And you are a miner!" she exclaimed in surprise. 5

"Yes. I went down when I was ten."*

She looked at him in wondering dismay.

"When you were ten!—and wasn't it very hard?" she asked.

"You soon get used to it. You live like th' mice, an' you pop out at night to see what's going on." 10

"It makes me feel blind," she frowned.

"Like a moudiwarp!" he laughed. "Yi, an' there's some chaps as does go round like moudiwarps." He thrust his face forward in the blind, snout-like way of a mole, seeming to sniff and peer for direction. "They dun though!" he protested naïvely. "Tha niver 15 seed such a way they get in. But tha mun let me ta'e thee down sometime, an' tha can see for thysen."

She looked at him startled. This was a new tract of life suddenly opened before her. She realised the life of the miners, hundreds of them toiling below earth and coming up at evening. He seemed to 20 her noble. He risked his life daily, and with gaiety. She looked at him, with a touch of appeal in her pure humility.

"Shouldn't ter like it?" he asked tenderly. "'Appen not, it 'ud dirty thee."

She had never been "thee'd" and "thou'd"* before. 25

The next Christmas they were married, and for three months she was perfectly happy: for six months she was very happy.

He had signed the pledge,* and wore the blue ribbon of a teetotaller: he was nothing if not showy. They lived, she thought, in his own house. It was small, but convenient enough, and quite nicely furnished, with 30 solid, worthy stuff that suited her honest soul. The women her neighbours were rather foreign to her, and Morel's mother and sisters were apt to sneer at her lady-like ways. But she could perfectly well live by herself, so long as she had her husband close.

Sometimes, when she herself wearied of love talk, she tried to 35 open her heart seriously to him. She saw him listen deferentially, but without understanding. This killed her efforts at a finer intimacy, and she had flashes of fear. Sometimes he was restless of an evening: it was not enough for him just to be near her, she realised. She was glad when he set himself to little jobs. 40

He was a remarkably handy man, could make or mend anything. So she would say:

"I do like that coal-rake of your mother's—it is small and natty."

"Does ter, my wench. Well, I made that, so I can make thee one."

"What—why it's a steel one—!"

"An' what if it is!—tha s'lt ha'e one very similar, if not exactly same."

She did not mind the mess, nor the hammering and noise. He was busy and happy.

But in the seventh month, when she was brushing his Sunday coat, she felt papers in the breast pocket, and, seized with a sudden curiosity, took them out to read. He very rarely wore the frock coat he was married in: and it had not occurred to her before to feel curious concerning the papers. They were the bills of the household furniture, still unpaid.

"Look here," she said at night, after he was washed and had had his dinner. "I found these in the pocket of your wedding coat. Haven't you settled the bills yet?"

"No—I haven't had a chance."

"But you told me all was paid. I had better go into Nottingham on Saturday and settle them, I don't like sitting on another man's chairs, and eating from an unpaid table."

He did not answer.

"I can have your bank book, can't I?"

"Tha can ha'e it, for what good it'll be to thee."

"I thought— —" she began. He had told her he had a good bit of money left over. But she realised it was no use asking questions. She sat rigid with bitterness and indignation.

The next day, she went down to see his mother.

"Didn't you buy the furniture for Walter?" she asked.

"Yes, I did," tartly retorted the elder woman.

"And how much did he give you to pay for it?"

The elder woman was stung with fine indignation.

"Eighty pound, if you're so keen on knowin'," she replied.

"Eighty pounds! But there are forty two pounds still owing!"

"I can't help that."

"But where has it all gone?"

"You'll find all the papers, I think, if you look—beside ten pound as he owed me, an' six pound as the wedding cost down here."

"Six pounds!" echoed Gertrude Morel. It seemed to her monstrous that, after her own father had paid so heavily for her wedding, six pounds more should have been squandered in eating and drinking at Walter's parents' house, at his expense.

"And how much has he sunk in his houses?" she asked.

"His houses—which houses?"

Gertrude Morel went white to the lips. He had told her the house he lived in, and the next one, was his own.

"I thought the house we live in—" she began.

"They're my houses, those two," said the mother-in-law. "And not clear either. It's as much as I can do to keep the mortgage interest paid."

Gertrude sat white and silent. She was her father now.

"Then we ought to be paying you rent," she said coldly.

"Walter is paying me rent," replied the mother.

"And what rent?" asked Gertrude.

"Six-and-six a week," retorted the mother.

It was more than the house was worth. Gertrude held her head erect, looked straight before her.

"It is lucky to be you," said the elder woman bitingly, "to have a husband as takes all the worry of the money, and leaves you a free hand."

The young wife was silent.

She said very little to her husband, but her manner had changed towards him. Something in her proud, honorable soul had crystallised out hard as rock.

When October came in, she thought only of christmas. Two years ago, at Christmas, she had met him. Last Christmas she had married him. This Christmas she would bear him a child.

Being of a friendly disposition, she soon got to know her neighbours, and often stood talking with them, only afraid lest, because of the difference in speech, they should consider, as did his people, that she put on airs. They always gave her the first say, but they liked her.

"You don't dance yourself, do you Missis?" asked her nearest neighbour, in October, when there was great talk of opening a dancing class over the Brick and Tile Inn, at Bestwood.

"No—I never had the least inclination to," Mrs Morel replied.

"Fancy! An' how funny as you should ha' married your Mester. You know he's quite a famous one for dancing."

"I didn't know he was famous," laughed Mrs Morel.

"Yea, he is though! Why, he run that dancing class in the Miners' Arms Club-room for over five year."

"Did he?"

"Yes, he did." The other woman was defiant. "An' it was 5 thronged every Tuesday, and Thursday, an' Sat'day—an' there *was* carryin's-on, accordin' to all accounts."

This kind of thing was gall and bitterness* to Mrs Morel, and she had a fair share of it. The women did not spare her, at first; for she was superior, though she could not help it.

10 He began to be rather late in coming home.

"They're working very late now, aren't they?" she said to her washer woman.

"No later than they allers do, I don't think. But they stop to have their pint at Ellen's,* an' they get talkin', an' there you are!—Dinner 15 stone cold—an' it serves 'em right."

"But Mr Morel does not take any drink."

The woman dropped the clothes, looked at Mrs Morel, then went on with her work, saying nothing.

Gertrude Morel was very ill when the boy was born. Morel was 20 good to her, as good as gold. But she felt very lonely, miles away from her own people. She felt lonely with him now, and his presence only made it more intense.

The boy was small and frail at first, but he came on quickly. He was a beautiful child, with dark gold ringlets, and dark blue eyes, 25 which changed gradually to a clear grey. His mother loved him passionately. He came just when her own bitterness of disillusion was hardest to bear; when her faith in life was shaken, and her soul felt dreary and lonely. She made much of the child, and the father was jealous.

30 At last Mrs Morel despised her husband. She turned to the child, she turned from the father. He had begun to neglect her, the novelty of his own home was gone. He had no grit, she said bitterly to herself. What he felt just at the minute, that was all to him. He could not abide by anything. There was nothing at the back of all his 35 show.*

There began a battle between the husband and wife, a fearful, bloody battle that ended only with the death of one. She fought to make him undertake his own responsibilities, to make him fulfil his obligations. But he was too different from her. His nature was 40 purely sensuous, and she strove to make him moral, religious. She tried to force him to face things. He could not endure it—it drove him out of his mind.

While the baby was still tiny, the father's temper had become so irritable that it was not to be trusted. The child had only to give a little trouble, when the man began to bully. A little more, and the hard hands of the collier hit the baby. Then Mrs Morel loathed her husband, loathed him for days: and he went out and drank: and she cared very little what he did. Only, on his return, she scathed him with her satire.

The estrangement between them caused him, knowingly or unknowingly, grossly to offend her where he would not have done. William, the baby, was just a year old, was just beginning to walk, and to say pretty things. He was a winsome child, still with a little mop of boy's curls, darkening now. He was fond of his father, who was very affectionate, indulgent and full of ingenuity to amuse the child, when it pleased him. The two played together, and Mrs Morel used to wonder which was the truer baby.

Morel always rose early, about five or six o'clock in the morning, whether holiday or work day. On Sunday morning he would get up and prepare breakfast. The fire was never let to go out. It was raked just at bed-time. That is, a great piece of coal, a raker, was placed so that it would be nearly burned through by morning. On Sunday mornings, the child would get up with his father, while the mother lay in bed for another hour or so. She was then more rested than at any other time: when father and child played and prattled together downstairs.

William was only one year old, and his mother was proud of him, he was so pretty. She was not well off now, but her sisters kept the boy in clothes. Then, with his little white hat curled with an ostrich feather, and his white coat, he was a joy to her, the twining wisps of hair clustering round his head. Mrs Morel lay listening, one Sunday morning, to the chatter of the two. Then she dozed off. When she came downstairs, a great fire glowed in the grate, the room was hot, the breakfast was roughly laid. And seated in his armchair, against the chimney piece, sat Morel, rather timid: and standing between his legs, the child—cropped like a sheep, with such an odd round poll—looking wondering at her: and on a newspaper spread out upon the hearth rug, a myriad of crescent-shaped curls, like the petals of a marigold scattered in the reddening firelight.

Mrs Morel stood still. It was her first baby. She went very white, and was unable to speak.

"What dost think on 'im?" Morel laughed uneasily.

She gripped her two fists, lifted them, and came forward. Morel
5 shrank back.

"I could kill you, I could!" she said. She choked with rage, her two fists uplifted.

"Yer non want ter make a wench on 'im," Morel said, in a frightened tone, bending his head to shield his eyes from hers. His
10 attempt at laughter had vanished.

The mother looked down at the jagged, close clipped head of her child. She put her hands on his hair, and stroked and fondled his head.

"Oh—my boy!—" she faltered. Her lip trembled, her face broke,
15 and, snatching up the child, she buried her face in his shoulder and cried painfully. She was one of those women who cannot cry: whom it hurts as it hurts a man. It was like ripping something out of her, her sobbing. Morel sat with his elbows on his knees, his hands gripped together till the knuckles were white. He gazed in the fire,
20 feeling almost stunned, as if he could not breathe.

Presently she came to an end, soothed the child—and cleared away the breakfast table. She left the newspaper littered with curls, spread upon the hearthrug. At last her husband gathered it up and put it at the back of the fire. She went about her work with closed
25 mouth and very quiet. Morel was subdued. He crept about wretchedly, and his meals were a misery that day. She spoke to him civilly, and never alluded to what he had done. But he felt something final had happened.

Afterwards, she said she had been silly, that the boy's hair would
30 have had to be cut, sooner or later. In the end, she even brought herself to say to her husband, it was just as well he had played barber when he did. But she knew, and Morel knew, that that act had caused something momentous to take place in her soul. She remembered the scene all her life, as one in which she had suffered the
35 most intensely.

This act of masculine clumsiness was the spear through the side* of her love for Morel. Before, while she had striven against him bitterly, she had fretted after him, as if he had gone astray from her. Now she ceased to fret for his love: he was an outsider to her. This
40 made life much more bearable.

Nevertheless, she still continued to strive with him. She still had her high moral sense, inherited from generations of Puritans. It was now a religious instinct, and she was almost a fanatic with him, because she loved him, or had loved him. If he sinned, she tortured him. If he drank, and lied, was often a poltroon, sometimes a knave, she wielded the lash unmercifully.*

The pity was, she was too much his opposite. She could not be content with the little he might be, she would have him the much that he ought to be. So, in seeking to make him nobler than he could be, she destroyed him. She injured and hurt and scarred herself, but she lost none of her worth. She also had the children.

He drank rather heavily, though not more than many miners, and always beer, so that whilst his health was affected, it was never injured. The week-end was his chief carouse. He sat in the Miners' Arms until turning out time every Friday, every Saturday, and every Sunday evening. On Monday and Tuesday he had to get up and reluctantly leave towards ten o'clock. Sometimes he stayed at home on Wednesday and Thursday evenings, or was only out for an hour. He practically never had to miss work owing to his drinking.

But although he was very steady at work, his wages fell off. He was blab-mouthed, a tongue-wagger. Authority was hateful to him, therefore he could only abuse the pit-managers.* He would say, in the Palmerston:

"Th' gaffer come down to our stall this morning, an' 'e says: 'You know, Walter, this 'ere'll not do. What about these props!' An' I says to him, 'Why what art talkin' about? What d'st mean about th' props?' 'It'll niver do, this 'ere,' 'e says. 'You'll be havin' th' roof in, one o' these days.' An' I says, 'Tha'd better stan' on a bit o' clunch, then, an' hold it up wi' thy 'ead.' So 'e wor that mad, 'e cossed* an' 'e swore, an' t'other chaps they did laugh." Morel was a good mimic. He imitated the manager's fat, squeaky voice, with its attempt at good English.

"'I shan't have it, Walter. Who knows more about it, me or you?' So I says 'I've niver fun out how much tha knows, Alfred. It'll 'appen carry thee ter bed an' back.'"

So Morel would go on, to the amusement of his boon companions. And some of this would be true. The pit-manager was not an educated man. He had been a boy along with Morel, so that, while the two disliked each other, they more or less took each other for granted. But Alfred Charlesworth did not forgive the butty* these public-house sayings. Consequently, although Morel was a good miner, sometimes earning as much as five pounds a week when he married, he came gradually to have worse and worse stalls, where the coal was thin, and hard to get, and unprofitable.

5 A butty is a contractor. Two or three butties are given a certain length along a seam of coal, which they are to mine forward to a certain distance. They were paid something like 3/4 for every ton of coal they turned out. Out of this, they had to pay the men, holers* and loaders, whom they hired by the day, and also for tools, 10 powder, and so on. If their stall was a good one, and the pit was turning full time, then they got a hundred or two tons of coal out, and made good money. If their stall was a poor one, they might work just as hard, and earn very little. Morel, for thirty years of his life, never had a good stall. But, as his wife said, it was his own 15 fault.

Also, in summer, the pits are slack.* Often, on bright sunny mornings, the men are seen trooping home again at ten, eleven, or twelve-o'clock. No empty trucks stand at the pit mouth. The women on the hill side look across as they shake the hearthrug 20 against the fence, and count the wagons the engine is taking along the line up the valley, to the pits.

"Seven," they say to each other, "either for Minton or Spinney Park. That's a fat lot to keep a pit going."

And the children, as they come from school at dinner-time, 25 looking down the fields and seeing the wheels on the headstocks standing, say:

"Minton's knocked off. My dad'll be at home."

And there is a sort of shadow over all, women and children and men, because money will be short at the end of the week.

30 Morel was supposed to give his wife thirty shillings a week, to provide everything, rent, food, clothes, clubs, insurance, doctors. Occasionally, if he were flush, he gave her thirty five. But these occasions by no means balanced those when he gave her twenty five. In winter, with a decent stall, the miner might earn fifty or fifty 35 five shillings a week. Then he was happy. On Friday night, Saturday, and Sunday, he spent royally, getting rid of his sovereign or thereabouts. And out of so much, he scarcely spared the children an extra penny, or bought them a pound of apples. It all went in drink. In the bad times, matters were more worrying, but he was 40 not so often drunk, so that Mrs Morel used to say:

"I'm not sure I wouldn't rather be short, for when he's flush, there isn't a minute of peace."

If he earned forty shillings,* he kept ten; from thirty five, he kept five; from thirty two, he kept four; from twenty eight, he kept three; from twenty four, he kept two; from twenty, he kept one and six; 5 from eighteen, he kept a shilling; from sixteen, he kept sixpence. He never saved a penny, and he gave his wife no opportunity of saving; instead, she had occasionally to pay his debts; not public-house debts, for those never were passed on to the women, but debts when he had bought a canary, or a fancy walking-stick. 10

At the Wakes time, Morel was working badly, and Mrs Morel was trying to save against her confinement.* So, it galled her bitterly to think he should be out taking his pleasure and spending money, whilst she remained at home, harassed. There were two days holiday. On the Tuesday morning, Morel rose early. He was in good 15 spirits. Quite early, before six o'clock she heard him whistling away to himself downstairs. He had a pleasant way of whistling, lively and musical. He nearly always whistled hymns. He had been a choir-boy with a beautiful voice, and had taken solos in Southwell cathedral. His morning whistling alone betrayed it. 20

His wife lay listening to him tinkering away in the garden, his whistling ringing out as he sawed and hammered away. It always gave her a sense of warmth and peace to hear him thus as she lay in bed, the children not yet awake, in the bright early morning happy in his man's fashion. 25

At nine o'clock, while the children with bare legs and feet were sitting playing on the sofa, and the mother was washing up, he came in from his carpentry, his sleeves rolled up, his waistcoat hanging open. He was still a good looking man, with black, wavy hair, and a large black moustache. His face was perhaps too much inflamed, 30 and there was about him a look almost of peevishness. But now he was jolly. He went straight to the sink where his wife was washing up.

"What, are thee there!" he said boisterously. "Sluther off an' let me wesh my-sen." 35

"You may wait till I've finished," said his wife.

"Oh mun I?—An' what if I shonna?"

This good-humoured threat amused Mrs Morel.

"Then you can go and wash yourself in the soft water tub."

"Ha! I can an' a', tha mucky little 'ussy." 40

With which he stood watching her a moment, then went away to
wait for her.

When he chose, he could still make himself again a real 'gallant.'
Usually he preferred to go out with a scarf round his neck. Now,
5 however, he made a toilet. There seemed so much gusto in the way he
puffed and swilled as he washed himself, so much alacrity with which
he hurried to the mirror in the kitchen, and, bending because it was
too low for him, scrupulously parted his wet black hair, that it irritated
Mrs Morel. He put on a turn-down collar, a black bow, and wore his
10 Sunday tail coat. As such, he looked spruce, and what his clothes
would not do, his instinct for making the most of his good looks would.

At half-past nine Jerry Purdy came to call for his pal. Jerry was
Morel's bosom friend, and Mrs Morel disliked him. He was a tall
thin man, with a rather foxy face, the kind of face that seems to lack
15 eyelashes. He walked with a stiff, brittle dignity, as if his head were
on a wooden spring. His nature was cold and shrewd. Generous
where he intended to be generous, he seemed to be very fond of
Morel, and more or less to take charge of him.

Mrs Morel hated him. She had known his wife, who had died of
20 consumption, and who had, at the end, conceived such a violent
dislike of her husband, that if he came into her room it caused her
hemorrhage. None of which Jerry had seemed to mind. And now his
eldest daughter, a girl of fifteen, kept a poor house for him, and
looked after the two younger children.

25 "A mean, wizzen-hearted stick!" Mrs Morel said of him.

"I've niver known Jerry mean in *my* life," protested Morel. "A
opener-handed and more freer chap you couldn't find anywhere,
accordin' to my knowledge."

"Open-handed to you," retorted Mrs Morel. "But his fist is shut
30 tight enough to his children, poor things."

"Poor things!—and what for are they poor things, I should like to
know."

But Mrs Morel would not be appeased on Jerry's score.

The subject of argument was seen, craning his thin neck over the
35 scullery curtain. He caught Mrs Morel's eye.

"Mornin' missis!—mester in?"

"Yes—he is."

Jerry entered unasked and stood by the kitchen doorway. He was
not invited to sit down, but stood there, coolly asserting the rights of
40 men and husbands.

"A nice day," he said to Mrs Morel.

"Yes."

"Grand out this morning—grand for a walk."

"Do you mean *you're* going for a walk?" she asked.

"Yes. We mean walkin' to Nottingham," he replied.   5

"Hm!"

The two men greeted each other, both glad, Jerry however full of assurance, Morel rather subdued, afraid to seem too jubilant in presence of his wife. But he laced his boots quickly, with spirit. They were going for a ten mile walk across the fields to Nottingham. 10 Climbing the hillside from the Bottoms, they mounted gaily into the morning. At the Moon and Stars they had their first drink, then on to the 'Old Spot.' Then a long five miles of drought, to carry them into Bulwell to a glorious pint of bitter. But they stayed in a field with some haymakers whose gallon bottle was full, so that, when they 15 came in sight of the city, Morel was sleepy. The town spread upwards before them, smoking vaguely in the midday glare, fridging the crest away to the south with spires and factory bulks and chimneys. In the last field Morel lay down under an oak-tree and slept soundly for over an hour. When he rose to go forward, he felt 20 queer.

The two had dinner in the Meadows, with Jerry's sister, then repaired to the 'Punch Bowl', where they mixed in the excitement of pigeon-racing. Morel never in his life played cards, considering them as having some occult, malevolent power: "the devil's pic- 25 tures,"* he called them. But he was a master of skittles and of dominoes. He took a challenge from a Newark man, on skittles. All the men in the old, long bar took sides, betting either one way or the other. Morel took off his coat. Jerry held the hat containing the money. The men at the tables watched. Some stood with their mugs 30 in their hands. Morel felt his big, wooden ball carefully, then launched it. He played havoc among the nine-pins, and won half-a-crown, which restored him to solvency.

By seven o'clock the two were in good condition. They caught the 7.30 train home.   35

Mrs Morel was depressed and wretched that day. She did what washing she could, but the ponching* was too much for her. William tidied up the house for her.

"Should I do anything else, mother?" he asked.

"No, there's nothing for you to do—except take Annie out."   40

"I don't want to."

"Want or not want, you must."

So the child went out, hampered with his sister, while his mother
worked. He was angry with her, for foisting the burden on him,
5 and yet grieved for her, because he knew something was the matter.
So, with his love for his mother vexing his young growth, he made
the best of things.

In the afternoon, the Bottoms was intolerable. Every inhabitant
remaining was out of doors. The women, in twos and threes,
10 bare-headed and in white aprons, gossiped in the alley between the
blocks. Men having a rest between drinks, sat on their heels and
talked. The place smelled stale, the slate roofs glistered in the arid
heat.

Mrs Morel took the little girl down to the brook, in the meadows
15 which were not more than two hundred yards away. The water ran
quickly over stones and broken pots. Mother and child leaned on the
rail of the old sheep-bridge, watching. Up at the dipping-hole,* at
the other end of the meadow, Mrs Morel could see the naked forms
of boys flashing round the deep yellow water, or an occasional bright
20 figure dart glittering over the blackish, stagnant meadow. She knew
William was at the dipping hole, and it was the dread of her life lest
he should get drowned. Annie played under the tall old hedge,
picking up alder cones, that she called currants. The child required
much attention, and the flies were teasing.

25   The children were put to bed at seven o'clock. Then she worked
awhile.

When Walter Morel and Jerry arrived at Bestwood, they felt a
load off their minds: a railway journey no longer impended, so they
could put the finishing touches to a glorious day. They entered the
30 'Nelson' with the satisfaction of returned travellers. Mrs Morel
always said the after-life would hold nothing in store for her
husband: he rose from the lower world into purgatory, when he
came home from pit, and passed on to heaven in the Palmerston
Arms.

35   As it grew cooler, the little garden at the Bottoms became frag-
rant. Mrs Morel went out to look at the flowers and to breathe the
evening. Mrs Kirk, her neighbour,* was not at home, or the two
might have talked together. So she was alone. The black swifts, that
the children call 'devilins,'* darted to and fro like black arrow-heads
40 just above her, veering round the corner of the house, flying in at the

broad eaves, then slipping out again and darting down the air with little cries, that seem to come out of the light, not from the noiseless birds. Some one had trodden the stone-crop, that was littered over with fallen white rose-leaves. She stooped and brushed it up to raise its little yellow heads again.   5

The next day was a work-day, and the thought of it put a damper on the men's spirits. Most of them, moreover, had spent their money. Some were already rolling dismally home, to sleep in preparation for the morrow. Mrs Morel, listening to their mournful singing, went indoors. Nine o'clock passed, and ten, and still "the 10 pair" had not returned. On a doorstep somewhere, a man was singing loudly, in a drawl, "Lead Kindly Light."* Mrs Morel was always indignant with the drunken men, that they must sing that hymn when they got maudlin.

"As if 'Geneviève'* weren't good enough," she said.   15

The kitchen was full of the scent of boiled herbs and hops. On the hob, a large black saucepan steamed slowly. Mrs Morel took a panchion, a great bowl of thick red earth, streamed a heap of white sugar into the bottom, and then, straining herself to the weight, was pouring in the liquor.   20

Just then, Morel came in. He had been very jolly in the 'Nelson', but coming home had grown irritable. He had not quite got over the feeling of irritability and pain, after having slept on the ground when he was so hot; and a bad conscience afflicted him as he neared the house. He did not know he was angry. But when the garden gate 25 resisted his attempts to open it, he kicked it and broke the latch. He entered just as Mrs Morel was pouring the infusion of herbs out of the saucepan. Swaying slightly, he lurched against the table. The boiling liquor pitched. Mrs Morel started back.*

"Good gracious," she cried, "coming home in his drunkenness!" 30

"Comin' home in his what—?" he snarled, his hat over his eye.

Suddenly her blood rose in a jet.

"Say you're *not* drunk!" she flashed.

She had put down her saucepan, and was stirring the sugar into the beer. He dropped his two hands heavily on the table, and thrust 35 his face forward at her.

"'Say you're not drunk'" he repeated. "Why, nobody but a nasty little bitch like you 'ud 'ave such a thought."

"Well you've been boozing all day, so if you're not drunk by eleven o'clock at night—" she replied, continuing to stir.   40

"I've not been boozing all day—I've *not* been boozing all day—it's where you make your mistake," he said, snarling.

"It looks as if I made a mistake," she replied.

"Does it—does it—Oh—Oh indeed!—oh!"

5 "Goes out at nine in the morning, comes rolling home at midnight. Besides, we know well enough what you do when you go out with your beautiful Jerry."

"'Your beautiful Jerry'—what?—why wha 'r' yer talkin' about, woman—eh?—what?"

10 He thrust his face forward at her.

"There's money to bezzle with, if there's money for nothing else."

"I've not spent a two-shillin' bit this day," he said.

"You don't get as drunk as a lord on nothing," she replied. "And," she cried, flashing into sudden fury, "if you've been sponging on 15 your beloved Jerry, why, let him look after his children, for they need it."

"'Let 'im look after his children'.—Why, what children's better looked after than hisn, I sh'd like to know."

"My sirs, not yours, if *you* had the looking after to do.—A man that 20 can afford to swill his belly from morn till night—"

"It's a lie, it's a lie," he cried, breaking into rage and banging the table.

"—Can't afford to keep his children," she continued.

"What's it got to do wi' you?" he shouted.

25 "'Got to do with me?'—why, a good deal.—Gives me a miserable twenty-five shillings to do everything with, and goes jaunting off for the day, coming rolling home at midnight—"

"It's a lie, woman, it's a lie!"

"And thinks I'm going to go on scraping and pedgilling and 30 contriving, while he guzzles and swills and jaunts to Nottingham carousing—"

"It's a lie, it's a lie—shut your face woman."

They were now at battle pitch. Each forgot everything save the hatred of the other, and the battle between them. She was fiery and 35 furious as he. They went on till he called her a liar.

"No," she cried, starting up scarce able to breathe. "Don't call *me* that—you, the most despicable liar that ever walked in shoe-leather." She forced the last words out of suffocated lungs.

"You're a liar!" he yelled, banging the table with his fist. "You're a 40 liar, you're a liar."

She stiffened herself, with clenched fists.

"I'd smite you down, you cowardly beast, if only I could," she said, in low, quivering tones.

Then, in the next wave, came out her passionate loathing of him. He raged at her, and banged the table till the house rang, while she poured over him all her contempt and hate of him.

"The house is filthy with you," she cried.

"Then get out on it—it's mine. Get out on it," he shouted. "It's ma as brings th' money whoam, not thee. It's my house, not thine. Then ger out on't—ger out on't!"

"And I would," she cried, suddenly shaken into tears of impotence. "Ah, wouldn't I, wouldn't I have gone long, long ago, but for those children. Ay, haven't I repented not going years ago, when I'd only the one—" suddenly drying into rage. "Do you think it's for *you* I stop—do you think I'd stop one minute for *you*—"

"Go then," he shouted, beside himself. "Go!"

"No!" she faced round. "No," she cried loudly, "you shan't have it *all* your own way: you shan't do *all* you like. I've got those children to see to. My word—" she laughed, "I should look well to leave them to you."

"Go," he cried thickly, lifting his fist. He was afraid of her. "Go!"

"I should be only too glad—I should laugh, laugh, my lord, if I could get away from you," she replied.

He came up to her, his red face, with its blood-shot eyes, thrust forward, and gripped her arms. She cried in fear of him, struggled to be free. Coming slightly to himself, panting, he pushed her roughly to the outer door, and thrust her forth, slotting the bolt behind her with a bang. Then he went back into the kitchen, dropped into his arm-chair, his head, bursting full of blood, sinking between his knees. Thus he dipped gradually into a stupor, from exhaustion and intoxication.

The moon was high and magnificent in the August night. Mrs Morel, seared with passion, shivered to find herself out there in a great, white light, that fell cold on her, and gave a shock to her inflamed soul. She stood for a few moments helplessly staring at the glistening great rhubarb leaves near the door. Then she got the air into her breast. She walked down the garden path, trembling in every limb, while the child boiled within her. For a while, she could not control her consciousness; mechanically she went over the last scene, then over it again, certain phrases, certain moments coming

each time like a brand red hot, down on her soul: and each time she
enacted again the past hour, each time the brand came down at the
same points, till the mark was burnt in, and the pain burnt out, and
at last she came to herself. She must have been half an hour in this
5 delirious condition. Then the presence of the night came again to
her. She glanced round in fear. She had wandered to the side
garden, where she was walking up and down the path beside the
currant bushes under the long wall. The garden was a narrow strip,
bounded from the road that cut transversely between the blocks, by
10 a thick thorn hedge.

She hurried out of the side garden to the front, where she could
stand as if in an immense gulf of white light, the moon streaming
high in face of her, the moonlight standing up from the hills in front,
and filling the valley where the Bottoms crouched, almost blind-
15 ingly. There, panting and half weeping in reaction from the stress,
she murmured to herself over and again: "The nuisance!—the
nuisance!"

She became aware of something about her. With an effort, she
roused herself, to see what it was that penetrated her consciousness.
20 The tall white lilies were reeling in the moonlight, and the air was
charged with their perfume, as with a presence. Mrs Morel gasped
slightly in fear. She touched the big, pallid flowers on their petals,
then shivered. They seemed to be stretching in the moonlight. She
put her hand into one white bin: the gold scarcely showed on her
25 fingers by moonlight. She bent down, to look at the bin-ful of yellow
pollen: but it only appeared dusky. Then she drank a deep draught
of the scent. It almost made her dizzy.

She looked round her. The privet hedge had a faint glitter among
its blackness. Various white flowers were out. In front, the hill rose
30 into indistinctness, barred by high black hedges, and nervous with
cattle moving in the dim moonlight. Here and there the moonlight
seemed to stir and ripple.

Mrs Morel leaned on the garden gate, looking out, and she lost
herself awhile. She did not know what she thought. Except for a
35 slight feeling of sickness, and her consciousness in the child, her self
melted out like scent into the shiny, pale air. After a time, the child
too melted with her in the mixing-pot of moonlight, and she rested
with the hills and lilies and houses, all swum together in a kind of
swoon.
40 When she came to herself, she was tired for sleep. Languidly, she

looked about her; the clumps of white phlox seemed like bushes
spread with linen; a moth ricochetted over them, and right across
the garden. Following it with her eye roused her. A few whiffs of the
raw strong scent of phlox invigorated her. She passed along the path
hesitating at the white rose-bush. It smelled sweet and simple. She 5
touched the white ruffles of the roses. Their fresh scent and cool,
soft leaves reminded her of the morning-time and sunshine. She
was very fond of them. But she was tired and wanted to sleep. In the
mysterious out-of-doors she felt forlorn.

There was no noise anywhere. Evidently the children had not 10
been wakened, or had gone to sleep again. A train, three miles away,
roared across the valley. The night was very large, and very strange,
stretching its hoary distances infinitely. And out of the silver-grey
fog of darkness came sounds vague and hoarse: a corncrake not far
off, sound of a train like a sigh, and distant shouts of men. 15

Her quietened heart beginning to beat quickly again, she hurried
down the side garden to the back of the house. Softly, she lifted the
latch: the door was still bolted, shut hard against her. She rapped
gently, waited, then rapped again. She must not rouse the children,
nor the neighbours. He must be asleep, and he would not wake 20
easily. Her heart began to burn to be indoors. She clung to the
door-handle. Now, it was cold: she would take a chill, and in her
present condition!

Putting her apron over her head and her arms, she hurried again
to the side garden, to the window of the kitchen. Leaning on the sill, 25
she could just see, under the blind, her husband's arms spread out
on the table, and his black head on the board. He was sleeping with
his face lying on the table. Something in his attitude made her feel
tired of things. The lamp was burning smokily, she could tell by the
copper colour of the light. She tapped at the window more and more 30
noisily. Almost it seemed as if the glass would break. Still he did not
wake up.

After vain efforts, she began to shiver, partly from contact with
the stone, and from exhaustion. Fearful always for the unborn child,
she wondered what she could do for warmth. She went down to the 35
coal-house, where was an old hearth-rug she had carried out for the
rag-man the day before. This she wrapped over her shoulders. It
was warm, if grimy. Then she walked up and down the garden path,
peeping every now and then under the blind, knocking, and telling
herself that in the end the very strain of his position must wake him. 40

At last, after about an hour, she rapped long and low at the window. Gradually the sound penetrated to him. When in despair she had ceased to tap, she saw him stir, then lift his face blindly. The labouring of his heart hurt him into consciousness. She rapped
5   imperatively at the window. He started awake. Instantly she saw his fists set and his eyes glare. He had not a grain of physical fear. If it had been twenty burglars, he would have gone blindly for them. He glared round, bewildered, but prepared to fight.

"Open the door Walter," she said coldly.
10   His hands relaxed—it dawned on him what he had done. His head dropped, sullen and dogged. She saw him hurry to the door, heard the bolt chock. He tried the latch. It opened—and there stood the silver grey night, fearful to him, after the tawny light of the lamp. He hurried back.

15   When Mrs Morel entered, she saw him almost running through the door to the stairs. He had ripped his collar off his neck, in his haste to be gone ere she came in, and there it lay with bursten button-holes. It made her angry.

She warmed and soothed herself. In her weariness forgetting
20   everything, she moved about at the little tasks that remained to be done, set his breakfast, rinsed his pit-bottle, put his pit-clothes on the hearth to warm, set his pit-boots beside them, put him out a clean scarf and snap-bag and two apples, raked the fire and went to bed. He was already dead asleep. His narrow black eyebrows were
25   drawn up in a sort of peevish misery, into his forehead, while his cheek's downstrokes, and his sulky mouth, seemed to be saying: "I don't care who you are nor what you are, I *shall* have my own way."

Mrs Morel knew him too well to look at him. As she unfastened her brooch at the mirror, she smiled faintly to see her face all
30   smeared with the yellow dust of lilies. She brushed it off, and at last lay down. For some time her mind continued snapping and jetting sparks, but she was asleep before her husband awoke from the first sleep of his drunkenness.

Chapter II

The Birth of Paul, and another Battle*

After such a scene as the last, Walter Morel was for some days abashed and ashamed, but he soon regained his old bullying indifference. Yet there was a slight shrinking, a diminishing in his assurance. Physically even, he shrank, and his fine full presence waned. He never grew in the least stout, so that, as he sank from his erect, assertive bearing, his physique seemed to contract along with his pride and moral strength.

But now he realised how hard it was for his wife to drag about at her work and, his sympathy quickened by penitence, hastened forward with his help. He came straight home from the pit, and stayed in at evening—till Friday, and then he could not remain at home. But he was back again by ten o'clock, almost quite sober.

He always made his own breakfast. Being a man who rose early and had plenty of time, he did not, as some miners do, drag his wife out of bed at six o'clock. At five, sometimes earlier, he woke, got straight out of bed and went downstairs. When she could not sleep, his wife lay waiting for this time, as for a period of peace. The only real rest seemed to be when he was out of the house.

He went downstairs in his shirt, and then struggled into his pit-trousers, which were left on the hearth to warm all night. There was always a fire, because Mrs Morel raked. And the first sound in the house was the bang, bang of the poker against the raker, as Morel smashed the remainder of the coal to make the kettle, which was filled and left on the hob,* finally boil. His cup and knife and fork, all he wanted except just the food, was laid ready on the table on a newspaper. Then he got his breakfast, made the tea, packed the bottom of the doors with rugs to shut out the draught, piled a big fire, and sat down to an hour of joy. He toasted his bacon on a fork and caught the drops of fat on his bread. Then he put the rasher on his thick slice of bread, and cut off chunks with a clasp knife, poured his tea into his saucer,* and was happy. With his family about, meals were never so pleasant. He loathed a fork. It is a modern introduction which has still scarcely reached the common people.* What

Morel preferred was a clasp knife. Then, in solitude, he ate, and
drank, often sitting, in cold weather, on a little stool with his back to
the warm chimney piece, his food on the fender, his cup on the
hearth. And then he read the last night's newspaper, what of it he
5   could, spelling it over laboriously. He preferred to keep the blinds
down and the candle lit, even when it was daylight. It was the habit
of the mine.

At a quarter to six he rose, cut two thick slices of bread and butter,
and put them in the white calico snap-bag. He filled his tin bottle
10   with tea. Cold tea without milk or sugar was the drink he preferred
for the pit. Then he pulled off his shirt, and put on his pit-singlet, a
vest of thick flannel cut low round the neck, and with short sleeves
like a chemise.

Then he went upstairs to his wife, with a cup of tea because she
15   was ill, and because it occurred to him.

"I've browght thee a sup o' tea, lass," he said.

"Well you needn't, for you know I don't like it," she replied.

"Drink it up, it'll pop thee off to sleep again."

She accepted the tea. It pleased him to see her take it and sip it.
20   "I'll back my life there's no sugar in," she said.

"Yi—there's one big un," he replied, injured.

"It's a wonder," she said, sipping again.

She had a winsome face when her hair was loose. He loved her to
grumble at him in this manner. He looked at her again, and went,
25   without any sort of leave taking. He never took more than two slices
of bread and butter to eat in the pit, so an apple or an orange was a
treat to him.* He always liked it when she put one out for him. He
tied a scarf round his neck, put on his great, heavy boots, his coat
with the big pocket that carried his snap-bag and his bottle of tea,
30   and went forth into the fresh, morning air, closing without locking
the door behind him. He loved the early morning. He always left the
house at six, though the men were not turned down* till about seven,
and he had only a half hour's walk. Usually he went over the fields,
and often, in summer, would look in the gin-close for mushrooms,
35   straying through the thick wet grass in his pit-boots, looking for the
lurking, white-fleshed things. If he found any, he stowed them
carefully in his pocket. It scarcely seemed hard to him, to leave the
fresh, cool air of morning, and go down. He was so used to it, it
came simply and naturally. So he appeared at the pit top, often with
40   a stalk from the hedge between his teeth, which he chewed all day to

keep his mouth moist, down the mine, feeling quite as happy as when he was in the field.

Later, when the time for the baby grew nearer, he would bustle round in his slovenly fashion, poking out the ashes, rubbing the fire-place, sweeping the house before he went to work. Then, 5 feeling very self-righteous, he went upstairs.

"Now I'n cleaned up for thee: that's no 'casions ter stir a peg all day, but sit and read thy books."

Which made her laugh, in spite of her indignation.

"And the dinner cooks itself?" she answered.   10

"Eh, I know nowt about th' dinner."

"You'd know if there weren't any."

"Ay, 'appen so," he answered, departing.

When she got downstairs, she would find the house tidy, but dirty. She could not rest until she had thoroughly cleaned. As she went 15 down to the ash-pit with her dust-pan, Mrs Kirk, spying her, would contrive to have to go to her own coal-place at that minute. Then, across the wooden fence, she would call:

"So you keep wagging on then?"

"Ay," answered Mrs Morel, deprecatingly. "There's nothing else 20 for it."

Mrs Kirk was a thin, nervous woman, apt to be hysterical. Mrs Morel liked her. The two women came together, one on either side of the fence, each holding her dust-pan, and they talked for awhile. Then: 25

"You may go on till you drop," said Mrs Kirk. "Won't your mester do a bit for you? Tom's not bad that way."

"Ay," answered the neighbour, "he came up this morning to tell me he'd cleaned up, so I'd nothing to do all day but sit and read."

"Eh, but isn't men great gawps!" exclaimed Mrs Kirk.   30

"And I found the fire-place thick with silt, and all th' dirt under the hearthrug."

Mrs Kirk laughed, her thin face showing her teeth.

"It's allers alike," she said. "They smarm a brush an' a duster across, an' bless you, it'll do for them."   35

"They don't care how they pig it," said Mrs Morel.

"They don't. Our Tom's just the same."

"All alike," said Mrs Morel.

"You've 'eered about Mrs Allsop?"

"No."   40

"Not?—her's has come."

"You don't mean it! When?"

"Night afore last—after that thunderstorm—"

"What—!"

5   And both women laughed heartily.*

. . . . .

"Have you seen Hose,"* called a very small woman from across the road. It was Mrs Anthony, a black haired, strange little body, who always wore a brown velvet dress, tight fitting.

10   "I haven't," said Mrs Morel.

"Eh, I wish he'd come. I've got a copperful of clothes,* an' I'm sure I heered his bell."

"Hark—he's at the end."

The two women looked down the Alley. At the end of the

15   Bottoms a man stood in a sort of old-fashioned trap, bending over bundles of cream-coloured stuff, while a cluster of women held up their arms to him, some with bundles. Mrs Anthony herself had a heap of creamy, undyed stockings hanging over her arm.

"I've done ten dozen this week," she said proudly to Mrs Morel.

20   "T-t-t!" went the other. "I don't know how you can find time."

"Eh!" said Mrs Anthony. "You can find time if you make time."

"I don't know how you do it," said Mrs Morel. "And how much shall you get for those many?"

"Tuppence-ha'penny a dozen," replied the other.

25   "Well!" said Mrs Morel, "I'd starve before I'd sit down and seam twenty four stockings for twopence ha'penny."

"Oh I don't know," said Mrs Anthony. "You can rip along with 'em."

. . . . .

30   'Hose' was coming along, ringing his bell. Women were waiting at the yard-ends with their seamed stockings hanging over their arms. The man, a common fellow, made jokes with them, tried to swindle them, and bullied them. Mrs Morel went up her yard disdainfully.

It was an understood thing that if one woman wanted her neigh-

35   bour, she should put the poker in the fire and bang at the back of the fire-place, which, as the fires were back to back, would make a great noise in the adjoining house. One morning Mrs Kirk, mixing a pudding, nearly started out of her skin as she heard the thud, thud, in her grate. With her hands all floury, she rushed to the fence.

40   "Did you knock, Mrs Morel?"

"If you wouldn't mind, Mrs Kirk."

Mrs Kirk climbed onto her copper, got over the wall onto Mrs Morel's copper, and ran in to her neighbour.

"Eh dear, how are you feeling?" she cried in concern.

"You might fetch Mrs Bower,"* said Mrs Morel.   5

Mrs Kirk went into the yard, lifted up her strong, shrill voice, and called:

"Ag-gìe*—Ag-gìe!"

The sound was heard from one end of the Bottoms to the other. At last, Aggie came running up, and was sent for Mrs Bower, whilst   10
Mrs Kirk left her pudding and stayed with her neighbour.

Mrs Morel went to bed. Mrs Kirk had Annie and William for dinner. Mrs Bower, fat and waddling, bossed the house.

"Hash some cold meat up for the master's dinner, and make him an apple-charlotte pudding," said Mrs Morel.   15

"He may go without pudding *this* day," said Mrs Bower.

Morel was not as a rule one of the first to appear at the bottom of the pit, ready to come up. Some men were there before four o'clock, when the whistle blew loose-all. But Morel, whose stall, a poor one, was at this time about a mile and a half away from the bottom,   20
worked usually till the first mate stopped, then he finished also. This day, however, the miner was sick of the work. At two o'clock he looked at his watch, by the light of the green candle—he was in a safe working*—and again at half past two. He was hewing at a piece of rock that was in the way for the next day's work. As he sat on his   25
heels, or kneeled, giving hard blows with his pick, 'Uszza—uszza!' he went.

"Shall ter finish, *Sorry?" cried Barker, his fellow butty.

"Finish—niver while the world stands!" growled Morel.

And he went on striking. He was tired.   30

"It's a heart-breaking job," said Barker.

But Morel was too exasperated, at the end of his tether, to answer. Still he struck and hacked with all his might.

"Tha might as well leave it, Walter," said Barker. "It'll do tomorrow, without thee hackin' thy guts out."   35

"I s'll lay no b— finger on this tomorrow, Isr'el," cried Morel.

"Oh well, if tha wunna, someb'dy else'll ha'e to," said Israel.

Then Morel continued to strike.

"Hey-up theer—*loose-a'*," cried the men, leaving the next stall.

* ('Sorry' is a common form of address. It is perhaps a corruption of 'Sirrah'.)   40

Morel continued to strike.

"Tha'll happen catch me up," said Barker, departing.

When he had gone, Morel, left alone, felt savage. He had not finished his job. He had overworked himself into a frenzy. Rising, 5 wet with sweat, he threw his tool down, pulled on his coat, blew out his candle, took his lamp and went. Down the main road, the lights of the other men went swinging. There was a hollow sound of many voices. It was a long, heavy tramp underground.

He sat at the bottom of the pit, where the great drops of water fell 10 plash. Many colliers were waiting their turns to go up, talking noisily. Morel gave his answers short and disagreeable.

"It's rainin', Sorry," said old Giles, who had had the news from the top. Morel found one comfort. He had his old umbrella, which he loved, in the lamp cabin. At last he took his stand on the chair, 15 and was at the top in a moment. Then he handed in his lamp and got his umbrella, which he had bought at an auction for one-and-six. He stood on the edge of the pit-bank for a moment, looking out. Over the fields, grey rain was falling. The trucks stood full of wet, bright coal. Water ran down the sides of the wagons, over the white 20 C. W. & Co. Colliers, walking indifferent to the rain, were streaming down the line and up the field, a grey, dismal host. Morel put up his umbrella, and took pleasure from the peppering of the drops thereon.

All along the road to Bestwood, the miners tramped, wet and grey 25 and dirty, but their red mouths talking with animation. Morel also walked with a gang, but he said nothing. He frowned peevishly as he went. Many men passed into the Prince of Wales, or into Ellen's. Morel, feeling sufficiently disagreeable to resist temptation, trudged along under the dripping trees that overhung the park wall, and 30 down the mud of Greenhill Lane.

Mrs Morel lay in bed, listening to the rain, and the feet of the colliers from Minton, their voices, and the bang! bang!! of the gates as they went through the stile up the field.

"There's some herb beer behind the pantry door," she said. "Th' 35 master 'll want a drink, if he doesn't stop."

But he was late, so she concluded he had called for a drink, since it was raining. What did he care about the child or her.

She was very ill when her children were born.

"What is it?" she asked, feeling sick to death.

40   "A boy."

And she took consolation in that. The thought of being the mother of men was warming to her heart. She looked at the child. It had blue eyes, and a lot of fair hair, and was bonny. Her love came up hot, in spite of everything. She had it in bed with her.

Morel, thinking nothing, dragged his way up the garden path, wearily, and angrily. He closed his umbrella, and stood it in the sink. Then he sluthered his heavy boots into the kitchen. Mrs Bower appeared in the inner doorway.

"Well," she said, "she's about as bad as she can be.—It's a boy-childt."

The miner grunted, put his empty snap-bag and his tin bottle on the dresser, went back into the scullery and hung up his coat, then came and dropped into his chair.

"Han yer got a drink?" he asked.

The woman went into the pantry. There was heard the pop of a cork. She set the mug with a little, disgusted rap, on the table before Morel. He drank, gasped, wiped his big moustache on the end of his scarf, drank, gasped, and lay back in his chair. The woman would not speak to him again—she set his dinner before him, and went upstairs.

"Was that the master?" asked Mrs Morel.

"I've gave him his dinner," replied Mrs Bower.

After he had sat with his arms on the table—he resented the fact that Mrs Bower put no cloth on for him, and gave him a little plate, instead of a full sized dinner-plate—he began to eat. The fact that his wife was ill, that he had another boy, was nothing to him at that moment. He was too tired, he wanted his dinner, he wanted to sit with his arms lying on the board, he did not like having Mrs Bower about. The fire was too small to please him.

After he had finished his meal, he sat for twenty minutes. Then he stoked up a big fire. Then, in his stocking feet,* he went reluctantly upstairs. It was a struggle to face his wife at this moment, and he was tired. His face was black, and smeared with sweat. His singlet had dried again, soaking the dirt in. He had a dirty woollen scarf round his throat. So, he stood at the foot of the bed.

"Well, how are ter then?" he asked.

"I s'll be all right," she answered.

"Hm!"

He stood at a loss what to say next. He was tired, and this bother was rather a nuisance to him, and he didn't quite know where he was.

"A lad, tha says," he stammered.

She turned down the sheet and showed the child.

"Bless him!" he murmured. Which made her laugh, because he blessed by rote—pretending paternal emotion, which he did not feel
5 just then.

"Go now," she said.

"I will my lass," he answered, turning away.

Dismissed, he wanted to kiss her, but he dared not. She half wanted him to kiss her, but could not bring herself to give any signs.
10 She only breathed freely when he was gone out of the room again, leaving behind him a faint smell of pit-dirt.

Mrs Morel had a visit every day from the Congregational clergyman. Mr Heaton* was young, and very poor. His wife had died at the birth of his first baby, so he remained alone in the manse. He
15 was a Bachelor of Arts of Cambridge, very shy, and no preacher. Mrs Morel was fond of him, and he depended on her. For hours, he talked to her, when she was well. He became the god-parent of the child.

The mother lay in bed thinking of her children. As she had no life
20 of her own, but was busy from morning till night cleaning, cooking, nursing, and sewing, she had to put her own living aside, put it in the bank, as it were, of her children. She thought and waited for them, dreamed what they would do, with herself behind them as motor force, when they grew up. Already William was a lover to her. If she
25 had neuralgia, from which she suffered badly at times, and she was pale and silent at her work:

"Have you got toothache mother?" he asked.

"Yes."

"Is it awful?"

30 She laughed, in spite of the pain. But sometimes, when she was suckling the baby, it was so bad she could scarcely move. Then her eldest son would be found lying weeping bitterly to himself in the front room, and when his father asked:

"Whativer's a matter, my duckie?" he replied:

35 "My mother's got toothache."

"Well," Mrs Morel would say, when she heard him, "*you* haven't got it, silly, so what are you crying for?"

Then he did not like the new baby.

"He looks nasty, mother," he said.

40 "Why?" asked the mother.

"He scowls," said William.

Then Mrs Morel kissed the baby quickly. It had a peculiar pucker on the forehead, as if something had startled its tiny consciousness before birth. When Mrs Morel looked at the infant, something hurt her, inside. But the baby was good. Often she sat singing nursery rhymes to it.

"He can't understand you, what do you sing to him for?" said William.

"Well, he likes the noise, I'm sure," said the mother, laughing with her rare warmth shining in her blue eyes, at the baby, worrying the tiny fingers with her lips; while William stood aside and fumed.

Occasionally the minister stayed to tea with Mrs Morel. Then she laid the cloth early, got out her best cups, with a little green rim, and hoped Morel would not come too soon. Indeed, if he stayed for a pint, she would not mind this day. She had always two dinners to cook, because she believed children should have their chief meal at mid-day, whereas Morel needed his at five o'clock. So Mr Heaton would hold the baby, whilst Mrs Morel beat up a batter pudding or peeled the potatoes, and he, watching her all the time, would discuss his next sermon. His ideas were quaint and fantastic, she brought him judiciously to earth. It was a discussion of the Wedding at Cana.*

"When He changed the water into wine at Cana," he said, "that is a symbol, that the ordinary life, even the blood, of the married husband and wife, which had before been uninspired, like water, became filled with the spirit, and was as wine, because, when love enters, the whole spiritual constitution of a man changes, is filled with the Holy Ghost, and almost his form is altered."

Mrs Morel thought to herself:

"Yes, poor fellow, his young wife is dead; that is why he makes his love into the Holy Ghost."

"No," she said aloud, "don't make things into symbols. Say: 'It was a wedding, and the wine ran out. Then the father-in-law was put about, because there was nothing to offer the guests, except water—there was no tea, no coffee, in those days, only wine. And how would he like to see all the people sitting with glasses of water in front of them. The host and his wife were ashamed, the bride was miserable, and the bridegroom was disagreeable. And Jesus saw them whispering together, and looking worried. And He knew they were poor. They were only, perhaps, farm-labouring people. So He thought to himself "What a shame!—all the wedding spoiled." And so He made wine, as quickly as he could.'—You can say, wine isn't beer, not so intoxicating—and people in the East never get drunk. It's getting drunk makes beer so bad."

5 The poor man looked at her. He wanted badly to say how human love is the presence of the Holy Ghost, making the lovers divine and immortal. Mrs Morel insisted on his making the bible real to the people, and on his having only bits of his own stuff in between. They both were very excited, and very happy. Suddenly William
10 appeared.

"Goodness!" exclaimed Mrs Morel, "is it so late?"

She popped the kettle on, and hurried with the only clean cloth, hoping her husband would not be early. William and Annie, with a piece of bread and butter each, went to play in the street. There
15 were radishes and jam and marmalade for tea. Everything looked clean and pretty. Mrs Morel was happy, bullying her clergyman over his sermons, sitting at tea with a gentleman, who passed her the bread and butter, who waited for her to begin.*

They were half way down their first cup of tea when they heard the
20 sluther of pit-boots.

"Good gracious!" exclaimed Mrs Morel, in spite of herself.

The minister looked rather scared. Morel entered. He was feeling rather savage. He nodded a 'How d'yer do' to the clergyman, who rose to shake hands with him.

25 "Nay," said Morel, showing his hand, "look thee at it! Tha niver wants ter shake hands wi' a hand like that, does ter? There's too much pick-haft and shovel dirt on it."

The minister flushed with confusion, and sat down again. Mrs Morel rose, carried out the steaming saucepan. Morel took off his
30 coat, dragged his arm-chair to table, and sat down, heavily.

"Are you tired?" asked the clergyman.

"Tired—I ham that," replied Morel. "*You* don't know what it is to be tired, as *I'm* tired."

"No," replied the clergyman.

35 "Why look yer 'ere," said the miner, showing the shoulders of his singlet. "It's a bit dry now, but it's wet as a clout with sweat even yet. Feel it."

"Goodness!" cried Mrs Morel. "Mr Heaton doesn't want to feel your nasty singlet."

40 The clergyman put out his hand gingerly.

"No, perhaps he doesn't," said Morel. "But it's all come out of *me*, whether or not. An' iv'ry day alike my singlet's wringing wet.— 'Aven't you got a drink, Missis, for a man when he comes home barkled up from the pit."

"You know you drank all the beer,' said Mrs Morel, pouring out his tea.

"An' was there no more to be got?"—turning to the clergyman. "A man gets that caked up wi' th' dust, you know, that clogged up, down a coal mine, he *needs* a drink when he comes home."

"I am sure he does," said the clergyman.

"But it's ten to one if there's owt for him."

"There's water—and there's tea," said Mrs Morel.

"Water—it's not water as'll clear his throat."

He poured out a saucerful of tea, blew it, and sucked it up through his great black moustache, sighing afterwards. Then he poured out another saucerful, and stood his cup on the table.

"My cloth!" said Mrs Morel, putting it on a plate.

"A man as comes home as I do 's too tired to care about cloths," said Morel.

"Pity!" exclaimed his wife, sarcastically.

The room was full of the smell of meat and vegetables, and pit-clothes.

He leaned over to the minister, his great moustache thrust forward, his mouth very red in his black face.

"Mr Heaton," he said, "a man as has been down the black hole all day, dingin' away at a coal face, yi, a sight harder than that wall—"

"Needn't make a moan of it," put in Mrs Morel.

"Needn't he—oh needn't 'e! We know *you'd* rather not hear." Then he turned away from her to the clergyman again. "—he comes home that tired he doesn't know what to do with himself." He looked at his dinner, which stood before him. "Yi, he's too tired to eat his dinner, that he is." Whereupon he laid his arms, black with coal dust, on the white cloth.

"Goodness man, it's a clean cloth!" exclaimed Mrs Morel involuntarily. It was the only clean cloth.

"Am I to have my dinner in the yard, like a dog?" he shouted.

"There was no question of the yard," replied his wife coldly.

He kept his arms on the table cloth.

"When a man's been drivin' a pick into 'ard rock all day, Mister Heaton, his arms is that tired, 'e doesn't know what to do with 'em."

"I can understand it," said the clergyman.

The miner was a sort of strange beast to him.

"There are arms to your chair," said Mrs Morel.

"Yer'd 'ave ter put *your* spoke in, would yer!" her husband said.

5   She would have scorned to say, how *she* must work and slave. The miner ate with his knife, shovelling the food into his mouth noisily. It made his wife's flesh creep. He was quite regardless of anyone's feelings. After a while he laid his knife down.

"Mester Heaton," he said, "can yer tell me owt for my 'ead?"

10   "I find cascara—"* faltered the minister.

"Tell him to drink less beer and keep his liver in order," said Mrs Morel.

" 'Drink less beer!' " Morel repeated. "Oh!—oh!—everything's the *beer*!—A man happens to drink a glass, Mester Heaton, an' he
15 never hears the last of it."

"I'm glad he drinks a glass," said Mrs Morel.

She hated her husband, because, whenever he had an audience, he whined and played for sympathy. William, sitting nursing the baby, hated him with a boy's hatred for false sentiment, and for the
20 stupid treatment of his mother. Annie had never liked him: she merely avoided him.

When the minister had gone, Mrs Morel looked at her cloth.

"A fine mess!" she said.

"Dos't think I'm goin' to sit wi' my arms danglin', cos tha's got a
25 parson for tea wi' thee?" he bawled.

They were both angry, but she said nothing. The baby began to cry, and Mrs Morel, picking up a saucepan from the hearth, accidentally knocked Annie on the head, whereupon the girl began to whine, and Morel to shout at her. In the midst of this pandemo-
30 nium, William looked up at the big, glazed text over the mantel-piece and read, distinctly:

"God Bless Our Home."

Whereupon Mrs Morel, trying to soothe the baby, jumped up, rushed at him, boxed his ears, saying:

35 "What are *you* putting in for?"

And then she sat down and laughed, till tears ran over her cheeks, while William kicked the stool he had been sitting on, and Morel growled:

"I canna see what there is so much to laugh at."

40 It was about this time Mrs Morel was destroying her husband's

authority. Until now, she had felt too much alone to stand away from him. But William was growing up, and all his young soul was his mother's. Annie too was against her father. Finally, there was this last baby. Mrs Morel had hated her husband during the year before it was born. They were poor, and Morel was mean. He had got in with a gang of pals, of whom one was Jerry, who insisted that a man did the work and should have the money wherewith to enjoy himself. They discussed the various degrees of subjection in which their wives were held. Morel found his wife was not sufficiently subdued. After one inflamed evening, when Jerry had been telling him 'not to put up with any b— woman's domineering, what was he a man for?', he shouted at her:

"I'll make you tremble at the sound of my footstep."

It was a historical phrase in her life. She had sat down and laughed till she was quite good-humoured and merry at the idea. He had stood bursting with fury and ignominy. And, by giving her as little money as possible, by drinking much and going out with men who brutalised him and his idea of women, he paid her back. Then she thought, he was taking his pleasure out of the lives of the children, so she threw herself on their side against him.

One evening directly after the parson's visit, feeling unable to bear herself after another display from her husband, she took Annie and the baby and went out. Morel had kicked William, and the mother would never forgive him.

She went over the sheep-bridge and across a corner of the meadow to the cricket ground. The meadows seemed one space of ripe, evening light, whispering with the distant mill-race. She sat on a seat under the alders in the cricket ground, and fronted the evening. Before her, level and solid, spread the big green cricket-field, like the bed of a sea of light. Children played in the bluish shadow of the pavilion. Many rooks, high up, came cawing home across the softly woven sky. They stooped in a long curve down into the golden glow, concentrating, cawing, wheeling like black flakes on a slow vortex, over a tree-clump that made a dark boss among the pasture.

A few gentlemen were practising, and Mrs Morel could hear the chock of the ball, and the voices of men suddenly roused; could see the white forms of men shifting silently over the green, upon which already the under-shadows were smouldering. Away at the grange, one side of the hay-stacks was lit up, the other sides blue-grey. A wagon of sheaves rocked small across the melting yellow light.

The sun was going down. Every open evening, the hills of Derbyshire were blazed over with red sunset. Mrs Morel watched the sun sink from the glistening sky, leaving a soft flower-blue overhead, while the western space went red, as if all the fire had swum down there, leaving the bell cast flawless blue. The mountain-ash berries across the field stood fierily out from the dark leaves, for a moment. A few shocks of corn in a corner of the fallow stood up as if alive: she imagined them bowing: perhaps her son would be a Joseph.* In the east, a mirrored sunset floated pink opposite the west's scarlet. The big haystacks on the hill-side that butted into the glare, went cold.

With Mrs Morel, it was one of those still moments when the small frets vanish, and the beauty of things stands out, and she had the peace and the strength to see herself. Now and again, a swallow cut close to her. Now and again, Annie came up with a handful of alder currants. The baby was restless on his mother's knee, clambering with his hands at the light.

Mrs Morel looked down at him. She had dreaded this baby like a catastrophe, because of her feeling for her husband. And now, she felt strangely towards the infant. Her heart was heavy because of the child, almost as if it were unhealthy, or malformed. Yet it seemed quite well. But she noticed the peculiar knitting of the baby's brows, and the peculiar heaviness of its eyes, as if it were trying to understand something that was pain. She felt, when she looked at the child's dark, brooding pupils, as if a burden were on her heart.

"He looks as if he was thinking about something—quite sorrowful," said Mrs Kirk.

Suddenly, looking at him, the heavy feeling at the mother's heart melted into passionate grief. She bowed over him, and a few tears shook swiftly out of her very heart. The baby lifted his fingers.

"My lamb!" she cried, softly.

And at that moment she felt, in some far inner place of her soul, that she and her husband were guilty.

The baby was looking up at her. It had blue eyes like her own, but its look was heavy, steady, as if it had realised something that had stunned some point of its soul.

In her arms lay the delicate baby. Its deep blue eyes, always

looking up at her unblinking, seemed to draw her innermost
thoughts out of her. She no longer loved her husband; she had not
wanted this child to come, and there it lay in her arms and pulled at
her heart. She felt as if the navel string that had connected its frail
little body with hers had not been broken. A wave of hot love went 5
over her to the infant. She held it close to her face and breast. With
all her force, with all her soul she would make up to it for having
brought it into the world unloved. She would love it all the more now
it was here, carry it in her love. Its clear, knowing eyes gave her pain
and fear. Did it know all about her? When it lay under her heart, had 10
it been listening then? Was there a reproach in the look? She felt the
marrow melt in her bones, with fear, and pain.

Once more she was aware of the sun lying red on the rim of the
hill opposite. She suddenly held up the child in her hands.

"Look!" she said. "Look, my pretty!" 15

She thrust the infant forward to the crimson, throbbing sun,
almost with relief. She saw him lift his little fist. Then she put him to
her bosom again, ashamed almost of her impulse to give him back
again whence he came.*

"If he lives," she thought to herself, "what will become of 20
him—what will he be?"

Her heart was anxious.

"I will call him 'Paul'," she said, suddenly, she knew not why.

After a while, she went home. A fine shadow was flung over the
deep green meadow, darkening all. 25

As she expected, she found the house empty. But Morel was
home by ten o'clock, and that day at least ended peacefully.

Walter Morel was, at this time, exceedingly irritable. His work
seemed to exhaust him. When he came home, he did not speak
civilly to anybody. If the fire were rather low, he bullied about that; 30
he grumbled about his dinner; if the children made a chatter, he
shouted at them in a way that made their mother's blood boil, and
made them hate him.

"You have no need to shout their heads off," Mrs Morel would
say. "We are none of us hard of hearing." 35

"I'll put my foot through 'em," he bawled.

If, whilst he was washing in the scullery, anyone entered or left
the house:

"Shut that doo-er!" he shouted, so that he could be heard down
the Bottoms. 40

"It's a pity, poor nesh creature!" Mrs Morel said quietly.

"I shonna ha'e my ribs blowed out o' my sides wi' that draught, for nob'dy!" he would shout. Whenever he was angry, he bawled.

"Goodness me man," said Mrs Morel at last. "There isn't a bit of peace while you're in the house."

"No, I know that. I know you're niver right till I'm out o' your sight."

"True," she said calmly to herself.

"Oh I know—I know what yer chunterin' 's about. You're niver satisfied till I'm down pit, none on yer. They ought ter keep me theer, like one o' th' 'osses."

"True," said Mrs Morel again, under her breath, as she turned with a tight-shut mouth.

He hurried to escape from the house, thrusting his head forward in determined rage.

"I'll pay the b— out!" he said to himself, meaning his wife.

He* was not home by eleven o'clock. The baby was unwell, and was restless, crying if he were put down. Mrs Morel, tired to death, and still weak, was scarcely under control.

"I wish the nuisance would come," she said wearily to herself.

The child at last sank down to sleep in her arms. She was too tired to carry him to the cradle.

"But I'll say nothing, whatever time he comes," she said. "It only works me up, I won't say anything." She did not trust herself, however. Time after time she had said the same, determined to refrain, and then her sudden anger had flashed out. She wished, with the loathing of weariness, that she might be spared seeing him when he came home. The reason she would not go to bed and leave him to come in when he liked—let any woman tell.

"I know if he does anything, it'll make my blood boil," she said pitiably to herself.

She sighed, hearing him coming, as if it were something she could not bear. He, taking his revenge, was nearly drunk. She kept her head bent over the child as he entered, not wishing to see him. But it went through her like a flash of hot fire when, in passing, he lurched against the dresser, setting the tins rattling, and clutched at the white pot knobs* for support. He hung up his hat and coat, then returned, stood glowering from a distance at her, as she sat bowed over the child.

"Is there nathing to eat in the house?" he asked, insolently, as if to a servant. In certain stages of his intoxication he affected the clipped, mincing speech of the towns. Mrs Morel hated him most in this condition.

"You know what there is in the house," she said, so coldly, it sounded impersonal.

He stood and glared at her without moving a muscle.

"I asked a civil question, and I expect a civil answer," he said, affectedly.

"And you got it," she said, still ignoring him.

He glowered again. Then he came unsteadily forward. He leaned on the table with one hand, and with the other jerked at the table drawer to get a knife to cut bread. The drawer stuck, because he pulled sideways. In a temper, he dragged at it so that it flew out bodily, and spoons, forks, knives, a hundred metallic things splashed with a clatter and a clang upon the brick floor. The baby gave a little convulsed start.

"What are you doing, clumsy drunken fool?" the mother cried.

"Then tha should get the flamin' thing thysen. Tha should get up like other women have to, an' wait on a man."

"Wait on you—wait on *you!*" she cried. "Yes, I see myself."

"Yis, an' I'll learn thee tha's got to. Wait on *me*, yes, tha sh'lt wait on *me*—"

"Never, milord. I'd wait on a dog at the door first."

"What—what?"

He was trying to fit in the drawer. At her last speech, he turned round. His face was crimson, his eyes bloodshot. He stared at her one silent second, in threat.

"P-h!" she went quickly, in contempt.

He jerked at the drawer in his excitement. It fell, cut sharply on his shin, and on the reflex, he flung it at her.

One of the corners caught her brow as the shallow drawer crashed into the fireplace. She swayed, almost fell stunned from her chair. To her very soul she was sick; she clasped the child tightly to her bosom. A few moments elapsed. Then, with an effort, she brought herself to. The baby was crying plaintively. Her left brow was bleeding rather profusely. As she glanced down at the child, her brain reeling, some drops of blood soaked into its white shawl. But the baby was at least not hurt. She balanced her head to keep equilibrium, so that the blood ran into her eye.

Walter Morel remained as he had stood, leaning on the table with

one hand, looking blank. When he was sufficiently sure of his balance, he went across to her, swayed, caught hold of the back of her rocking-chair, almost tipping her out. Then, leaning forward over her and swaying as he spoke, he said, in a tone of wondering
5 concern:

"Did it catch thee?"

He swayed again, as if he would pitch onto the child. With the catastrophe, he had lost all balance.

"Go away!" she said, struggling to keep her presence of mind.
10 He hiccoughed. "Let's—let's look at it," he said, hiccoughing again.

"Go away," she cried.

"Lemme—lemme look at it lass."

She smelled him of drink, felt the unequal pull of his swaying
15 grasp on the back of her rocking-chair.

"Go away," she said, and weakly she pushed him off.

He stood, uncertain in balance, gazing upon her.

Summoning all her strength, she rose, the baby on one arm. By a cruel effort of will, moving as if in sleep, she went across to the
20 scullery, where she bathed her eye for a minute in cold water. But she was too dizzy. Afraid lest she should swoon, she returned to her rocking-chair, trembling in every fibre. By instinct, she kept the baby clasped.

Morel, bothered, had succeeded in pushing the drawer back into
25 its cavity, and was on his knees, groping with numb paws for the scattered spoons.

Her brow was still bleeding. Presently Morel got up and came craning his neck towards her.

"What has it done to thee, lass?" he asked, in a very wretched,
30 humble tone.

"You can see what it's done," she answered.

He stood bending forward, supported on his hands, which grasped his legs just above the knee. He peered to look at the wound. She drew away from the thrust of his face, with its great
35 moustache, averting her own face as much as possible. As he looked at her, who was cold and impassive as stone, with mouth shut tight, he sickened with feebleness and hopelessness of spirit. He was turning drearily away, when he saw a drop of blood fall from the averted wound into the baby's fragile, glistening hair. Fascinated, he
40 watched the heavy dark drop hang in the glistening cloud, and pull

down the gossamer. Another drop fell. It would soak through to the baby's scalp. He watched fascinated, feeling it soak in. Then, finally, his manhood broke.

"What of this child?" was all his wife said to him. But her low, intense tones brought his head lower. She softened:

"Get me some wadding out of the middle drawer," she said.

He stumbled away very obediently, presently returning with a pad, which she singed before the fire, then put on her forehead, as she sat with the baby on her lap.

"Now that clean pit-scarf."

Again he rummaged and fumbled in the drawer, returning presently with a red, narrow scarf. She took it, and with trembling fingers proceeded to bind it round her head.

"Let me tie it for thee," he said humbly.

"I can do it myself," she replied.

When it was done she went upstairs, telling him to rake the fire and lock the door.

In the morning, Mrs Morel said:

"I knocked against the latch of the coal-place, when I was getting a raker in the dark, because the candle blew out." Her two small children looked up at her with wide, dismayed eyes. They said nothing, but their parted lips seemed to express the unconscious tragedy they felt.

Walter Morel lay in bed next day until nearly dinner time. He did not think of the previous evening's work. He scarcely thought of anything, but he would not think of that. He lay and suffered like a sulking dog. He had hurt himself most. And he was the more damaged, because he would never say a word to her, or express his sorrow. He tried to wriggle out of it.

"It was her own fault," he said to himself. Nothing, however, could prevent his inner consciousness inflicting on him the punishment which ate into his spirit like rust, and which he could only alleviate by drinking.

He felt as if he had not the initiative to get up, or to say a word, or to move, but could only lie like a log. Moreover he had himself violent pains in the head. It was Saturday. Towards noon he rose, cut himself food in the pantry, ate it with his head dropped, then pulled on his boots and went out, to return at three o'clock, slightly tipsy, and relieved; then once more straight to bed. He rose again at six in the evening, had tea, and went straight out.

Sunday was the same: bed till noon, the 'Palmerston Arms' till
2.30, dinner and bed; scarcely a word spoken. When Mrs Morel
went upstairs, towards four o'clock, to put on her Sunday dress, he
was fast asleep. She would have felt sorry for him, if he had once
5 said: "Wife, I'm sorry." But no, he insisted to himself it was her
fault. And so he broke himself. So she merely left him alone. There
was this deadlock of passion between them, and she was stronger.

The family began tea. Sunday was the only day when all sat down
to meals together.

10 "Isn't my father going to get up?" asked William.

"Let him lie," the mother replied.

There was a feeling of misery over all the house. The children
breathed the air that was poisoned, and they felt dreary. They
were rather disconsolate, did not know what to do, what to play
15 at.

Immediately Morel woke he got straight out of bed. That was
characteristic of him, all his life. He was all for activity. The
prostrated inactivity of two mornings was stifling him.

It was near six o'clock when he got down. This time he entered
20 without hesitation, his wincing sensitiveness having hardened again.
He did not care any longer what the family thought or felt.

The tea-things were on the table. William was reading aloud from
The Child's Own,* Annie listening and asking eternally 'Why?' Both
children hushed into silence as they heard the approaching thud of
25 their father's stockinged feet, and shrank as he entered. Yet he was
usually indulgent to them.

Morel made the meal alone, brutally. He ate and drank more
noisily than he had need. No one spoke to him. The family life
withdrew, shrank away and became hushed as he entered. But he
30 cared no longer about his alienation.

Immediately he had finished tea he rose with alacrity to go out. It
was this alacrity, this haste to be gone, which so sickened Mrs
Morel. As she heard him sousing heartily in cold water, heard the
eager scratch of the steel comb on the side of the bowl, as he wetted
35 his hair, she closed her eyes in disgust. As he bent over, lacing his
boots, there was a certain vulgar gusto in his movement that divided
him from the reserved, watchful rest of the family. He always ran
away from the battle with himself. Even in his own heart's privacy,
he excused himself, saying, 'If she hadn't said so-and-so, it would
40 never have happened. She asked for what she's got.' The children

waited in restraint during his preparations. When he had gone, they sighed with relief.

He closed the door behind him, and was glad. It was a rainy evening. The 'Palmerston' would be the cosier. He hastened forward in anticipation. All the slate roofs of the Bottoms shone black with wet. The roads, always dark with coal dust, were full of blackish mud. He hastened along. The Palmerston windows were steamed over. The passage was paddled with wet feet. But the air was warm, if foul, and full of the sound of voices and the smell of beer and smoke.

"What shollt ha'e, Walter?" cried a voice, as soon as Morel appeared in the doorway.

"Oh, Jim, my lad, wheriver has thee sprung fro'?"

The men made a seat for him, and took him in warmly. He was glad. In a minute or two, they had thawed all responsibility out of him, all shame, all trouble, and he was clear as a bell, for a jolly night.

But the next evening, as he was sitting on his heels at the garden gate, smoking, and calling across to the miners on the other side the alley, watching the youths, still unwashed from the pit, playing football, Mrs Kirk came out of her yard.

"Evenin' Missis!" said Morel, in his gallant, hearty fashion.

"You lookin' well, aren't yer?" said Mrs Kirk.

"Why, what's amiss?" cried Morel.

"Lettin' your Missis split 'er 'ead open like she has done," said Mrs Kirk.

"Yes, it was a nasty accident," said Morel, only thankful his wife had not told her neighbours.

"I can't think how she did it," said Mrs Kirk.

"No, nor me," answered Morel.

"At any rate, she'll be scarred for life."

"Ay it was a nasty bang," said Morel. "Yes—it's a great pity! I want her to go to th' doctor with it, but she won't."

"Your mester says he wants you to go to the doctor's with that eye of yours," said Mrs Kirk to Mrs Morel.

"Does he?" answered Mrs Morel.

On the Wednesday following, Morel was penniless. He dreaded his wife. Having hurt her, he hated her. He did not know what to do with himself that evening, having not even twopence with which to go to the Palmerston, and being already rather deeply in debt. So,

while his wife was down the garden with the child, he hunted in the top drawer of the dresser where she kept her purse, found it, and looked inside. It contained a half crown, two halfpennies, and a sixpence. So he took the sixpence, put the purse carefully back, and
5 went out.

The next day, when she wanted to pay the greengrocer, she looked in the purse for her sixpence, and her heart sank to her shoes. Then she sat down and thought: "*Was* there a sixpence?—I hadn't spent it, had I?—and I hadn't left it anywhere else?"
10 She was much put about. She hunted round everywhere for it. And, as she sought, the conviction came into her heart that her husband had taken it. What she had in her purse was all the money she possessed. But that he should sneak it from her thus was unbearable. He had done so twice before. The first time, she had
15 not accused him, and at the week end he had put the shilling again into her purse. So that was how she had known he had taken it. The second time he had not paid back.

This time, she felt it was too much. When he had had his dinner—he came home early that day—she said to him coldly:
20 "Did you take sixpence out of my purse last night?"

"Me!" he said, looking up in an offended way, "No, I didna! I niver clapped eyes on your purse."

But she could detect the lie.

"Why you know you did," she said quietly.
25 "I tell you I didna," he shouted. "Yer at me again, are yer? I've had about enough on't."

"So you filch sixpence out of my purse while I'm taking the clothes in."

"I'll may yer pay for this," he said, pushing back his chair in
30 desperation. He bustled and got washed, then went determinedly upstairs. Presently he came down dressed, and with a big bundle in a blue-checked enormous handkerchief.

"And now," he said, "you'll see me again when you do."

"It'll be before I want to," she replied, and at that, he marched out
35 of the house with his bundle. She sat trembling slightly, but her heart brimming with contempt. What would she do if he went to some other pit, obtained work, and got in with another woman? But she knew him too well—he couldn't. She was dead sure of him. Nevertheless her heart was gnawed inside her.
40 "Where's my Dad?" said William, coming in from school.

"He says he's run away," replied the mother.

"Where to?"

"Eh, I don't know. He's taken a bundle in the blue handkerchief, and says he's not coming back."

"What shall we do?" cried the boy.   5

"Eh never trouble, he won't go far."

"But if he doesn't come back," wailed Annie.

And she and William retired to the sofa and wept. Mrs Morel sat and laughed.

"You pair of gabeys!" she exclaimed. "*You'll* see him before the   10
night's out."

But the children were not to be consoled. Twilight came on. Mrs Morel grew anxious from very weariness. One part of her said, it would be a relief to see the last of him: another part fretted because of keeping the children: and inside her, as yet, she could not quite   15
let him go. At the bottom, she knew very well he could *not* go.

When she went down to the coal-place at the end of the garden, however, she felt something behind the door. So she looked. And there in the dark lay the big blue bundle. She sat on a piece of coal, in front of the bundle, and laughed. Every time she saw it, so fat and   20
yet so ignominious, slunk into its corner in the dark, with its ends flopping like dejected ears from the knots, she laughed again.*

She went up with her coal to the house. Annie and William were having a fresh weep because she had gone out.

"Silly pair of babies," she said. "Go down to the coalplace and   25
look behind the door, and *then* you'll see how far he's gone."

"What?" exclaimed William, rather pathetically.

"Go and see," said his mother.

And he slunk out, followed by Annie, who trotted sniffing up her tears. Directly he reappeared in great excitement, hugging the   30
bundle.

"He won't go now, will he mother?" he cried.

"No—and I knew he never would.—My only fear was that he'd pawn something. But take it back—go and put it where you found it."   35

"But—!" faltered William. "What's in it?"

"Go and put it back!" she insisted, "and never mind."

The boy lugged the fat bundle down the yard again, and dropped it behind the coal-place door. Then, relieved but not yet at ease, the children went to bed.   40

Mrs Morel sat waiting. He had not any money, she knew, so if he stopped, he was running up a bill. She was very tired of him, tired to death. He had not even the courage to carry his bundle beyond the yard end.

5　　As she meditated, at about nine o'clock, he opened the door and came in, slinking, and yet sulky. She said not a word. He took off his coat and slunk to his arm-chair, where he began to take off his boots.

"You'd better fetch your bundle before you take your boots off," she said, quietly.

10　　"You may thank your stars I've come back tonight," he said, looking up from under his dropped head, sulkily, trying to be impressive.

"Why where should you have gone? You daren't even get your parcel through the yard-end," she said.

15　　He looked such a fool she was not even angry with him. He continued to take his boots off and prepare for bed.

"I don't know what's in your blue handkerchief," she said. "But if you leave it the children shall fetch it in the morning."

Whereupon he got up and went out of the house, returning 20　presently and crossing the kitchen with averted face, hurrying upstairs. As Mrs Morel saw him slink quickly through the inner doorway, holding his bundle, she laughed to herself—but her heart was bitter, because she had loved him.

Chapter III

The Casting off of Morel, the Taking on of William*

During the next week Morel's temper was almost unbearable. Like all miners, he was a great lover of medicines, which, strangely 5 enough, he would often pay for himself.

"You mun get me a drop o' laxy vitral,"* he said. "It's a winder as we canna ha'e a sup i' th'ouse."

So Mrs Morel bought him elixir of vitriol, his favourite first medicine. And he made himself a jug of wormwood tea. He had 10 hanging in the attic great bunches of dried herbs: wormwood, rue, horehound, elder-flowers, parsley-purt, marsh-mallow, hyssop, dandelion and centaury.* Usually there was a jug of one or other decoction standing on the hob, from which he drank largely.

"Grand!" he said, smacking his lips after wormwood. "Grand!" 15 And he exhorted the children to try.

"It's better than any of your tea or your cocoa stews," he vowed. But they were not to be tempted.

This time, however, neither pills nor vitriol nor all his herbs would shift the "nasty peens in his head." He was sickening for an attack of 20 an inflammation of the brain. He had never been well since his sleeping on the ground when he went with Jerry to Nottingham. Since then he had drunk and stormed. Now he fell seriously ill, and Mrs Morel had him to nurse. He was one of the worst patients imaginable. But, in spite of all, and putting aside the fact that he was 25 bread-winner, she never quite wanted him to die. Still there was one part of her wanted him for herself.

The neighbours were very good to her: occasionally some had the children in to meals, occasionally some would do the downstairs work for her, one would mind the baby for a day. But it was a great 30 drag, nevertheless. It was not every day the neighbours helped. Then she had nursing of baby and husband, cleaning and cooking, everything to do. She was quite worn out, but she did what was wanted of her.

And the money was just sufficient. She had seventeen shillings a 35 week from clubs, and every Friday, Barker and the other butty put

by a portion of the stall's profits for Morel's wife. And the neighbours made broths, and gave eggs, and such invalids' trifles. If they
had not helped her so generously in those times, Mrs Morel would
never have pulled through, without incurring debts that would have
5 dragged her down.*
    The weeks passed, Morel, almost against hope, grew better. He
had a fine constitution, so that, once on the mend, he went straight
forward to recovery. Soon he was pottering about downstairs.
During his illness his wife had spoilt him a little. Now he wanted her
10 to continue. He often put his hand to his head, pulled down the
corners of his mouth, and shammed pains he did not feel. But there
was no deceiving her. At first she merely smiled to herself. Then she
scolded him sharply.
    "Goodness man, don't be so lachrymose."
15   That wounded him slightly, but still he continued to feign
sickness.
    "I wouldn't be such a mardy baby," said his wife shortly.
    Then he was indignant, and cursed under his breath, like a boy.
He was forced to resume a normal tone, and to cease to whine.
20   Nevertheless, there was a state of peace in the house for some
time. Mrs Morel was more tolerant of him, and he, depending on
her almost like a child, was rather happy. Neither knew that she was
more tolerant because she loved him less. Up till this time, in spite of
all, he had been her husband, and her man. She had felt that, more
25 or less, what he did to himself he did to her. Her living depended on
him. There were many, many stages in the ebbing of her love for
him, but it was always ebbing.
    Now, with the birth of this third baby, her self no longer set
towards him, helplessly, but was like a tide that scarcely rose,
30 standing off from him. After this she scarcely desired him. And
standing more aloof from him, not feeling him so much part of
herself, but merely part of her circumstances she did not mind so
much what he did, could leave him alone.
    There was the halt, the wistfulness about the ensuing year, which
35 is like autumn in a man's life. His wife was casting him off, half
regretfully, but relentlessly; casting him off and turning now for love
and life to the children. Henceforward he was more or less a husk.
And he half acquiesced, as so many men do, yielding their place to
their children.
40   During his recuperation, when it was really over between them,

both made an effort to come back somewhat to the old relationship
of the first months of their marriage. He sat at home, and, when the
children were in bed, and she was sewing—she did all her sewing by
hand, made all shirts and children's clothing—he would read to her
from the newspaper, slowly pronouncing and delivering the words 5
like a man pitching quoits. Often she hurried him on, giving him a
phrase in anticipation. And then he took her words humbly.

The silences between them were peculiar. There would be the
swift, slight 'cluck' of her needle, the sharp 'pop' of his lips as he let
out the smoke, the warmth, the sizzle on the bars as he spat in the 10
fire. Then her thoughts turned to William. Already he was getting a
big boy. Already he was top of the class, and the master said he was
the smartest lad in the school. She saw him a man, young, full of
vigour, making the world glow again for her.

And Morel sitting there, quite alone, and having nothing to think 15
about, would be feeling vaguely uncomfortable. His soul would
reach out in its blind way to her, and find her gone. He felt a sort of
emptiness, almost like a vacuum in his soul. He was unsettled and
restless. Soon he could not live in that atmosphere, and he affected
his wife. Both felt an oppression on their breathing, when they were 20
left together for some time. Then he went to bed, and she settled
down to enjoy herself alone, working, thinking, living.

So, having to get into an atmosphere where he could live, not
being able to acquiesce in his own obliteration, Morel faltered back
to the Palmerston and to Jerry, and his wife, in her heart of hearts, 25
was relieved to have him go.

He had lost his game now. Though, of course, he recurred again
and again to his old selves, still had his moments of dominance and
authority and pride. But they were like echoes. The baby Paul,
towards whom he also felt strangely moved, would not be touched by 30
him. The infant had a gathering in the ear, when he was eight
months old, and was very fretful. Morel wanted to hold the child, to
soothe him. It would have done the man good to be able to nurse his
sick baby. But the child would not be nursed by him. It would stiffen
in his arms, and, although usually a quiet baby, would scream, draw 35
back from the father's hands. And Morel, seeing the small fists
clenched, the baby face averted, the wet blue eyes turned frantically
to the mother, would say in a kind of impatient despair:

"Here, come an' ta'e him!"

"It's your moustache frightens him," she replied, as she took the 40 child and pressed it to her bosom. Nevertheless her heart hurt with pain. And Morel was afraid of the child.

Meanwhile another infant was coming, fruit of this little peace and tenderness between the separating parents. Paul was seventeen
5 months old when the new baby was born. He was then a plump, pale child, quiet, with heavy blue eyes and still the peculiar slight knitting of the brows. The last child was also a boy, fair and bonny. Mrs Morel was sorry when she knew she was with child, both for economic reasons, and because she did not love her husband; but
10 not for the sake of the infant.

They called the baby Arthur. He was very pretty, with a mop of gold curls, and he loved his father from the first. Mrs Morel was glad this child loved the father. Hearing the miner's footsteps, the baby would put up his arms and crow. And if Morel were in a good
15 temper, he called back immediately, in his hearty, mellow voice:

"What then, my beauty—I sh'll come to thee, in a minute."

And as soon as he had taken off his pitcoat, Mrs Morel would put an apron round the child, and give him to his father.

"What a sight the lad looks!" she would exclaim sometimes,
20 taking back the baby, that was smutted on the face from his father's kisses and play. Then Morel laughed joyfully.

"He's a little collier, bless his bit o' mutton,"* he exclaimed. And these were the happy moments of her life now, when the children included the father in her heart.

25 Meanwhile William grew bigger and stronger and more active, while Paul, always rather delicate and quiet, got slimmer, and trotted after his mother like her shadow. He was usually active and interested, but sometimes he would have fits of depression. Then the mother would find the boy of three or four crying on the sofa.

30 "What's the matter?" she asked, and got no answer.

"What's the matter?" she insisted, getting cross.

"I don't know," sobbed the child.

So she tried to reason him out of it, or to amuse him, but without effect. It made her feel beside herself. Then the father, always
35 impatient, would jump from his chair and shout:

"If he doesn't stop I'll smack him till he does."

"You'll do nothing of the sort," said the mother coldly.

And then she carried the child into the yard, plumped him into his little chair, and said:

40 "Now cry there, Misery!"

And then a butterfly on the rhubarb leaves perhaps caught his eye, or at last he cried himself to sleep. These fits were not often, but they caused a shadow in Mrs Morel's heart, and her treatment of Paul was different from that of the other children.

One morning Mrs Morel, hearing 'Barm-O',* went down into the   5
alley with her mug. 'Barm-O' was not yet up to her gate, so she stood waiting, listening to the snatches of hymns the man was singing as he dipped the can into his barrels and filled the pots the women gave him. He was a cheerful old man, with a rather bulbous comic face surrounded with white whiskers. In his decrepit old cart   10
were two barrels of brewer's yeast, covered with a wet sack. As he went along, he sang snatches of hymns, since he had been converted three months before.

"We shall meet beyond the river,
Where the surges cease to roll*—Barm-O!"   15

came his big, half wicked cry down the alley. And he chaffed the women as he served them their ha'porths of barm. Suddenly Mrs Morel heard a voice calling her. It was the thin little Mrs Anthony in brown velvet.

"Here, Mrs Morel, I want to tell you about your Willie."   20
"Oh do you?" replied Mrs Morel.*

Mrs Anthony did not come close, but stood and shouted across the alley.

"D'you reckon he's got any right to rip our Alfie's collar off'n his back?"   25

"Why, has he done?" Mrs Morel called back. Both women scorned to go near each other.

"He has that—and if you don't believe me, I'll go an' fetch it you."

"I think you've no need," said Mrs Morel. "But how do you know   30
our William did it?"

"What, do you think our Alfie doesn't tell the truth then? There isn't a more truthful spoken lad in the Bottoms. All right, ask Annie Bower an' a lot more of 'em. He got hold of my lad's collar an' ripped it clean off his back. And *I* can't afford to buy new collars   35
when their own's ripped up by folks—."

"I know you can't," said Mrs Morel.

"An' what I say," said Mrs Anthony, hotly, "is, he ought to have a good thrashing, that's what he ought."

"'At the Cross at the cross, where I found—'* Barm-O!—Barm-
OO!—How much this dip Missis?"

"A ha-porth 'll do," said Mrs Morel, handing up her mug.

"A ha-porth in this mug, an' 'ere you are, all fresh an' drippin',
5 an' God's blessin' on you," replied Barm-O. He and his cart stood
between the two women.

"'Consider the lilies how they grow'—Yes Mrs Anthony—a
ha-porth. All ha'porths! Never mind. 'They toil not neither do they
spin. Yet not even Solerman—'* Thank yer—"

10 He moved on, having made not the slightest impression on the
two women. Mrs Anthony was rather more indignant than ever.

"—A lad as gets 'old of another an' rips his clothes off'n 'is
back," she repeated.*

"Your Alfred's as old as my William," said Mrs Morel.

15 "'Appen 'e is, but that doesn't give him a right to get hold of the
boy's collar, an' fair rip it clean off his back."

"Well," said Mrs Morel, "I don't thrash my children, and even if
I did, I should want to hear their side of the tale."

"They'd happen be a bit better if they did get a good hiding,"
20 retorted Mrs Anthony, "when it comes ter rippin' a lad's clean
collar off'n 'is back a purpose—"

"I'm sure he didn't do it on purpose," said Mrs Morel.

"Make me a liar!" shouted Mrs Anthony.

Mrs Morel moved away and closed her gate. Her hand trembled
25 as she held her mug of barm.

"But I s'll let your mester know," Mrs Anthony cried after her.

At dinner time, when William had finished his meal and wanted
to be off again—he was then eleven years old—his mother said to
him:

30 "What did you tear Alfred Anthony's collar for?"

"When did I tear his collar?"

"I don't know when, but his mother says you did."

"Why—it was yesterday—an' it was torn a'ready."

"But you tore it more."

35 "Well, I'd got a cobbler as 'ad licked seventeen—an' Alfy Ant'ny
'e says:

> 'Adam an' Eve an' Pinch-me,
> Went down to a river to bade.
> Adam an' Eve got drownded,
40 > Who d'yer think got saved—?'*

An' so I says 'Oh, Pinch-*you*', an' so I pinched 'im, an' 'e was mad, an' so he snatched my cobbler an' run off with it. An' so I run after 'im, an' when I was gettin' hold of him, 'e dodged an' it ripped 'is collar. But I got my cobbler—"

He pulled from his pocket a black old horse-chestnut hanging on a string. This old cobbler had 'cobbled'—hit and smashed—seventeen other cobblers on similar strings. So the boy was proud of his veteran.

"Well," said Mrs Morel, "you know you've got no right to rip his collar."

"Well our mother!" he answered. "I never meant tr'a done it—an' it was on'y an old indirrubber* collar as was torn a'ready."

"Next time," said his mother, "*you* be more careful. I shouldn't like it if you came home with *your* collar torn off."

"I don't care, our mother, I never did it a-purpose."

The boy was rather miserable at being reprimanded.

"No—well you be more careful."

William fled away, glad to be exonerated. And Mrs Morel, who hated any bother with the neighbours, thought she would explain to Mrs Anthony, and the business would be over.

But that evening, Morel came in from the pit looking very sour. He stood in the kitchen and glared round, but did not speak for some minutes. Then:

"Wheer's that Willy?" he asked.

"What do you want *him* for?" asked Mrs Morel, who had guessed.

"I'll let 'im know when I get him," said Morel, banging his pit-bottle onto the dresser.

"I suppose Mrs Anthony's got hold of you and been yarning to you about their Alfy's collar," said Mrs Morel, rather sneering.

"Niver mind who's got hold of me," said Morel. "When I get hold of '*im* I'll make his bones rattle."

"It's a poor tale," said Mrs Morel, "that you're so ready to side with any snipey vixen who likes to come telling tales against your own children."

"I'll learn 'im!" said Morel. "It none matters to me whose lad 'e is, 'e's none goin' rippin' an' tearin' about just as he's a mind."

"'Ripping and tearing about!'" repeated Mrs Morel.—"He was running after that Alfy, who'd taken his cobbler, and he accidentally got hold of his collar—because the other dodged—as an Anthony would."

"I know—" shouted Morel, threateningly.

"You would, before you're told," replied his wife bitingly.

"Niver you mind," stormed Morel. "I know my business."

"That's more than doubtful," said Mrs Morel, "supposing some
loud-mouthed creature had been getting you to thrash your own
children."

"I know," repeated Morel.

And he said no more, but sat and nursed his bad temper.

Suddenly William ran in, saying:

"Can I have my tea mother?"

"Tha can ha'e more than that," shouted Morel.

"Hold your noise man," said Mrs Morel. "And don't look so
ridiculous."

"He'll look ridiculous before I've done wi' him!" shouted Morel,
rising from his chair and glaring at his son. William, who was a tall
lad for his years, but very sensitive, had gone pale and was looking in
a sort of horror at his father.

"Go out!" Mrs Morel commanded her son.

William had not the wit to move. Suddenly Morel clenched his
fist, and crouched.

"I'll *gi'e* him go out!" he shouted, like an insane thing.

"What!" cried Mrs Morel, panting with rage. "You shall not
touch him for *her* telling, you shall not."

"Shonna I?" shouted Morel. "Shonna I?"

And, glaring at the boy, he ran forward. Mrs Morel sprang in
between them, with her fist lifted.

"Don't you *dare*!" she cried.

"What!" he shouted, baffled for the moment. "What!"

She spun round to her son.

"*Go* out of the house!" she commanded him in fury. The boy, as
if hypnotised by her, turned suddenly and was gone. Morel rushed
to the door, but was too late. He returned, pale under his pit-dirt
with fury. But now his wife was fully roused.

"Only dare!" she said, in a loud, ringing voice. "Only
dare, milord, to lay a finger on that child. You'll regret it for
ever."

He was afraid of her. In a towering rage, he sat down.

"No, you've done it before, but you shall do it no more!" she
began suddenly, after a pause. "I don't forget the time you kicked
him, and made great bruises on him, because of old Mother Sharp's

spite against him—you shall do it no more," she panted. She was quite breathless with passion.

"Shonna I? Shonna I?" repeated Morel.

"You bully, you miserable coward and bully!" she cried. "Haven't you more stomach than to be ordered about by any common cat like that Anthony, when she comes bidding you to thrash your children. Is *she* to decide for you, when you're to come home and knock the lad about?—and you to do it, you coward, and you bully!—No, not while I'm here!"

"Tha'lt see what'll 'appen while tha'rt here," threatened Morel.

"Never again, milord, never again do you lay a finger on my children."

"Oh!—Oh!!" he snarled.

And that night he went out and got drunk, and that week-end he did not give William his weekly penny.

"You are better without it," said Mrs Morel to her son.

When the children were old enough to be left, Mrs Morel joined the Women's Guild.* It was a little club of women attached to the Co-operative Wholesale Society,* which met on Monday night in the long room over the grocery shop of the Bestwood "Co-op." The women were supposed to discuss the benefits to be derived from Co-operation, and other social questions. Sometimes Mrs Morel read a paper. It seemed queer to the children to see their mother, who was always busy about the house, sitting writing in her rapid fashion, thinking, referring to books, and writing again. They felt for her on such occasions the deepest respect.

But they loved the 'Guild.' It was the only thing to which they did not grudge their mother: and that partly because she enjoyed it, partly because of the treats they derived from it. The guild was called by some hostile husbands, who found their wives getting too independent, the "clat-fart" shop: that is, the gossip shop. It is true, from off the basis of the guild, the women could look at their homes, at the conditions of their own lives, and find fault. So, the colliers found their women had a new standard of their own, rather disconcerting. And also, Mrs Morel always had a lot of news on Monday nights, so that the children liked William to be in when their mother came home, because she told him things.

Then, when the lad was thirteen, she got him a job in the Co-op. office. He was a very clever boy, frank, with rather rough features and real viking blue eyes.

"What dost want ter ma'e a stool-harsed Jack on 'im for?" said Morel. "All he'll do is to wear his britches behind out an' earn nowt. What's 'e startin' wi'?"

"It doesn't matter what he's starting with," said Mrs Morel.

5 "It wouldna! Put 'im i' th' pit wi'* me, an' 'e'll earn a easy ten shillin' a wik* from th' start. But six shillin' wearin' his truck-end out on a stool's better than ten shillin' i' th' pit wi' me, I know."

"He is *not* going in the pit," said Mrs Morel, "and there's an end of it."

10 "It wor good enough for me, but it's non good enough for 'im."

"If your mother put you in the pit at twelve, it's no reason why I should do the same with my lad."

"Twelve!—it wor a sight afore that!"

"Whenever it was," said Mrs Morel.

15 She was very proud of her son. He went to the night-school, and learned shorthand, so that by the time he was sixteen, he was the best short-hand clerk and book-keeper on the place, except one. Then he taught in the nightschools. But he was so fiery, that only his good-nature and his size protected him.

20 All the things that men do—the decent things—William did. He could run like the wind. When he was twelve, he won a first prize in a race: an inkstand of glass, shaped like an anvil. It stood proudly on the dresser, and gave Mrs Morel a keen pleasure. The boy only ran for her. He flew home with his anvil, breathless, with a:

25 "Look mother!"

That was the first real tribute to herself. She took it like a queen.

"How pretty!" she exclaimed.

The children of the Bottoms, playing round the stile, used to shout, as William came along:

30 "Jump it Willy—jump it."

And he would leap over the fence, some four or five feet, grandly.

"Sithee at that!" the small boys shouted.

He also could throw farther than any youth in Bestwood. His comrades and rivals were very jealous of these feats, and they vowed

35 that his stones were not those that lay furthest, beyond the hedge. So William disdainfully marked them with a W.M.

When he was seventeen, he won a bicycle race at Ilkeston. Morel, in one of his bursts of bragging, had challenged his son against any champion there in the public house. William felt it his duty to fulfil

40 his father's boasts. Mrs Morel did not approve.

"See me lick 'em, mother!" he cried, smacking the calves of his
legs. All that day Mrs Morel sat in suspense and misery. He might
be killed or hurt. She was sure his heart was not strong enough for
cycle-racing. Then he came home at night with a little oak writing
desk.

"Here you are, mother!" he said. "Didn't I tell you I'd bring it
you?"

But she made him promise not to enter a cycle-race again.

He had pupils, and taught short-hand at home. But he was so
furious and fiery, that only the youths who were students by nature,
could stand him. He and his pupil sat at the table in the kitchen. It
was warm and lamp-lit, and very still. The red chintz cushions on
the sofa were soft, the red cotton table-cloth seemed cosy. As a rule,
the pupil, a lad of thirteen or fourteen, sat anxiously, while William,
rapid and energetic, corrected the exercise. There were snorts of
impatience and disgust from the teacher. Then suddenly he would
cry:

"Why you doddering blockhead, you had it right in the last
sentence, and now—"

The poor pupil blew his nose nervously on his red handkerchief
as he peered over William's elbow. Sometimes Mrs Morel sat
sewing in her rocking-chair. Then the lesson-proper began.
William grew more and more impatient, until he burst forth:

"You great booby, you block-head, you thundering idiot and fool,
what have I told you a thousand times—?"

"William! William!" cried his mother. "Be ashamed of yourself! I
wonder anyone puts up with you.—Take no notice of him Robert,
it's his own impatience that's the matter, not you. *You're* quick
enough." And Robert would give a glance of shame and gratitude at
Mrs Morel, while William continued:

"Come on—and for Goodness sake don't be a blockhead.
Look—!"

At last Mrs Morel made it a rule, always to go out of the house
when these lessons took place, in order to spare the feelings of the
poor lads.

William had to be at his office at eight, so his mother got up at
seven o'clock to prepare him. He was usually late, or on the verge of
lateness. But nothing could hurry him. He loved these breakfasts
alone with his mother. Then, being jolly, he rattled away to her, and
teased her.

One morning he asked her for his clean shirt. He stood on the
hearthrug as she gave it him. Then she sat down to her cup of tea.
He held up the woollen shirt, that was largely patched, open in front
of him.

5 "What do you call this, mother?" he asked.

"A shirt," she replied, beginning to laugh.

"'A rose would smell as sweet—'!"* he quoted, whimsically.

"Well—you're such a rip—and I'd no more stuff like the shirt—
besides, who'll see it?"

10 "Are you sure it won't show through my breeks—I feel as if it
would shine through," he said, still surveying the shirt doubtfully.

"Put it on—look at the time!" she commanded, laughing in spite
of herself, as she sat in her rocking-chair, sipping her tea. He stood
just before her, a big, strong youth, holding out his patchwork-shirt.

15 "My Joseph's-Coat!"* he addressed it, "I don't think anybody'll
be jealous of you—one, two, three, four—which is the original stuff,
mother?"

"Put it on!" commanded his mother.

"But suppose I have an accident, and am taken to the hospital,
20 and recover consciousness to see four nurses holding out the tail of
my shirt—" he grumbled.

"They will say what good looking-after you have," she laughed.

He struggled into the shirt, saying, with his face yet muffled up:

"'Not even Solomon in all his glory—'"

25 "No," laughed Mrs Morel, "I don't suppose anybody would put
as many stitches in for Solomon—."

William peered over his shoulder quizzically:

"My tail of woe!"* he lamented.

Mrs Morel was now shaking with laughter. She struggled with
30 herself, recovered sufficiently to bang the table with her fist, and cry:

"*Will* you get dressed, sir! There it is a quarter to eight."

"You don't expect me to hurry, clad about with all these patches,
do you mother?"

"Oh you looney and gabey!" she cried. "You'll go breaking your
35 neck on that bicycle—"

"Yes, if I were dead I shouldn't be ashamed of my shirt," he
interrupted.

She jumped up, seized the hair-brush, and rapped his head with
it.

40 "Brush that hair of yours," she commanded.

They left each other glowing warm: he made her feel warm inside, and she him.

Then he began to get ambitious. He gave all his money to his mother. When he earned fourteen shillings a week, she gave him back two for himself, and, as he never drank, he felt himself rich. He went about with the bourgeois of Bestwood. The townlet contained nothing higher than the clergyman. Then came the bank-manager, then the doctors, then the tradespeople, and after that, the hosts of colliers. William began to consort with the sons of the chemist, the schoolmaster, and the tradesmen. He played billiards in the Mechanics' Hall.* Also he danced, this in spite of his mother. All the life that Bestwood offered, he enjoyed, from the sixpenny-hops down Church Street, to sports and billiards.

"Waltz!" exclaimed his father. "Dost reckon *tha* can waltz? When I was a bit nimbler, I could turn on a threp'ny bit."*

"I'll bet you could," said William sceptically.

"I could an' all!" protested Morel, with pride.

"Go on then—let's have a look at you."

But Morel was afraid to dance before his children.

"Nay, that I niver sholl! It's a fool's game altogether, an' I canna see what good it'll do thee."

"You see I'm following in my father's footsteps," he said.

"An' more fool thee," said his father, "if iver tha does that."

"That's all right when you're too stiff to dance any more," said William.

"I've niver danced for twenty year," cried Morel hotly.

"An' I'll bet you found it hard work to give it up."

But William persisted. He was a great favourite with the ladies.

"'Postle,'* he used to say to his brother Paul, after a dance, as the two lay in bed together. "'Postle—a girl in white satin—d'yer hear, white satin down to her slippers—lives at Sutton—dead gone on me!* I'm going to see her tomorrow."

After a fortnight Paul would ask of him:

"What about that white-satin lady?"

"Don't care for her 'Postle—no cop! But there's a little gem from Ripley—faintly scented with cherry-blossom—fair as a lily—"

Paul was treated to dazzling descriptions of all kinds of flower-like ladies, most of whom lived like cut blooms in William's heart, for a brief fortnight.

Occasionally some flame would come in pursuit of her errant

swain. Mrs Morel would find a strange girl at the door, and immediately she sniffed the air.

"Is Mr Morel in?" the damsel would ask appealingly.

"My husband is at home," Mrs Morel replied.

5 "I—I mean *young* Mr Morel," repeated the maiden, painfully.

"Which one—there are several?"

Whereupon much blushing and stammering from the fair one.

"I—I met Mr Morel—at Ripley," she explained.

"Oh—at a dance!"

10 "Yes."

"I don't approve of the girls my son meets at dances. And he is *not* at home."

Mrs Morel hated the cheap dances her son went to.

"Do you think," she said to him, "I don't know the brazen hussies 15 that go there?"

"Well mother, *I'm* not brazen, as you see."

"I'm not so sure," laughed his mother.

"You don't think I shall fall in love with 'em, do you? I shan't. I only want a bit of fun with them."

20 "But they don't merely want a bit of fun with *you*. And it is not right."

"Why? I shan't get married. Don't you fret, Mater,* I shan't get married till I meet a woman like you—an' that'll be a long time first.—And then—I s'll get married at thirty, when I'm sick of 25 romping about."

"We s'll see, my son," replied his mother.

Then he came home angry with his mother for having turned the girl away so rudely. He was a careless, yet eager-looking fellow, who walked with long strides, sometimes frowning, often with his cap 30 pushed jollily to the back of his head. Now he came in frowning. He threw his cap onto the sofa, and took his strong jaw in his hand, and glared down at his mother. She was small, with her hair taken straight back from her forehead. She had a quiet air of authority, and yet of rare warmth. Knowing her son was angry, she trembled 35 inwardly.

"Did a lady call for me yesterday, mother?" he asked.

"I don't know about a lady—there was a girl came."

"And why didn't you tell me?"

"Because I forgot, simply."

40 He fumed a little.

"A good-looking girl—seemed a lady?"

"I didn't look at her."

"Big brown eyes—!"

"Yes."

Again he fumed.

"And what did you tell her?"

"That you were not at home."

"And what else?"

"Merely that I didn't approve of girls you had met once coming to your mother's house for you."

"Well you needn't have said that," he replied. "Her father's well off—they keep two servants—"

"They weren't with her, so I didn't know."

"But why need you be nasty—there was no wrong in her coming, was there."

"I thought she was a brazen hussy."

"She wasn't—she wasn't—her father—"

"Keeps two servants," chimed in Mrs Morel.

"No—he's the vet for Woodlinton—besides mother—"

"She was a brazen hussy."

"She wasn't.—And she *was* pretty, wasn't she?"

"I didn't look."

"But you must have done—own up—"

"I did *not* look. And tell your girls, my son, that when they're running after you, they're not to come and ask your mother for you—tell them that—brazen baggages you meet at dancing classes."

"I'm sure she was a nice girl—"

"And I'm sure she wasn't."

There ended the altercation. Over the dancing there was a great strife between the mother and the son. The grievance reached its height when William said he was going to Hucknall Torkard—considered a low town—to a fancy dress ball. He was to be a Highlander. There was a dress he could hire, which one of his friends had had, and which fitted him perfectly. The Highland suit came home. Mrs Morel received it coldly, and would not unpack it.

"My suit come?" cried William.

"There's a parcel in the front room."

He rushed in and cut the string.

"How do you fancy your son in this!" he said enraptured, showing her the suit.

"You know I don't want to fancy you in it."

On the evening of the dance, when he had come home to dress, Mrs Morel put on her coat and bonnet.

"Aren't you going to stop and see me, mother?" he asked.

5 "No—I don't want to see you," she replied.

She was rather pale, and her face was closed and hard. She was afraid of her son's going the same way as his father. He hesitated a moment, and his heart stood still with anxiety. Then he caught sight of the Highland bonnet with its ribbons. He picked it up gleefully,
10 forgetting her. She went out.

He never knew how disappointed he was. The excitement of the moment, and of anticipation, was enough to carry him through the present. But all his pride was built on *her* seeing him. And afterwards, it always hurt him to think back on this ball.

15 However, he went upstairs in great excitement. Paul helped him to dress.

"This is a fancy dress set 'Postle," he said. "Give me those things." He struggled into a pair of black, tight drawers, very short. Then he stood in front of his mother's looking glass with glee.

20 "See me in my black shorts!" he said, twisting round. Then he added: "You see, 'Postle, a real Highlander doesn't wear drawers—he covers his nakedness with a kilt. But if I happened to kick rather high, and all those ladies there—why—it wouldn't do!"

25 The small boy thought it wouldn't, though it didn't seem to him as serious as all that.

"Fine pair of legs there, 'Postle! Fine legs! They've won four prizes in running for me, and two bicycle races. Not a bad pair!" He slapped his strong young thighs. "Muscle, my lad!—There's one
30 fault though, I can't quite make my knees touch. I'm a smite bandy, 'Postle. But it makes for strength.—Nicholas Nickleby*—he had fine legs—he could make his knees touch, according to the picture. And I guess, so could Mr Good. Was it Mr Good who had the 'beautiful white legs' in *King Solomon's Mines*.* Fasten me that. This suit
35 doesn't half look well on me, does it 'Postle?"

"No," said Paul, reverently.

"A real Highlander," continued William, "has to fold his kilt. I wish this was one of that sort—I should like to have a go at arranging it. You see, 'Postle, I can wear a kilt, because I'm a tidy
40 size round where it sits. You'd be no good—as flat as [a] box-lid.

You must pray to the Lord for development in that quarter, or you'll
never be able to wear a kilt."

Paul wondered vaguely why he should ever want to wear a kilt. He
could not aspire to his brother's brawn and stature, being slight and
small himself.

"Now how do my knees look!—all right, don't they? Ripping
knees they are—ripping knees—legs altogether! The chaps had a
bet on the other day in the office, that I was padded. So Vickers
crept up while I was writing and stuck a pin in. I nearly yelled the
ceiling down, and I jumped and punched his head, I can tell you.—I
wish I hadn't knocked that bit of skin off with my bike."

"Happen you could put a bit of your pink toothpowder on,"
suggested Paul.

"Happen I could—it says antiseptic—but will it give me gyp! You
know, I've a real highland figure—ginger hair, blue eyes, and fierce,
'Postle, fierce—besides brawn to back it up.—If ever I enlisted it'ud
be in the Black Watch.*—That tooth-powder's a nobby idea—."

When he was dressed, a tribe of children came in to see him, and
several neighbours. Then he set off. He had a high good time; and
yet, when he remembered it, it seemed a pain. His mother was cool
with him for a day or two. But he was so adorable—! And yet—a
tinge of loneliness was creeping in again, between her and him.

About this time he began to study. With a friend of his, he set off
to learn French and Latin, and other things. Soon he grew pale.
After the office, he would go to Fred Simpson's house, and the two
would work together until midnight, almost till one o'clock. Mrs
Morel remonstrated, got violently angry, implored him to take more
care of his health.

"When we're at it," he says, "I can*not* remember the time—
neither of us can—till Fred's mother shouts downstairs."

These nights of study were mixed with 'soirées' and dances. As he
grew older, he got leaner, and the carelessness went out of his eyes.

His mother, watching for him and waiting for him, felt a little chill
at her heart. Was he going to 'come off'? A grain of anxiety mingled
with her pride in him. And she had waited so long for him, she could
not bear it if he failed. She did not know what she wanted him to do.
Perhaps she only wanted him to be himself, to develop and bring to
fruit all that she had put into him. In him, she wanted to see her life's
fruition, that was all. And with all the strength of her soul she tried to
keep him strong and balanced and moving straight forwards. But he

was baffling, without clarity of purpose. Sometimes he lapsed and was purely like his father. It made her heart sink with dismay and apprehension.

He had had dozens of flirtations, but not anything approaching a
5 love affair. She did not mind flirtations, so long as he went straight forward with his career. But she dreaded lest he should come a cropper over some shallow hussy.*

When he was nineteen, he suddenly left the 'Co-op' office, and got a situation in Nottingham. In his new place he had thirty
10 shillings a week, instead of eighteen. This was indeed a rise. His mother and his father were brimmed up with pride. Everybody praised William. It seemed he was going to get on rapidly. Mrs Morel hoped, with his aid, to help her younger sons. Annie was now studying to be a teacher. Paul, also very clever, was getting on well,
15 having lessons in French and German from his Godfather, the clergyman who was still a friend to Mrs Morel. Arthur, a spoilt and very good-looking boy, was at the board school, but there was talk of his trying to get a Scholarship for the High School* in Nottingham.

William remained a year at his new post in Nottingham. He was
20 studying hard, and growing serious. Something seemed to be fretting him. Still he went out to the dances and the river parties. He did not drink. The children were all rabid teetotallers. He came home very late at night, and sat yet longer studying. His mother implored him to take more care, to do one thing or another.

25 "Dance if you want to dance, my son, but don't think you can work in the office, and then amuse yourself, and *then* study on top of all. You can't, the human frame won't stand it. Do one thing or the other—amuse yourself or learn Latin—but don't try to do both."

Then he got a place in London, at a hundred and twenty* a year.
30 This seemed a fabulous sum. His mother doubted almost whether to rejoice or to grieve.

"They want me in Lime Street on Monday week, mother," he cried, his eyes blazing, as he read the letter. Mrs Morel felt everything go silent inside her. He read the letter. "—'and will you reply by
35 Thursday whether you accept—Yours faithfully—' —they want me, mother, at a hundred and twenty a year, and don't even ask to see me. Didn't I tell you I could do it! Think of me in London!—And I can give you twenty pounds a year, Mater—we s'll all be rolling in money."

"We shall, my son," she answered sadly.
40 It never occurred to him that she might be more hurt at his going

away, than glad of his success. Indeed, as the days drew near for his
departure, her heart began to close and grow dreary with despair.
She loved him so much. More than that, she hoped in him so much.
Almost she lived by him. She liked to do things for him: she liked to
put a cup for his tea and to iron his collars, of which he was so proud.   5
It was a joy to her to have him proud of his collars. There was no
laundry. So she used to rub away at them with her little convex iron,
to polish them,* till they shone from the sheer pressure of her arm.
Now she would not do it for him. Now he was going away. She felt
almost as if he were going as well out of her heart. He did not seem   10
to leave her inhabited with himself. That was the grief and the pain
to her. He took nearly all himself away.

A few days before his departure—he was just twenty—he burned
his love-letters. They had hung on a file at the top of the kitchen
cupboard. From some of them he had read extracts to his mother.   15
Some of them she had taken the trouble to read herself. But most
were too trivial.

Now, on the Saturday morning he said:

"Come on, 'Postle, let's go through my letters, and you can have
the birds and flowers."   20

Mrs Morel had done her Saturday's work on the Friday, because
he was having a last day's holiday. She was making him a rice cake,
which he loved, to take with him. He was scarcely conscious that she
was so miserable.

He took the first letter off the file. It was mauve-tinted, and had   25
purple and green thistles. William sniffed the page:

"Nice scent—smell—!"

And he thrust the sheet under Paul's nose.

"Um!" said Paul, breathing in. "What d'you call it?"

"That's Jockey Club," said William, though he did not know in   30
the least.

"It couldn't be thistle," said Paul, "because thistles don't smell."

"Listen—'Dear One—' —hark Mater."

"I dont want to hear the silly hussies," said Mrs Morel.

"Listen though! 'Dear One—You *did not* tell me your first name,   35
so I can only call you what you *are*. I have to write to you, or I think I
shall go off my head—' think of that, Mater."

"Yes the silly lunatics! It's little head they've got, to *go* off.—And
they don't know what a rod they're making for their backs puffing
you up."   40

"That's not puffing me up. She *was* gone on me."

"And if she was, is it anything to be proud of? A silly thing!"

"You shouldn't say 'puffing him up to make a rod for her own back,' mother," interrupted Paul.

5 "*You* would be right, of course," laughed his mother.

"'I fairly *love* Scotch things since I saw you in that kilt. It suited you *awfully*. I think I *never* saw anybody look so nice, with that *kilt* and those *stockings*—' It's my knees—I know it's my knees Mater. They can't escape 'em."

10 "They can't, if they're common cats."

"Clip the thistle out, Postle. It's a nice one, isn't it?"

Paul loved the pretty little embellishments to the love-letters. William burned the letter. The next was pink, with cherry blossom in the corner.

15 "Cherry blossom!" said Paul, sniffing deeply. "Grand—smell mother."*

His mother ducked her small, fine nose down to the paper.

"*I* don't want to smell their rubbish," she said, sniffing.

"This girl's father," said William, "is as rich as Crœsus. He owns 20 property without end.—She calls me Lafayette,* because I know French.—'You will see, I've forgiven you.'—I like *her* forgiving me.—'I told mother about you this morning, and she will have much pleasure if you come to tea on Sunday, but she will have to get father's consent also. I sincerely hope he will agree. I will let you 25 know how it transpires. If however you—'"

"'Let you know how it' what?" interrupted Mrs Morel.

"'Transpires'—oh yes!"*

"'Transpires!'" repeated Mrs Morel, mockingly. "I thought she was so well-educated!"

30 William felt slightly uncomfortable, and abandoned this maiden, giving Paul the corner with the cherry-blossom.* He continued to read extracts from his letters, some of which amused his mother, some of which saddened her and made her anxious for him.

"My lad," she said, "they're very wise. They know they've only 35 got to flatter your vanity, and you press up to them like a dog that has its head scratched."

"Well, they can't go on scratching for ever," he replied. "And when they've done, I trot away."

"But one day you'll find a string round your neck, that you can't 40 pull off," she answered.

"Not me! I'm equal to any of 'em, Mater, they needn't flatter themselves."

"You flatter *yourself*," she said quietly.

Soon there was a heap of twisted black pages, all that remained of the file of scented letters: except that Paul had thirty or forty pretty 5 tickets from the corners of the notepaper, swallows and forget-me-nots and ivy sprays. And William went to London, to start a new file.

Chapter IV

The young Life of Paul*

Paul would be built like his mother, slightly, and rather small. His fair hair went reddish, and then dark brown: his eyes were grey. He was a pale, quiet child, with eyes that seemed to listen, and with a full, dropping underlip.

As a rule, he seemed old for his years. He was so conscious of what other people felt, particularly his mother. When she fretted, he understood, and could have no peace. His soul seemed always attentive to her.

As he grew older, he became stronger. William was too far removed from him to accept him as a companion. So the smaller boy belonged at first almost entirely to Annie. She was a tom-boy and a 'flybie-skybie,' as her mother called her. But she was intensely fond of her second brother. So Paul was towed round at the heels of Annie, sharing her game. She raced wildly at lerky,* with the other young wild-cats of the Bottoms. And always Paul flew beside her, living her share of the game, having as yet no part of his own. He was quiet and not noticeable. But his sister adored him. He always seemed to care for things if she wanted him to.

She had a big doll of which she was fearfully proud, though not so fond. So she laid the doll on the sofa, and covered it with an antimacassar, to sleep. Then she forgot it. Meantime Paul must practise jumping off the sofa arm. So he jumped crash into the face of the hidden doll. Annie rushed up, uttered a loud wail, and sat down to weep a dirge. Paul remained quite still.

"You couldn't tell it was there, mother: you couldn't tell it was there," he repeated over and over. So long as Annie wept for the doll he sat helpless with misery. Her grief wore itself out. She forgave her brother, he was so much upset. But a day or two afterwards she was shocked.

"Let's make a sacrifice of Arabella," he said. "Let's burn her." She was horrified, yet rather fascinated. She wanted to see what the boy would do. He made an altar of bricks, pulled some of the shavings out of Arabella's body, put the waxen fragments into the

hollow face, poured on a little paraffin, and set the whole thing
alight. He watched with wicked satisfaction the drops of wax melt off
the broken forehead of Arabella, and drop like sweat into the flame.
So long as the stupid big doll burned, he rejoiced in silence. At the
end, he poked among the embers with a stick, fished out the arms   5
and legs, all blackened, and smashed them under stones.

"That's the sacrifice of Missis Arabella," he said. "An' I'm glad
there's nothing left of her."

Which disturbed Annie inwardly, although she could say nothing.
He seemed to hate the doll so intensely, because he had broken it.   10

All the children, but particularly Paul, were peculiarly *against*
their father, along with their mother. Morel continued to bully and
to drink. He had periods, months at a time, when he made the whole
life of the family a misery. Paul never forgot coming home from the
Band of Hope,* one Monday evening, and finding his mother with   15
her eye swollen and discoloured, his father standing on the hearthrug, feet astride, his head down, and William, just home from work,
glaring at his father. There was a silence as the young children
entered, but none of the elders looked round.

William was white to the lips, and his fists were clenched. He   20
waited until the children were silent, watching with children's rage
and hate, then he said:

"You coward, you daren't do it when I was in."

But Morel's blood was up. He swung round on his son. William
was bigger, but Morel was hard-muscled, and mad with fury.   25

"Dossn't I?" he shouted. "Dossn't I? Ha'e much more o' thy
chelp, my young jockey, an' I'll rattle my fist about thee. Ay an' I
sholl that, dost see."

Morel crouched at the knees and showed his fist in an ugly,
almost beast-like fashion. William was white with rage.   30

"Will yer!" he said, quiet and intense. "It'ud be the last time,
though."

Morel danced a little nearer, crouching, drawing back his fist to
strike. William put his fists ready. A light came into his blue eyes,
almost like a laugh. He watched his father. Another word, and the   35
men would have begun to fight. Paul hoped they would. The three
children sat pale on the sofa.

"Stop it both of you," cried Mrs Morel, in a hard voice. "We've
had enough for *one* night.—And *you*," she said, turning onto her
husband, "look at your children."   40

Morel glanced at the sofa.

"Look at the children, you nasty little bitch," he sneered, "why what have *I* done to the children, I should like to know. But they're like yourself—you've put 'em up to your own tricks and nasty
5 ways—you've learned 'em in it, you 'ave."

She refused to answer him. No one spoke. After a while, he threw his boots under the table and went to bed.

"Why didn't you let me have a go at him," said William, when his father was upstairs. "I could easily have beaten him."
10 "A nice thing, your own father," she replied.

"'*Father*!'" repeated William. "Call *him my* father!"

"Well he is—and so—"

"But why don't you let me settle* him, I could do easily."

"The idea!" she cried. "It hasn't come to *that* yet."
15 "No," he said, "it's come to worse—look at yourself. *Why* didn't you let me give it him."

"Because I couldn't bear it, so never think of it," she cried quickly.

And the children went to bed, miserably.
20 When William was growing up, the family moved from the Bottoms to a house* on the brow of the hill, commanding a view of the valley, which spread out like a convex cockle shell, or a clamp shell, before it. In front of the house was a huge old ash-tree. The west wind, sweeping from Derbyshire, caught the houses with full
25 force, and the tree shrieked again. Morel liked it.

"It's music," he said. "It sends me to sleep."

But Paul and Arthur and Annie hated it. To Paul, it became almost a demoniacal noise. The winter of their first year in the new house, their father was very bad. The children played in the street,
30 on the brim of the wide dark valley, until eight o'clock. Then they went to bed. Their mother sat sewing below. Having such a great space in front of the house gave the children a feeling of night, of vastness, and of terror. This terror came in from the shrieking of the tree and the anguish of the home discord. Often Paul would wake
35 up, after he had been asleep a long time, aware of thuds downstairs. Instantly he was wide awake. Then he heard the booming shouts of his father, come home nearly drunk, then the sharp replies of his mother, then the bang, bang of his father's fist on the table, and the nasty snarling shout as the man's voice got higher. And then the
40 whole was drowned in a piercing medley of shrieks and cries from

the great, wind-swept ash-tree. The children lay silent in suspense, waiting for a lull in the wind to hear what their father was doing. He might hit their mother again. There was a feeling of horror, a kind of bristling in the darkness, and a sense of blood. They lay with their hearts in the grip of an intense anguish. The wind came through the tree fiercer and fiercer. All the cords of the great harp hummed, whistled, and shrieked. And then, came the horror of the sudden silence: silence everywhere, outside, and downstairs. What was it?—was it a silence of blood? What had he done.

The children lay and breathed the darkness. And then, at last, they heard their father throw down his boots and tramp upstairs in his stocking feet. Still they listened. Then at last, if the wind allowed, they heard the water of the tap drumming into the kettle, which their mother was filling for morning, and they could go to sleep in peace.

So they were happy in the morning, happy, very happy, playing, dancing at night round the lonely lamppost in the midst of the darkness. But they had one tight place of anxiety in their hearts, one darkness in their eyes, which showed all their lives.

Paul hated his father. As a boy, he had a fervent private religion.

"Make him stop drinking," he prayed every night.

"Lord, let my father die," he prayed very often.

"Let him be* killed at pit," he prayed when, after tea, the father did not come home from work.

That was another time when the family suffered intensely. The children came from school and had their teas. On the hob, the big black saucepan was simmering, the stew-jar was in the oven, ready for Morel's dinner. He was expected at five o'clock. But, for months, he would stop and drink every night on his way from work.

In the winter nights, when it was cold, and grew dark early, Mrs Morel would put a brass candlestick on the table, light a tallow candle to save the gas. The children finished their bread and butter, or dripping, and were ready to go out to play. But if Morel had not come, they faltered. The sense of his sitting in all his pit-dirt, drinking, after a long day's work, not coming home and eating and washing, but sitting getting drunk on an empty stomach, made Mrs Morel unable to bear herself. From her, the feeling was transmitted to the children. She never suffered alone any more: the children suffered with her.

Paul went out to play with the rest. Down in the great trough of twilight, tiny clusters of lights burned where the pits were. A few last

colliers straggled up the dim field-path. The lamp-lighter came
along. No more colliers came. Darkness shut down over the valley,
work was gone, it was night.

Then Paul ran anxiously into the kitchen. The one candle still
5 burned on the table, the big fire glowed red, Mrs Morel sat alone.
On the hob the saucepan steamed: the dinner plate lay waiting on
the table. All the room was full of the sense of waiting, waiting, for
the man who was sitting in his pit-dirt, dinnerless, some mile away
from home, across the darkness, drinking himself drunk. Paul stood
10 in the doorway.

"Has my Dad come?" he asked.

"You can see he hasn't," said Mrs Morel, cross with the futility of
the question.

Then the boy dawdled about, near his mother. They shared the
15 same anxiety. Presently Mrs Morel went out and strained the
potatoes.

"They're ruined and black," she said, "but what do I care." Not
many words were spoken. Paul almost hated his mother for suffering
because his father did not come home from work.

20 "What do you bother yourself for?" he said. "If he wants to stop
and get drunk, why don't you let him?"

"Let him!" flashed Mrs Morel. "You may well say 'let him.'" She
knew that the man who stops on the way home from work is on a
quick way to ruining himself and his home. The children were yet
25 young, and depended on the bread-winner. William gave her the
sense of relief, providing her at last with someone to turn to, if
Morel failed. But the tense atmosphere of the room on these waiting
evenings was the same.

The minutes ticked away. At six o'clock, still the cloth lay on the
30 table, still the dinner stood waiting, still the same sense of anxiety
and expectation in the room. The boy could not stand it any longer.
He could not go out and play. So he ran in to Mrs Inger, next door
but one, for her to talk to him. She had no children. Her husband
was good to her, but he was in a shop, and came home late. So, when
35 she saw the lad at the door, she called:

"Come in, Paul."

The two sat talking for some time, when suddenly the boy rose,
saying:

"Well, I'll be going and seeing if my mother wants an errand
40 doing."

He pretended to be perfectly cheerful, and did not tell his friend what ailed him. Then he ran indoors.

Morel, at these times, came in churlish and hateful.

"This is a nice time to come home," said Mrs Morel.

"Wha's it matter to yo', what time I come whoam," he shouted.

And everybody in the house was still, because he was dangerous. He ate his food in the most brutal manner possible, and when he had done, pushed all the pots in a heap away from him, to lay his arms on the table. Then, he went to sleep.

Paul hated his father so. The collier's small, mean head with its black hair slightly soiled with grey, lay on the bare arms, and the face, dirty and inflamed, with a fleshy nose and thin, paltry brows, was turned sideways, asleep with beer and weariness and nasty temper. If anyone entered suddenly, or a noise were made, the man looked up and shouted:

"I'll lay my fist about thy y'ead, I'm tellin' thee, if tha doesna stop that clatter. Dost hear!"

And the two last words, shouted in a bullying fashion, usually at Annie, made the family writhe with hate of the man.

He was shut out from all family affairs. No one told him anything. The children, alone with their mother, told her all about the day's happenings, everything. Nothing had really taken place in them, until it was told to their mother. But as soon as the father came in, everything stopped. He was like the scotch* in the smooth, happy machinery of the home. And he was always aware of this fall of silence on his entry, the shutting off of life, the unwelcome. But now it was gone too far to alter.

He would dearly have liked the children to talk to him, but they could not. Sometimes Mrs Morel would say:

"You ought to tell your father."

Paul won a prize in a competition in a child's paper. Everybody was highly jubilant.

"Now you'd better tell your father when he comes in," said Mrs Morel. "You know how he carries on and says he's never told anything."

"All right," said Paul. But he would almost rather have forfeited the prize than have to tell his father.

"I've won a prize in a competition, Dad," he said.

Morel turned round to him.

"Have you, my boy—what sort of a competition?"

"Oh nothing—about famous women."

"And how much is the prize, then, as you've got?"

"It's a book."

"Oh indeed!"

5　"About birds."

"Hm—hm!"

And that was all. Conversation was impossible between the father and any other member of the family. He was an outsider. He had denied the God in him.

10　The only times when he entered again into the life of his own people was when he worked, and was happy at work. Sometimes, in the evening, he cobbled the boots or mended the kettle or his pit-bottle. Then he always wanted several attendants, and the children enjoyed it. They united with him in the work, in the actual

15　doing of something, when he was his real self again.

He was a good workman, dexterous, and one who, when he was in a good humour, always sang. He had whole periods, months, almost years, of friction and nasty temper. Then sometimes he was jolly again. It was nice to see him run with a piece of red-hot iron into the

20　scullery, crying:

"Out of my road, out of my road!"

Then he hammered the soft, red-glowing stuff on his iron goose,* and made the shape he wanted. Or he sat absorbed for a moment, soldering. Then the children watched with joy as the metal sank

25　suddenly molten, and was shoved about against the nose of the soldering iron, while the room was full of a scent of burnt resin and hot tin, and Morel was silent and intent for a minute. He always sang when he mended boots, because of the jolly sound of hammering. And he was rather happy when he sat putting great patches on his

30　moleskin* pit trousers, which he would often do, considering them too dirty, and the stuff too hard, for his wife to mend.

But the best time for the young children was when he made fuses. Morel fetched a sheaf of long sound wheat straws from the attic. These he cleaned with his hand, till each one gleamed like a stalk of

35　gold. After which he cut the straws into lengths of about six inches, leaving if he could a notch at the bottom of each piece. He always had a beautifully sharp knife, that could cut a straw clean without hurting it. Then he set in the middle of the table a heap of gunpowder, a little pile of black grains upon the white-scrubbed

40　board. He made and trimmed the straws while Paul and Annie filled and plugged them. Paul loved to see the black grains trickle down a crack in his palm, into the mouth of the straw, peppering jollily downwards till the straw was full. Then he bunged up the mouth with a bit of soap—which he got on his thumb nail from a pat in a saucer—and the straw was finished. 5

"Look Dad!" he said.

"That's right, my beauty," replied Morel, who was peculiarly lavish of endearments to his second son. Paul popped the fuse into the powder tin, ready for the morning, when Morel would take it to the pit, and use it to fire a shot that would blast the coal down. 10

Meantime Arthur, still fond of his father, would lean on the arm of Morel's chair and say:

"Tell us about down-pit, Daddy."

This Morel loved to do.

"Well, there's one little 'oss, we call 'im Taffy," he would begin. 15 "An' he's a fawce* un!"

Morel had a warm way of telling a story. He made one feel Taffy's cunning.

"He's a brown un," he would answer,* "an' not very high. Well, he comes i' th' stall wi' a rattle, an' then yo' 'ear 'im sneeze. 20

''Ello Taff,' you say, 'what art sneezin' for. Bin ta'ein' some snuff?'

An'e sneezes again. Then he slives up an' shoves 'is 'ead on yer, that cadin'.

'What's want, Taff?' yo' say." 25

"And what does he?" Arthur always asked.

"He wants a bit o' bacca, my duckey."

This story of Taffy would go on interminably, and everybody loved it.

Or sometimes it was a new tale. 30

"An' what dost think, my darlin'. When I went to put my coat on at snap time, what should go runnin' up my arm but a mouse.

'Hey up, theer!' I shouts.

An' I wor just in time ter get 'im by th' tail."

"And did you kill it?" 35

"I did, for they're a nuisance. The place is fair snied wi' 'em."

"An' what do they live on?"

"The corn as the 'osses drops—an' they'll get in your pocket an' eat your snap, if you'll let 'em—no matter where yo' hing your coat—the slivin' nibblin' little nuisances, for they are—" 40

These happy evenings could not take place unless Morel had some job to do. And then, he always went to bed very early, often before the children. There was nothing remaining for him to stay up for, when he had finished tinkering, and had skimmed the head lines
5   of the newspaper.

And the children felt secure when their father was in bed. They lay and talked softly awhile. Then they started as the lights went suddenly sprawling over the ceiling, from the lamps that swung in the hands of the colliers tramping by outside, going to take the nine
10 o'clock shift. They listened to the voices of the men, imagined them dipping down into the dark valley. Sometimes they went to the window and watched the three or four lamps growing tinier and tinier, swaying down the fields in the darkness. Then it was a joy to rush back to bed and cuddle closely in the warmth.

15 Paul was rather a delicate boy, subject to bronchitis. The others were all quite strong, so this was another reason for his mother's difference in feeling for him. One day he came home at dinner time feeling ill. But it was not a family to make any fuss.

"What's the matter with *you?*" his mother asked sharply.
20 "Nothing," he replied.

But he ate no dinner.

"If you eat no dinner you're not going to school," she said.

"Why?" he asked.

"That's why."

25 So after dinner he lay down on the sofa, on the warm chintz cushions the children loved. Then he fell into a kind of doze. That afternoon, Mrs Morel was ironing. She listened to the small, restless noise the boy made in his throat, as she worked. Again rose in her heart the old, almost weary feeling towards him. She had never
30 expected him to live. And yet he had a great vitality in his young body. Perhaps it would have been a little relief to her if he had died. She always felt a mixture of anguish in her love for him.

He, in his semi-conscious sleep, was vaguely aware of the clatter of the iron on the iron-stand, of the faint thud, thud on the
35 ironing-board. Once, roused, he opened his eyes to see his mother standing on the hearthrug with the hot iron near her cheek, listening as it were to the heat. Her still face, with the mouth closed tight from suffering and disillusion and self-denial, and her nose the smallest bit on one side, and her blue eyes so young, quick, and warm, made
40 his heart contract with love. When she was quiet, so, she looked

brave and rich with life, but as if she had been done out of her rights. It hurt the boy keenly, this feeling about her, that she had never had her life's fulfilment: and his own incapability to make up to her hurt him with a sense of impotence, yet made him patiently dogged inside. It was his childish aim. 5

She spat on the iron, and a little ball of spit bounded, raced off the dark glossy surface. Then, kneeling, she rubbed the iron on the sack lining of the hearthrug, vigorously. She was warm in the ruddy firelight. Paul loved the way she crouched and put her head on one side. Her movements were light and quick. It was always a pleasure 10 to watch her. Nothing she ever did, no movement she ever made, could have been found fault with by her children.—The room was warm, and full of the scent of hot linen. Later on, the clergyman came and talked softly with her.

Paul was laid up with an attack of bronchitis. He did not mind 15 much. What happened, happened, and it was no good kicking against the pricks.* He loved the evenings, after eight o'clock, when the light was put out, and he could watch the fire flames spring over the darkness of the walls and ceiling; could watch huge shadows waving and tossing, till the room seemed full of men who battled silently. 20

On retiring to bed, the father would come into the sick-room. He was always very gentle if anyone were ill. But he disturbed the atmosphere for the boy.

"Are ter asleep, my darlin'?" Morel asked softly.

"No—is my mother comin'?" 25

"She's just finishin' foldin' the clothes. Do you want anything?" Morel rarely "thee'd" his son.

"I don't want nothing.—But how long will she be?"

"Not long, my duckie."

The father waited undecidedly on the hearthrug for a moment or 30 two. He felt his son did not want him. Then he went to the top of the stairs and said to his wife:

"That childt's axin' for thee—how long art goin' to be?"

"Until I've finished, good gracious! Tell him to go to sleep."

"She says you're to go to sleep," the father repeated gently to 35 Paul.

"Well, I want *her* to come," insisted the boy.

"He says he can't go off till you come," Morel called downstairs.

"Eh dear! I shan't be long. And do stop shouting downstairs. There's the other children—" 40

Then Morel came again, and crouched before the bedroom fire.
He loved a fire dearly.

"She says she won't be long," he said.

He loitered about indefinitely. The boy began to get feverish with
5   irritation. His father's presence seemed to aggravate all his sick
impatience. At last Morel, after having stood looking at his son
awhile, said softly:

"Goodnight my darling."

"Goodnight," Paul replied, turning round in relief to be alone.
10   Paul loved to sleep with his mother. Sleep is still most perfect, in
spite of hygienists, when it is shared with a beloved. The warmth,
the security and peace of soul, the utter comfort from the touch of
the other, knits the sleep,* so that it takes the body and soul
completely in its healing. Paul lay against her and slept, and got
15   better;—whilst she, always a bad sleeper, fell later on into a profound sleep that seemed to give her faith.

In convalescence he would sit up in bed, see the fluffy horses
feeding at the troughs in the field, scattering their hay on the
trodden yellow snow; watch the miners troop home, small, black
20   figures trailing slowly in gangs across the white field. Then the night
came up in dark blue vapor from the snow. .

In convalescence everything was wonderful. The snowflakes,
suddenly arriving on the window pane, clung there a moment like
swallows, then were gone, and a drop of water was crawling down
25   the glass. The snowflakes whirled round the corner of the house,
like pigeons dashing by. Away across the valley, the little black train
crawled doubtfully over the great whiteness.

While they were so poor, the children were delighted if they could
do anything to help, economically. Annie and Paul and Arthur went
30   out early in the morning, in summer, looking for mushrooms,
hunting through the wet grass, from which the larks were rising, for
the white skinned, wonderful naked bodies crouched secretly in the
green. And if they got half a pound, they felt exceedingly happy:
there was the joy of finding something, the joy of accepting some-
35   thing straight from the hand of nature, and the joy of contributing to
the family exchequer.

But the most important harvest, after gleaning for frumenty,* was
the blackberries. Mrs Morel must buy fruit for puddings, on the
Saturdays; also she liked blackberries. So Paul and Arthur scoured
40   the coppices and woods and old quarries, so long as a blackberry

was to be found, every week end going on their search. In that region of mining villages, blackberries became a comparative rarity. But Paul hunted far and wide. He loved being out in the country, among the bushes. But he also could not bear to go home to his mother empty. That, he felt, would disappoint her, and he would have died rather.

"Good gracious!" she would exclaim as the lads came in, late, and tired to death, and hungry. "Wherever have you been ?"

"Well," replied Paul, "there wasn't any, so we went over Misk Hills.—And look here, our mother."

She peeped into the basket.

"Now those are fine ones," she exclaimed.

"And there's over two pounds—isn't there over two pounds?"

She tried the basket.

"Yes," she answered, doubtfully.

Then Paul fished out a little spray. He always brought her one spray, the best he could find.

"Pretty!" she said, in a curious tone, of a woman accepting a love-token.

The boy walked all day, went miles and miles, rather than own himself beaten, and come home to her empty-handed. She never realised this, whilst he was young. She was a woman who waited for her children to grow up. And William occupied her chiefly.

But when William went to Nottingham, and was not so much at home, the mother made a companion of Paul. The latter was unconsciously jealous of his brother, and William was jealous of him. At the same time, they were good friends.

Mrs Morel's intimacy with her second son was more subtle and fine, perhaps not so passionate as with her eldest. It was the rule that Paul should fetch the money on Friday afternoons. The colliers of the five pits were paid on Fridays, but not individually. All the earnings of each stall were put down to the chief butty, as contractor, and he divided the wages again, either in the public house, or in his own home. So that the children could fetch the money, school closed early on Friday afternoons. Each of the Morel children, William, then Annie, then Paul, had fetched the money on Friday afternoons, until they went themselves to work. Paul used to set off at half past three, with a little calico bag in his pocket. Down all the paths, women, girls, children and men were seen trooping to the Offices.

These offices were quite handsome: a new, red-brick building, almost like a mansion, standing in its own well-kept grounds at the end of Greenhill Lane. The waiting room was the hall, a long, bare room paved with blue brick, and having a seat all round, against the
5 wall. Here sat the colliers in their pit-dirt. They had come up early. The women and children usually loitered about on the red gravel paths. Paul always examined the grass border, and the big grass bank, because in it grew tiny pansies and tiny forget me nots. There was a sound of many voices. The women had on their Sunday hats.
10 The girls chattered loudly. Little dogs ran here and there. The green shrubs were silent all around.

Then, from inside came the cry "Spinney Park—Spinney Park." All the folk for Spinney Park trooped inside. When it was time for Bretty to be paid, Paul went in among the crowd. The pay-room was
15 quite small. A counter went across, dividing it into half. Behind the counter stood two men, Mr Braithwaite and his clerk, Mr Winterbottom. Mr Braithwaite was large, somewhat of the stern patriarch in appearance, having a rather thin white beard. He was usually muffled in an enormous silk neckerchief, and right up to the hot
20 summer, a huge fire burned in the open grate. No window was open. Sometimes in winter, the air scorched the throats of the people, coming in from the freshness.—Mr Winterbottom was rather small and fat and very bald. He made remarks that were not witty, whilst his chief launched forth patriarchal admonitions against the colliers.
25 The room was crowded with miners in their pit dirt, men who had been home and changed, and women, and one or two children, and usually a dog. Paul was quite small, so it was often his fate to be jammed behind the legs of the men, near the fire which scorched him. He knew the order of the names—they went according to stall
30 number.

"Holliday," came the ringing voice of Mr Braithwaite. Then Mrs Holliday stepped silently forward, was paid, drew aside.

"Bower—John Bower."

A boy stepped to the counter. Mr Braithwaite, large and irascible,
35 glowered at him over his spectacles.

"John Bower!" he repeated.

"It's me," said the boy.

"Why you used to 'ave a different nose than that," said glossy Mr Winterbottom, peeering over the counter. The people tittered,
40 thinking of John Bower senior.

"How is it your father's not come?" said Mr Braithwaite, in a large and magisterial voice.

"He's badly," piped the boy.

"You should tell him to keep off the drink," pronounced the great cashier. 5

"An' niver mind if he puts his foot through yer," said a mocking voice from behind.

All the men laughed. The large and important cashier looked down at his next sheet.

"Fred Pilkington!" he called, quite indifferent. 10

Mr Braithwaite was an important shareholder in the firm.

Paul knew his turn was next but one, and his heart began to beat. He was pushed against the chimney piece. His calves were burning. But he did not hope to get through the wall of men.

"Walter Morel!" came the ringing voice. 15

"Here!" piped Paul, small and inadequate.

"Morel—Walter Morel!" the cashier repeated, his finger and thumb on the invoice, ready to pass on.

Paul was suffering convulsions of self consciousness, and could not or would not shout. The backs of the men obliterated him. Then 20 Mr Winterbottom came to the rescue.

"He's here—where is he! Morel's lad?"

The fat, red, bald little man peered round with keen eyes. He pointed at the fireplace. The colliers looked round, moved aside, and disclosed the boy. 25

"Here he is!" said Mr Winterbottom.

Paul went to the counter.

"'Seventeen pounds eleven and fivepence'—Why don't you shout up when you're called?" said Mr Braithwaite. He banged onto the invoice a five pound bag of silver, then, in a delicate and pretty 30 movement, picked up a little ten-pound column of gold, and plumped it beside the silver. The gold slid in a bright stream over the paper. The cashier finished counting off the money, the boy dragged the whole down the counter to Mr Winterbottom, to whom the stoppages for rent, and tools, must be paid. Here he suffered again. 35

"Sixteen an' six," said Mr Winterbottom.

The lad was too much upset to count. He pushed forward some loose silver and half a sovereign.

"How much do you think you've given me?" asked Mr Winterbottom. 40

The boy looked at him, but said nothing. He had not the faintest notion.

"Haven't you got a tongue in your head?"

Paul bit his lip and pushed forward some more silver.

5 "Don't they teach you to count at the Board School?" he asked.

"Nowt but algìbbra an' French," said a collier.

"An' cheek an' impidence," said another.

Paul was keeping someone waiting. With trembling fingers he got his money into the bag, and slid out. He suffered the tortures of the 10 damned on these occasions.

His relief, when he got outside, and was walking along the Mansfield Road, was infinite. On the Park Wall the mosses were green. There were some gold and some white fowls pecking under the apple trees of an orchard. The colliers were walking home in a 15 stream. The boy went near the wall, self consciously. He knew many of the men, but could not recognise them in their dirt. And this was a new torture to him.

When he got down to the New Inn, at Bretty, his father was not yet come. Mrs Wharmby, the landlady, knew him. His grandmother, 20 Morel's mother, had been Mrs Wharmby's friend.

"Your father's not come yet," said the landlady, in the peculiar half scornful, half patronising voice of a woman who talks chiefly to grown men. "Sit you down."

Paul sat down on the edge of the bench in the bar. Some colliers 25 were "reckoning"—sharing out their money—in a corner; others came in. They all glanced at the boy, without speaking. At last Morel came: brisk and with something of an air, even in his blackness.

"Hello," he said, rather tenderly, to his son. "Have you bested me? Shall you have a drink of something?"

30 Paul, and all the children, were bred up fierce anti-alcoholists. And he would have suffered more in drinking a lemonade before all the men, than in having a tooth drawn.

The landlady looked at him *de haut en bas,** rather pitying, and at the same time resenting his clear, fierce morality. Paul went home, 35 glowering. He entered the house silently. Friday was baking day, and there was usually a hot bun. His mother put it before him.

Suddenly he turned on her in a fury, his eyes flashing.

"I'm *not* going to the Office any more," he said.

"Why, what's the matter?" his mother asked in surprise. His 40 sudden rages rather amused her.

"I'm *not* going any more," he declared.

"Oh very well, tell your father so."

He chewed his bun as if he hated it.

"I'm not—I'm not going to fetch the money."

"Then one of Carlin's children* can go. They'd be glad enough 5 of the sixpence," said Mrs Morel.

This sixpence was Paul's only income. It mostly went in buying birthday presents. But it *was* an income, and he treasured it. But:

"They can have it then!" he said. "I don't want it."

"Oh very well," said his mother. "But you needn't bully *me* 10 about it."

"They're hateful, and common, and hateful, they are, and I'm not going any more. Mr Braithwaite drops his 'h's', an' Mr Winterbottom says 'you was'."

"And is that why you won't go any more?" smiled Mrs Morel. 15

The boy was silent for some time. His face was pale, his eyes dark and furious. His mother moved about at her work, taking no notice of him.

"They always stan' in front of me, so's I can't get out," he said.

"Well my lad, you've only to *ask* them," she replied. 20

"An' then Alfred Winterbottom says 'What do they teach you at the board school?'"

"They never taught *him* much," said Mrs Morel, "that is a fact—neither manners nor wit—and his cunning he was born with." 25

"An' they say 'Nowt but algìbbra an' French.' They *don't* teach me French at the board school."

"And if they did," smiled his mother, "you needn't get into a state about it.—You're such a baby, my boy, if anyone says a word."

"Well—!"—he looked at her almost in tears, and still with more 30 rage and hate than grief.

"You're such a silly," she said. "You can't simply say 'it's my turn now', you let yourself be passed over, and then get into a fury. It's all your own fault."

So, in her own way, she soothed him. His ridiculous hyper- 35 sensitiveness made her heart ache. And sometimes, the fury in his eyes roused her, made her sleeping soul lift up its head a moment, surprised.

"What was the cheque?" she asked.

"Seventeen pounds eleven and fivepence, and sixteen and six 40 stoppages," replied the boy. "It's a good week, and only five shillings stoppages for my father."

So she was able to calculate how much her husband had earned, and could call him to account if he gave her short money. Morel
5 always kept to himself the secret of the week's amount.

Friday was baking night and market night. It was the rule that Paul should stay at home and bake. He loved to stop in and draw or read: he was very fond of drawing. Annie always "gallivanted" on Friday nights, Arthur was enjoying himself as usual. So the boy remained
10 alone.

Mrs Morel loved her marketing. In the tiny market-place on the top of the hill, where four roads, from Nottingham and Derby, Ilkeston and Mansfield meet, many stalls were erected. Brakes ran in from surrounding villages. The market-place was full of women, the
15 streets packed with men. It was amazing to see so many men everywhere in the streets. Mrs Morel usually quarrelled with her lacewoman, sympathised with her fruit man, who was a gabey, but his wife was a bad un, laughed with the fish man, who was a scamp but so droll, put the linoleum man in his place, was cold with the odd-wares
20 man, and only went to the crockery man when she was driven—or drawn by the cornflowers on a little dish. Then she was coldly polite.

"I wondered how much that little dish was," she said.

"Sevenpence to you."

"Thank you."

25 She put the dish down and walked away. But she could not leave the market place without it. Again she went by where the pots lay coldly on the floor, and she glanced at the dish, furtively, pretending not to.

She was a little woman in a bonnet and a black costume. Her
30 bonnet was in its third year; it was a great grievance to Annie.

"Mother!" the girl implored, "don't wear that nubbly little bonnet."

"Then what else shall I wear," replied the mother, tartly. "And I'm sure it's right enough."

35 It had started with a tip:* then had had flowers: now was reduced to black lace and a bit of jet.

"It looks rather come down," said Paul. "Couldn't you give it a pick me up."

"I'll jowl your head for impudence," said Mrs Morel, and she tied
40 the strings of the black bonnet valiantly under her chin.

She glanced at the dish again. Both she and her enemy, the pot-man, had an uncomfortable feeling, as if there were something between them. Suddenly he shouted:

"Do you want it for fivepence?"

She started. Her heart hardened. But then she stooped and took 5
up her dish.

"I'll have it," she said.

"Yer'll do me the favour, like?" he said. "Yer'd better spit in it, like yer do when y'ave something give yer."*

Mrs Morel paid him the fivepence in a cold manner. 10

"I don't see you give it me," she said. "You wouldn't let me have it for fivepence if you didn't want to."

"In this flamin' scrattlin' place you may count yerself lucky if you can give your things away," he growled.

"Yes, there are bad times, and good," said Mrs Morel. 15

But she had forgiven the pot man. They were friends. She dare now finger his pots. So she was happy.

Paul was waiting for her. He loved her homecoming. She was always her best so, triumphant, tired, laden with parcels, feeling rich in spirit. He heard her quick light step in the entry and looked up 20
from his drawing.

"Oh!" she sighed, smiling at him from the doorway.

"My word you *are* loaded!" he exclaimed, putting down his brush.

"I am!" she gasped. "That brazen Annie said she'd meet me. *Such* a weight!" 25

She dropped her string bag, and her packages, on the table.

"Is the bread done?" she asked, going to the oven.

"The last one is soaking," he replied. "You needn't look, I've not forgotten it."

"Oh that pot man!" she said, closing the oven door. "You know 30
what a wretch I've said he was. Well, I don't think he's quite so bad."

"Don't you?"

The boy was attentive to her. She took off her little black bonnet.

"No—I think he can't make any money—well, it's everybody's cry alike nowadays—and it makes him disagreeable." 35

"It would *me*," said Paul.

"Well, one can't wonder at it.—And he let me have—how much do you think he let me have *this* for?"

She took the dish out of its rag of newspaper, and stood looking on it with joy. 40

"Show me!" said Paul.

The two stood together gloating over the dish.

"I *love* cornflowers on things," said Paul.

"Yes, and I thought of the teapot you bought me—"

5   "One and three," said Paul.

"Fivepence!"

"It's not enough, mother."

"No. Do you know, I fairly sneaked off with it. But I'd been extravagant, I couldn't afford any more. And he needn't have let me

10 have it if he hadn't wanted to."

"No, he needn't, need he," said Paul, and the two comforted each other from the fear of having robbed the pot-man.

"We c'n have stewed fruit in it," said Paul.

"Or custard, or a jelly," said his mother.

15 "Or radishes and lettuce," said he.

"Don't forget that bread," she said, her voice bright with glee.

Paul looked in the oven—tapped the loaf on the base.

"It's done," he said, giving it to her.

She tapped it also.

20 "Yes," she replied, going to unpack her bag.—"Oh, and I'm a wicked extravagant woman—I know I s'll come to want."

He hopped to her side eagerly, to see her latest extravagance. She unfolded another lump of newspaper and disclosed some roots of pansies and of crimson daisies.

25 "Four penn'orth!" she moaned.

"How *cheap*!" he cried.

"Yes, but I couldn't afford it *this* week of all weeks."

"But lovely!" he cried.

"Aren't they!" she exclaimed, giving way to pure joy. "Paul—

30 look at this yellow one—isn't it—!—and a face just like an old man!"

"Just!" cried Paul, stooping to sniff. "And smells that nice! But he's a bit splashed."

He ran in the scullery, came back with the flannel, and carefully

35 washed the pansy.

"*Now* look at him now he's wet!" he said.

"Yes!" she exclaimed, brimful of satisfaction.

The children of Scargill Street* felt quite select. At the end where the Morels lived, there were not many young things. So the

40 few were more united. Boys and girls played together, the girls

joining in the fights and the rough games, the boys taking part in the
dancing games and rings* and make belief of the girls.

Annie and Paul and Arthur loved the winter evenings, when it was
not wet. They stayed indoors till the colliers were all gone home, till
it was thick dark, and the street would be deserted. Then they tied 5
their scarves round their necks, for they scorned overcoats, as all the
colliers' children did, and went out. The entry was very dark, and at
the end, the whole great night opened out, in a hollow, with a little
tangle of lights below where Minton pit lay, and another far away
opposite, for Selby. The farthest tiny lights seemed to stretch out the 10
darkness forever. The children looked anxiously down the road at
the one lamp-post, which stood at the end of the field path. If the
little, luminous space were deserted, the two boys felt genuine
desolation. They stood with their hands in their pockets under the
lamp, turning their backs on the night, quite miserable, watching the 15
dark houses. Suddenly a pinafore under a short coat was seen, and a
long legged girl came flying up.

"Wheer's Billy Pillins an' your Annie an' Eddie Dakin?"

"I don't know."

But it did not matter so much—there were three now. They set up 20
a game round the lamp-post, till the others rushed up yelling. Then
the play went fast and furious.

There was only this one lamp-post. Behind, was the great
scoop of darkness, as if all the night were there. In front, another
wide, dark way opened over the hill brow. Occasionally somebody 25
came out of this way and went into the field down the path. In a
dozen yards, the night had swallowed them. The children played
on.

They were brought exceedingly close together, owing to their
isolation. If a quarrel took place, the whole play was spoilt. Arthur 30
was very touchy, and Billy Pillins, really Philips, was worse. Then
Paul had to side with Arthur, and on Paul's side went Alice, while
Billy Pillins always had Emmie Limb and Eddie Dakin to back him
up. Then the six would fight, hate with a fury of hatred, and flee
home in terror. Paul never forgot, after one of these fierce interne- 35
cine fights, seeing a big red moon lift itself up, slowly, between the
waste road over the hill-top; steadily, like a great bird. And he
thought of the bible, that the moon should be turned to blood.* And
the next day he made haste to be friends with Billy Pillins. And then
the wild, intense games went on again under the lamp post, sur- 40

rounded by so much darkness. Mrs Morel, going into her parlour, would hear the children singing away:

> "My shoes are made of Spanish leather
> My socks are made of silk;
> I wear a ring on every finger
> I wash myself in milk."*

They sounded so perfectly absorbed in the game, as their voices came out of the night, that they had the feel of wild creatures singing. It stirred the mother. And she understood when they came in at eight o'clock, ruddy, with brilliant eyes, and quick passionate speech.

They all loved the Scargill Street house for its openness, for the great scallop of the world it had in view. On summer evenings, the women would stand against the field fence, gossiping, facing the west, watching the sunsets flare quickly out, till the Derbyshire hills ridged across the crimson, far away, like the black crest of a newt.

In this summer season, the pits never turned full time, particularly the soft coal. Mrs Dakin, who lived next door to Mrs Morel, going to the field fence to shake her hearth-rug, would spy men coming slowly up the hill. She saw at once they were colliers. Then she waited, a tall, thin, shrew faced woman, standing on the hill brow almost like a menace to the poor colliers who were toiling up. It was only eleven o'clock. From the far-off, wooded hills the haze that hangs like fine black crape at the back of a summer morning had not yet dissipated. The first man came to the stile. 'Chock-chock!' went the gate under his thrust.

"What, han' yer knocked off?" cried Mrs Dakin.

"We han, Missis."

"It's a pity as they letn yer goo," she said, sarcastically.

"It is that," replied the man.

"Nay, you know you're flig to come up again," she said.

And the man went on. Mrs Dakin, going up her yard, spied Mrs Morel taking the ashes to the ash-pit.

"I reckon Minton's knocked off, Missis," she cried.

"Isn't it sickenin'!" exclaimed Mrs Morel in wrath.

"Ha!—But I'n just seed Jont Hutchly."

"They might as well have saved their shoe-leather," said Mrs Morel, and both women went indoors disgusted.

The colliers, their faces scarcely blackened, were trooping home again. Morel hated to go back. He loved the sunny morning. But he had gone to pit to work, and to be sent home again spoilt his temper.

"Good gracious, at this time!" exclaimed his wife, as he entered.

"Can I help it woman!" he shouted.

"And I've not done half enough dinner."   5

"Then I'll eat my bit o' snap as I took with me," he bawled, pathetically. He felt ignominious and sore.

And the children coming home from school, would wonder to see their father eating with his dinner the two thick slices of rather dry and dirty bread and butter, that had been to pit and back.   10

"What's my Dad eating his snap for now?" asked Arthur.

"I should ha'e it holled at me if I didna," snorted Morel.

"What a story!" exclaimed his wife.

"An' is it goin' to be wasted?" said Morel. "I'm not such a extravagant mortal as you lot, with your waste. If I drop a bit of bread   15
at pit, in all the dust an' dirt, I pick it up an' eat it."

"The mice would eat it," said Paul. "It wouldn't be wasted."

"Good bread an' butter's not for mice, neither," said Morel. "Dirty or not dirty, I'd eat it rather than it should be wasted."

"You might leave it for the mice and pay for it out of your next   20
pint," said Mrs Morel.

"Oh might I!" he exclaimed.

They were very poor that autumn. William had just gone away to London, and his mother missed his money. He sent ten shillings once or twice, but he had many things to pay for at first. His letters   25
came regularly, once a week. He wrote a good deal to his mother, telling her all his life, how he made friends, and was exchanging lessons with a Frenchman, how he enjoyed London. His mother felt again he was remaining to her just as when he was at home. She wrote to him every week her direct, rather witty letters. All day long,   30
as she cleaned the house, she thought of him. He was in London: he would do well. Almost, he was like her knight who wore *her* favour in the battle.

He was coming at Christmas for five days. There had never been*
such preparations. Paul and Arthur scoured the land for holly and   35
evergreens. Annie made the pretty paper hoops in the old-fashioned way. And there was unheard-of extravagance in the larder. Mrs Morel made a big and magnificent cake. Then, feeling queenly, she showed Paul how to blanche almonds. He skinned the long nuts reverently, counting them all, to see not one was lost. It was said that   40

eggs whisked better in a cold place. So the boy stood in the scullery, where the temperature was nearly at freezing point, and whisked and whisked, and flew in excitement to his mother as the white of egg grew stiffer and more snowy.

5   "Just look, mother—isn't it lovely?"

And he balanced a bit on his nose, then blew it in the air.

"Now don't waste it," said the mother.

Everybody was mad with excitement. William was coming on Christmas Eve. Mrs Morel surveyed her pantry. There was a big
10 plum cake, and a rice cake: jam tarts, lemon tarts, and mince pies, two enormous dishes. She was finishing cooking:—Spanish tarts* and cheese-cakes. Everywhere was decorated. The kissing-bunch,* of berried holly hung with bright and glittering things, spun slowly over Mrs Morel's head as she trimmed her little tarts in the kitchen.
15 A great fire roared. There was a scent of cooked pastry. He was due at seven o'clock, but he would be late. The three children had gone to meet him. She was alone. But at a quarter to seven, Morel came in again. Neither wife nor husband spoke. He sat in his arm-chair, quite awkward with excitement, and she quietly went on with her
20 baking. Only by the careful way in which she did things could it be told how much moved she was. The clock ticked on.

"What time dost say he's coming?" Morel asked, for the fifth time.

"The train gets in at half past six," she replied, emphatically.
25   "Then he'll be here at ten past seven."

"Eh bless you, it'll be hours late, on the Midland," she said, indifferently. But she hoped, by expecting him late, to bring him early. Morel went down the entry to look for him. Then he came back.
30   "Goodness man!" she said. "You're like an ill-sitting hen."

"Hadna you better be gettin' him summat t'eat ready?" asked the father.

"There's plenty of time," she answered.

"There's not so much as *I* can see on," he answered, turning
35 crossly in his chair. She began to clear her table. The kettle was singing. They waited and waited.

Meantime the three children were on the platform at Lethley Bridge, on the Midland main line, two miles from home. They waited one hour. A train came—he was not there. Down the line the
40 red and green lights shone. It was very dark and very cold.

"Ask him if the London train's come," said Paul to Annie, when they saw a man in a tip cap.

"I'm not," said Annie. "You be quiet—he might send us off."

But Paul was dying for the man to know they were expecting someone by the London train: it sounded so grand. Yet he was much 5 too much scared of broaching any man, let alone one in a peaked cap, to dare to ask. The three children could scarcely go into the waiting room, for fear of being sent away, and for fear something should happen whilst they were off the platform. Still they waited in the dark and cold. 10

"It's an hour an' a half late," said Arthur, pathetically.

"Well," said Annie, "it's Christmas eve."

They all grew silent. He wasn't coming. They looked down the darkness of the railway. There was London! It seemed the uttermost of distance. They thought, anything might happen, if one came from 15 London. They were all too troubled to talk. Cold, and unhappy, and silent, they huddled together on the platform.

At last, after more than two hours, they saw the lights of an engine veering round, away down the darkness. A porter ran out. The children drew back with beating hearts. A great train, bound for 20 Manchester, drew up. Two doors opened—and from one of them, William. They flew to him. He handed parcels to them cheerily, and immediately began to explain that this great train had stopped for *his* sake, at such a small station as Lethley* Bridge: it was not booked to stop. 25

Meanwhile the parents were getting anxious. The table was set, the chop was cooked, everything was ready. Mrs Morel put on her black apron. She was wearing her best dress. Then she sat, pretending to read. The minutes were a torture to her.

"Hm!" said Morel. "It's an hour an' a ha'ef." 30

"And those children waiting!" she said.

"Th' train canna ha' come in yit," he said.

"I tell you, on Christmas Eve they're *hours* wrong."

They were both a bit cross with each other, so gnawed with anxiety. The ash-tree moaned outside in a cold, raw wind. And all 35 that space of night from London home! Mrs Morel suffered. The slight click of the works inside the clock irritated her: it was getting so late: it was getting unbearable.

At last there was a sound of voices, and a footstep in the entry.

"He's here!" cried Morel, jumping up. 40

Then he stood back. The mother ran a few steps towards the door, and waited. There was a rush and a patter of feet, the door burst open, William was there. He dropped his gladstone bag and took his mother in his arms.

5 "Mater!" he said.

"My boy!" she cried.

And for two seconds, no longer, she clasped him and kissed him. Then she withdrew and said, trying to be quite normal:

"But how late you are!"

10 "Aren't I!" he cried, turning to his father.

"Well Dad!"

The two men shook hands.

"Well my lad!"

Morel's eyes were wet.

15 "We thought tha'd niver be commin'," he said.

"Oh I'd come," exclaimed William.

Then the son turned round to his mother.

"But you look well," she said proudly, laughing.

"Well!" he exclaimed. "I should think so—coming home."

20 He was a fine fellow, big, straight, and fearless looking. He looked round, at the evergreens and the kissing bunch and the little tarts that lay in their tins on the hearth.

"By jove, mother, it's not different," he said, as if in relief.

Everybody was still for a second. Then he suddenly sprang
25 forward, picked a tart from the hearth, and pushed it whole into his mouth.

"Well did iver you see such a parish oven!"* the father exclaimed.

He had brought them endless presents. Every penny he had, he had spent on them. There was a sense of luxury overflowing in the
30 house. For his mother, there was an umbrella with gold on the pale handle. She kept it to her dying day, and would have lost anything rather than that. Everybody had something gorgeous, and besides, there were pounds of unknown sweets: Turkish delight, crystallised pineapple, and such like things which, the children thought, only the
35 splendour of London could provide. And Paul boasted of these sweets among his friends.

"Real pineapple, cut off in slices, and then turned into crystal—fair grand!"

Everybody was mad with happiness in the family. Home was
40 home, and they loved it with a passion of love, whatever the suffering

had been. There were parties, there were rejoicings. People came in to see William, to see what difference London had made to him. And they all found him "such a gentleman, and *such* a fine fellow, my word!"

When he went away again the children retired to various places to 5 weep alone, Morel went to bed in misery, and Mrs Morel felt as if she were numbed by some drug, as if her feelings were paralysed. She loved him passionately.

He was in the office of a lawyer connected with a large shipping firm, and at the midsummer, his chief offered him a trip in the 10 Mediterranean, on one of the boats, for quite a small cost. Mrs Morel wrote: "Go, go, my boy, you may never have a chance again, and I should love to think of you cruising there in the Mediterranean almost better than to have you at home." But William came home for his fortnight's holiday. Not even the Mediterranean, which 15 pulled at all his young man's desire to travel, and at his poor man's wonder at the glamorous south, could take him away when he might come home. That compensated his mother for much.

Chapter V

Paul Launches into Life*

Morel was rather a heedless man, careless of danger. So, he had endless accidents.* Now, when Mrs Morel heard the rattle of an
5 empty coal-cart cease at her entry-end, she ran into the parlour to look, expecting almost to see her husband seated in the wagon, his face grey under his dirt, his body limp and sick with some hurt or other. If it were he she would run out to help.

About a year after William went to London, and just after Paul
10 had left school, before he got work, Mrs Morel was upstairs and her son was painting in the kitchen—he was very clever with his brush—when there came a knock at the door. Crossly, he put down his brush to go. At the same moment his mother opened a window upstairs and looked down.

15 A pit lad in his dirt stood on the threshold.

"Is this Walter Morel's?" he asked.

"Yes!" said Mrs Morel. "What is it?"

But she had guessed already.

"Your mester's got hurt," he said.

20 "Eh dear me!" she exclaimed. "It's a wonder if he hadn't, lad. And what's he done this time?"

"I don't know for sure, but it's 'is leg somewhere. They ta'ein' 'im ter th'ospital."

"Good gracious me!" she exclaimed. "Eh dear, what a one he is!
25 There's not five minutes of peace, I'll be hanged if there is! His thumb's nearly better, and now—Did you see him?"

"I seed him at th' bottom. An' I seed 'em bring 'im up in a tub, an' 'e wor in a dead faint. But he shouted like anythink when Doctor Fraser examined him i'th' lamp cabin—an' cossed an' swore—an'
30 said as 'e wor goin' to be ta'en whoam—'e worn't goin' ter th'ospital—!" The boy faltered to an end.

"He *would* want to come home, so that I can have all the bother.—Thank you, my lad.—Eh dear, if I'm not sick—sick and surfeited, I am!"

35 She came downstairs. Paul had mechanically resumed his painting.

"And it must be pretty bad if they've taken him to the hospital,"
she went on. "But what a *careless* creature he is! *Other* men don't
have all these accidents.—Yes, he *would* want to put all the burden
on me.—Eh dear, just as we *were* getting easy a bit at last.—Put
those things away, there's no time to be painting now.—What time is 5
there a train? I know I s'll have to go trailing to Keston.—I s'll have
to leave that bedroom."

"I can finish it," said Paul.

"You needn't—I shall catch the seven o'clock back, I should
think.—Oh my blessed heart, the fuss and commotion he'll make! 10
And those granite setts at Tinder Hill—he might well call them
kidney pebbles—they'll jolt him almost to bits. I wonder why they
can't mend them, the state they're in, an' all the men as go across in
that ambulance.—You'd think they'd have a hospital here.—The
men bought the ground, and, my Sirs, there'd be accidents enough 15
to keep it going. But no, they must trail them ten miles in a slow
ambulance, to Nottingham. It's a crying shame!—Oh and the fuss
he'll make, I know he will! I wonder who's with him—Barker, I s'd
think. Poor beggar, he'll wish himself anywhere rather. But he'll
look after him, I know. Now there's no telling how long he'll be 20
stuck in that hospital—and *won't* he hate it! But if it's only his leg it's
not so bad."

All the time, she was getting ready. Hurriedly taking off her
bodice, she crouched at the boiler while the water ran slowly into her
lading can. 25

"I wish this boiler was at the bottom of the sea!" she exclaimed,
wriggling the handle impatiently. She had very handsome, strong
arms, rather surprising on a smallish woman.

Paul cleared away, put on the kettle, and set the table.

"There isn't a train till four-twenty," he said. "You've time 30
enough."

"Oh no I haven't!" she cried, blinking at him over the towel as she
wiped her face.

"Yes you have—you must drink a cup of tea at any rate. Should I
come with you to Keston?" 35

"Come with me, what for I should like to know!—Now what have
I to take him? Eh dear!—His clean shirt—and it's a blessing it *is*
clean. But it had better be aired—and stockings—he won't want
them—and a towel, I suppose—and handkerchiefs—now what
else?" 40

"A comb, a knife and fork and spoon," said Paul. His father had been in the hospital before.

"Goodness knows what sort of state his feet were in," continued Mrs Morel, as she combed her long brown hair, that was fine as silk,
5   and was touched now with grey. "He's very particular to wash himself to the waist, but below he thinks doesn't matter. But there, I suppose they see plenty like it."

Paul had laid the table. He cut his mother one or two pieces of very thin bread and butter.
10   "Here you are," he said, putting her cup of tea in her place.

"I can't be bothered," she exclaimed, crossly.

"Well you've got to, so there, now it's put out ready," he insisted.

So she sat down and sipped her tea, and ate a little, in silence. She was thinking.
15   In a few minutes she was gone, to walk the two and a half miles to Keston Station. All the things she was taking him she had in her bulging string bag. Paul watched her go up the road between the hedges, a little, quick-stepping figure, and his heart ached for her, that she was thrust forward again into pain and trouble. And she,
20   tripping so quickly in her anxiety, felt at the back of her her son's heart waiting on her, felt him bearing what part of the burden he could, even supporting her. And when she was at the hospital, she thought, "It *will* upset that lad when I tell him how bad it is—I'd better be careful." And when she was trudging home again, she felt
25   she was coming to share her burden.

"Is it bad?" asked Paul, as soon as she entered the house.

"It's bad enough," she replied.

"What?"

She sighed and sat down, undoing her bonnet strings. Her son
30   watched her face as it was lifted, and her small, work-hardened hands fingering at the bow under her chin.

"Well," she answered, "it's not really dangerous—but the nurse says it's a dreadful smash. You see, a great piece of rock fell on his leg—here—and it's a compound fracture—there are pieces of bone
35   sticking through—"

"Ugh—how horrid!" exclaimed the children.

"And," she continued, "of course he says he's going to die—it wouldn't be him if he didn't. 'I'm done for, my lass!' he said, looking at me. 'Don't be so silly,' I said to him. 'You're not going to die of a
40   broken leg, however badly it's smashed.'—'I s'll niver come out of

'ere but in a wooden box,' he groaned. 'Well!' I said, 'if you want
them to carry you into the garden in a wooden box, when you're
better, I've no doubt they will.'—'If we think it's good for him'—said
the Sister. She's an awfully nice Sister, but rather strict."
Mrs Morel took off her bonnet. The children waited in silence.   5
"Of course he *is* bad," she continued, "and he will be. It's a great
shock, and he's lost a lot of blood—and of course, it *is* a very
dangerous smash. It's not at all sure that it will mend so easily. And
then there's the fever and the mortification*—if it took bad ways he'd
quickly be gone—. But there, he's a clean blooded man, with   10
wonderful healing flesh, and so I see no reason why it *should* take bad
ways.—Of course, there's a wound—"
She was pale now with emotion and anxiety. The three children
realised that it was very bad for their father, and the house was silent,
anxious.   15
"But he always gets better," said Paul, after a while.
"That's what I tell him," said the mother.
Everybody moved about in silence. ·
"And he really looked nearly done for," she said. "But the Sister
says that is the pain."   20
Annie took away her mother's coat and bonnet.
"And he looked at me when I came away—! I said 'I s'll have to go
now, Walter, because of the train—and the children—'—and he
looked at me.—It seems hard—"
Paul took up his brush again and went on painting. Arthur went   25
outside for some coal. Annie sat looking dismal. And Mrs Morel, in
her little rocking-chair, that her husband had made for her when the
first baby was coming, remained motionless, brooding. She was
grieved, and bitterly sorry for the man who was hurt so much. But
still, in her heart of hearts, where the love should have burned, there   30
was a blank. Now, when all her woman's pity was roused to its full
extent, when she would have slaved herself to death to nurse him and
to save him, when she would have taken the pain herself, if she could,
somewhere far away inside her she felt indifferent to him and to his
suffering. It hurt her most of all, this failure to love him, even when   35
he roused her strong emotions. She brooded awhile.
"And there!" she said suddenly, "when I'd got half way to Keston,
I found I'd come out in my working boots—and *look* at them." They
were an old pair of Paul's, brown and rubbed through at the toes. "I
didn't know what to do with myself, for shame," she added.   40

In the morning, when Annie and Arthur were at school, Mrs
Morel talked again to her son, who was helping her with her
house-work.

"I found Barker at the hospital. He did look bad, poor little
5   fellow. 'Well,' I said to him, 'what sort of a journey did you have with
him?' 'Dunna ax me, missis!' he said. 'Ay,' I said, 'I know what he'd
be.'—'But it *wor* bad for him, Mrs Morel, it *wor* that!' he said. 'I
know,' I said. 'At ivry jolt I thought my 'eart would ha' flown clean
out o' my mouth,' he said. 'An' the scream 'e give sometimes—
10 missis, not for a fortune would I go through wi' it again.' 'I can quite
understand it,' I said. 'It's a nasty job, though,' he said, 'an' one as'll
be a long while afore it's right again.' 'I'm afraid it will,' I said. I like
Mr Barker—I *do* like him. There's something so manly about him."

Paul resumed his task silently.

15 "And of course," Mrs Morel continued, "for a man like your
father, the hospital *is* hard. He *can't* understand rules and regula-
tions. And he won't let anybody else touch him, not if he can help it.
When he smashed the muscles of his thigh, and it had to be dressed
four times a day, *would* he let anybody but me or his mother do
20 it—he wouldn't. So of course he'll suffer in there, with the
nurses.—And I didn't like leaving him. I'm sure, when I kissed him
an' came away, it seemed a shame—"

So she talked to her son, almost as if she were thinking aloud to
him, and he took it in as best he could, by sharing her trouble to
25 lighten it. And in the end, she shared almost everything with him,
without knowing.

Morel had a very bad time; for a week he was in a critical
condition. Then he began to mend. And then, knowing he was going
to get better, the whole family sighed with relief, and proceeded to
30 live happily.

They were not badly off whilst Morel was in the hospital. There
were fourteen shillings a week from the pit, ten shillings from the
sick club, and five shillings from the Disability Fund;* and then
every week the butties had something for Mrs Morel, five or seven
35 shillings, so that she was quite well to do. And whilst Morel was
progressing favourably in the hospital, the family was extraordinarily
happy and peaceful. On Saturdays and Wednesdays Mrs Morel
went to Nottingham to see her husband. Then she always brought
back some little thing: a small tube of paints, for Paul, or some thick
40 paper—a couple of post-cards for Annie, that the whole family

rejoiced over for days before the girl was allowed to send them away—or a fret-saw for Arthur, or a bit of pretty wood. She described her adventures into the big shops with joy. Soon the folk in the picture shop knew her, and knew about Paul. The girl in the book shop took a keen interest in her. Mrs Morel was full of information when she got home from Nottingham. The three sat round till bed-time, listening, putting-in, arguing. Then Paul often raked the fire.

"I'm the man in the house now," he used to say to his mother, with joy. They learned how perfectly peaceful the home could be. And they almost regretted—though none of them would have owned to such callousness—that their father was soon coming back.

Paul was now fourteen, and was looking for work. He was a rather small and rather finely-made boy, with dark brown hair and light blue eyes. His face had already lost its youthful chubbiness, and was becoming somewhat like William's, rough-featured, almost rugged, and it was extraordinarily mobile. Usually he looked as if he saw things, was full of life, and warm; then his smile, like his mother's, came suddenly and was very lovable; and then, when there was any clog in his soul's quick running, his face went stupid and ugly. He was the sort of boy that becomes a clown and a lout as soon as he is not understood, or feels himself held cheap; and again is adorable at the first touch of warmth.

He suffered very much from the first contact with anything. When he was seven, the starting school had been a nightmare and a torture to him. But afterwards he liked it. And now that he felt he had to go out into life, he went through agonies of shrinking self consciousness. He was quite a clever painter, for a boy of his years. And he knew some French and German and mathematics, that Mr Heaton had taught him.* But nothing he had was of any commercial value. He was not strong enough for heavy manual work, his mother said. He did not care for making things with his hands, preferred racing about, or making excursions into the country, or reading, or painting.

"What do you want to be?" his mother asked.

He had not the faintest notion. He would have liked to go on painting, but that never occured to him, since it was impossible. He quite strongly did not want to do anything. But it was urgent now that he should begin to earn. And since he did not feel that he was of high monetary value in the world, and since he knew that at any job a man makes thirty shillings or thirty five shillings a week, he invariably replied:

"Anything."

"That is no answer," said Mrs Morel.

5 But it was quite truthfully the only answer he could give. His ambition, as far as this world's gear went,* was quietly to earn his thirty or thirty-five shillings a week, somewhere near home, and then, when his father died, have a cottage with his mother, paint and go out as he liked, and live happy ever after. That was his pro-

10 gramme as far as doing things went. But he was proud within himself, measuring people against himself, and placing them, inexorably. And he thought that *perhaps* he might also make a painter, the real thing. But that he left alone.

"Then," said his mother, "you must look in the paper for the

15 advertisements."

He looked at her. It seemed to him a bitter humiliation and an anguish to go through. But he said nothing. When he got up in the morning, his whole being was knotted up over this one thought:

"I've got to go and look for advertisements for a job."

20 It stood in front of the morning, that thought, killing all joy and even life, for him. His heart felt like a tight knot.

And then, at ten o'clock, he set off. He was supposed to be a queer, quiet child. Going up the sunny street of the little town, he felt as if all the folk he met said to themselves: "He's going to the

25 Co-op Reading Room to look in the papers for a place. He can't get a job. I suppose he's living on his mother." Then he crept up the stone stairs behind the drapery shop at the Co-op, and peeped in the reading room. Usually one or two men were there, either old useless fellows, or colliers 'on the club.'* So he entered, full of shrinking and

30 suffering when they looked up, seated himself at the table, and pretended to scan the news. He knew they would think, "What does a lad of thirteen want in a reading room, with a newspaper," and he suffered.

Then he looked wistfully out of the window. Already he was a

35 prisoner of industrialism. Large sunflowers stared over the old red wall of the garden opposite, looking in their jolly way down on the women who were hurrying with something for dinner. The valley was full of corn, brightening in the sun. Two collieries, among the fields, waved their small white plumes of steam. Far-off on the hills

40 were the woods of Aldersley,* dark and fascinating. Already his heart

went down. He was being taken into bondage. His freedom in the beloved home valley, was going now.

The brewers' wagons came rolling up from Keston, with enormous barrels, four a side, like beans in a burst bean-pod. The wagoner, throned aloft, rolling massively in his seat, was not so much below Paul's eye. The man's hair, on his small, bullet head, was bleached almost white by the sun, and on his thick red arms, rocking idly on his sack apron, the white hairs glistened. His red face shone and was almost asleep with sunshine. The horses, handsome and brown, went on by themselves, looking by far the masters of the show.

Paul wished he were stupid. "I wish," he thought to himself, "I was fat like him, and like a dog in the sun. I wish I was a pig, and a brewer's wagoner."

Then, the room being at last empty, he would hastily copy an advertisement on a scrap of paper, then another, and slip out in immense relief. His mother would scan over his copies.

"Yes," she said, "you may try."

William had written out a letter of application,* couched in admirable business language, which Paul copied, with variations. The boy's handwriting was execrable, so that William, who did all things well, got into a fever of impatience.

The elder brother was becoming quite swanky. In London, he found that he could associate with men far above his Bestwood friends in station. Some of the clerks in the office had studied for the law, and were more or less going through a kind of apprenticeship. William always made friends among men, wherever he went, he was so jolly. Therefore he was soon visiting and staying in houses of men who, in Bestwood, would have looked down on the unapproachable Bank Manager, and would merely have called indifferently on the Rector. So he began to fancy himself as a great gun. He was indeed rather surprised at the ease with which he became a gentleman.

His letters to his mother often ran in a pleased vein.

> "'The Myrmidons'
> Limpsfield

My dear Mater,

It is one o'clock, a.m. Imagine your son seated on an ancient oak chair, with a latest pattern electric lamp in front of him, on the table, writing to you. He is wearing evening clothes, and the gold studs you gave him for his 21st, and he thinks no end of himself. He only wishes you could see him. Solomon in all his glory must have felt dowdy in comparison.

I am staying the week-end with Loosemore, and seize this opportunity of writing to you.— —"

5   His mother was glad, he seemed so pleased. And his lodging in Walthamstow was so dreary. But now there seemed to come a kind of fever into the young man's letters. He was unsettled by all the change, he did not stand firm on his own feet, but seemed to spin rather giddily on the quick current of the new life. His mother was
10 anxious for him. She could feel him losing himself. He had danced and gone to the theatre, boated on the river, been out with friends; and she knew he sat up afterwards in his cold bedroom, grinding away at Latin, because he intended to get on in his office, and in the Law as much as he could. He never sent his mother any money now.
15 It was all taken, the little he had, for his own life. And she did not want any, except sometimes, when she was in a tight corner, and when ten shillings would have saved her much worry. She still dreamed of William, and of what he would do, with herself behind him. Never for a minute would she admit to herself, how heavy and
20 anxious her heart was because of him.

Also he talked a good deal now of a girl* he had met at a dance, a handsome brunette, quite young, and a lady, after whom the men were running thick and fast.

"I wonder if you would run my boy," his mother wrote to him,
25 "unless you saw all the other men chasing her too. You feel safe enough and vain enough in a crowd. But take care, and see how you feel when you find yourself alone, and in triumph—"

William resented these things, and continued the chase. He had taken the girl on the river—"if you saw her, mother, you would
30 know how I feel. Tall, and elegant, with the clearest of clear transparent olive complexions, hair as black as jet, and such grey eyes, bright, mocking, like lights on water at night. It is all very well to be a bit satirical, till you see her. And she dresses as well as any woman in London. I tell you your son doesn't half put his head up,
35 when she goes walking down Piccadilly with him."

Mrs Morel wondered, in her heart, if her son did not go walking down Piccadilly with an elegant figure and fine clothes, rather than with a woman who was near to him. But she congratulated him, in her doubtful fashion. And, as she stood over the washing tub, the
40 mother brooded over her son. She saw him saddled with an elegant

and expensive wife, earning little money, dragging along and getting draggled in some small ugly house in a suburb. "But there," she told herself, "I am very likely a silly—meeting trouble half way." Nevertheless, the load of anxiety scarcely ever left her heart, lest William should do the wrong thing by himself. 5

Presently, Paul was bidden call upon Thomas Jordan,* manufacturer of surgical appliances, at 21 Spaniel Row, Nottingham. Mrs Morel was all joy.

"There you see!" she cried, her eyes shining. "You've only written four letters, and the third is answered. You're lucky, my boy, 10
as I always said you were."

Paul looked at the picture of a wooden leg, adorned with elastic stockings and other appliances, that figured on Mr Jordan's notepaper, and he felt alarmed. He had not known that elastic stockings existed. And he seemed to feel the business world, with its regulated 15
system of values, and its impersonality, and he dreaded it. It seemed monstrous also that a business could be run on wooden legs.

Mother and son set off together one Tuesday morning. It was August and blazing hot. Paul walked with something screwed up tight inside him. He would have suffered much physical pain rather 20
than this unreasonable suffering at being exposed to strangers to be accepted or rejected. Yet he chattered away with his mother. He would never have confessed to her how he suffered over these things, and she only partly guessed. She was gay, like a sweetheart. She stood in front of the ticket office at Bestwood, and Paul watched 25
her take from her purse the money for the tickets. As he saw her hands in their old, black kid gloves, getting the silver out of the worn purse, his heart contracted with pain of love of her.

She was quite excited, and quite gay. He suffered because she *would* talk aloud in presence of the other travellers. 30

"Now look at that silly cow!" she said. "Careering round as if it thought it was a circus."

"It's most likely a bott fly," he said, very low.

"A what?" she asked, brightly, and unashamed.

They thought awhile. He was sensible all the time of having her 35
opposite him. Suddenly their eyes met, and she smiled to him, a rare, intimate smile, beautiful with brightness and love. Then each looked out of the window.

And suddenly she turned to him and said, distinctly:

"And I really think you'll get it.—And if you don't, well, you can't 40

grumble if you don't get the *third* place you apply for, can you? But I
think you will. You are lucky, though you don't deserve to
be."—She *would* talk so that the other people could hear!

The sixteen slow miles of railway journey passed. The mother
5   and son walked down Station Street, feeling the excitement of lovers
having an adventure together. In Carrington Street they stopped to
hang over the parapet and look at the barges on the canal below.

"It's just like Venice," he said, seeing the sunshine on the water,
that lay between high factory walls.

10   "Perhaps," she answered, smiling.

They enjoyed the shops immensely.

"Now you see that blouse," she would say, "wouldn't that just suit
our Annie?—And for one and eleven three.* Isn't that cheap!"

"And made of needlework as well," he said.

15   "Yes."

They had plenty of time, so they did not hurry. The town was
strange and delightful to them. But the boy was tied up inside in a
knot of apprehension. He dreaded the interview with Thomas
Jordan.

20   It was nearly eleven o'clock by St. Peter's Church. They turned
up a narrow street that led to the Castle. It was gloomy and
old-fashioned, having low dark shops and dark-green house-doors
with brass knockers, and yellow ochred doorsteps projecting onto
the pavement, then another old shop whose small window looked
25   like a cunning, half-shut eye. Mother and son went cautiously,
looking everywhere for 'Thomas Jordan and Son.' It was like
hunting in some wild place. They were on tiptoe of excitement.

Suddenly they spied a big dark archway, in which were names of
various firms, Thomas Jordan among them.

30   "Here it is," said Mrs Morel. "But now *where* is it?"

They looked round. On one side was a queer, dark cardboard-
factory, on the other a Commercial Hotel.

"It's up the entry," said Paul.

And they ventured under the archway, as into the jaws of the
35   dragon. They emerged into a wide yard, like a well, with buildings
all round. It was littered with straw and boxes and cardboard. The
sunshine actually caught one crate whose straw was streaming onto
the yard like gold. But elsewhere the place was like a pit. There were
several doors, and two flights of steps. Straight in front, on a dirty
40   glass door at the top of a staircase, loomed the ominous words

"Thomas Jordan and Son—Surgical Appliances." Mrs Morel went first, her son followed her. Charles the First mounted his scaffold* with a lighter heart than had Paul Morel as he followed his mother up the dirty steps to the dirty door.

She pushed open the door, and stood in pleased surprise. In front of her was a big warehouse, with creamy paper parcels everywhere, and clerks with their shirt sleeves rolled back, were going about in an at-home sort of way. The light was subdued, the glossy cream parcels seemed luminous, the counters were of dark brown wood. All was quiet and very homely. Mrs Morel took two steps forward, then waited. Paul stood behind her. She had on her Sunday bonnet and a black veil, he wore a boy's broad white collar and a norfolk suit.*

One of the clerks looked up. He was thin and tall, with a small face. His way of looking was alert. Then he glanced round to the other end of the room, where was a glass office. And then he came forward. He did not say anything, but leaned in a gentle, inquiring fashion towards Mrs Morel.

"Can I see Mr Jordan?" she asked.

"I'll fetch him," answered the young man.

He went down to the glass office. A red faced, white whiskered old man looked up. He reminded Paul of a pomeranian dog. Then the same little man came up the room. He had short legs, was rather stout, and wore an alpaca jacket. So, with one ear up, as it were, he came stoutly and inquiringly down the room.

"Goodmorning!" he said, hesitating before Mrs Morel, in doubt as to whether she were a customer or not.

"Goodmorning—I came with my son, Paul Morel—you asked him to call this morning."

"Come this way," said Mr Jordan, in a rather snappy little manner intended to be business like.

They followed the manufacturer into a grubby little room, upholstered in black American leather, glossy with the rubbing of many customers. On the table was a pile of trusses, yellow wash-leather hoops tangled together. They looked new and living. Paul sniffed the odor of new wash-leather. He wondered what the things were. By this time he was so much stunned that he only noticed the outside things.

"Sit down!" said Mr Jordan, irritably pointing Mrs Morel to a horse hair chair. She sat on the edge, in an uncertain fashion. Then the little old man fidgeted, and found a paper.

"Did you write this letter?" he snapped, thrusting what Paul recognised as his own note-paper in front of him.

"Yes," he answered.

5 At that moment, he was occupied in two ways: first, in feeling guilty for telling a lie, since William had composed the letter, second, in wondering why his letter seemed so strange and different, in the fat, red hand of the man, from what it had been when it lay on the kitchen table. It was like part of himself, gone astray. He resented the way the man held it.

10 "Where did you learn to write?" said the old man, crossly.

Paul merely looked at him shamedly, and did not answer.

"He *is* a bad writer," put in Mrs Morel, apologetically. Then she pushed up her veil. Paul hated her for not being prouder with this common little man, and he loved her face, clear of the veil.

15 "And you say you know French?" inquired the little man, still sharply.

"Yes," said Paul.

"What school did you go to?"

"The board school."

20 "And did you learn it there?"

"No—I—" the boy went crimson, and got no further.

"His god-father gave him lessons," said Mrs Morel, half pleading, and rather distant.

Mr Jordan hesitated. Then, in his irritable manner—he always 25 seemed to keep his hands ready for action—he pulled another sheet of paper from his pocket, unfolded it. The paper made a crackling noise. He handed it to Paul.

"Read that," he said.

It was a note in French, in thin, flimsy foreign handwriting that 30 the boy could not decipher. He stared blankly at the paper.

"'Monsieur,'" he began, then looked in great confusion at Mr Jordan.

"It's the—it's the——."

He wanted to say 'handwriting', but his wits would no longer work 35 even sufficiently to supply him with the word. Feeling an utter fool, and hating Mr Jordan, he turned desperately to the paper again.

"'Sir—Please send me'—er—er—I can't tell the——er—'two pairs—*gris fil bas*—grey thread stockings—er—er—*sans*—without—' er I can't tell the words—er—'doigts—fingers'—er—I 40 can't tell the——"

He wanted to say handwriting, but the word still refused to come. Seeing him stuck, Mr Jordan snatched the paper from him.

"'Please send by return two pairs grey thread stockings without *toes*—'"

"Well," flashed Paul, "'doigts' mean fingers—as well—as a rule—"

The little man looked at him. He did not know whether 'doigts' meant 'fingers', he knew that for all *his* purposes, it meant 'toes.'

"Fingers to stockings!" he snapped.

"Well it *does* mean fingers," the boy persisted.

He hated the little man, who made such a clod of him. Mr Jordan looked at the pale, stupid, defiant boy, then at the mother, who sat quiet and with that peculiar shut-off look of the poor who have to depend on the favour of others.

"And when could he come?" he asked.

"Well," said Mrs Morel, "as soon as you wish. He has finished school now."

"He would live in Bestwood?"

"Yes—but he could be in—at the station—at quarter to eight—"

"Hm!"

It ended by Paul's being engaged as junior spiral clerk, at eight shillings a week. The boy did not open his mouth to say another word, after having insisted that 'doigts' meant 'fingers'. He followed his mother down the stairs. She looked at him with her bright blue eyes full of love and joy.

"I think you'll like it," she said.

"'Doigts' does mean 'fingers', mother—and it was the writing—I couldn't read the writing."

"Never mind, my boy.—I'm sure he'll be all right, and you won't see much of him.—Wasn't that first young fellow nice—I'm sure you'll like them."

"But wasn't Mr Jordan common, mother? Does he own it all?"

"I suppose he was a workman, who has got on," she said. "You mustn't mind people so much. They're not being disagreeable to *you*—it's their way—you always think people are meaning things for you. But they don't."

It was very sunny. Over the big, desolate space of the market-place, the blue sky shimmered, and the granite cobbles of the paving glistened. Shops down the Long Row were deep in obscurity, and the shadow was full of colour. Just where the horse trams trundled

across the market, was a row of fruit stalls, with fruit blazing in the
sun, apples and piles of reddish oranges, small greengage plums,
and bananas. There was a warm scent of fruit as mother and son
passed. Gradually his feeling of ignominy and of rage sank.

5   "Where should we go for dinner?" asked the mother.

"Should we buy something, and eat it in the Arboretum?"

"No, we shan't."

"Should we go to Morley's?"

"Their tea's stewed. No—you've got the place—we'll go and have
10 some proper dinner."*

It was felt to be a reckless extravagance. Paul had only been in an
eating house once or twice in his life, and then only to have a cup of
tea and a bun. Most of the people of Bestwood considered that tea
and bread and butter, and perhaps potted beef, was all they could
15 afford to eat in Nottingham. Real cooked dinner was considered
great extravagance. Paul felt rather guilty.

They found a place that looked quite cheap. But when Mrs Morel
scanned the bill of fare, her heart was heavy, things were so dear. So
she ordered kidney pies and potatoes, as the cheapest available dish.

20   "We oughtn't to have come here, mother," said Paul.

"Never mind," she said. "We won't come again."

She insisted on his having a small currant tart, because he liked
sweets.

"I don't want it, mother," he pleaded.

25   "Yes," she insisted, "you'll have it."

And she looked round for the waitress. But the waitress was busy,
and Mrs Morel did not like to bother her then. So the mother and
son waited for the girl's pleasure, whilst she flirted among the men.

"Brazen hussy," said Mrs Morel to Paul. "Look now, she's taking
30 that man *his* pudding, and he came long after us."

"It doesn't matter mother," said Paul.

Mrs Morel was angry. But she was too poor, and her orders were
too meagre, so that she had not the courage to insist on her rights
just then. They waited and waited.

35   "Should we go, mother?" he said.

Then Mrs Morel stood up. The girl was passing near.

"Will you bring one currant tart," said Mrs Morel clearly.

The girl looked round insolently.

"Directly," she said.

40   "We have waited quite long enough," said Mrs Morel.

In a moment the girl came back with the tart. Mrs Morel asked coldly for the bill. Paul wanted to sink through the floor. He marvelled at his mother's hardness. He knew that only years of battling had taught her to insist even so little on her rights. She shrank as much as he. 5

"It's the last time I go *there* for anything!" she declared, when they were outside the place, thankful to be clear.

"We'll go," she said, "and look at Keep's, and Boot's, and one or two places, shall we?"

They had discussions over the pictures, and Mrs Morel wanted to 10 buy him a little sable brush,* that he hankered after. But this indulgence he refused. He stood in front of milliners' shops, and drapers' shops, almost bored, but content for her to be interested. They wandered on.

"Now just look at those black grapes!" she said. "They make your 15 mouth water.—I've wanted some of those for years, but I s'll have to wait a bit before I get them."

Then she rejoiced in the florist's, standing in the doorway, sniffing.

"Oh!—Oh!—isn't it simply lovely!" 20

Paul saw, in the darkness of the shop, an elegant young lady in black peering over the counter curiously.

"They're looking at you," he said, trying to draw his mother away.

"But what *is* it?" she exclaimed, refusing to be moved.

"Stocks!" he answered, sniffing hastily. "Look, there's a tub-ful." 25

"So there is—red and white!—but really, I never knew stocks to smell like it!" And, to his great relief, she moved out of the doorway, but only to stand in front of the window.

"Paul!" she cried to him, who was trying to get out of sight of the elegant young lady in black, the shop-girl. "Paul! Just look here!" 30

He came reluctantly back.

"Now, just look at that fuchsia!" she exclaimed, pointing.

"Hm!"—he made a curious, interested sound. "You'd think every second as the flowers was going to fall off, they hang so big an' heavy." 35

"And such an abundance!" she cried.

"And the way they drop downwards with their threads and knots—!"

"Yes!" she exclaimed. "Lovely!"

"I wonder who'll buy it!" he said. 40

"I wonder!" she answered. "Not us."

"It would die in our parlour."

"Yes, beastly cold sunless hole, it kills every bit of a plant you put in—and the kitchen chokes them to death—"

They bought a few things, and set off towards the station. Looking up the canal, through the dark pass of the buildings, they saw the Castle on its bluff of brown, green-bushed rock, in a positive miracle of delicate sunshine.

"Won't it be nice for me to come out at dinner-times!" said Paul. "I can go all round here and see everything. I s'll love it."

"You will," assented his mother.

He had spent a perfect afternoon with his mother. They arrived home in the mellow evening, happy, and glowing, and tired. In the morning he filled in the form for his season ticket, and took it to the station. When he got back, his mother was just beginning to wash the floor. He sat crouched up on the sofa.

"He says it'll be here by Saturday," he said.

"And how much will it be?"

"About one pound eleven," he said.

She went on washing her floor in silence.

"Is it a lot?" he asked.

"It's no more than I thought," she answered.

"An' I s'll earn eight shillings a week," he said.

She did not answer, but went on with her work. At last she said:

"That William promised me, when he went to London, as he'd give me a pound a month. He has given me ten shillings—twice: and now I know he hasn't a farthing if I asked him. Not that I want it. Only just now, you'd think he might be able to help with this ticket, which I'd never expected."

"He earns a lot," said Paul.

"He earns a hundred and thirty pounds. But they're all alike. They're large in promises, but it's precious little fulfilment you get."

"He spends over fifty shillings a week on himself," said Paul.

"And I keep this house on less than thirty," she replied, "and am supposed to find money for extras. But they don't care about helping you, once they've gone. He'd rather spend it on that dressed-up creature."

"She should have her own money, if she's so grand," said Paul.

"She should, but she hasn't. I asked him.—And I know he

doesn't buy her a gold bangle for nothing. I wonder who ever bought *me* a gold bangle."

"Well, you never wanted one."

"No, I didn't—but it would have been all the same if I had."

"Didn't my father ever buy you things?" 5

"Yes—one half-pound of apples—and that was all—every penny he spent on me, before we were married."

"Why?"

"Because I was silly, and when he said 'What should I buy thee?' I told him 'Nothing'. But bring me anything!—it never occurred to 10 him. And William wouldn't buy gold bangles, except for a fol-de-lol who makes great pretensions."

"And I'll bet she'd got plenty," said the boy.

"Got plenty, ay! But he'd have to give her another, to seem grand as well. What does he care, really! I can keep him while he's earning 15 a few shillings, and then, as soon as his money is anything like, and one might feel a bit of peace and security, he goes away, and it's the same struggle over again, nowhere to turn to when there's anything needed, nobody to do you a hand's turn."

"You should ask him." 20

"Yes, and he'd have to borrow it. I could borrow it myself, if it came to that. I'm sure I'm not going to be beholden to him for anything I have to ask him for. He needn't write to me, singing her praises, and saying the operas they've been to. I don't want to hear. A fat lot of thought he has for me, I must say.—But there, they don't care! 25 They've got their own lives to live, and their own way to go, and what am I to him. But a nuisance I will never be, nor ask him for anything.—And I hope your father will live long enough, till I'm gone. For it's a poor tale, if you have to be dependent on your children."

"Well mother—I s'll be earning soon—an' you can always have 30 my money, 'cause I s'll never get married."

"It's an old tale, and one William was always preaching. Wait a bit, and your tune will alter."

"It won't."

"Very well." 35

She went on washing her floor of red brick, in silence.

"What shall you do?" asked Paul.

"I suppose I s'll have to draw out of the Co-op—and that'll break into my share, so I shan't get full dividend. And I *didn't* want to break into it again." 40

The boy was very miserable, rather angry. It was for him the money was needed, and it galled him.

"Well," he said, "I s'll soon get a raise, and you can have all my money."

5 "That's all very well," she said. "But that doesn't provide thirty shillings for Saturday morning."

William was succeeding with his "Gipsy", as he called her. He asked the girl—her name was Louisa Lily Denys Western—for a photograph to send to his mother. The photo came—a handsome
10 brunette, taken in profile, smirking slightly—and, it might be, quite naked, for on the photograph not a scrap of clothing was to be seen, only a naked bust.

"Yes," wrote Mrs Morel to her son, "the photograph of Louie is very striking, and I can see she must be attractive. But do you think,
15 my boy, it was very good taste of a girl, to give her young man that photo to send to his mother, the first. Certainly the shoulders are beautiful, as you say. But I hardly expected to see so much of them at the first view—."

Morel found the photograph standing on the chiffonnier in the
20 parlour. He came out with it between his thick thumb and finger.

"Who dost reckon this is?" he asked of his wife.

"It's the girl our William is going with," replied Mrs Morel.

"Hm! 'Er's a bright spark, from th' look on 'er—an' one as wunna do him owermuch good neither.—Who is she?"

25 "Her name is Louisa Lily Denys Western."

"An' come again tomorrer!" exclaimed the miner. "An' is 'er an actress?"

"She is not. She's supposed to be a lady."

"I'll bet," he exclaimed, still staring at the photo. "A lady, is she?
30 An' how much does she reckon ter keep up this sort o' game on?"

"On nothing—she lives with an old aunt, whom she hates, and takes what bit of money's given her."

"Hm!" said Morel, laying down the photograph. "Then he's a fool to ha' ta'en up wi' such a one as that."

35 "Dear Mater," William replied. "I'm sorry you didn't like the photograph. It never occurred to me, when I sent it, that you mightn't think it decent. However, I told Gyp that it didn't quite suit your prim and proper notions, so she's going to send you another, that I hope will please you better. She's always being photographed.
40 In fact, the photographers *ask* her if they may take her, for nothing."

Presently the new photograph came, with a little silly note from the girl. This time the young lady was seen in a black satin evening bodice, cut square, with little puff sleeves, and black lace hanging down her beautiful arms.

"I wonder if she ever wears anything except evening clothes," said Mrs Morel sarcastically. "I'm sure I *ought* to be impressed."

"You *are* disagreeable, mother," said Paul. "I think the first one with bare shoulders is lovely."

"Do you," answered his mother. "Well, I don't."

On the Monday morning, the boy got up at six, to start work. He had the season-ticket which had cost such bitterness, in his waistcoat pocket. He loved it, with its bars of yellow across. His mother packed his dinner in a small, shut up basket, and he set off at a quarter to seven to catch the 7.15 train. Mrs Morel came to the entry end to see him off.

It was a perfect morning. From the ash-tree, the slender green fruits that the children call 'pigeons' were twinkling gaily down on a little breeze, into the front gardens of the houses. The valley was full of a lustrous dark haze, through which the ripe corn shimmered, and in which the steam from Minton pit melted swiftly. Puffs of wind came. Paul looked over the high woods of Aldersley, where the country gleamed, and home had never pulled at him so powerfully.

"Goodmorning mother," he said, smiling, but feeling very unhappy.

"Goodmorning," she replied, cheerfully and tenderly.

She stood in her white apron on the open road, watching him as he crossed the field. He had a small, compact body, that looked full of life. She felt, as she saw him trudging over the field, that where he determined to go, he would get. She thought of William. He would have leaped the fence, instead of going round to the stile. He was away in London, doing well. Paul would be working in Nottingham. Now she had two sons in the world. She could think of two places, great centres of industry, and feel that she had put a man into each of them, that these men would work out what *she* wanted; they were derived from her, they were of her, and their works also would be hers. All the morning long she thought of Paul.

At eight o'clock he climbed the dismal stairs of Jordan's Surgical Appliance Factory, and stood helplessly against the first great parcel-rack, waiting for somebody to pick him up. The place was still not awake. Over the counters were great dust sheets. Two men

only had arrived, and were heard talking in a corner, as they took off
their coats and rolled up their shirt sleeves. It was ten past eight.
Evidently there was no rush of punctuality. Paul listened to the
voices of the two clerks. Then he heard someone cough, and saw in
5 the office at the end of the room, an old, decaying clerk in a round
smoking cap of black velvet embroidered with red and green,
opening letters. He waited and waited. One of the junior clerks went
to the old man, greeted him cheerily and loudly. Evidently the old
'chief' was deaf. Then the young fellow came striding importantly
10 down to his counter. He spied Paul.

"Hello!" he said. "You the new lad?"

"Yes," said Paul.

"Hm! What's your name?"

"Paul Morel."

15   "Paul Morel?—All right, you come on round here."

Paul followed him round the rectangle of counters. The room was
second storey. It had a great hole in the middle of the floor, fenced
as with a wall of counters, and down this wide shaft the lifts went,
and the light for the bottom storey. Also there was a corresponding
20 big, oblong hole in the ceiling, and one could see above, over the
fence of the top floor, some machinery. And right away overhead
was the glass roof, and all light for the three storeys came downwards, getting dimmer, so that it was always night on the ground
floor, and rather gloomy on the second floor. The factory was the
25 top floor, the warehouse the second, the storehouse the ground
floor. It was an insanitary ancient place.

Paul was led round to a very dark corner.

"This is the 'Spiral' corner," said the clerk. "You're Spiral, with
Pappleworth. He's your boss, but he's not come yet. He doesn't get
30 here till half past eight. So you can fetch the letters, if you like, from
Mr Melling down there."

The young man pointed to the old clerk in the office.

"All right," said Paul.

"Here's a peg to hang your cap on—here are your entry
35 ledgers—Pappleworth won't be long."

And the thin young man stalked away with long, busy strides, over
the hollow wooden floor.

After a minute or two, Paul went down and stood in the door of
the glass office. The old clerk in the smoking cap looked down over
40 the rim of his spectacles.

"Good—mòrning," he said, kindly and impressively. "You want the letters for the Spiral department, Thomas?"

Paul resented being called Thomas. But he took the letters and returned to his dark place, where the counter made an angle, where the great parcel-rack came to an end, and where there were three 5 doors in the corner. He sat on a high stool and read the letters, those whose handwriting was not too difficult. They ran as follows:

"Will you please send me at once a pair of lady's silk, spiral thigh hose, without feet, such as I had from you last year—length—thigh to knee— —etc" 10

or "Major Chamberlain wishes to repeat his previous order for a silk, non-elastic suspensory bandage."

Many of these letters, some of them in French or Norwegian, were a great puzzle to the boy. He sat on his stool nervously awaiting the arrival of his "boss." He suffered tortures of shyness 15 when, at half past eight, the factory girls for upstairs trooped past him.

Mr Pappleworth arrived chewing a chlorodyne* gum, at about twenty to nine, when all the other men were at work. He was a thin, sallow man with a red nose, quick, staccato, and smartly but stiffly 20 dressed. He was about thirty six years old. There was something rather 'doggy', rather 'smart', rather 'cute and shrewd, and something warm, and something slightly contemptible about him.

"You my new lad?" he said.

Paul stood up and said he was. 25

"Fetched the letters?"

Mr Pappleworth gave a chew to his gum.

"Yes."

"Copied 'em?"

"No." 30

"Well come on then, let's look slippy. Changed your coat?"

"No."

"You want to bring an old coat, and leave it here"—he pronounced the last words with the chlorodyne gum between his side teeth. He vanished into darkness behind the great parcel rack, 35 re-appeared coatless, turning up a smart striped shirt cuff over a thin and hairy arm. Then he slipped into his coat. Paul noticed how thin he was, and that his trousers were in folds behind. He seized a stool, dragged it beside the boy's, and sat down.

"Sit down," he said. Paul took a seat. Mr Pappleworth was very 40

close to him. The man seized the letters, snatched a long entry book
out of a rack in front of him, flung it open, seized a pen, and said:
"Now look here—you want to copy these letters in here."
He sniffed twice, gave a quick chew at his gum, stared fixedly at a
5 letter, then went very still and absorbed, and wrote the entry rapidly,
in a beautiful flourishing hand. He glanced quickly at Paul.
"See that?"
"Yes."
"Think you can do it all right?"
10 "Yes."
"All right then—let's see you."
He sprang off his stool. Paul took a pen. Mr Pappleworth disappeared. Paul rather liked copying the letters, but he wrote slowly,
laboriously, and exceedingly badly. He was doing the fourth letter,
15 and feeling quite busy and happy, when Mr Pappleworth
reappeared.
"Now then—how'r'yer getting on—done 'em?"
He leaned over the boy's shoulder, chewing, and smelling of
chlorodyne.
20 "Strike my bob,* lad, but you're a beautiful writer!" he exclaimed,
satirically. "Ne'er mind, how many h'yer done? Only three! I'd 'a
eaten 'em. Get on, my lad, an' put numbers on 'em—here look! Get
on!"
Paul ground away at the letters, whilst Mr Pappleworth fussed
25 over various jobs. Suddenly the boy started as a shrill whistle
sounded near his ear. Mr Pappleworth came, took a plug out of a
pipe, and said, in an amazingly cross and bossy voice:
"Yes!"
Paul heard a faint voice, like a woman's, out of the mouth of the
30 tube. He gazed in wonder, never having seen a speaking tube before.
"Well," said Mr Pappleworth, disagreeably, into the tube, "you'd
better get some of your back work done then."
Again the woman's tiny voice was heard, sounding pretty and
cross.
35 "I've not time to stand here while you talk," said Mr Pappleworth,
and he pushed the plug into the tube.
"Come my lad," he said, imploringly, to Paul, "there's Polly
crying out for them orders. Can't you buck up a bit? Here—come
out."
40 He took the book, to Paul's immense chagrin, and began the

copying himself. He worked quickly and well. This done, he seized some strips of long yellow paper, about three inches wide, and made out the day's orders for the work girls.

"You'd better watch me," he said to Paul, working all the while rapidly. Paul watched the weird little drawings of legs and thighs and ankles, with the strokes across and the numbers, and the few brief directions, which his chief made upon the yellow paper. Then Mr Pappleworth finished and jumped up.

"Come on with me," he said, and, the yellow papers flying in his hands, he dashed through a door and down some stairs, into the basement where the gas was burning. They crossed the cold, damp store-room, then a long dreary room with a long table on trestles, into a smaller cosy apartment, not very high, which had been built-on to the main building. In this room a small woman with a red serge blouse, and her black hair done on top of her head, was waiting like a proud little bantam.

"Here y'are!" said Pappleworth.

"I think it is 'here you are'!" exclaimed Polly. "The girls have been here nearly half an hour waiting. Just think of the time wasted!"

"*You* think of getting your work done and not talking so much," said Mr Pappleworth. "You could ha' been finishing off."

"You know quite well we finished everything off on Saturday," cried Polly, flying at him, her dark eyes flashing.

"Tu-tu-tu-tu-terterter!" he mocked. "Here's your new lad. Don't ruin him as you did the last."

"'As we did the last!'" repeated Polly. "Yes, *we* do a lot of ruining, we do. My word, a lad would *take* some ruining after he'd been with you."

"It's time for work now, not for talk," said Mr Pappleworth severely and coldly.

"It was time for work some time back," said Polly, marching away with her head in the air. She was an erect little body of forty.

In that room were two round spiral machines on the bench under the window. Through the inner doorway was another, longer room, with six more machines. A little group of girls, nicely dressed and in white aprons, stood talking together.

"Have you nothing else to do but talk?" said Mr Pappleworth.

"Only wait for you," said one handsome girl, laughing.

"Well, get on, get on," he said. "Come on my lad. You'll know your road down here again."

And Paul ran upstairs after his chief. He was given some checking and invoicing to do. He stood at the desk, labouring in his execrable handwriting. Presently Mr Jordan came strutting down from the glass office, and stood behind him, to the boy's great discomfort.
5 Suddenly a red and fat finger was thrust on the form he was filling in.

"*Mr* J.A.Bates Esquire!" exclaimed the cross voice just behind his ear.

Paul looked at "Mr J.A.Bates Esquire," in his own vile writing,
10 and wondered what was the matter now.

"Didn't they teach you any better than *that* while they were at it. If you put 'Mr' you don't put 'Esquire'—a man can't be both at once."

The boy regretted his too-much generosity in disposing of honors, hesitated, and with trembling fingers, scratched out the
15 "Mr." Then all at once Mr Jordan snatched away the invoice.

"Make another! Are you going to send *that* to a gentleman?" and he tore up the blue form irritably.

Paul, his ears red with shame, began again. Still Mr Jordan watched.
20 "I don't know what they *do* teach in school. You'll have to write better than that. Lads learn nothing nowadays, but how to recite poetry and play the fiddle.—Have you seen his writing?" he asked of Mr Pappleworth.

"Yes—prime, isn't it?" replied Mr Pappleworth indifferently.
25 "He'll come on all right."*

Mr Jordan gave a little grunt, not unamiable. Paul divined that his master's bark was worse than his bite. Indeed, the little manufacturer, although he spoke bad English, was quite gentleman enough to leave his men alone, and to take no notice of trifles. But he knew
30 he did not look like the boss and owner of the show, so he had to play his rôle of proprietor at first, to put things on a right footing.

"Let's see, *what's* your name?" asked Mr Pappleworth of the boy.

"Paul Morel."

It is curious that children suffer so much at having to pronounce
35 their own names.

"Paul Morel is it! All right, you Paul-Morel through them things there, and then—"

Mr Pappleworth subsided onto a stool, and began writing. A girl came up from out of a door just behind, put some newly pressed
40 elastic web appliances on the counter, and returned. Mr Papple-

worth picked up the whitey-blue knee-band, examined it and its yellow order-paper quickly, and put it on one side. Next was a flesh-pink 'leg'. He went through the few things, wrote out a couple of orders, and called to Paul to accompany him. This time they went through the door whence the girl had emerged. There Paul found himself at the top of a little wooden flight of steps, and below him saw a room with windows round two sides, and at the further end, half a dozen girls sitting bending over the benches, in the light from the window, sewing. They were singing together "Two Little Girls in Blue."* Hearing the door opened, they all turned round, to see Mr Pappleworth and Paul looking down on them from the far end of the room. They stopped singing.

"Can't you make a bit less row?" said Mr Pappleworth. "Folk'll think we keep cats."

A hunchback woman on a high stool turned her long, rather heavy face towards Mr Pappleworth and said, in a contralto voice:

"They're all tom-cats then."

In vain Mr Pappleworth tried to be impressive for Paul's benefit. He descended the steps into the finishing-off room, and went to the hunchback Fanny. She had such a short body, on her high stool, that her head, with its great bands of bright brown hair, seemed over large, as did her pale, heavy face. She wore a dress of green-black cashmere, and her wrists, coming out of the narrow cuffs, were thin and flat, as she put down her work nervously. He showed her something that was wrong with a knee-cap.

"Well," she said, "you needn't come blaming it onto me—it's not my fault." Her colour mounted to her cheek.

"I never said it *was* your fault—will you do as I tell you!" replied Mr Pappleworth shortly.

"You don't say it's my fault, but you'd like to make out as it was," the hunch-back woman cried, almost in tears. Then she snatched the knee-cap from her "boss," saying: "Yes, I'll do it for you, but you needn't be snappy."

"Here's your new lad," said Mr Pappleworth.

Fanny turned, smiling very gently on Paul.

"Oh!" she said.

"Yes—don't make a softy of him between you."

"It's not us as 'ud make a softy of him," she said indignantly.

"Come on then Paul," said Mr Pappleworth.

"*Au revoy*,* Paul," said one of the girls.

There was a titter of laughter. Paul went out, blushing deeply, not having spoken a word.

The day was very long. All morning, the work people were coming to speak to Mr Pappleworth, Paul was writing, or learning to make up parcels, ready for the mid-day post. At one o'clock, or rather at a quarter to one, Mr Pappleworth disappeared to catch his train: he lived in the suburbs. At one o'clock, Paul, feeling very lost, took his dinner basket down into the stack room in the basement, that had the long table on trestles, and ate his meal hurriedly, alone in that cellar of gloom and desolation. Then he went out of doors. The brightness and the freedom of the streets made him feel adventurous and happy. But at two o'clock he was back in the corner of the big room. Soon the work girls went trooping past, making remarks. It was the commoner girls, who worked upstairs at the heavy tasks of truss-making and the finishing of artificial limbs. He waited for Mr Pappleworth, not knowing what to do, sitting scribbling on the yellow order paper. Mr Pappleworth came at twenty minutes to three. Then he sat and gossiped with Paul, treating the boy entirely as an equal, even in age.

In the afternoon there was never very much to do, unless it were near the week end, and the accounts had to be made up. At five o'clock all the men went down into the dungeon with the table on trestles, and there they had tea, eating bread and butter on the bare, dirty boards, talking with the same kind of ugly haste and slovenliness with which they ate their meal. And yet upstairs the atmosphere among them was always jolly and clear. The cellar and the trestles affected them.

After tea, when all the gases were lighted, work* went more briskly. There was the big evening post to get off. The hose came up warm and newly pressed from the workrooms. Paul had made out the invoices. Now he had the packing up and addressing to do, then he had to weigh his stack of parcels on the scales. Everywhere voices were calling weights, there was the chink of metal, the rapid snapping of string, the hurrying to old Mr Melling for stamps. And at last the postman came with his sack, laughing and jolly. Then everything slacked off, and Paul took his dinner basket, and ran to the station to catch the eight twenty train. The day in the factory was just twelve hours long.

His mother sat waiting for him rather anxiously. He had to walk from Keston, so was not home until about twenty past nine. And he

left the house before seven in the morning. Mrs Morel was rather
anxious about his health. But she herself had had to put up with so
much, that she expected her children to take the same odds. They
must go through with what came. And Paul stayed at Jordan's,
although all the time he was there, his health suffered from the 5
darkness, and lack of air, and the long hours.

He came in pale and tired. His mother looked at him. She saw he
was rather pleased, and her anxiety all went.

"Well, and how was it?" she asked.

"Ever so funny, mother," he replied. "You don't have to work a 10
bit hard, and they're nice with you."

"And did you get on all right?"

"Yes—they only say my writing's bad. But Mr Pappleworth—he's
my man, said to Mr Jordan I should be all right. I'm Spiral, mother.
You must come and see. It's ever so nice.— —" 15

He told her everything, all he had observed, all he thought, giving
her every scrap of his experience. The only thing he hid from her
was the fact that he had put "Mr J.A.Bates Esquire." Of that he
would have been very much ashamed, if she had known. And he
never told her anything disagreeable that was said to him, only the 20
nice things, trying always to make her believe he was happy and
well-liked, and that the world went well with him—which as a rule it
did. He brought her everything, except his small shames or ignomi-
nies; he could never have borne to make her feel ashamed or
ignominious for him. 25

Soon he liked Jordan's. Mr Pappleworth, who had a certain
'saloon bar' flavour about him, was always natural, and treated him
as if he had been a comrade. Sometimes the 'Spiral boss' was
irritable, and chewed more lozenges than ever. Even then, however,
he was not offensive, but one of those people who hurt themselves 30
by their own irritability, more than they hurt other people.

"Haven't you done that *yet*?" he would cry. "Go on, be a month of
Sundays."

Again, and Paul could understand him least then, he was jocular
and in high spirits. 35

"I'm going to bring my little Yorkshire terrier bitch tomorrow,"
he said jubilantly to Paul.

"What's a Yorkshire terrier?"

"*Don't* know what a Yorkshire terrier is?—*don't know* a
Yorkshire—!" Mr Pappleworth was aghast. 40

"Is it a little silky one—colours of iron and rusty silver?"

"*That's* it my lad. She's a gem. She's had five pounds' worth of pups already, and she's worth over seven pounds herself: and she doesn't weigh twenty ounces—."

5   The next day the bitch came. She was a shivering miserable morsel. Paul did not care for her, she seemed so like a wet rag that would never dry. Then a man called for her, and began to make coarse jokes. But Mr Pappleworth nodded his head in the direction of the boy, and the talk went on sotto voce.

10   Mr Jordan only made one more excursion to watch Paul, and then the only fault he found was, seeing the boy lay his pen on the counter:

"Put your pen in your ear, if you're going to be a clerk. Pen in your ear!"

15   And one day he said to the lad:

"*Why* don't you hold your shoulders straighter? Come down here." When he took him into the glass office and fitted him with special braces for keeping the shoulders square.

But Paul liked the girls best. The men seemed common and
20   rather dull. He liked them all, but they were uninteresting. Polly, the little brisk overseer downstairs, finding Paul eating in the cellar, asked him if she could cook him anything on her little stove. Next day his mother gave him a dish that could be heated up. He took it into the pleasant, clean room, to Polly. And very soon it grew to be
25   an established custom that he should have dinner with her. When he came in at eight in the morning he took his basket to her, and when he came down at one o'clock, she had his dinner ready.

He was not very tall, and pale, with thick chestnut hair, irregular features, and a wide full mouth. She was like a small bird. He often
30   called her a 'robinet.' Though naturally rather quiet, he would sit and chatter with her for hours, telling her about his home. The girls all liked to hear him talk. They often gathered in a little circle, while he sat on a bench, and held forth to them, laughing. Some of them regarded him as a curious little creature, so serious, yet so bright and
35   jolly, and always so delicate in his way with them. They all liked him, and he adored them. Polly he felt he belonged to. Then Connie, with her mane of red hair, her face of apple-blossom, her murmuring voice, such a lady in her shabby black frock, appealed to his romantic side.
40   "When you sit winding," he said, "it looks as if you were spinning

at a spinning-wheel—it looks ever so nice. You remind me of Elaine in the *Idylls of the King.** I'd draw you if I could." And she glanced at him, blushing shyly. And later on, he had a sketch he prized very much: Connie sitting on the stool before the wheel, her flaming mane of red hair on her rusty black frock, her red mouth shut and 5 serious, running the scarlet thread off the hank onto the reel.

With Louie, handsome and brazen, who always seemed to thrust her hip at him, he usually joked.

"What are you making?"

"What do you want to know for?" she replied, putting her head up 10 mockingly.

"Because I don't believe you know yourself."

"Why not?" She found him piquant.

"Because you don't look as if you do."

"How do I look then?" 15

"You look as if you were thinking of something. What were you thinking about?"

She looked at him sideways, burst into a laugh, saying:

"You'd like to know, wouldn't you!"

"Come out," he said, "let's give your stocking a turn." 20

And he seized the handle of her machine and began to grind.

She suddenly snatched him away.

"It'll be wrong," she cried.

They looked at each other, laughing.

Emma was rather plain, rather old, and condescending. But to 25 condescend to him made her happy, and he did not mind.

"How do you put needles in?" he asked.

"Go away and don't bother."

"But I ought to know how to put needles in."

She ground at her machine all the while, steadily. 30

"There are many things you ought to know," she replied.

"Tell me then how to stick needles in the machine."

"Oh, the boy, what a nuisance he is!—Why, *this* is how you do it—"

He watched her attentively. Suddenly a whistle piped. Then Polly 35 appeared, and said in a clear voice:

"Mr Pappleworth wants to know how much longer you're going to be down here playing with the girls, Paul."

Paul flew upstairs, calling "Goodbye!", and Emma drew herself up: 40

"It wasn't *me* who wanted him to play with the machine," she said.

"What yer been doin'?" asked Mr Pappleworth, as the boy appeared.

"Just talking to Emma, and learning how to set needles."

5   "You'd better take your work an' go an' live down there."

"Well, there's nothing particular to do, is there?"

"Th' boss was looking for you a minute since. You'll catch it! And what about this ledger?"

Paul buckled to work quite cheerfully.

10   As a rule, when all the girls came back, at two o'clock, he ran upstairs* to Fanny, the hunchback, in the finishing-off room. Mr Pappleworth did not appear till twenty to three, and he often found his boy sitting beside Fanny, talking, or drawing, or singing with the girls.

15   "Come Paul, my darling," Fanny would cry. "We thought you wasn't coming today. We thought you was going to stop down there, because we wasn't good enough for you."

"I've been in the town."

"What have you been in the town for, my duck?"

20   "For a keg of cranberries for my mother."

"And did you get it?"

Then the talk had started, and it went on endlessly. He was very fond of Fanny, and the hunchback loved him. She was twenty nine years old, and had suffered too much. He loved to sit beside her

25 looking out of her window and making sketches of all the weird jungle of chimney pots and roof-ridges, ancient and peaked, that filled the prospect. Then he would say:

"Sing Fanny."

"Now look here, you don't want me to sing," she answered, as she

30 stitched rapidly and nervously with her thin hands. "You only want to make game of me."

"Why I don't! I was only telling my mother how you could sing—."

"I don't know what your mother'd think of *me*, Paul, if she saw

35 me. She'd think it was a monkey on a stick."

"She knows what you're like, because I've told her. And she likes you. Sing 'There is a Tavern—.'* This is going to be a grand sketch I'm doing."

Then, after a minute's hesitation, Fanny would begin to sing. She

40 had a fine contralto voice. Everybody joined in the chorus, and it

went well. Paul was not at all embarrassed, sitting* in the room with
the half dozen work-girls.

At the end of the song Fanny would say:

"I know you've been laughing at me."

"Don't be so soft, Fanny!" cried one of the girls. 5

Once there was mention of Connie's red hair.

"Fanny's is better, to my fancy," said Emma.

"You needn't try to make a fool of me," said Fanny, flushing
deeply.

"No but she has, Paul, she's got beautiful hair." 10

"It's a treat of a colour," said he. "That coldish colour, like earth,
and yet shiny. It's like bog-water."

"Goodness me!" exclaimed one girl, laughing.

"How I do but get criticised," said Fanny.

"But you should see it down, Paul," cried Emma earnestly. "It's 15
simply beautiful. Put it down for him, Fanny, if he wants something
to paint."

Fanny would not. And yet she wanted to.

"Then I'll take it down myself," said the lad.

"Well, you can if you like," said Fanny. 20

And he carefully took the pins out of the knot, and the rush of
hair, of uniform dark brown, slid over the humped back.

"What a lovely lot!" he exclaimed.

The girls watched. There was silence. The youth shook the hair
loose from the coil. 25

"It's splendid," he said, smelling its perfume. "I'll bet it's worth
pounds."

"I'll leave it you when I die, Paul," said Fanny, half joking.

"You look just like anybody else, sitting drying their hair," said
one of the girls to the long-legged hunch-back. 30

Poor Fanny was morbidly sensitive, always imagining insults.
Polly was curt and business like. The two departments were for ever
at war, and Paul was always finding Fanny in tears. Then he was
made the recipient of all her woes, and he had to plead her cause
with Polly. 35

Mr Jordan's daughter was a painter.* She had Connie for a model.
Connie told her about Paul, and Miss Jordan asked to see some of
his sketches. Then she came to see him. She was dry and business-
like, but she took some interest in the boy.

So the time went along happily enough. The factory had a homely 40

feel. No one was rushed or driven. Paul always enjoyed it when the work got faster, towards post-time, and all the men united in labour. He liked to watch his fellow clerks at work. The man was the work, and the work was the man, one thing, for the time being. It was
5 different with the girls. The real woman never seemed to be there at the task, but as if left out, waiting.

From the train going home at night, he used to watch the lights of the town, sprinkled thick on the hills, fusing together in a blaze in the valleys. He felt rich in life and happy. Drawing further off, there
10 was a patch of lights at Bulwell, like myriad petals shaken to the ground from the shed stars; and beyond was the red glare of the furnaces, playing like hot breath on the clouds.

He had to walk two and more miles from Keston home, up two long hills, down two short hills. He was often tired, and he counted
15 the lamps climbing the hill above him, how many more to pass. And from the hill-top, on pitch dark nights, he looked round on the villages five or six miles away, that shone like swarms of glittering living things, almost a heaven against his feet. Marlpool and Heanor scattered the far off darkness with brilliance. And occasionally, the
20 black valley space between was traced, violated by a great train rushing south to London, or north to Scotland. The trains roared by like projectiles level on the darkness, fuming and burning, making the valley clang with their passage. They were gone, and the lights of the towns and villages glittered in silence.
25 And then he came to the corner at home, which faced the other side of the night. The ash tree seemed a friend now. His mother rose with gladness as he entered. He put his eight shillings proudly on the table.

"It'll help, mother?" he asked, wistfully.
30 "There's precious little left," she answered, "after your ticket and dinners and such are taken off."

Then he told her the budget of the day. His life-story, like an *Arabian Nights,** but much duller, was told night after night to his mother. It was almost as if it were her own life.

Chapter VI

Death in the Family

Arthur Morel was growing up. He was a quick, careless, impulsive boy, a good deal like his father. He hated study, made a great moan if he had to work, and escaped as soon as possible to his sport again.   5

In appearance, he remained the flower of the family, being well made, graceful, and full of life. His dark brown hair and fresh colouring, and his exquisite dark blue eyes shaded with long lashes, together with his generous manner and fiery temper, made him a favourite. But as he grew older his temper became uncertain. He   10 flew into rages over nothing, seemed unbearably raw and irritable.

His mother, whom he loved, wearied of him sometimes. He thought only of himself. When he wanted amusement, all that stood in his way he hated, even if it were she. When he was in trouble, he moaned to her ceaselessly.   15

"Goodness boy," she said, when he groaned about a master who, he said, hated him, "if you don't like it, alter it, and if you can't alter it, put up with it."

And his father, whom he had loved and who had worshipped him, he came to detest. As he grew older, Morel fell into a slow ruin. His   20 body, which had been beautiful in movement and in being, shrank, did not seem to ripen with the years, but to get mean and rather despicable. There came over him a look of meanness, and of paltriness. And when the mean-looking elderly man bullied or ordered the boy about, Arthur was furious. Moreover, Morel's   25 manners got worse and worse, his habits somewhat disgusting. When the children were growing up, and in the crucial stage of adolescence, the father was like some ugly irritant to their souls. His manners in the house were the same as he used among the colliers down pit.   30

"Dirty nuisance!" Arthur would cry, jumping up and going straight out of the house, when his father disgusted him.

And Morel persisted the more, because his children hated it. He seemed to take a kind of satisfaction in disgusting them, and driving them nearly mad, while they were so irritably sensitive, at the age of   35 fourteen or fifteen. So that Arthur, who was growing up when his father was degenerate and elderly, hated him worst of all.

Then, sometimes, the father would seem to feel the contemptuous hatred of his children.

5 "There's not a man tries harder for his family," he would shout. "He does his best for them, and then gets treated like a dog.—But I'm not going to stand it, I tell you!"

But for the threat, and the fact that he did not try so hard as he imagined, they would have felt sorry. As it was, the battle now went 10 on nearly all between father and children, he persisting in his dirty and disgusting ways, just to assert his independence. They loathed him.

Arthur was so inflamed and irritable at last that, when he won a scholarship for the Grammar School* in Nottingham, his mother 15 decided to let him live in town, with one of her sisters, and only come home at week-ends.

Annie was still a junior teacher in the Board School, earning about four shillings a week. But soon she would have fifteen shillings, since she had passed her examination, and there would be 20 financial peace in the house.

Mrs Morel clung now to Paul. He was quiet and not brilliant. But still he stuck to his painting, and still he stuck to his mother. Everything he did, was for her. She waited for his coming home in the evening, and then she unburdened herself of all she had pon-25 dered or of all that had occurred to her during the day. He sat and listened with his earnestness. The two shared lives.

William was engaged now to his brunette, and had bought her an engagement ring that cost eight guineas. The children gasped at such a fabulous price.

30 "Eight guineas!" said Morel. "More fool him!—If he'd gen me some on't, it 'ud ha' looked better on 'im."

"Given *you* some of it," cried Mrs Morel. "Why give *you* some of it!"

She remembered he had bought no engagement ring at all, and 35 she preferred William, who was not mean, if he were foolish. But now the young man talked only of the dances to which he went with his betrothed, and the different resplendent clothes she wore; or he told his mother with glee, how they went to the theatre, like great swells.

40 He wanted to bring the girl home. Mrs Morel said she should

come at the Christmas. This time, William arrived with a lady, but with no presents. Mrs Morel had prepared supper. Hearing footsteps she rose and went to the door. William entered.

"Hello mother!"—he kissed her hastily, then stood aside, to present a tall, handsome girl, who was wearing a costume of fine 5 black-and-white check, and furs.

"Here's Gyp!"

Miss Western held out her hand and she showed her teeth in a small smile.

"Oh, how do you do, Mrs Morel!" she exclaimed. 10

"I am afraid you will be hungry," said Mrs Morel.

"Oh no, we had dinner in the train.—Have you got my gloves, Chubby?"

William Morel, big and raw-boned, looked at her quickly.

"How should I?" he said. 15

"Then I've lost them. Don't be cross with me—."

A frown went over his face, but he said nothing. She glanced round the kitchen. It was small and curious to her, with its glittering kissing-bunch, its evergreens behind the pictures, its wooden chairs and little deal table. At that moment Morel came in. 20

"Hello Dad!"

"Hello my son—tha's let on me!"*

The two shook hands, and William presented the lady. She gave the same smile that showed her teeth.

"How do you do, Mr Morel?" 25

Morel bowed obsequiously.

"I'ne very well, and I hope so are you.—You must make yourself very welcome."

"Oh thank you," she replied, rather amused.

"You will like to go upstairs," said Mrs Morel. 30

"If you don't mind—but not if it is any trouble to you."

"It is no trouble—Annie will take you.—Walter, carry up this box."

"And don't be an hour dressing yourself up," said William to his betrothed. 35

Annie took a brass candlestick, and, too shy almost to speak, preceded the young lady to the front bedroom, which Mr and Mrs Morel had vacated for her. It too was small, and cold by candlelight. The colliers' wives only lit fires in bedrooms, in case of extreme illness. 40

"Shall I unstrap the box?" asked Annie.

"Oh thank you very much!"

Annie played the part of maid, then went downstairs for hot water.

"I think she's rather tired, mother," said William. "It's a beastly
5 journey, and we had such a rush."

"Is there anything I can give her?" asked Mrs Morel.

"Oh no—she'll be all right."

But there was a chill in the atmosphere. After half an hour, Miss
Western came down, having put on a purplish coloured dress, very
10 fine for the collier's kitchen.

"I told you you'd no need to change," said William to her.

"Oh Chubby!—" then she turned with that sweetish smile to Mrs
Morel. "Don't you think he's always grumbling, Mrs Morel?"

"Is he?" said Mrs Morel. "That's not very nice of him."

15 "It isn't, really!"

"You are cold," said the mother, "won't you come near the fire."

Morel jumped out of his arm-chair.

"Come and sit you here," he cried, "come and sit you here."

"No Dad—keep your own chair—sit on the sofa, Gyp," said
20 William.

"No no!" cried Morel. "This cheer's warmest. Come and sit
here, Miss Wesson."

"Thank you *so* much," said the girl, seating herself in the collier's
arm-chair, the place of honor. She shivered, feeling the warmth of
25 the kitchen penetrate her.

"Fetch me a hanky, Chubby dear!" she said, putting up her
mouth to him, and using the same intimate tone, as if they were
alone: which made the rest of the family feel as if they ought not to
be present. The young lady evidently did not realise them as people:
30 they were creatures to her, for the present. William winced.

In such a household, in Streatham, Miss Western would have
been a lady condescending to her inferiors. These people were, to
her, certainly clownish—in short, the working classes. How was she
to adjust herself?

35 "I'll go," said Annie.

Miss Western took no notice, as if a servant had spoken. But
when the girl came downstairs again with the handkerchief, she
said:

"Oh thank you," in a gracious way.

40 She sat and talked: about the dinner on the train, which had been

so poor; about London, about dances. She was really very nervous, and chattered from fear. Morel sat all the time smoking his thick-twist tobacco, watching her, and listening to her glib London speech, as he puffed. Mrs Morel, dressed up in her best black-silk blouse, answered quietly and rather briefly. The three children sat round in silence and admiration. Miss Western was the princess. Everything of the best was got out for her: the best cups, the best spoons, the best table-cloth, the best coffee-jug. The children thought she must find it quite grand. She felt strange, not able to realise the people, not knowing how to treat them. William joked, and was slightly uncomfortable.

At about ten o'clock, he said to her:

"Aren't you tired, Gyp?"

"Rather, Chubby," she answered, at once in the intimate tones, and putting her head slightly on one side.

"I'll light her the candle, mother?" he said.

"Very well," replied the mother.

Miss Western stood up, held out her hand to Mrs Morel.

"Goodnight, Mrs Morel," she said.

Paul sat at the boiler, letting the water run from the tap into a stone beer-bottle. Annie swathed the bottle in an old flannel pit singlet, and kissed her mother goodnight. She was to share the room with the lady, because the house was full.

"You wait a minute," said Mrs Morel to Annie. And Annie sat nursing the hot water bottle. Miss Western shook hands all round, to everybody's discomfort, and took her departure, preceded by William. In five minutes he was downstairs again. His heart was rather sore, he did not know why. He talked very little till everybody had gone to bed but himself and his mother. Then he stood with his legs apart, in his old attitude on the hearth-rug, and said hesitatingly:

"Well mother?"

"Well, my son!"

She sat in the rocking-chair, feeling somehow hurt and humiliated, for his sake.

"Do you like her?"

"Yes," came the slow answer.

"She's shy yet, mother—she's not used to it. It's different from her Aunt's house, you know."

"Of course it is, my boy—and she must find it difficult."

"She does." Then he frowned swiftly. "If only she wouldn't put on her *blessed* airs!"

"It's only her first awkwardness, my boy. She'll be all right."

"That's it, mother," he replied, gratefully. But his brow was
5 gloomy. "You know she's not like you, mother—she's not serious—and she can't think."

"She's young, my boy."

"Yes!—And she's had no sort of show. Her mother died when she was a child. Since then she's lived with her aunt, whom she can't
10 bear. And her father was a rake.—She's had no love."

"No!—Well, you must make up to her."

"And so—you have to forgive her a lot of things."

"*What* do you have to forgive her, my boy?"

"I dunno—when she seems shallow, you have to remember she's
15 never had anybody to bring her deeper side out.—And she's *fearfully* fond of me."

"Anybody can see that."

"But you know mother—she's—she's different from us. Those sort of people, like those she lives amongst—they don't seem to have
20 the same principles."

"You mustn't judge too hastily," said Mrs Morel.

But he seemed uneasy within himself.

In the morning, however, he was up singing and larking round the house.

25 "Hello!" he called, sitting on the stairs. "Are you getting up?"

"Yes," her voice called, faintly.

"Merry Christmas!" he shouted to her.

Her laugh, pretty and tinkling, was heard in the bedroom. She did
30 not come down in half an hour.

"Was she *really* getting up when she said she was?" he asked of Annie.

"Yes, she was," replied Annie.

He waited awhile, then went to the stairs again.

35 "Happy New Year!" he called.

"Thank you Chubby Dear!" came the laughing voice, far away.

"Buck up!" he implored.

It was nearly an hour, and still he was waiting for her. Morel, who always rose before six, looked at the clock.

40 "Well it's a winder!" he exclaimed.

The family had breakfasted, all but William. He went to the foot of the stairs.

"Shall I have to send you an Easter Egg up there?" he called, rather crossly. She only laughed. The family expected, after that time of preparation, something like magic. At last she came, looking very nice in a blouse and skirt.

"Have you *really* been all this time getting ready?" he asked.

"Chubby dear!—That question is not permitted, is it, Mrs Morel?"

She played the grand lady at first. When she went with William to Chapel, he in his frock coat and silk hat, she in her furs and London-made costume, Paul and Arthur and Annie expected everybody to bow to the ground in admiration. And Morel, standing in his Sunday Suit at the end of the road, watching the gallant pair go, felt he was the father of princes and princesses.

And yet she was not so grand. For a year now, she had been a sort of secretary, or clerk, in a London office.

But while she was with the Morels she queened it: she sat and let Annie or Paul wait on her as if they were her servants. She treated Mrs Morel with a certain glibness, and Morel with patronage. But after a day or so, she began to change her tune.

William always wanted Paul, or Annie, to go along with them on their walks. It was so much more interesting. And Paul really *did* admire 'Gypsy,' whole heartedly. In fact, his mother scarcely forgave the boy for the adulation with which he treated the girl.

On the second day, when Lily said:

"Oh Annie, do you know where I left my muff?"

William replied:

"You know it is in your bedroom. Why do you ask Annie?"

And Lily went upstairs, with a cross, shut mouth. But it angered the young man, that she made a servant of his sister.

On the third evening, William and Lily were sitting together in the parlour, by the fire, in the dark. At a quarter to eleven, Mrs Morel was heard raking the fire. William came out to the kitchen, followed by his beloved.

"Is it as late as that, mother?" he said. She had been sitting alone.

"It is not *late*, my boy—but it is as late as I usually sit up."

"Won't you go to bed, then?" he asked.

"And leave you two?—No, my boy, I don't believe in it."

"Can't you trust us, mother?"

"Whether I can or not, I won't do it.—You can stay till eleven if you like, and I can read."

"Go to bed, Gyp," he said to his girl. "We won't keep Mater waiting."

"Annie has left the candle burning, Lily," said Mrs Morel. "I think you will see."

"Yes thank you. Goodnight, Mrs Morel."

William kissed his sweetheart at the foot of the stairs, and she went. He returned to the kitchen.

"Can't you trust us, mother?" he repeated, rather offended.

"My boy, I tell you I don't *believe* in leaving two young things like you alone downstairs, when everyone else is in bed."

And he was forced to take this answer. He kissed his mother goodnight.

At Easter, he came over alone. And then he discussed his sweetheart endlessly, with his mother.

"You know mother—when I'm away from her, I don't care for her a bit—I shouldn't care if I never saw her again.—But then when I'm with her in the evenings, I am awfully fond of her."

"It's a queer sort of love, to marry on," said Mrs Morel. "If she holds you no more than that!"

"It *is* funny!" he exclaimed. It worried and perplexed him. "But yet—there's so much between us now—I couldn't give her up."

"You know best," said Mrs Morel. "But if it is as you say, I wouldn't call it *love*—at any rate it doesn't look much like it."

"Oh I don't know, mother. She's an orphan, and—."

They never came to any sort of conclusion. He seemed puzzled, and rather fretted. She was rather reserved. All his strength and money went in keeping this girl. He could scarcely afford to take his mother to Nottingham, when he came over.

Paul's wages had been raised at Christmas to ten shillings, to his great joy. He was quite happy at Jordan's, but his health suffered from the long hours and the confinement. His mother, to whom he became more and more significant, thought how to help.

His half-day holiday was on Monday afternoon. On a Monday morning in May, as the two sat alone at breakfast, she said:

"I think it will be a fine day."

He looked up in surprise. This meant something.

"You know Mr Leivers has gone to live on a new farm. Well he asked me last week if I wouldn't go and see Mrs Leivers,* and I promised to bring you on Monday, if it's fine. Shall we go?"

"I say, little woman, how lovely!" he cried. "And we'll go this afternoon?"

"If you won't be too tired—it's a long way."   5

"How far?"

"Four miles."

"Pooh—it's not me that'll be tired with walking four miles, it's you. Can you do it?"

"Of course I can."   10

"Jolly—jolly!" he cried. "I'll make haste home. And is it pretty?"

"He says so—you must see for yourself."

"I don't know Mrs Leivers, mother—do you?"

"Why you do know her—a little pathetic woman with great brown eyes, used to sit opposite us in Chapel."   15

"I can't remember."

"I should have thought you could remember her hat, if nothing else,—for she never had a new one all the six years *I've* known her: a little black object with a scrap of lace stuck on it by accident: I'm sure, when I used to see it perched on her head, Sunday after   20 Sunday, and still it came again, I used to feel as if I could pull it off. Yet he's so smart, and a good looking man."

"She was happen poor," said Paul.

"And if she was! *I* know she was no worse off than *I* was. But she *wouldn't* have anything new, because she wouldn't."   25

"But is she nice?"

"Yes, I *always* liked her—except that she *won't* manage to make herself look decent for that man.—And it's pride that does it, nothing else."

"Why?"   30

"Well, she's a little, delicate, refined woman, with great pathetic brown eyes—rather soulful. And *I* know she's had a hard, dragging time, with seven children and Alfred Leivers' bit of money. I think *he* doesn't like hard work—though perhaps—. But so, because she's come down, and is made a veritable drudge of, she's too proud to   35 keep up appearances level with any other ordinary woman, she must go about an old fashioned object—yet she's pretty."

"Is she proud, mother?"

"Well no, not to other people. But to herself, she's as proud as they're made. Her poverty and drudging galls her soul, so she sticks   40 to that bit of a black hat, to spite her poverty—or him—Goodness knows. But *you'll* like her—and *I* like her."

"Well," said Paul, "if we go to see her in a farm, she won't have a hat on at all."

5   "Let's hope not," said Mrs Morel. "Not but what it's a scandal and a shame to put such a burden on a little body like her, but then she needn't make a fright of herself, for spite. How he must feel—!"

Paul hurried off to the station, jubilant. Down Derby Road was a cherry tree that glistened. The old brick wall by the Statutes ground
10 burned scarlet, spring was a very flame of green. And the steep swoop of highroad lay, in its cool morning dust, splendid with patterns of sunshine and shadow, perfectly still. The trees sloped their great green shoulders proudly. And inside the warehouse all morning, the boy had a vision of spring outside.

15 When he came home at dinner-time, his mother was rather excited.

"Are we going?" he asked.

"When I'm ready," she replied.

"But you've done your work?"

20 "Yes."

He sat down to dinner. She took the frying pan.

"Now what business had you to be making rhubarb fritters," he said to her, "when you've no time?"

"Because I choose to make fritters," she said. "And I shall be
25 ready as soon as you are."

She made the fritters because he was only home for dinner this one week-day, and he liked them.

"No you won't—go away and let me do them," he said.

He got up, tried to take the handle of the frying-pan from her.

30 "I shall do nothing of the sort!" she said, waving her fork. "I shall be in plenty of time."

He retired discomfited to his dinner, whilst she went on cooking.

"It's just like a woman," he said, "to go dabbling in the frying pan when she ought to be getting ready to go somewhere."

35 "And it's just like a boy, to think he knows everything," she said. She put the sweets in front of him.

"And you've burned your face like one-o'clock," he said; "and you know what a rising sun you'll look by the time you get there."

"Then I shan't ask *you* to look at me."

40 "I wouldn't if you did ask me," he said.

"Ingratitude!"

"Red-face!"

She sniffed, and drew herself up, in the way he called "turtling."

"Are you washed?" he asked.

"Yes I am."

"Well you don't look it, for you've got a smut on your nose as usual."

She went to the glass to see.

"What a nuisance!" she exclaimed.

Presently he got up.

"Go and get dressed while I wash up," he said.

She did so. He washed the pots, straightened, and then took her boots. They were quite clean. Mrs Morel was one of those naturally exquisite people who can walk in mud without dirtying their shoes. But Paul had to clean them for her. They were kid boots at eight shillings a pair. He however, thought them the most dainty boots in the world, and he cleaned them with as much reverence as if they had been flowers.

Suddenly she appeared in the inner doorway, rather shyly. She had got a new cotton blouse on. Paul jumped up and went forward.

"Oh my stars!" he exclaimed, "what a bobby-dazzler!"

She sniffed in a little, haughty way, and put her head up.

"It's not a bobby dazzler at all!" she replied. "It's very quiet."

She walked forward, whilst he hovered round her.

"Well," she asked, quite shy, but pretending to be high and mighty. "Do you like it?"

"Awfully! You *are* a fine little woman, to go jaunting out with!"

He went and surveyed her from the back.

"Well!" he said, "if I was walking down the street behind you, I should say: 'Doesn't *that* little person fancy herself.'"

"Well she doesn't," replied Mrs Morel. "She's not sure it suits her."

"Oh no!—she wants to be in dirty black, looking as if she was wrapped in burnt paper. It *does* suit you, and *I* say you look nice."

She sniffed in her little way, pleased, but pretending to know better.

"Well," she said, "it's cost me just three shillings. You couldn't have got it ready made for that price, could you?"

"I should think you couldn't," he replied.

"And you know, it's good stuff."

"Awfully pretty," he said.

The blouse was white, with a little sprig of heliotrope and black.

"Too young for me, though, I'm afraid," she said.

"Too young for you!" he exclaimed in disgust. "Why don't you
5 buy some false white hair, and stick it on your head."

"I s'll soon have no need," she replied. "I'm going white fast
enough."

"Well, you've no business to," he said. "What do I want with a
white haired mother."

10 "I'm afraid you'll have to put up with one, my lad," she said,
rather strangely.

They set off in great style, she carrying the umbrella William had
given her, because of the sun. Paul was considerably taller than she,
though he was not big. He fancied himself.

15 On the fallow land the young wheat shone silkily. Minton pit
waved its plumes of white steam, coughed and rattled hoarsely.

"Now look at that!" said Mrs Morel. Mother and son stood on the
road to watch. Along the ridge of the great pit-hill crawled a little
group in silhouette against the sky, a horse, a small truck, and a man.
20 They climbed the incline against the heavens: at the end the man
tipped the wagon; there was an undue rattle as the waste fell down
the sheer slope of the enormous bank.

"You sit a minute, mother," he said, and she took a seat on a
bank, whilst he sketched rapidly. She was silent whilst he worked,
25 looking round at the afternoon, the red cottages shining among their
greenness.

"The world is a wonderful place," she said, "and wonderfully
beautiful."

"And so's the pit," he said. "Look how it heaps together, like
30 something alive, almost—a big creature that you don't know."

"Yes," she said. "Perhaps!"

"And all the trucks standing waiting, like a string of beasts to be
fed," he said.

"And very thankful I am they *are* standing," she said, "for that
35 means they'll turn middling time this week."

"But I like the feel of *men* on things, while they're alive. There's a
feel of men about trucks, because they've been handled with men's
hands, all of them."

"Yes," said Mrs Morel.

40 They went along under the trees of the high road. He was

constantly informing her, but she was interested. They passed the end of Nethermere, that was tossing its sunshine like petals lightly in its lap. Then they turned on a private road, and in some trepidation approached a big farm. A dog barked furiously. A woman came out to see.

"Is this the way to Willey Farm?" Mrs Morel asked.

Paul hung behind, in terror of being sent back. But the woman was amiable, and directed them. The mother and son went through the wheat and oats, over a little bridge into a wild meadow. Peewits with their white breasts glistening wheeled and screamed about them. The lake was still and blue. High overhead a heron floated. Opposite, the wood heaped on the hill, green and still.

"It's a wild road, mother," said Paul. "Just like Canada."

"Isn't it beautiful!" said Mrs Morel, looking round.

"See that heron—see—see her legs?"

He directed his mother, what she must see, and what not. And she was quite content.

"But now," she said, "which way?—He told me, through the wood." The wood, fenced and dark, lay on their left.

"I can feel a bit of a path this road," said Paul. "You've got town feet, somehow or other, you have."

They found a little gate, and soon were in a broad green alley of the wood, with a new thicket of fir and pine on one hand, an old oak glade, dipping down on the other. And among the oaks the bluebells stood in pools of azure, under the new green hazels, upon a pale fawn floor of oak-leaves. He found flowers for her.

"Here's a bit of new-mown hay," he said, then again he brought her forgetmenots. And again his heart hurt with love, seeing her hand, used with work, holding the little bunch of flowers he gave her. She was perfectly happy.

But at the end of the riding was a fence to climb. Paul was over in a second.

"Come," he said, "let me help you."

"No—go away. I will do it in my own way."

He stood below, with his hands up ready to help her. She climbed cautiously.

"What a way to climb!" he exclaimed scornfully, when she was safely to earth again.

"Hateful stiles!" she cried.

"Duffer of a little woman," he replied, "who can't get over 'em."

In front, along the edge of the wood, was a cluster of low, red farm buildings. The two hastened forward. Flush with the wood was the apple-orchard, where blossom was falling on the grind stone. The pond was deep under a hedge, and overhanging oak-

5 trees. Some cows stood in the shade. The farm and buildings, three sides of a quadrangle, embraced the sunshine towards the wood. It was very still.

Mother and son went into the small railed garden, where was a scent of red gillivers. By the open door were some floury loaves, put

10 out to cool. A hen was just coming to peck them. Then, in the doorway suddenly appeared a girl in a dirty apron. She was about fourteen years old, had a rosy dark face, a bunch of short black curls, very fine and free, and dark eyes; shy, questioning, a little resentful of the strangers. She disappeared. In a minute another

15 figure appeared, a small, frail woman, rosy, with great dark brown eyes.

"Oh!" she exclaimed, smiling with a little glow, "you've come then. I *am* glad to see you." Her voice was intimate, and rather sad.

The two women shook hands.

20 "Now are you sure we're not a bother to you?" said Mrs Morel. "I know what a farming life is."

"Oh no. We're only too thankful to see a new face, it's so lost up here."

"I suppose so," said Mrs Morel.

25 They were taken through into the parlour, a long, low room, with a great bunch of guelder-roses in the fire-place. There the women talked, whilst Paul went out to survey the land. He was in the garden smelling the gillivers and looking at the plants, when the girl came out quickly to the heap of coal which stood by the fence.

30 "I suppose these are cabbage roses," he said to her, pointing to the bushes along the fence. She looked at him with startled, big brown eyes.

"I suppose they are cabbage roses, when they come out?" he said.

"I don't know," she faltered. "They're white, with pink middles."

35 "Then they're maiden-blush."

Miriam* flushed. She had a beautiful warm colouring.

"I don't know," she said.

"You don't have *much* in your garden," he said.

"This is our first year here," she answered, in a distant, rather

40 superior way, drawing away* and going indoors. He did not notice,

but went his round of exploration. Presently his mother came out, and they went through the buildings. Paul was hugely delighted.

"And I suppose you have the fowls and calves and pigs to look after?" said Mrs Morel to Mrs Leivers.

"No," replied the little woman. "I can't find time to look after cattle, and I'm not used to it. It's as much as I can do to keep going in the house."

"Well, I suppose it is," said Mrs Morel.

Presently the girl came out.

"Tea is ready, mother," she said, in a musical, quiet voice.

"Oh thank you, Miriam, then we'll come," replied her mother, almost ingratiatingly. "Would you *care* to have tea now, Mrs Morel?"

"Of course," said Mrs Morel. "Whenever it's ready."

Paul and his mother and Mrs Leivers had tea together. Then they went out into the wood, that was flooded with bluebells, while fumy forgetmenots were in the paths. The mother and son were in ecstasy together.

When they got back to the house, Mr Leivers and Edgar, the eldest son, were in the kitchen. Edgar was about eighteen. Then Geoffrey and Maurice,* big lads of twelve and thirteen were in from school. Mr Leivers was a good-looking man in the prime of life, with a golden-brown moustache and blue eyes screwed up against the weather.

"Have you had a look round?" he asked of Paul, heartily.

"Not everywhere," the boy replied.

Then he went out with Geoffrey and Maurice.

"Where do *you* work?" asked Geoffrey of Paul. They were all three shy.

"In Jordan's Surgical Appliance Factory in Nottingham."

"And what do you do there?"

"I'm a clerk."

"And what do you do?"

"I copy the letters, and make orders, and make out invoices."

"What sort of letters do you copy?"

"Oh—any sort—mostly orders for elastic stockings."

"Elastic stockings!—what's them?"

There followed many explanations.

"And some of the letters are from France, and other places," said Paul.

"And do you copy them?"

"Yes."

"In French?"

"No—translate them."

"Why, do you reckon *you* know French?"

5   "I know some—and German as well."

"Why who learnt you that?"

"My Godfather—and algebra and Euclid."

"I don't want *my* 'ead full of that stuff," said Geoffrey.

The boys were amazingly superior. But* Paul scarcely observed it.

10 They went round for eggs, scrambling into all sorts of places. As
they were feeding the fowls, Miriam came out. The boys took no
notice of her. One hen with her yellow chickens was in a coop.
Maurice took his hand full of corn and let the hen peck from it.

"Durst you do it?" he asked of Paul.

15   "Let's see," said Paul.

He had a small hand, warm, and rather capable-looking. Miriam
watched. He held the corn to the hen. The bird eyed it with her hard
bright eye, and suddenly made a peck into his hand. He started, and
laughed. 'Rap-rap-rap!' went the bird's beak in his palm. He

20 laughed again, and the other boys joined.

"She knocks you, and nips you, but she never hurts," said Paul,
when the last corn had gone.

"Now Miriam," said Maurice, "you come an' 'ave a go."

"No," she cried, shrinking back.

25   "Ha! Baby. The mardy-kid!" said her brothers.

"It doesn't hurt a bit," said Paul. "It only just nips rather nicely."

"No," she still cried, shaking her black curls and shrinking.

"She dursn't," said Geoffrey. "She niver durst do anything
except recite poitry."

30   "Dursn't jump off a gate—dursn't tweedle—dursn't go on a
slide—dursn't stop a girl hittin' her—she can do nowt but go about
thinkin' herself somebody—'The Lady of the Lake'*—yah!" cried
Maurice.

Miriam was crimson with shame and misery.

35   "I dare do more than you," she cried. "You're never anything but
cowards and bullies."

"Oh 'cowards and bullies!'" they repeated, mincingly mocking
her speech.

        "'Not such a clown shall anger me
40   A boor is answered silently'"*

he quoted against her, shouting with laughter.

She went indoors. Paul went with the boys into the orchard, where they had rigged up a parallel bar. They did feats of strength. He was more agile than strong, but it served. He fingered a piece of apple-blossom, that hung low on a swinging bough.

"I wouldn't get the apple-blossom," said Edgar, the eldest brother. "There'll be no apples next year."

"I wasn't going to get it," replied Paul, going away.

The boys felt hostile to him. They were more interested in their own pursuits. He wandered back to the house to look for his mother. As he went round the back, he saw Miriam kneeling in front of the hen coop, some maize in her hand, biting her lip, and crouching in an intense attitude. The hen was eyeing her wickedly. Very gingerly she put forward her hand. The hen bobbed for her. She drew back quickly with a cry, half of fear, half of chagrin.

"It won't hurt you," said Paul.

She flushed crimson and started up.

"I only wanted to try," she said, in a low voice.

"See, it doesn't hurt," he said, and, putting only two corns in his palm, he let the hen peck, peck, peck at his bare hand. "It only makes you laugh," he said.

She put her hand forward, and dragged it away, tried again, and started back with a cry. He frowned.

"Why I'd let her take corn from my face," said Paul, "only she bumps a bit. She's ever so neat. If she wasn't, look how much ground she'd peck up every day."

He waited grimly, and watched. At last Miriam let the bird peck from her hand. She gave a little cry, fear, and pain because of fear, rather pathetic. But she had done it, and she did it again.

"There you see," said the boy. "It doesn't hurt, does it."

She looked at him with dilated dark eyes.

"No," she laughed, trembling.

Then she rose and went indoors. She seemed to be in some way resentful of the boy.

"He thinks I'm only a common girl," she thought, and she wanted to prove she was a grand person like the 'Lady of the Lake.'

Paul found his mother ready to go home. She smiled on her son. He took the great bunch of flowers. Mr and Mrs Leivers walked down the fields with them. The hills were golden with evening: deep in the wood showed the darkening purple of bluebells: it was everywhere perfectly still, save for the rustling of leaves and birds.

"But it is a beautiful place," said Mrs Morel.

"Yes," answered Mr Leivers. "It's a nice little place, if only it weren't for the rabbits. The pasture's bitten down to nothing. I dunno if ever I s'll get the rent off it."

He clapped his hands, and the field broke into motion, near the woods, brown rabbits hopping everywhere.

"Would you believe it!" exclaimed Mrs Morel.

She and Paul went on alone together.

"Wasn't it lovely, mother?" he said, quietly. A thin moon was coming out. His heart was full of happiness till it hurt. His mother had to chatter, because she too wanted to cry with happiness.

"Now *wouldn't* I help that man!" she said. "*Wouldn't* I see to the fowls and the young stock. And *I'd* learn to milk, and *I'd* talk with him, and *I'd* plan with him. My word, if I were his wife, the farm would be run, I know.—But there, she hasn't the strength—she simply hasn't the strength. She ought never to have been burdened like it, you know. I'm sorry for her, and I'm sorry for him too. My word if *I'd* had him, I shouldn't have thought him a bad husband.—Not that she does either.—And she's very lovable."

William came home again with his sweetheart at the Whitsuntide. He had one of his week's holidays then. It was beautiful weather. As a rule, William and Lily and Paul went out in the morning together, for a walk. William did not talk to his beloved much, except to tell her things from his boyhood. Paul talked endlessly to both of them. They lay down, all three, in a meadow by Minton Church. On one side, by the Castle farm, was a beautiful quivering screen of poplars. Hawthorn was dropping from the hedges: penny daisies and ragged robin were in the field, like laughter. William, a big fellow of twenty three, thinner now and even a bit gaunt, lay back in the sunshine and dreamed, while she fingered with his hair. Paul went gathering the big daisies. She had taken off her hat. Her hair was black as a horse's mane. Paul came back and threaded daisies in her jet black hair, big spangles of white and yellow, and just a pink touch of ragged robbin.

"Now you look like a young witch-woman," the boy said to her. "Doesn't she William?"

Lily laughed. William opened his eyes and looked at her. In his gaze was a certain baffled look of misery and fierce appreciation.

"Has he made a sight of me?" she asked, laughing down on her lover.

"That he has!" said William, smiling. And as he lay he continued to look at her. His eyes never sought hers. He did not want to meet her eyes. He only wanted to look at her, not to come together with

her in her gaze. And the fact that he wanted to avoid her was in his
eyes like misery. He turned away again. She let her slim dark hand,
whereon the diamonds sparkled, stray in his hair a moment longer.
Then she said:

"Paul knows how to do things." 5

"All right," said he. "So long as he makes you happy. He'll do for
mornings, and I for evenings."

She turned laughing to the boy.

"I want to put three more over your ear," he said, standing above
her. "Then you'll be finished." 10

She submitted. He threaded in the daisies.

"Can't you smell the sun on your hair?" he said. "Now, that's how
you ought to go to a ball."

"Thank you," she laughed.

Presently they rose to go. 15

"Don't wear a hat yet," said Paul.

"Shall I?" she asked of William. "May I go like this."

William looked at her again. Her beauty seemed to hurt him. He
glanced at her flower-decked head and frowned.

"You look nice enough, if that's what you want to know," he said. 20

And she walked without her hat. In a little while, William recovered, and was rather tender to her. Coming to a bridge, he carved
her initials, and his, in a heart.

25

She watched his strong, nervous hand, with its glistening hairs
and freckles, as he carved, and she seemed fascinated by it.

All the time, there was a feeling of sadness, and warmth, and a
certain tenderness in the house, whilst William and Lily were at
home. But often he got irritable. She had brought, for an eight days' 30
stay, five dresses and six blouses.

"Oh would you mind," she said to Annie, "washing me these two
blouses—and these things."

And Annie stood washing when William and Lily went out, the
next morning. Mrs Morel was furious. And sometimes the young 35
man, catching a glimpse of his sweetheart's attitude towards his
sister, hated her.

On Sunday morning she looked very beautiful, in a dress of

foulard,* silky and sweeping, and blue as a jay-bird's feather, and in a large cream hat covered with many roses, mostly crimson. Nobody could admire her enough. But in the evening, when she was going out, she asked again:

5 "Chubby, have you got my gloves?"

"Which?" asked William.

"My new black suède?"

"No."

There was a hunt. She had lost them.

10 "Look here, mother," said William. "That's the fourth pair she's lost since Christmas—at five shillings a pair."

"You only gave me *two* of them," she remonstrated.

And in the evening, after supper, he stood on the hearth-rug, whilst she sat on the sofa, and he seemed to hate her. In the
15 afternoon he had left her, whilst he went to see some old friend. She had sat looking at a book. After supper, William wanted to write a letter.

"Here is your book, Lily," said Mrs Morel. "Would you care to go on with it for a few minutes?"

20 "No thank you," said the girl. "I will sit still."

"But it is so dull—"

William scribbled irritably at a great rate. As he sealed the envelope, he said:

"Read a book!—Why she's never read a book in her life."

25 "Oh go along!" said Mrs Morel, cross with the exaggeration.

"It's true mother—she hasn't," he cried, jumping up and taking his old position on the hearthrug. "She's never read a book in her life."

"'Er's like me," chimed in Morel. "'Er canna see what there is i'
30 books, ter sit borin' your nose in 'em for, nor more can I!"

"But you shouldn't say these things," said Mrs Morel to her son.

"But it's true mother—she *can't* read—what did you give her?"

"Well I gave her a little thing of Annie Swan's.* Nobody wants to read dry stuff on Sunday afternoon."

35 "Well I'll bet she didn't read ten lines of it."

"You are mistaken," said his mother.

All the time, Lily sat miserably on the sofa. He turned to her swiftly.

"*Did* you read any?" he asked.

40 "Yes, I did," she replied.

"How much?"

"I don't know how many pages—"

"Tell me *one thing* you read."

She could not.

"Be quiet, William," said his mother. "The very idea!"

"But she can't mother!" he cried, bitterly. "She can't take it in, when she reads. She can't read, and she can't talk. There's not a thing you can talk to her about. She only thinks in frocks and how folk admire her."

"Take no notice of him, Lily," said Mrs Morel.

"It's only fools as sits wi' their noses stuck i' books, that's what *I* say," added Morel.

And the poor girl remained in ignominy. He seemed to hate her. Later Mrs Morel found her a very simple book, and it was pathetic to see her, on a wet afternoon, wading in misery through a few lines. She never got beyond the second page. He read a great deal, and had a quick, active intelligence. She could understand nothing but love making and chatter. He was accustomed to having all his thoughts sifted through his mother's mind. So, when he wanted companionship, and was asked in reply to be the billing and twittering lover, he hated his betrothed.

"You know, mother," he said, when he was alone with her at night, "she's no idea of money, she's so wessel-brained.* When she's paid, she'll suddenly buy such rot as *marrons glacés.** And then *I* have to buy her season-ticket, and her extras, even her underclothing. And she wants to get married—And I think myself we might as well get married next year. But at this rate—!"

"A fine mess of a marriage it would be," replied his mother. "I should consider it again, my boy."

"Oh well—I've gone too far to break off now," he said. "And so I shall get married as soon as I can."

"Very well, my boy. If you will you will, and there's no stopping you.—But I tell you, *I* can't sleep when I think about it."

"Oh, she'll be all right, mother. We shall manage."

"And she lets you buy her underclothing?" asked the mother.

"Well," he began, apologetically. "She didn't ask me. But one morning—and it *was* cold—I found her on the station, shivering, not able to keep still. So I asked her if she was well wrapped up. She said, 'I think so.' So I said 'Have you got warm underthings on?' And she said, no, they were cotton. I asked her why on earth she hadn't

got something thicker on, in weather like that, and she said, because she *had* nothing. And there she is a bronchial subject!—I *had* to take her and get some warm things.—Well mother, I shouldn't mind the money, if we had any.—And you know, she *ought* to keep enough to
5 pay for her season ticket. But no—she comes to me about that, and I have to find the money—"

"It's a poor look-out," said Mrs Morel bitterly.

He was pale, and his rugged face, that used to be so perfectly careless and laughing, was stamped with conflict and despair.

10 "But I can't give her up, now, it's gone too far," he said. "And besides, for *some* things, I couldn't do without her—."

"My boy, remember you're taking your life in your hands," said Mrs Morel. "*Nothing* is as bad as a marriage that's a hopeless failure. Mine was bad enough, God knows, and ought to teach you
15 something.—But it might have been worse by a long chalk."

He leaned with his back against the side of the chimney piece, his hands in his pockets. He was a big, raw-boned man, who looked as if he would go to the world's end, if he wanted to. But she saw the despair on his face.

20 "I couldn't give her up now," he said.

"Well," she said. "Remember there are worse wrongs than breaking off an engagement."

They remained in silence, he staring across the room. Only his mother could help him now. And yet, he would not let her decide for
25 him. He stuck to what he had done.

"And of course," added Mrs Morel, "there's a great deal more nobility in breaking off in order to avoid doing more wrong, than in keeping on because you've said you would."

He was stock still, staring across the room.

30 "I can't give her up *now*," he said.

The clock ticked on. Mother and son remained in silence, a conflict between them. But he would say no more. At last she said:

"Well, go to bed, my son—you'll feel better in the morning—and perhaps you'll know better."

35 He kissed her, and went. She raked the fire. Her heart was heavy now as it had never been. Before, with her husband, things had seemed to be breaking down in her, but they did not destroy her power to live. Now, her soul felt lamed in itself. It was her hope that was struck.

40 And so often, William manifested the same hatred towards his

betrothed. On the last evening at home, he was railing against her.

"Well," he said, "if you don't believe me, what she's like, would you believe she has been confirmed* three times!"

"Nonsense," laughed Mrs Morel.

"Nonsense or not, she *has*! That's what confirmation means for her—a bit of a theatrical show where she can cut a figure."

"I haven't, Mrs Morel," cried the girl. "I haven't. It is not true."

"What!" he cried, flashing round on her. "Once in Bromley, once in Beckenham, and once somewhere else."

"Nowhere else!" she said, in tears. "Nowhere else."

"It *was*! And if it wasn't, why were you confirmed *twice*?"

"Once I was only fourteen, Mrs Morel," she pleaded, tears in her eyes.

"Yes," said Mrs Morel. "I can quite understand it, child. Take no notice of him. You ought to be ashamed, William, saying such things."

"But it's true. She's religious—she has blue velvet prayerbooks—and she's not as much religion, or anything else, in her than that table leg. Gets confirmed three times, for show, to show herself off. And that's how she is in *everything, everything*!"

The girl sat on the sofa, crying. She was not strong.*

"As for *love*!" he cried. "You might as well ask a fly to love you. It'll love settling on you—"

"Now say no more," commanded Mrs Morel. "If you want to say these things, you must find another place than this. I am ashamed of you, William. Why don't you be more manly. To do nothing but find fault with a girl—and then pretend you're engaged to her—!" Mrs Morel subsided in wrath and indignation.

William was silent. And later he repented, kissed and comforted the girl. Yet it was true, what he had said. He hated her.*

When they were going away, Mrs Morel accompanied them as far as Nottingham. It was a long way to Keston station.

"You know mother," he said to her, "Gyp's shallow—nothing goes deep with her."

"William I *wish* you wouldn't say these things," said Mrs Morel, very uncomfortable for the girl who walked beside her.

"But it doesn't mother.—She's very much in love with me *now*.—But if I died, she'd have forgotten me in three months."

Mrs Morel was afraid. Her heart beat furiously, hearing the quiet bitterness of her son's last speech.

"How do you know!" she replied. "You *don't* know—and therefore you've no right to say such a thing."

"He's always saying these things!" cried the girl.

"In three months after I was buried, you'd have somebody else,
5 and I should be forgotten," he said. "And that's your love!"

Mrs Morel saw them into the train in Nottingham, then she returned home.

"You know," she said pathetically to Paul, "it's no good, and it never will be any good. What it will be like if ever they *do* marry, is
10 too much for me to think of. If *only* he'd let her go, he wouldn't torment her half so much, I'm sure. But they'll hang on to each other till they kill each other. And I felt, when he said *that*, going to Keston, as if I couldn't walk another stride. Poor thing, I'm sorry for her. But she's not fit for him, she isn't. I'm sure, it seems a wicked thing to say,
15 but she's delicate, and I'd rather she died than he married her."

All summer long Mrs Morel thought about her son. He seemed now to be making a ruin of his life. But still the marriage was a long way off.

"There's one comfort," she said to Paul, "he'll never have any
20 money to marry on, that I *am* sure of. And so she'll save him that way."

So she took cheer. Matters were not yet very desperate. She firmly believed William would never marry his Gipsy. She waited, and she kept Paul near to her.

All summer long William's letters had a feverish tone. He seemed
25 unnatural and intense. Sometimes he was exaggeratedly jolly, usually he was flat and bitter in his letter.

"Ay," his mother said, "I'm afraid he's ruining himself against that creature, who isn't worthy of his love, no, no more than a rag doll."

30 He wanted to come home. The midsummer holiday was gone. It was a long while to Christmas. He wrote in wild excitement saying he could come for Saturday and Sunday at Goose Fair,* the first week in October.

"You are not well, my boy," said his mother when she saw him.
35 She was almost in tears at having him to herself again.

"No, I've not been well," he said, "I've seemed to have a dragging cold all the last month. But it's going, I think."

It was sunny October weather. He seemed wild with joy like a schoolboy escaped. Then again he was silent, and reserved. He was
40 more gaunt than ever, and there was a haggard look in his eyes.

"You are doing too much," said his mother to him.

He was doing extra work, trying to make some money to marry on, he said. He only talked to his mother once, on the Saturday night. Then he was sad and tender about his beloved.

"And yet, you know mother, for all that, if I died she'd be broken-hearted for two months, and then she'd start to forget me. You'd see, she'd never come home here to look at my grave, not even once."

"Why William," said his mother, "you're not going to die, so why talk about it."

"But whether or not—" he replied.

"And she can't help it—she is like that—and if you choose her, well, you can't grumble," said his mother.

On the Sunday morning, as he was putting his collar on:

"Look," he said to his mother, holding up his chin, "what a rash my collar's made under my chin!"

Just at the junction of chin and throat was a big red inflammation.

"It ought not to do that," said his mother. "Here, put a bit of this soothing ointment on. You should wear different collars."

He went away on Sunday midnight, seeming better and more solid for his two days at home.

On Tuesday morning came a telegram from London, that he was ill. Mrs Morel got off her knees from washing the floor, read the telegram, called a neighbour, went to her landlady and borrowed a sovereign, put on her things and set off. She hurried to Keston, caught an express for London in Nottingham. She had to wait in Nottingham nearly an hour. A small figure in her black bonnet, she was anxiously asking the porters, if they knew how to get to Elmers End. The journey was three hours. She sat in her corner in a kind of stupor, never moving. At King's Cross still no one could tell her how to get to Elmers End.—Carrying her string bag, that contained her nightdress, comb and brush, she went from person to person. At last they sent her underground to Cannon Street.

It was six o'clock when she arrived at William's lodging. The blinds were not down.

"How is he?" she asked.

"No better," said the landlady.

She followed the woman upstairs. William lay on the bed, with blood-shot eyes, his face rather discoloured. The clothes were tossed about, there was no fire in the room, a glass of milk stood on the stand at his bedside. No one had been with him.

"Why, my son!" said the mother bravely.

He did not answer. He looked at her, but did not see her.

Then he began to say, in a dull voice, as if repeating a letter from dictation: "Owing to a leakage in the hold of the vessel, the sugar
5 had set, and become converted into rock. It needed hacking—"

He was quite unconscious. It had been his business to examine some such cargo of sugar in the Port of London.

"How long has he been like this?" the mother asked the landlady.

10 "He got home at six o'clock on Monday morning, and he seemed to sleep all day. Then in the night we heard him talking, and this morning he asked for you. So I wired, and we fetched the doctor."

"Will you have a fire made?"

Mrs Morel tried to soothe her son, to keep him still.

15 The doctor came. It was pneumonia, and, he said, a peculiar erysipelas,* which had started under the chin where the collar chafed, and was spreading over the face. He hoped it would not get to the brain.

Mrs Morel settled down to nurse. She prayed for William,
20 prayed that he would recognise her. But the young man's face grew more discoloured. In the night she struggled with him. He raved, and raved, and would not come to consciousness. At two o'clock, in a dreadful paroxysm, he died.

Mrs Morel sat perfectly still for an hour, in the lodging bedroom.
25 Then she roused the house-hold.

At six o'clock, with the aid of the char-woman, she laid him out. Then she went round the dreary London village, to the registrar and the doctor.

At nine o'clock, to the cottage on Scargill Street, another wire.
30 "William died last night. Let father come—bring money."

Annie, Paul, and Arthur were at home. Mr Morel was gone to work. The three children said not a word. Annie began to whimper with fear. Paul set off for his father.

It was a beautiful day. At Bretty pit the white steam melted slowly
35 in the sunshine of a soft blue sky, the wheels of the headstocks twinkled high up, the screen, shuffling its coal into the trucks, made a busy noise.

"I want my father—he's got to go to London," said the boy to the first man he met on the bank.

40 "Tha wants Walter Morel?—Go in theer an' tell Joe Ward."

Paul went into the little top office.

"I want my father—he's got to go to London."

"Thy feyther—is he down—what's his name?"

"Mr Morel."

"What, Walter? Is owt amiss?" 5

"He's got to go to London."

The man went to the telephone and rang up the bottom office.

"Walter Morel's wanted—Number 42 Hard.* Summat's amiss—there's his lad here."

Then he turned round to Paul. 10

"He'll be up in a few minutes," he said.

Paul wandered out to the pit top. He watched the chair come up, with its wagon of coal. The great iron cage sank back on its rests, a full carfle was hauled off, an empty tram run onto the chair, a bell 'ting-ed' somewhere, the chair heaved, then dropped like a stone. 15

Paul did not realise William was dead—it was impossible, with such a bustle going on. The puller-off swung the small truck onto the turn-table, another man ran with it along the bank, down the curving lines. "And William is dead, and my mother's in London, and what will she be doing?" The boy asked himself, as if it were a 20 conundrum.

He watched chair after chair come up, and still no father. At last, standing beside a wagon, a man's form! The chair sank on its rests, Morel stepped off. He was slightly lame from an accident.

"Is it thee Paul!—is 'e worse?" 25

"You've got to go to London."

The two walked off the pit bank, where men were watching curiously. As they came out, and went along the railway, with the sunny autumn field on one side, and a wall of trucks on the other, Morel said, in a frightened voice: 30

"'E's niver gone, child?"

"Yes."

"When wor't?"

The miner's voice was terrified.

"Last night—we had a telegram from my mother." 35

Morel walked on a few strides, then leaned up against a truck side, his hand over his eyes. He was not crying. Paul stood looking round, waiting. On the weighing machine a truck trundled slowly. Paul saw everything, except his father leaning against the truck as if he were tired. 40

Morel had only once before been to London. He set off, scared and peaked, to help his wife. That was on Tuesday. The children were left alone in the house. Paul went to work, Arthur went to school, and Annie had in a friend to be with her.

On Saturday night, as Paul was turning the corner, coming home from Keston, he saw his mother and father, who had come to Lethley Bridge station. They were walking in silence in the dark, tired, straggling apart. The boy waited.

"Mother!" he said, in the darkness.

Mrs Morel's small figure seemed not to observe. He spoke again.

"Paul!" she said, uninterestedly. She let him kiss her, but she seemed unaware of him.

In the house she was the same, small, white, and mute. She noticed nothing, she said nothing, only:

"The coffin will be here tonight, Walter. You'd better see about some help." Then, turning to the children: "We're bringing him home."

Then she relapsed into the same mute looking into space, her hands folded on her lap. Paul, looking at her, felt he could not breathe. The house was dead silent.

"I went to work, mother," he said, plaintively.

"Did you," she answered, dully.

After half an hour, Morel, troubled and bewildered, came in again.

"Wheer s'll we ha'e him when he *does* come?" he asked his wife.

"In the front room."

"Then I'd better shift th'table?"

"Yes."

"An' ha'e him across th' chairs?"

"You know there—yes—I suppose so."

Morel and Paul went, with a candle, into the parlour. There was no gas there. The father unscrewed the top of the big, mahogany, oval table, and cleared the middle of the room. Then he arranged six chairs opposite each other, so that the coffin could stand on their beds.

"You niver seed such a length as he is!" said the miner, watching anxiously as he worked.

Paul went to the bay window and looked out. The ash-tree stood monstrous and black, in front of the wide darkness. It was a faintly luminous night. Paul went back to his mother.

At ten o'clock, Morel called:

"He's here!"

Everyone started. There was a noise of unbarring and unlocking the front door, which opened straight from the night into the room.

"Bring another candle," called Morel. 5

Annie and Arthur went. Paul followed with his mother. He stood with his arm round her waist, in the inner doorway. Down the middle of the cleared room waited six chairs, face to face. In the window, against the lace curtains, Arthur held up one candle—and by the open door, against the night, Annie stood leaning forward, her brass 10 candlestick glittering.

There was the noise of wheels. Outside in the darkness of the street below, Paul could see horses and a black vehicle, one lamp, and a few pale faces. Then some men, miners, all in their shirt sleeves, seemed to struggle in the obscurity. Presently, two men 15 appeared, bowed beneath a great weight. It was Morel and his neighbour.

"Steady!" called Morel, out of breath.

He and his fellow mounted the steep garden step, heaved into the candle light with their gleaming coffin-end. Limbs of other men 20 were seen struggling behind. Morel and Burns, in front, staggered. The great, dark weight swayed.

"Steady, steady!" cried Morel, as if in pain.

All the six bearers were up in the small garden, holding the great coffin aloft. There were three more steps to the door. The yellow 25 lamp of the carriage shone alone down in the black road.

"Now then!" said Morel.

The coffin swayed, the men began to mount the three steps with their load. Annie's candle flickered, and she whimpered as the first men appeared, and the limbs and bowed heads of six men struggled 30 to climb into the room, bearing the coffin that rode like sorrow on their living flesh.

"Oh my son—my son!"* Mrs Morel sang softly. And each time the coffin swung to the unequal climbing of the men:

"Oh my son—my son—my son!" 35

"Mother!" Paul whimpered, his hand round her waist. "Mother!"

She did not hear.

"Oh my son, my son!" she repeated.

Paul saw drops of sweat fall from his father's brow. Six men were in the room, six coatless men with yielding, struggling limbs filling 40

the room and knocking against the furniture. The coffin veered, and
was gently lowered onto the chairs. The sweat fell from Morel's face
on its boards.

"My word, he's a weight!" said a man, and the five miners sighed,
5   bowed, and trembling with the struggle, descended the steps again,
closing the door behind them.

The family was alone in the parlour, with the great polished box,
William, when laid out, was six feet four inches long. Like a
monument lay the bright brown, ponderous coffin. Paul thought it
10   would never be got out of the room again. His mother was stroking
the polished wood.

They buried him, on the Monday,* in the little cemetery on the
hillside, that looks over the fields at the big church and the houses. It
was sunny, and the white chrysanthemums frilled themselves in the
15   warmth.

Mrs Morel could not be persuaded, after this, to talk and take her
old bright interest in life. She remained shut off. All the way home,
in the train, she had said to herself: "If only it could have been
me."

20   When Paul came home at night, he found his mother sitting, her
day's work done, with hands folded in her lap, upon her coarse
apron. She always used to have changed her dress, and put on a
black apron, before. Now Annie set his supper, and his mother sat
looking blankly in front of her, her mouth shut tight. Then he beat
25   his brains for news to tell her.

"Mother, Miss Jordan was down today, and she said my sketch of
a colliery at work was beautiful—"

But Mrs Morel took no notice. Night after night he forced himself
to tell her things, although she did not listen. It drove him almost
30   insane to have her thus. At last:

"What's a-matter, mother?" he asked. She did not hear.

"What's a-matter?" he persisted. "Mother, what's a-matter?"

"You know what's the matter," she said, irritably, turning away.

The lad—he was sixteen years old, went to bed drearily. He was cut
35   off and wretched through October, November, and December. His
mother tried, but she could not rouse herself. She could only brood
on her dead son. He had been let to die so cruelly.

At last, on the 23rd of December, with his five shillings Christmas
box in his pocket, Paul wandered blindly home. His mother looked
40   at him, and her heart stood still.

"What's the matter?" she asked.

"I'm badly, mother!" he replied. "Mr Jordan gave me five shillings for a Christmas box."

He handed it to her with trembling hands. She put it on the table.

"You aren't glad," he reproached her.

But he trembled violently.

"Where hurts you?" she said, unbuttoning his overcoat.

It was the old question.

"I feel badly, mother."

She undressed him and put him to bed. He had pneumonia, dangerously, the doctor said.

"Might he never have had it if I'd kept him at home, not let him go to Nottingham?" was one of the first things she asked.

"He might not have been so bad," said the doctor.

Mrs Morel stood condemned on her own ground.

"I should have watched the living, not the dead," she told herself.

Paul was very ill. His mother lay in bed at nights with him. They could not afford a nurse. He grew worse, and the crisis approached. One night he tossed into consciousness, in the ghastly, sickly feeling of dissolution, when all the cells in the body seem in intense irritability to be breaking down, and consciousness makes a last flare of struggle, like madness.

"I s'll die, mother!" he cried, heaving for breath on the pillow.

She lifted him up, crying in a small voice:

"Oh, my son, my son!"

That brought him to. He realised her. His whole will rose up and arrested him. He put his head on her breast, and took ease of her, for love.

"For some things," said his aunt, "it was a good thing Paul was ill that Christmas. I believe it saved his mother."

Paul was in bed for seven weeks. He got up white and fragile. His father had bought him a pot of scarlet and gold tulips. They used to flame in the window, in the March sunshine, as he sat on the sofa chattering to his mother. The two knitted together in perfect intimacy. Mrs Morel's life now rooted itself in Paul.

William had been a prophet. Mrs Morel had a little present and a letter from Lily at Christmas. Mrs Morel's sister had a letter at the New Year.

"I was at a ball last night. Some delightful people were there and I enjoyed myself thoroughly," said the letter. "I had every dance— did not sit out one—"*

Mrs Morel never heard any more of her.

5   Morel and his wife were gentle with each other for some time after the death of their son. He would go into a kind of daze, staring wide-eyed and blank across the room. Then he got up suddenly and hurried out to the "Three Spots," returning in his normal state. But never in his life would he go for a walk up
10   Shepstone, past the office where his son had worked, and he always avoided the cemetery.*

PART II

Chapter VII

Lad-and-Girl Love*

Paul had been many times up to Willey Farm, during the Autumn. He was friends with the two younger* boys. Edgar, the eldest, would not condescend at first. And Miriam also refused to be approached. She was afraid of being set at nought, as by her own brothers. The girl was romantic in her soul. Everywhere was a Walter Scott heroine being loved by men with helmets or with plumes in their caps. She herself was something of a princess turned into a swine girl,* in her own imagination. And she was afraid lest this boy, who nevertheless looked something like a Walter Scott hero, who could paint and speak French and knew what algebra meant, and who went by train to Nottingham every day, might consider her simply as the swine girl, unable to perceive the princess beneath, so she held aloof.

Her great companion was her mother. They were both brown-eyed and inclined to be mystical, such women as treasure religion inside them, breathe it in their nostrils, and see the whole of life in a mist thereof. So, to Miriam Christ and God made one great figure, which she loved tremblingly and passionately when a tremendous sunset burned out the western sky; and Ediths and Lucys and Rowenas, Brian de Bois Guilberts, Rob Roys and Guy Mannerings* rustled the sunny leaves in the morning, or sat in her bedroom, aloft, alone, when it snowed. That was life to her. For the rest, she drudged in the house, which work she would not have minded had not her clean red floor been mucked-up immediately by the trampling farm-boots of her brothers; she madly wanted her little brother of four to let her swathe him and stifle him in her love; she went to church, reverently, with bowed head, and quivered in anguish from the vulgarity of the other choir-girls, and from the common-sounding voice of the curate;* she fought with her brothers, whom she considered brutal louts; and she held not her father in too high

173

esteem, because he did not carry any mystical ideals cherished in his heart, but only wanted to have as easy a time as he could, and his meals when he was ready for them.

She hated her position as swine-girl. She wanted to be considered. She wanted to learn, thinking that if she could read, as Paul said he could read, 'Colomba' or the *Voyage Autour de ma Chambre,** the world would have a different face for her, and a deepened respect. She could not be princess by wealth or standing. So, she was mad to have learning whereon to pride herself. For she was different from other folk, and must not be scooped up among the common fry. Learning was the only distinction to which she thought to aspire.

Her beauty, that of a shy, wild, quiveringly sensitive thing, seemed nothing to her. Even her soul, so strong for rhapsody,* was not enough. She must have something to reinforce her pride, because she felt different from other people. Paul she eyed rather wistfully. On the whole she scorned the male sex. But here was a new specimen, quick, light, graceful, who could be gentle and who could be sad, and who was clever and who knew a lot, and who had a death in the family. The boy's poor morsel of learning exalted him almost sky-high in her esteem. Yet she tried hard to scorn him, because he would not see in her the princess, but only the swinegirl.

And he scarcely observed her.

Then he was so ill, and she felt he would be weak. Then she would be stronger than he. Then she could love him. If she could be mistress of him in his weakness, take care of him, if he could depend on her, if she could, as it were, have him in her arms, how she would love him!

As soon as the skies brightened, and plum blossom was out, Paul drove off in the milk-man's heavy float up to Willey Farm. Mr Leivers shouted in a kindly fashion at the boy, then clicked to the horse as they climbed the hill, slowly, in the freshness of the morning. White clouds went on their way, crowding to the back of the hills that were rousing in the springtime. The water of Nethermere lay below, very blue against the seared meadows and the thorn trees.

It was four and a half miles' drive. Tiny buds on the hedges, vivid as copper-green, were opening into rosettes, and thrushes called, and black-birds shrieked and scolded. It was a new, glamorous world.

Miriam, peeping through the kitchen window, saw the horse walk through the big white gate into the farmyard that was backed by the oak-wood, still bare. Then a youth, in a heavy overcoat, climbed down. He put up his hands for the whip and the rug, that the good-looking ruddy farmer handed down to him. 5

Miriam appeared in the doorway. She was nearly sixteen, very beautiful, with her warm colouring, her gravity, her eyes dilating suddenly like an ecstasy.

"I say," said Paul, turning shyly aside, "your daffodils are nearly out. Isn't it early? But don't they look cold?" 10

"Cold!" said Miriam, in her musical, caressing voice.

"The green on their buds—" and he faltered into silence, timidly.

"Let me take the rug," said Miriam, over gently.

"I can carry it," he answered, rather injured. But he yielded it to her. 15

Then Mrs Leivers appeared.

"I'm sure you're tired and cold," she said. "Let me take your coat. It *is* heavy—you mustn't walk far in it."

She helped him off with his coat. He was quite unused to such attention. She was almost smothered under its weight. 20

"Why mother," laughed the farmer, as he passed through the kitchen swinging the great milk churns: "You've got almost more than you can manage there." She beat up the sofa cushions for the youth.

The kitchen was very small and irregular. The farm had been 25 originally a laborer's cottage. And the furniture was old and battered. But Paul loved it, loved the sack bag that formed the hearthrug, and the funny little corner under the stairs, and the small window deep in the corner, through which, bending a little, he could see the plum-trees in the back garden, and the lovely round hills beyond. 30

"Won't you lie down?" said Mrs Leivers.

"Oh no—I'm not tired," he said. "Isn't it lovely coming out, don't you think? I saw a sloe-bush in blossom, and a lot of celandines. I'm glad it's sunny."

"Can I give you anything to eat or to drink?" 35

"No thank you."

"How's your mother?"

"I think she's tired now—I think she's had too much to do. Perhaps in a little while she'll go to Skegness with me. Then she'll be able to rest. I s'll be glad if she can." 40

"Yes," replied Mrs Leivers. "It's a wonder she isn't ill herself."

Miriam was moving about preparing dinner. Paul watched everything that happened. His face was pale and thin, but his eyes were
quick and bright with life as ever. He watched the strange, almost
5 rhapsodic way in which the girl moved about, carrying a great
stew-jar to the oven, or looking in the saucepan. The atmosphere
was different from that of his own home, where everything seemed
so ordinary. When Mr Leivers called loudly outside to the horse,
that was reaching over to feed on the rose bushes in the garden, the
10 girl started, looking round with dark eyes, as if something had come
breaking in on her world. There was a sense of silence inside the
house and out. Miriam seemed as in some dreamy tale, a maiden in
bondage, her spirit dreaming in a land far away and magical. And
her discoloured, old blue frock, and her broken boots, seemed only
15 like the romantic rags of King Cophetua's beggar maid.*

She suddenly became aware of his keen blue eyes upon her, taking
her all in. Instantly her broken boots and her frayed old frock hurt
her. She resented his seeing everything. Even he knew that her
stocking was not pulled up. She went into the scullery, blushing
20 deeply. And afterwards her hands trembled slightly at her work, she
nearly dropped all she handled. When her inside dream was shaken,
her body quivered with trepidation. She resented that he saw so
much.

Mrs Leivers sat for some time talking to the boy, although she was
25 needed at her work. She was too polite to leave him. Presently she
excused herself, and rose. After a while she looked into the tin
saucepan:

"Oh *dear* Miriam," she cried, "these potatoes have boiled dry!"

Miriam started as if she had been stung.

30 "*Have* they mother!" she cried.

"I shouldn't care Miriam," said the mother, "if I hadn't trusted
them to you." She peered into the pan.

The girl stiffened as if from a blow. Her dark eyes dilated, she
remained standing in the same spot.

35 "Well," she answered, gripped tight in self-conscious shame,
"I'm sure I looked at them five minutes since."

"Yes," said the mother. "I know it's easily done."

"They're not much burned," said Paul. "It doesn't matter, does
it?"

40 Mrs Leivers looked at the youth with her brown, hurt eyes.

"It wouldn't matter but for the boys," she said to him. "Only Miriam knows what a trouble they make if the potatoes are caught."

"Then," thought Paul to himself, "you shouldn't let them make a trouble."

After a while, Edgar came in. He wore leggings, and his boots were covered with earth. He was rather small, rather formal for a farmer. He glanced at Paul, nodded to him distantly, and said: "Dinner ready?"

"Nearly Edgar," replied the mother apologetically.

"I'm ready for mine," said the young man, taking up the newspaper and reading. Presently the rest of the family trooped in. Dinner was served. The meal went rather brutally. The over gentleness and apologetic tone of the mother brought out all the brutality of manners in the sons. Edgar tasted the potatoes, moved his mouth quickly like a rabbit, looked indignantly at his mother, and said:

"These potatoes are burnt, mother!"

"Yes Edgar—I forgot them for a minute. Perhaps you'll have bread if you can't eat them."

Edgar looked in anger across at Miriam.

"What was Miriam doing that she couldn't attend to them?" he said.

Miriam looked up. Her mouth opened, her dark eyes blazed and winced, but she said nothing. She swallowed her anger and her shame, bowing her dark head.

"I'm sure she was trying hard," said the mother.

"She hasn't got sense even to boil the potatoes," said Edgar. "What is she kept at home for?"

"On'y for eating everything that's left in th' pantry," said Maurice.

"They don't forget that potato-pie against our Miriam," laughed the father. She was utterly humiliated The mother sat in silence, suffering, like some saint out of place at the brutal board.

It puzzled Paul. He wondered vaguely why all this intense feeling went running because of a few burnt potatoes. The mother exalted everything, even a bit of housework, to the plane of a religious trust. The sons resented this; they felt themselves cut away underneath, and they answered with brutality, and also with a sneering superciliousness.

Paul was just opening out from childhood into manhood. This

atmosphere, where everything took a religious value, came with a subtle fascination to him. There was something in the air. His own mother was logical. Here there was something different, something he loved, something that at times he hated.

5   Miriam quarrelled with her brothers, fiercely. Later in the afternoon, when they had gone away again, her mother said:

"You disappointed me at dinner-time, Miriam."

The girl dropped her head.

"They are such *brutes!*" she suddenly cried, looking up with
10 flashing eyes.

"But hadn't you promised not to answer them?" said the mother. "And I believed in you. I *can't* stand it, when you wrangle."

"But they're so hateful!" cried Miriam. "And—and *low.*"

"Yes dear. But how often have I asked you not to answer Edgar
15 back. Can't you let him say what he likes?"

"But why should he say what he likes!"

"Aren't you strong enough to bear it, Miriam, if even for my sake.* Are you so weak that you must wrangle with them."

Mrs Leivers stuck unflinchingly to this doctrine of "the other
20 cheek." She could not instil it at all into the boys. With the girls she succeeded better, and Miriam was the child of her heart. The boys loathed the other cheek when it was presented to them. Miriam was often sufficiently lofty to turn it. Then they spat on her* and hated her. But she walked in her proud humility, living within herself.

25 There was always this feeling of jangle and discord in the Leivers family. Although the boys resented so bitterly the eternal* appeal to their deeper feelings of resignation and proud humility, yet it had its effect on them. They could not establish between themselves and an outsider just the ordinary human feeling, and unexaggerated friend-
30 ship: they were always restless for the something deeper. Ordinary folk seemed shallow to them, trivial and inconsiderable. And so they were unaccustomed, painfully uncouth in the simplest social intercourse, suffering, and yet insolent in their superiority. Then beneath was the yearning for the soul intimacy to which they could not attain,
35 because they were too dumb, and every approach to close connexion was blocked by their clumsy contempt of other people. They wanted genuine intimacy, but they could not get even normally near to anyone, because they scorned to take the first steps, they scorned the triviality which forms common human intercourse.

40 Paul fell under Mrs Leivers' spell. Everything had a religious and

intensified meaning, when he was with her. His soul, hurt, highly
developed, sought her as if for nourishment. Together, they seemed
to sift the vital fact from an experience.

Miriam was her mother's daughter. In the sunshine of the afternoon, mother and daughter went down the fields with him. They
looked for nests. There was a jenny wren's in the hedge by the
orchard.

"I *do* want you to see this," said Mrs Leivers.

He crouched down, and carefully put his finger through the
thorns into the round door of the nest.

"It's almost as if you were feeling inside the live body of the bird,"
he said, "it's so warm. They say a bird makes its nest round like a
cup with pressing its breast on it.* Then how did it make the ceiling
round, I wonder." The nest seemed to start into life for the two
women. After that, Miriam came to see it every day. It seemed so
close to her. Again, going down the hedge side with the girl, he
noticed the celandines, scalloped splashes of gold, on the side of the
ditch.

"I like them," he said, "when their petals go flat back with the
sunshine. They seem to be pressing themselves at the sun." And
then the celandines ever after drew her with a little spell. Anthropo-
morphic as she was, she stimulated him into appreciating things
thus, and then they lived for her. She seemed to need things kindling
in her imagination or in her soul, before she felt she had them. And
she was cut off from ordinary life, by her religious intensity, which
made the world for her either a nunnery garden, or a Paradise where
sin and knowledge were not, or else an ugly, cruel thing.

So it was in this atmosphere of subtle intimacy, this meeting in
their common feeling for some thing in nature, that their love
started.

Personally, he was a long time before he realised her. For ten
months he had to stay at home, after his illness. For a while he went
to Skegness with his mother, and was perfectly happy. But even
from the seaside he wrote long letters to Mrs Leivers, about the
shore and the sea. And he brought back his beloved sketches of the
flat Lincoln coast, anxious for them to see. Almost, they would
interest the Leivers more than they interested his mother. It was not
his art Mrs Morel cared about, it was himself, and his achievement.
But Mrs Leivers, and her children, were almost his disciples. They
kindled him, and made him glow to his work, whereas his mother's

influence was to make him quietly determined, patient, dogged, unwearied.

He soon was friends with the boys, whose rudeness was only superficial. They had all, when they could trust themselves, a
5 strange gentleness and loveableness.

"Will you come with me onto the fallow?" asked Edgar, rather hesitatingly. Paul went joyfully, and spent the afternoon helping to hoe, or to single turnips, with his friend. He used to lie with the three brothers on* the hay piled up in the barn, and tell them about
10 Nottingham and about Jordan's. In return they taught him to milk, and let him do little jobs, chopping hay or pulping turnips, just as much as he liked. At midsummer he worked all through hay harvest with them, and then he loved them. The family was so cut off from the world, actually. They seemed somehow like 'les derniers fils
15 d'une race épuisée.'* Though the lads were strong and healthy, yet they had all that over-sensitiveness and hanging-back which made them so lonely, yet also such close, delicate friends once their intimacy was won. Paul loved them dearly, and they him.

Miriam came later. But he had come into her life before she
20 made any mark on his. One dull afternoon, when the men were on the land, and the rest at school, only Miriam and her mother at home, the girl said to him, after having hesitated for some time:

"Have you seen the swing?"

25 "No," he answered. "Where?"

"In the cowshed," she replied.

She always hesitated to offer or to show him anything. Men have such different standards of worth from women, and her dear things, the valuable things to her, her brothers had so often mocked or
30 flouted.

"Come on then," he replied, jumping up.

There were two cowsheds, one on either side of the barn. In the lower, darker shed, there was standing for four cows. Hens flew scolding over the manger wall as the youth and girl went forward for
35 the great thick rope which hung from the beam in the darkness overhead, and was pushed back over a peg in the wall.

"It's something like a rope!" he exclaimed, appreciatively, and he sat down in it, anxious to try it. Then immediately he rose.

"Come on then, and have first go," he said to the girl.

40 "See," she answered, going into the barn, "we put some bags on

the seat." And she made the swing comfortable for him. That gave
her pleasure. He held the rope.

"Come on then," he said to her.

"No, I won't go first," she answered.

She stood aside in her still, aloof fashion.   5

"Why?"

"You go," she pleaded.

Almost for the first time in her life, she had the pleasure of
giving-up to a man, of spoiling him. Paul looked at her.

"All right," he said, sitting down. "Mind out!"   10

He set off with a spring, and in a moment was flying through the
air, almost out of the door of the shed, the upper half of which was
open, showing outside the drizzling rain, the filthy yard, the cattle
standing disconsolate against the black cart-shed, and at the back of
all, the grey-green wall of the wood. She stood below in her crimson 15
tam-o'-shanter,* and watched. He looked down at her, and she saw
his blue eyes sparkling.

"It's a treat of a swing," he said.

"Yes."

He was swinging through the air, every bit of him swinging, like a   20
bird that swoops for joy of movement. And he looked down at her.
Her crimson cap hung over her dark curls, her beautiful warm face,
so still in a kind of brooding, was lifted towards him. It was dark and
rather cold in the shed. Suddenly a swallow came down from the
high roof, and darted out of the door.   25

"I didn't know a bird was watching," he called.

He swung negligently. She could feel him falling and lifting
through the air, as if he were lying on some force.*

"Now I'll die," he said, in a detached, dreamy voice, as though he
were the dying motion of the swing. She watched him fascinated.   30
Suddenly he put on the brake and jumped out.

"I've had a long turn," he said. "But it's a treat of a swing, it's a
real treat of a swing."

Miriam was amused that he took a swing so seriously, and felt so
warmly over it.   35

"No, you go on," she said.

"Why—don't you want one?" he asked, astonished.

"Well—not much. I'll have just a little."*

She sat down, whilst he kept the bags in place for her.

"It's so ripping," he said, setting her in motion. "Keep your heels 40 up or they'll bang the manger wall."

She felt the accuracy with which he caught her, exactly at the right moment, and the exactly proportionate strength of his thrust, and she was afraid. Down to her bowels went the hot wave of fear. She
5 was in his hands. Again, firm and inevitable came the thrust at the right moment. She gripped the rope, almost swooning.

"Ha!" she laughed in fear. "No higher!"

"But you're not a *bit* high," he remonstrated.

"But no higher."

10 He heard the fear in her voice and desisted. Her heart melted in hot pain when the moment came for him to thrust her forward again. But he left her alone. She began to breathe.

"Won't you really go any further?" he asked. "Should I keep you there?"

15 "No, let me go by myself," she answered.

He moved aside and watched her.

"Why you're scarcely moving," he said.

She laughed silently with shame, and in a moment got down.

"They say if you can swing you won't be sea-sick," he said as he
20 mounted again. "I don't believe I should ever be sea sick."

Away he went. There was something fascinating to her in him. For the moment he was nothing but a piece of swinging stuff, not a particle of him that did not swing. She could never lose herself so, nor could her brothers. It roused a warmth in her. It were almost as
25 if he were a flame that had lit a warmth in her, whilst he swung in the middle air.*

And gradually, the intimacy with the family concentrated for Paul on three persons: the mother, Edgar, and Miriam. To the mother he went for that sympathy and that appeal which seemed to draw him
30 out. Edgar was his very close friend. And to Miriam he more or less condescended, because she seemed so humble.

But the girl gradually sought him out. If he brought up his sketch book, it was she who pondered longest over the last picture. Then she would look up at him. Suddenly, her dark eyes alight like water
35 that shakes with a stream of gold in the dark, she would ask:

"Why do I like this so?"

Always something in his breast shrank from these close, intimate dazzled looks of hers.

"Why *do* you?" he asked.

40 "I don't know—it seems so true."

"It's because—it's because there is scarcely any shadow in it—it's more shimmery—as if I'd painted the shimmering protoplasm in the leaves and everywhere, and not the stiffness of the shape. That seems dead to me. Only this shimmeriness is the real living. The shape is a dead crust.* The shimmer is inside, really."   5

And she, with her little finger in her mouth, would ponder these sayings.* They gave her a feeling of life again, and vivified things which had meant nothing to her. She managed to find some meaning in his struggling, abstract speeches. And they were the medium through which she came distinctly at her beloved objects.   10

Another day she sat at sunset whilst he was painting some pine-trees which caught the red glare from the west. He had been quiet.

"There you are!" he said suddenly. "I wanted that. Now look at them and tell me, are they pine trunks or are they red coals,   15 standing-up pieces of fire in that darkness. There's God's burning bush,* for you, that burned not away."

Miriam looked, and was frightened. But the pine trunks were wonderful to her, and distinct. He packed his box and rose. Suddenly he looked at her.   20

"Why are you always sad?" he asked her.

"Sad!" she exclaimed, looking up at him with startled, wonderful brown eyes.

"Yes," he replied. "You are always, always sad."

"I am not—Oh, not a bit!" she cried.   25

"But even your joy is like a flame coming off of sadness," he persisted. "You're never jolly, or even just all right."

"No," she pondered. "I wonder—why—."

"Because you're not—because you're different inside—like a pine tree—and then you flare up—but you're not just like an   30 ordinary tree, with fidgety leaves and jolly—"

He got tangled up in his own speech; but she brooded on it, and he had a strange, roused sensation, as if his feelings were new. She got so near him. It was a strange stimulant.

Then sometimes he hated her. Her youngest brother was only   35 five. He was a frail lad, with immense brown eyes in his quaint, fragile face; one of Reynolds' 'Choir of Angels,'* with a touch of elf. Often Miriam knelt to the child, and drew him to her.

"Eh my Hubert!" she sang, in a voice heavy and surcharged with love. "Eh my Hubert!"   40

And folding him in her arms, she swayed slightly from side to side with love, her face half lifted, her eyes half closed, her voice drenched with love.

"Don't!" said the child, uneasy. "Don't Miriam."

5 "Yes you love me, don't you!" she murmured deep in her throat, almost as if she were in a trance, and swaying also as if she were swooned in an ecstasy of love.

"Don't!" repeated the child, a frown on his clear brow.

"You love me, don't you?" she murmured.

10 "What do you make such a *fuss* for!" cried Paul, all in suffering because of her extreme emotion. "Why can't you be ordinary with him?"

She let the child go, and rose, and said nothing. Her intensity, which would leave no emotion on a normal plane, irritated the youth

15 into a frenzy. And this fearful naked contact of her soul* on small occasions, shocked him. He was used to his mother's reserve. And on such occasions, he was thankful in his heart and soul, that he had his mother, so sane and wholesome.

All the life of Miriam's body was in her eyes, which were usually

20 dark as a dark church, but could flame with light like a conflagration. Her face scarcely ever altered from its look of brooding. She might have been one of the women who went with Mary when Jesus was dead.* Her body was not flexible and living. She walked with a swing, rather heavily, her head bowed forward, pondering. She was not

25 clumsy, and yet none of her movements seemed quite *the* movement. Often, when wiping the dishes, she would stand in bewilderment and chagrin, because she had pulled in two halves a cup or a tumbler. It was as if, in her fear and self mistrust, she put too much strength into the effort. There was no looseness or abandon about

30 her. Everything was gripped stiff with intensity, and her effort, overcharged, closed in on itself.

She rarely varied from her swinging, forward, intense walk. Occasionally she ran with Paul down the fields. Then her eyes blazed naked in a kind of ecstasy, that frightened him. But she was

35 physically afraid. If she were getting over a stile, she gripped his hands in a little hard anguish, and began to lose her presence of mind. And he could not persuade her to jump from even a small height. Her eyes dilated, became exposed and palpitating.

"No!" she cried half laughing in terror, "No!"

40 "You shall!" he cried once, and, jerking her forward, he brought

her falling from the fence. But her wild "Ah!" of pain, as if she were losing consciousness, cut him. She landed on her feet safely, and afterwards, had courage in this respect.

Often they walked together, Paul and Miriam, down the fields to Nethermere. He was naturally agile and very active. He went dancing from one thing to another. But she kept her regular course, almost unmovable. And gradually he fell in beside her, took her pace, and walked head-down with her. Till they came to the water. The margin of the lake was littered with white feathers from the swans. They sat on a pebbly bank. Suddenly he caught sight of a nice flat stone, and, jumping up, began to make ducks and drakes on the water.

"Can *you* skim?" he asked.

"Not very well," she replied, shaking her head. She remained seated, watching him.

"See that!" he cried. "Four hops!"

"Yes," she said, commending him. "That was very good." But soon he desisted, came and sat down again beside her.

"Why don't *you* want to do ducks and drakes as well?" he asked.

"I don't know," she replied.

"You never want to *do* things," he said.

"Well, you see, I have to work in the house."

He did not continue the argument. They fell into a discussion of books.

She was very much dissatisfied with her lot.

"Don't you like being at home?" Paul asked her, surprised.

"Who would!" she answered, low and intense. "What is it! I'm all day cleaning what the boys make just as bad in five minutes. I don't *want* to be at home."

"What do you want then?"

"I want to do something. I want a chance like anybody else. Why should I, because I'm a girl, be kept at home and not allowed to be anything. What chance *have* I?"

"Chance of what?"

"Of knowing anything—of learning—of doing anything. It's not fair, because I'm a woman."

She seemed very bitter. Paul wondered. In his own home, Annie was almost glad to be a girl. She had not so much responsibility, things were lighter for her. She never wanted to be other than a girl. But Miriam almost fiercely wished she were a man. And yet she hated men, at the same time.

"But it's as well to be a woman as a man," he said, frowning.

"Ha!—is it! Men have everything."

"I should think women ought to be as glad to be women, as men are to be men," he answered.

5 "No!" she shook her head. "No! Everything, the men have."

"But what do you want?" he asked.

"I want to learn. Why *should* it be that I know nothing!"

"What—such as mathematics and French—?"

"Why *shouldn't* I know mathematics!—Yes!" she cried, her eyes

10 expanding in a kind of defiance.

"Well you can learn as much as I know," he said. "I'll teach you if you like."

Her eyes dilated. She mistrusted him as teacher.

"Would you?" he asked.

15 Her head had dropped and she was sucking her finger broodingly.

"Yes," she said, hesitatingly.

He used to tell his mother all these things.

"Did *you* want to be a man, mother?" he asked.

20 "Sometimes I have—but it's silly—and no, I don't really want to be anything but myself, and never did."

"What did you want to be a man for, even sometimes?"

"Well my boy," she laughed, "I thought I could make a great deal better job of it than most men do—which isn't to be wondered at."

25 "I don't want to be a woman," he replied thoughtfully. "And I don't think I could be a woman better than a woman is one herself."

"No," laughed his mother. "I don't suppose you could.—But it makes us sometimes feel that we could do better than men."

"Perhaps you could, mother," he said.

30 "Well—!" she replied, with her little amused sniff—"And my boy," she continued, "anything that is natural is pleased to be itself. And when a woman wants very badly to be a man, you may back your life she's not much good as a woman."

"I hate it when a woman wants to be a man," he said.

35 "It shows her pride as a woman is pretty low," she answered. He always came to his mother, making her the touchstone.

"I'm going to teach Miriam algebra," he said.

"Well," replied Mrs Morel. "I hope she'll get fat on it."

When he went up to the farm on the Monday evening, it was

40 drawing twilight. Miriam was just sweeping up the kitchen, and was

kneeling at the hearth when he entered. Everyone was out but her. She looked round at him, flushed, her dark eyes shining, her fine hair falling about her face.

"Hello," she said, soft and musical, "I knew it was you."

"How?"

"I knew your step. Nobody treads so quick and firm."

He sat down, sighing.

"Ready to do some algebra?" he asked, drawing a little book from his pocket.

"But—!" He could feel her backing away.

"You said you wanted," he insisted.

"Tonight though—?" she faltered.

"But I came on purpose. And if you want to learn it, you must begin."

She took up her ashes in the dustpan, and looked at him, half tremulously laughing.

"Yes but—tonight!—you see I haven't thought of it."

"Well my goodness—take the ashes, and come."

He went and sat on the stone bench in the back yard, where the big milk cans were standing, tipped up, to air. The men were in the cowsheds. He could hear the little sing song of the milk spurting into the pails. Presently she came, bringing some big greenish apples.

"You know you like them," she said.

He took a bite.

"Sit down," he said with his mouth full.

She was short sighted, and peered over his shoulder. It irritated him. He gave her the book quickly.

"Here," he said. "It's only letters for figures. You put down *a* instead of '2' or '6.' "

They worked, he talking, she with her head down on the book. He was quick and hasty. She never answered. Occasionally when he demanded of her:

"Do you see?"

She looked up at him, her eyes wide with the half laugh that comes of fear.

"Don't you!" he cried.

He had been too fast. But she said nothing. He questioned her more, then got hot. It made his blood rouse to see her there, as it were at his mercy, her mouth open, her eyes dilated with laughter that was afraid, apologetic, ashamed. Then Edgar came along with two buckets of milk.

"Hello!" he said. "What are you doing?"

"Algebra," replied Paul.

5   "Algebra!" repeated Edgar, curiously. Then he passed on with a laugh. Paul took a bite at his forgotten apple, looked at the miserable cabbages in the garden, pecked into lace by the fowls, and he wanted to pull them up. Then he glanced at Miriam. She was poring over the book, seemed absorbed in it, yet trembling lest she could not get

10 at it. It made him cross. She was ruddy and beautiful. Yet her soul seemed to be intensely supplicating the algebra book. She closed, shrinking, knowing he was angered. And at the same instant he grew gentle, seeing her hurt because she did not understand.

"Tell me what seems hard?" he asked, tenderly.

15 The new note made her look at him suddenly, with dark eyes that seemed to try so hard. It hurt him, and a wave of tenderness went over him.

"You see it seems easy to me," he said. "I'm used to it, and I forget. See—"

20 Then patiently, gently, he went over it again. Edgar had come and was standing behind him. Miriam's dark head was beneath Paul's eyes. She had a small head, with black curls floating short like silk. She seemed to try so hard. His voice was a caress all the time.

"I see!" exclaimed Edgar suddenly from behind. "But—this—"

25 And his thick forefinger came down on the book. Miriam winced away. Paul looked round at his friend. Edgar was good-looking, and his brown eyes, sound and healthy, looked interested. It was like breathing fresh air, to explain to him.

Paul taught Miriam regularly. The lessons usually took place in

30 the parlour. There the youth began brightly. She always had learned and knew what task he had set from the week before. Often, she knew it more accurately than he. But things came slowly to her. And when she held herself in a grip, seemed so utterly humble before the lesson, it made his blood rouse. He stormed at her, got ashamed,

35 continued the lesson, and grew furious again, abusing her. She listened in silence. Occasionally, very rarely, she defended herself. Her liquid dark eyes blazed at him.

"You don't give me time to learn it," she said.

"All right," he answered, throwing the book on the table, and

40 lighting a cigarette. Then after a while he went back to her repent-

ant. So the lessons went. He was always either in a rage, or very gentle.

"What do you tremble your *soul* before it for?" he cried. "You don't learn algebra with your blessed soul. Can't you look at it with your clear simple wits?"

Often, when he went again into the kitchen, Mrs Leivers would look at him reproachfully, saying:

"Paul, don't be so hard on Miriam. She may not be quick—but I'm sure she tries."

"I can't help it," he said, rather pitiably. "I go off like it."

"You don't mind me, Miriam, do you?" he asked of the girl, later.

"No," she reassured him, in her beautiful deep tones. "No, I don't mind."

"Don't mind me, it's my fault."

But in spite of himself, his blood began to boil with her. It was strange that no-one else made him in such fury. He flared against her. Once he threw the pencil in her face. There was a silence. She turned her face slightly aside.

"I didn't—" he began, but got no further, feeling weak in all his bones. She never reproached him, or was angry with him. He was often cruelly ashamed. But still again his anger burst like a bubble surcharged. And still, when he saw her eager, silent, as it were blind face, he felt he wanted to throw the pencil in it. And still, when he saw her hand trembling and her mouth parted with suffering, his heart was scalded with pain for her. And because of the intensity to which she roused him, he sought her.

Then he often avoided her and went with Edgar. Miriam and her brother were naturally antagonistic. Edgar was a rationalist,* who was curious, and had a sort of scientific interest in life. It was a great bitterness to Miriam to see herself deserted by Paul for Edgar, who seemed so much lower. But the youth was very happy with her elder brother. The two men spent afternoons together on the land, or in the loft, doing carpentry when it rained. And they talked together, or Paul taught Edgar the songs he himself had learned from Annie at the piano. And often all the men, Mr Leivers as well, had bitter debates on the nationalising of the land,* and similar problems. Paul had already heard his mother's views, and as these were as yet his own, he argued for her. Miriam attended and took part, but was all the time waiting until it should be over, and a personal communication might begin.

"After all," she said within herself, "if the land were nationalised, Edgar and Paul and I would be just the same."

So she waited for the youth to come back to her.

He was studying for his painting. He loved to sit at home, alone with his mother at night, working and working. She sewed or read. Then, looking up from his task, he would rest his eyes for a moment on her face, that was bright with living warmth, and he returned gladly to his work.

"I can do my best things when you sit there in your rocking-chair, mother," he said.

"I'm sure!" she exclaimed, sniffing with mock scepticism. But she felt it was so, and her heart quivered with brightness. For many hours she sat still, slightly conscious of him labouring away, whilst she worked or read her book. And he, with all his soul's intensity directing his pencil, could feel her warmth inside him like strength. They were both very happy so, and both unconscious of it. These times, that meant so much, and which were real living, they almost ignored.

He was conscious only when stimulated. A sketch finished, he always wanted to take it to Miriam. Then he was stimulated into knowledge of the work he had produced unconsciously. In contact with Miriam, he gained insight, his vision went deeper. From his mother he drew the life warmth, the strength to produce; Miriam urged this warmth into intensity like a white light.

When he returned to the factory the conditions of work were better. He had Wednesday afternoon off to go to the Art School— Miss Jordan's provision—returning in the evening. Then the factory closed at six instead of at eight on Thursday and Friday evenings.

In Bestwood was a decent little library, the subscription to which was only four-and-six a year. Mrs Morel and Mrs Leivers had both joined when their children were growing up. The library was open in two rooms in the Mechanics Hall, on Thursday evenings from 7.0 till 9.0. Paul always fetched the books for his mother, who read a considerable amount, and Miriam trudged down with five or six volumes, for her family. It became the custom for the two to meet in the library.

Paul knew the two small rooms, with books all round the walls. It was warm with a great fire in the corner. Mr Sleath, the librarian, had white whiskers round his child-like face. He was tall and inqui-

sitive, but very affectionate, knew everybody and everybody's
affairs.* Mr Smedley was plump and bald and knowing.

Paul stood waiting whilst Mr Sleath finished his gossip with the
last subscriber. Then he plumped his books onto the counter. Mr
Sleath looked at him with lively but unseeing old blue eyes.   5

"Twenty-two fifty seven," said Paul.

The librarian—who was one of the chief clerks of the Colliery
Company, and quite a gentleman in comparison with the youth,
repeated the numbers cheerily, turning the leaves of his great
ledger.   10

"Ha!—Ha!" he exclaimed, glancing at the page. Then he looked
warmly and welcoming at the youth, rubbed his hands, and said:

"Ha!—Well Paul!—Ha! How's your mother?"

"Very well," replied Paul. "Thank you."

"That's right! She wasn't at chapel on Sunday night."   15

"No, she had an inflammation in her eyes."

"Oh dear—oh dear—sorry to hear that!"

"I thought you said," put in Mr Smedley, "that she was very
well." Paul did not answer, or look at the little man behind the
counter. Mr Sleath was ticking off the books in his great ledger. Mr   20
Smedley put some more coal on the fire. Several folk were talking
freely as they stood about the shelves. Their heels clicked as they
walked on the paddled brick floor.*

"But she'll be able to get out this week-end?" asked Mr Sleath,
having ticked off the books.   25

"Yes," said Paul.

"That's right—that's right. I wondered where she could be."

It was an understood thing that folk should enquire after his
mother, but his father was never mentioned.

He moved away to the book-shelves. Folk kept coming in, putting 30
their umbrellas in the passage, exchanging pleasant greetings. The
youth knew everybody, and everybody's history. They did not interest him. Perhaps Miriam would not come, because of the rain. He
gazed at the book in his hand, did not see it for some moments,
thinking of her, then saw it again. The time went by like a sleep.   35
There were noises of people going, but no one entered. If she did
not come? Then at the thought, he could see the night ahead,
dreary and profitless. But she would come. It still felt warm and
rich, just in front, and night went no further than the moment when
she would arrive.   40

"Nasty night, Alfred, nasty night," said Mr Sleath, turning round for someone to talk to. The library was empty.

"Seems like it," replied Mr Smedley.

Then Mr Sleath caught sight of Paul.

5   "Hello Paul!" he exclaimed. "Not found what you want yet, eh?"

"It's not books as Paul's waiting for, I think," said Mr Smedley.

"Oh—oh—!" exclaimed Mr Sleath.

"I think there's a young lady at the back of it," said Mr Smedley. "But it's a bad night to come from Willey Woods."

10   A footstep was heard in the passage. The young man listened. It was not she. A boy entered. When Paul saw the lad in the doorway where she should have been, he hated him. Yet she would come. She was so dependable. One of her great charms for the youth, was that she was not held by conventions. If she wanted to come, she

15   would come in spite of rain. And it was not so very bad. He listened for the sound of the weather. He heard the boy say that it was pouring. The boy was objectionable. She *would* come, in spite of him. He clung to the hope of her. He could feel her, across the night, wanting to come. And she never failed him.* With her, the

20   inner life counted for everything, the outer for nothing.

He heard her step in the hall and his suspense relaxed. He watched. In the doorway she hung back a moment. Her red cap was glistening with rain, her hair was revelling in dewy curliness, her face glowed. She was searching anxiously for him. Then her short-

25   sighted eyes met his. A flame came up in her that burned him too. She went, satisfied, to the counter. He turned his back to her.

Then she came hesitatingly forward.

"Am I late?" she asked.

"As usual," he replied. "Are you wet?"

30   "No—nothing."

"Did you come down the railway?" he said.

"Yes. Were you afraid I shouldn't come?"

"A bit."

He gave her a little smile.

35   "Come and see what books I found you," he said. She followed him implicitly. Books did not matter to her. But he insisted on her approving. She gazed over his arm, not seeing. But she touched him.

"Will it do?" he asked.

"Yes," she answered.*

40   Then, when her books were entered, the two went quickly out of

the library. They rejoiced in the darkness. They were excitedly happy. Paul had a great black mackintosh, under the cape of which he carried the books. They walked side by side down Mansfield road, in the rainy darkness, under the dripping trees.

The conversation started quick and vigorous, and immediately it 5 was a discussion of a book. He held forth passionately, she listened and her soul expanded. From the book, they inevitably came to a discussion of beliefs, very intimate.

"It seems as if it didn't matter, one more or less, among the lot," he said.   10

"No," she replied, gravely, questioning.

"I used to believe that about a sparrow falling—and hairs of the head—"

"Yes," she said. "And now?"

"Now I think that the race of sparrows* matters, but not one 15 sparrow: all my hair, but not one hair."

"Yes," she said, questioningly.

"And people matter. But *one* isn't so very important. Look at William."

"Yes," she pondered.   20

"I call it only wasted," he said. "Waste, no more."

"Yes," she said, very low.

It was her belief that the more people there were, the less they mattered. But to hear him talk was like life to her: like starting the breathing in a new-born baby.   25

"Yet," he said, "I reckon we've got a proper way to go—and if we go it, we're all right—and if we go near it. But if we go wrong, we die. I'm sure our William went wrong somewhere."

"And if we follow the course of our lives, we don't die?" she asked.

"No we don't. What we are inside makes us so that we ought to go 30 one particular way, and no other."

"But do we know when we're following the true course?" she asked.

"Yes! *I* do. I know I'm following mine."

"You do?" she asked.   35

"Yes—I'm certain."

He had stood under a lamp to think. His mackintosh shone wet. She looked at his face. His eyes, so certain and so steady, gazed into hers. He was quite firm. It fascinated her. She went on home, her heart glowing.   40

But when he turned round to go back, he forgot her in the knowledge that his mother would be angry with him for walking so far and getting wet. He hurried home, glowing nevertheless from the contact with Miriam. He had got some satisfaction from the
5   night.

"Do you mean to say you've been walking home with Miriam Leivers on a night like this?" asked his mother, looking up suddenly at him, a minute after he had been in the house.

"I stopped in the library ever such a long time," replied Paul.
10   "What, she came did she!" exclaimed Mrs Morel, quietly, scathingly. Paul winced.

"She has nothing to read all week if she doesn't come," he said.

"I don't know what her mother's doing, to let her trapse about ten miles in the pouring rain."
15   "It doesn't rain much," he said. "Not hard."

"I've only to look at your mackintosh and boots," she answered.

"Look what I brought you," he said, but she was too cross to condescend.

One evening in the summer Miriam and he went over the fields
20   by Herod's Farm on their way from the library home. So, it was only three miles to Willey Farm. There was a yellow glow over the mowing grass, and the sorrel heads burned crimson. Gradually as they walked along the high land the gold in the west sank down to red, the red to crimson, and then the chill blue crept up against the
25   glow.

They came out upon the high-road to Alfreton, which ran white between the darkening fields. There Paul hesitated. It was two miles home for him, one mile forward for Miriam. They both looked up the road, that ran in shadow right under the glow of the north-west
30   sky. On the crest of the hill Selby with its stark houses and the up-pricked headstocks of the pit stood in black silhouette small against the sky.

He looked at his watch.

"Nine o'clock!" he said.
35   The pair stood loth to part, hugging their books.

"The wood is so lovely now," she said. "I wanted you to see it."

He followed her slowly across the road to the white gate.

"They grumble so if I'm late," he said.

"But you're not doing anything wrong," she answered, impatient-
40   ly. He followed her across the nibbled pasture in the dusk. There

was a coolness in the wood, a scent of leaves, of honeysuckle, and a twilight. The two walked in silence. Night came wonderfully there, among the throng of dark tree-trunks. He looked round, expectant.

She wanted to show him a certain wild-rose bush she had discovered. She knew it was wonderful. And yet, till he had seen it, 5 she felt it had not come into her soul. Only he could make it her own, immortal. She was dissatisfied.

Dew was already on the paths. In the old oak-wood a mist was rising and he hesitated, wondering whether one whiteness were a strand of fog or only campion flowers, pallid in a cloud. 10

By the time they came to the pine-trees Miriam was getting very eager, and very tense. Her bush might be gone. She might not be able to find it. And she wanted it so much. Almost passionately, she wanted to be with him when she stood before the flowers. They were going to have a communion together, something that thrilled her, 15 something holy. He was walking beside her in silence. They were very near to each other. She trembled, and he listened, vaguely anxious.

Coming to the edge of the wood, they saw the sky in front like mother-of-pearl, and the earth growing dark. Somewhere on the 20 outermost branches of the pine-wood the honeysuckle was streaming scent.

"Where?" he asked.

"Down the middle path," she murmured, quivering.

When they turned the corner of the path she stood still. In the 25 wide walk between the pines, gazing rather frightened, she could distinguish nothing for some moments, the greying light robbed things of their colour. Then she saw her bush.

"Ah!" she cried, hastening forward.

It was very still. The tree was tall and straggling. It had thrown its 30 briars over a hawthorn bush, and its long streamers trailed thick, right down to the grass, splashing the darkness everywhere with great spilt stars, pure white. In bosses of ivory and in large splashed stars the roses gleamed on the darkness of foliage and stems and grass. Paul and Miriam stood close together, silent, and watched. 35 Point after point, the steady roses shone out to them, seeming to kindle something in their souls. The dusk came like smoke around, and still did not put out the roses.

Paul looked into Miriam's eyes. She was pale and expectant with wonder, her lips were parted, and her dark eyes lay open to him. His 40 look seemed to travel down into her. Her soul quivered. It was the communion she wanted. He turned aside, as if pained. He turned to the bush.

"They seem as if they walk like butterflies, and shake themselves," he said.

She looked at her roses. They were white, some incurved and holy, others expanded in an ecstasy. The tree was dark as a shadow. She lifted her hand impulsively to the flowers, she went forward and touched them in worship.

"Let us go," he said.

There was a cool scent of ivory roses, a white, virgin scent. Something made him feel anxious and imprisoned. The two walked in silence.

"Till Sunday," he said quietly, and left her, and she walked home slowly, feeling her soul satisfied with the holiness of the night. He stumbled down the path. And as soon as he was out of the wood, in the free open meadow where he could breathe, he started to run as fast as he could. It was like a delicious delirium in his veins.

Always, when he went with Miriam, and it grew rather late, he knew his mother was fretting and getting angry about him, why he could not understand. As he went into the house, flinging down his cap, his mother looked up at the clock. She had been sitting, thinking, because the* chill to her eyes prevented her reading. She could feel Paul being drawn away by this girl. And she did not care for Miriam. "She is one of those who will want to suck a man's soul out till he has none of his own left," she said to herself, "and he is just such a gaby as to let himself be absorbed. She will never let him become a man, she never will." So, while he was away with Miriam, Mrs Morel grew more and more worked up.

She glanced at the clock, and said, coldly, and rather tired:

"You have been far enough tonight."

His soul, warm and exposed from contact with the girl, shrank.

"You must have been right home with her," his mother continued.

He would not answer. Mrs Morel, looking at him quickly, saw his hair was damp on his forehead with haste, saw him frowning in his heavy fashion, resentfully.

"She must be wonderfully fascinating, that you can't get away from her, but must go trailing eight miles at this time of night."

He was hurt between the past glamour with Miriam and the

knowledge that his mother fretted. He had meant not to say anything, to refuse to answer. But he could not harden his heart to
ignore his mother.

"I *do* like to talk to her," he answered irritably.

"Is there nobody else to talk to?"   5

"You wouldn't say anything if I went with Edgar."

"You know I should. You know, whoever you went with, I should
say it was too far for you to go trailing, late at night, when you've been
to Nottingham.—Besides—" her voice suddenly flashed into anger
and contempt, "it is disgusting, bits of lads and girls courting."   10

"It is *not* courting," he cried.

"I don't know what else you call it."

"It's not! Do you think we *spoon* and do?* We only talk."

"Till Goodness knows what time and distance," was the sarcastic
rejoinder. Paul snapped at the laces of his boots, angrily.   15

"What are you so mad about?" he asked. "Because you don't like
her."

"I don't say I don't like her. But I don't hold with children keeping
company, and never did."

"But you don't mind our Annie going out with Jim Inger."   20

"They've more sense than you two."

"Why?"

"Our Annie's not one of the deep sort."

He failed to see the meaning of this remark. But his mother looked
tired. She was never so strong after William's death. And her eyes   25
hurt her.

"Well," he said, "it's so pretty in the country.—Mr Sleath asked
about you. He said he'd missed you.—Are you a bit better?"

"I ought to have been in bed a long time ago," she replied.

"Why mother, you know you wouldn't have gone before quarter   30
past ten."

"Oh yes I should!"

"Oh little woman, you'd say anything now you're disagreeable
with me, wouldn't you?"

He kissed her forehead, that he knew so well: the deep marks   35
between the brows, the rising of the fine hair, greying now, and the
proud setting of the temples. His hand lingered on her shoulder after
his kiss. Then he went slowly to bed. He had forgotten Miriam; he
only saw how his mother's hair was lifted back from her warm, broad
brow. And somehow, she was hurt.   40

Then the next time he saw Miriam, he said to her:

"Don't let me be late tonight—not later than ten o'clock. My mother gets so upset."

Miriam dropped her head, brooding.

5 "Why does she get upset?" she asked.

"Because she says I oughtn't to be out late when I have to get up early."

"Very well!" said Miriam, rather quietly, with just a touch of a sneer. He resented that. And he was usually late again.

10 That there was any love growing between him and Miriam, neither of them would have acknowledged. He thought he was too sane for such sentimentality, and she thought herself too lofty. They both were late in coming to maturity, and psychical ripeness was much behind even the physical. Miriam was exceedingly sensitive, as 15 her mother had always been. The slightest grossness made her recoil almost in anguish. Her brothers were brutal, but never coarse in speech. The men did all the discussing of farm matters outside. But, perhaps because of the continual business of birth and of begetting which goes on upon every farm, Miriam was the more hypersensitive 20 to the matter, and her blood was chastened almost to disgust of the faintest suggestion of such intercourse. Paul took his pitch from her, and their intimacy went on in an utterly blanched and chaste fashion. It could never be mentioned that the mare was in foal.

When he was nineteen, he was earning only twenty shillings a 25 week, but he was happy. His painting went well, and life went well enough. On the Good Friday he organised a walk to the Hemlock Stone. There were three lads of his own age, then Annie and Arthur, Miriam and Geoffrey. Arthur, apprenticed as an electrician in Nottingham, was home for the holiday. Morel, as usual, was up 30 early, whistling and sawing in the yard. At seven o'clock the family heard him buy three-pennyworth of hot cross buns, he talked with gusto to the little girl who brought them, calling her 'my darling'. He turned away several boys who came with more buns, telling them they had been "kested"* by a little lass. Then Mrs Morel got up, and 35 the family straggled down. It was an immense luxury to everybody, this lying in bed just beyond the ordinary time, on a week-day. And Paul and Arthur read before breakfast, and had the meal unwashed, sitting in their shirt sleeves. This was another holiday luxury. The room was warm. Everything felt free of care and anxiety. There was a 40 sense of plenty in the house.

While the boys were reading, Mrs Morel went into the garden. They were now in another house, an old one, near the Scargill street home, which had been left soon after William had died. Directly came an excited cry from the garden:

"Paul—Paul—come and look!" 5

It was his mother's voice. He threw down his book and went out. There was a long garden that ran to a field. It was a grey, cold day with a sharp wind blowing out of Derbyshire. Two fields away Bestwood began, with a jumble of roofs and red house-ends, out of which rose the church tower and the spire of the congregational 10 chapel. And beyond went woods and hills, right away to the pale grey heights of the Pennine Chain.

Paul looked down the garden for his mother. Her head appeared among the young currant bushes.

"Come here!" she cried. 15

"What for?" he answered.

"Come and see."

She had been looking at the buds on the currant trees. Paul went up.

"To think," she said, "that here I might never have seen them!" 20

Her son went to her side. Under the fence, in a little bed, was a ravel of poor grassy leaves, such as come from very immature bulbs, and three scillas in bloom. Mrs Morel pointed to the deep blue flowers.

"Now just see those!" she exclaimed. "I was looking at the 25 currant bushes, when thinks I to myself 'there's something very blue—is it a bit of sugar-bag?' And there behold you! Sugar-bag! Three Glories of the Snow,* and *such* beauties! But where on earth did they come from?"

"*I* don't know," said Paul. 30

"Well that's a marvel now! I *thought* I knew every weed and blade in this garden. But *haven't* they done well? You see that gooseberry bush just shelters them. Not nipped, not touched!"

He crouched down and turned up the bells of the blue little* flowers. 35

"They're a glorious colour!" he said.

"Aren't they!" she cried. "I guess they come from Switzerland where they say they have such lovely things. Fancy them against the snow! But where have they come from? They can't have *blown* here, can they?" 40

Then he remembered having set here a lot of little trash of bulbs,
to mature.

"And you never told me," she said.

"No, I thought I'd leave it till they might flower."

5   "And now you see! I might have missed them. And I've never had
a Glory of the Snow in my garden in my life."

She was full of excitement and elation. The garden was an
endless joy to her. Paul was thankful for her sake at last to be in a
house with a long garden that went down to the field. Every morning
10 after breakfast she went out and was happy pottering about in it. And
it was true, she knew every weed and blade.

Everybody turned up for the walk. Food was packed, and they set
off, a merry, delighted party. They hung over the wall of the mill
race, dropped paper in the water on one side the tunnel and watched
15 it shoot out on the other. They stood on the footbridge over
Boathouse Station, and looked at the metals gleaming coldly.

"You should see the Flying Scotchman come through at half past
six," said Leonard,* whose father was a signalman. "Lad, but she
doesn't half buzz!" And the little party looked up the lines one way,
20 to London, and the other way, to Scotland, and they felt the touch of
these two magical places.

In Ilkeston the colliers were waiting in gangs for the public houses
to open. It was a town of idleness and lounging. At Stanton Gate the
iron foundry blazed. Over everything there were great discussions.
25 At Trowell they crossed again from Derbyshire into Nottinghamshire. They came to the Hemlock Stone at dinner time. Its field
was crowded with folk from Nottingham and Ilkeston.

They had expected a venerable and dignified monument. They
found a little, gnarled, twisted stump of rock, something like a
30 decayed mushroom, standing out pathetically on the side of a field.
Leonard and Dick immediately proceeded to carve their initials,
L.W. and R.P., in the old red sandstone, but Paul desisted, because
he had read in the newspaper satirical remarks about initial-carvers
who could find no other road to immortality. Then all the lads
35 climbed to the top of the rock to look round.

Everywhere in the field below, factory girls and lads were eating
lunch or sporting about. Beyond was the garden of an old manor. It
had yew hedges, and thick clumps and borders of yellow crocuses
round the lawn.

40   "See," said Paul to Miriam, "what a quiet garden."

She saw the dark yews and the golden crocuses, then she looked at him gratefully. He had not seemed to belong to her among all these others; he was different then, not her Paul who understood the slightest quiver of her innermost soul, but something else, speaking another language than hers. How it hurt her and deadened her very 5 perceptions. Only when he came right back to her, leaving his other, his lesser self as she thought, would she feel alive again. And now he asked her to look at this garden wanting the contact with her again. Impatient of the set in the field, she turned to the quiet lawn surrounded by sheaves of shut-up crocuses. A feeling of stillness, 10 almost of ecstasy came over her. It felt almost as if she were alone with him in this garden.

Then he left her again, and joined the others. Soon they started home. Miriam loitered behind, alone. She did not fit in with the others; she could very rarely get into human relations with anyone: 15 so her friend, her companion, her lover was nature. She saw the sun declining wanly. In the dusky, cold hedgerows were some red leaves. She lingered to gather them, tenderly, passionately. The love in her finger-tips caressed the leaves, the passion in her heart came to a glow upon the leaves. 20

Suddenly she realised she was alone in a strange road, and she hurried forward. Turning a corner in the lane, she came upon Paul who stood bent over something, his mind fixed on it, working away steadily, patiently, a little hopelessly. She hesitated in her approach, to watch. 25

He remained concentrated in the middle of the road. Beyond, one rift of rich gold in that colourless grey evening seemed to make him stand out in dark relief. She saw him slender and firm, as if the setting sun had given him to her. A deep pain took hold of her, and she knew she must love him. And she had discovered him, dis- 30 covered in him a rare potentiality, discovered his loneliness. Quivering as at some 'Annunciation',* she went slowly forward.

At last he looked up.

"Why," he exclaimed gratefully, "have you waited for me!"

She saw a deep shadow in his eyes. 35

"What is it?" she asked.

"The spring broken here."

And he showed her where his umbrella was injured. Instantly, with some shame, she knew he had not done the damage himself, but that Geoffrey was responsible. 40

"It is only an old umbrella, isn't it?" she asked.

She wondered why he, who did not usually trouble over trifles, made such a mountain of this molehill.

5 "But it was William's—an' my mother can't help but know," he said quietly, still patiently working at the umbrella. The words went through Miriam like a blade. This then was the confirmation of her vision of him! She looked at him. But there was about him a certain reserve, and she dared not comfort him, not even speak softly to him.

10 "Come on," he said. "I can't do it."

And they went in silence along the road.

That same evening they were walking along under the trees by Nether Green. He was talking to her, fretfully, seemed to be struggling to convince himself.

15 "You know," he said, with an effort, "if one person loves, the other does."

"Ah!" she answered, "like mother said to me when I was little: 'Love begets love'."

"Yes—something like that—I think it *must* be."

20 "I hope so—because if it were not, love might be a very terrible thing," she said.

"Yes but it *is*—at least with most people," he answered.

And Miriam, thinking he had assured himself, felt strong in herself. She always regarded that sudden coming upon him in the 25 lane as a revelation. And this conversation remained graven in her mind, as one of the letters of the Law.*

Now she stood with him and for him. When, about this time, he outraged the family feeling at Willey Farm, by some overbearing insult, she stuck to him and believed he was right.

30 And at this time she dreamed dreams of him, vivid, unforgettable. These dreams came again later on, developed to a more subtle psychological stage.

On the Easter Monday the same party took an excursion to Wingfield Manor. It was great excitement to Miriam to catch a train 35 at Lethley Bridge, amid all the bustle of the Bank Holiday crowd. They left the train at Alfreton. Paul was interested in the street, and in the colliers with their dogs. Here was a new race of miners. Miriam did not live till they came to the church. They were all rather timid of entering, with their bags of food, for fear of being turned 40 out. Leonard, a comic, thin fellow, went first, Paul, who would have died rather than be sent back, went last. The place was decorated for Easter. In the font hundreds of white narcissi seemed to be growing. The air was dim, and coloured from the windows, and thrilled with a subtle scent of lilies and narcissi. In that atmosphere Miriam's soul came into a glow. Paul was afraid of the things he mustn't do. And he was sensitive to the feel of the place. Miriam turned to him. He answered. They were together. He would not go beyond the communion rail. She loved him for that. Her soul expanded into prayer beside him. He felt the strange fascination of shadowy religious places. All his latent mysticism quivered into life. She was drawn to him. He was a prayer along with her.

In the church-yard daffodils and jonquils were out, and so bright in the sunshine that they seemed to flutter. Lambs in the park were making the air tremble with their many tiny bleats. Leonard and Dick went into a public-house for a drink, much to the disgust of Paul and Annie.

"What did you go in a pub for?" asked Paul, crossly.

"Well," laughed Dick. "We only went for a lemonade."

"Even then you could have got it in a shop," said Annie.

"Shop!" cried Leonard. "Can you see our stout British hearts drinking lemonade in a shop?"

"No," said Paul, "but I can see your stout British mug."

"What's my mug done amiss?" said Leonard, wiping his wide mouth.

Miriam very rarely talked to the other lads. They at once became awkward in conversation with her. So usually she was silent.

It was past mid-day when they climbed the steep path to the manor. All things shone softly in the sun, which was wonderfully warm and enlivening. Celandines and violets were out. Everybody was tip-top full with happiness. The glitter of the ivy, the soft, atmospheric grey of the castle walls, the gentleness of everything near the ruin was perfect.

The manor is of hard, pale-grey stone, and the outer walls are blank and calm. The young folk were in raptures. They went in trepidation, almost afraid that the delight of exploring this ruin might be denied them. In the first courtyard, within the high, broken walls, were farm-carts with their shafts lying idle on the ground, the tyres of the wheels brilliant with gold-red rust. It was very still.

All eagerly paid their sixpences, and went timidly through the fine clean arch of the inner courtyard. They were shy. Here on the pavement where the hall had been, an old thorn-tree was budding. All kinds of strange openings and broken rooms were in the shadow around them.

"Isn't this all right!" exclaimed Leonard.

5 "Isn't it just!" added Paul.

And they rushed off to explore.

"Lad!" cried Leonard. "Here's an oven for you!"

And he promptly crept in the cavern. Dick and Paul crawled in after him, and the three sat and bellowed as if from the bowels of the 10 earth.

"They could cook an ox or two in here," said Dick.

"*And* a deer or two," added Paul.

"*And* a hass or two," added Leonard.

Whereupon he brayed loudly, while the other two punched him.

15 Paul made a dive for the open air, and the exploration continued. At last they came upon Geoffrey and the girls again. Geoffrey was eating.

"I reckon it *is* about snap-time," said Leonard.

"I've begun," said Geoffrey. He had been eating, more or less, 20 since the party set out.

"Where shall we sit?" asked Miriam.

"Let's go in the banqueting chamber," said Paul.

"How d'you know it's a banqueting chamber?" asked Leonard.

"Because I saw it on a picture."

25 "Right then, we'll banquet," said Leonard.

In the big, ruined apartment, with its raw edges high up against the blue sky, they sat in the sunshine to eat, looking up at the birds that twittered in the tracery of the big window.

"Now Lord Fuzzball,"* said Leonard to Paul, "willst thou partake 30 of this venison pasty?"

"No, Sir Staybone," replied Paul. "I will e'en have of this haunch of bread and cheese."

"And prithee," said Geoffrey, "hutch up an' make a bit more room."

35 "A million pardons, Gracious Sir," said Leonard. "Thou sprottlest so."

"Paul," said Annie, "here's your hard-boiled egg."

"Today we have, my hearty nobles, a feast of phœnix eggs, laid by our only phœnix, and bearing all our crest, as printed there by our 40 most accommodating fowl—" said Paul.

"Namely, a bit of dirt," said Leonard.

"Which has been our proud crest for generations Amen!" said Annie.

"A smut rampant,"* added Paul, which made Miriam laugh.

After lunch, they set off once more to explore the ruin. This time the girls went with the boys, who could act as guides and expositors. There was one tall tower in a corner, rather tottering, where they say Mary Queen of Scots was imprisoned.

"Think of the queen going up here," said Miriam, in a low voice, as she climbed the hollow stairs.

"If she could get up," said Paul, "for she had rheumatism like anything. I reckon they treated her rottenly."

"You don't think she deserved it?" asked Miriam.

"No I don't. She was only lively."*

They continued to mount the winding stair-case. A high wind blowing through the loopholes went rushing up the shaft and filled the girl's skirts like a balloon, so that she was ashamed, until he took the hem of her dress, and held it down for her. He did it perfectly simply, as he would have picked up her glove. She remembered this always.

Round the broken top of the tower the ivy bushed out, old and handsome. Also there were a few chill gillivers, in pale cold bud. Miriam wanted to lean over for some ivy, but he would not let her. Instead she had to wait behind him, and take from him each spray as he gathered it and held it to her, each one separately, in the purest manner of chivalry. The tower seemed to rock in the wind. They looked over miles and miles of wooded country, and country with gleams of pasture.

The crypt underneath the manor was beautiful and in perfect preservation. Paul made a drawing. Miriam stayed with him. She was thinking of Mary Queen of Scots looking with her strained hopeless eyes, that could not understand misery, over the hills where no help came,* or sitting in this crypt being told of a God as cold as the place she sat in.

They set off again gaily, looking round on their beloved manor that stood so clean and big on its hill.

"Supposing you could have *that* farm," said Paul to Miriam.

"Yes!"

"Wouldn't it be lovely to come and see you!"

They were now in the bare country of stone walls, which he loved, and which, though only ten miles from home, seemed so foreign to Miriam. The party was straggling now. As they were crossing a large meadow that sloped away from the sun, along a path embedded with innumerable tiny glittering points, Paul, walking alongside, laced his fingers in the strings of the bag Miriam was carrying, and instantly she felt Annie behind, watchful and jealous. But the meadow was bathed in a glory of sunshine, and the path was jewelled, and it was seldom that he gave her any sign. She held her fingers very still among the strings of the bag, his fingers touching. And the place was golden as a vision.

At last they came into the straggling grey village of Crich, that lies high. Beyond the village was the famous Crich Stand, that Paul could see from the garden at home. The party pushed on. Great expanse of country spread around and below. The lads were eager to get to the top of the hill. It was capped by a round knoll, half of which was by now cut away, and on the top of which stood an ancient monument, sturdy and squat, for signalling in old days far down into the level lands of Nottinghamshire and Leicestershire.

It was blowing so hard, high up there in the exposed place, that the only way to be safe was to stand nailed by the wind to the wall of the tower. At their feet fell the precipice where the limestone was quarried away. Below was a jumble of hills and tiny villages— Matlock, Ambergate, Stoney Middleton. The lads were eager to spy out the Church of Bestwood, far away among the rather wooded* country on the left. They were disgusted that it seemed to stand on a plain. They saw the hills of Derbyshire fall into the monotony of the midlands, that swept away south.

Miriam was somewhat scared by the wind, but the lads enjoyed it. They went on, miles and miles, to Whatstandwell. All the food was eaten, everybody was hungry and there was very little money to get home with. But they managed to procure a loaf and a currant loaf, which they hacked into pieces with shut-knives, and ate sitting on the wall near the bridge, watching the bright Derwent rushing by, and the brakes from Matlock pulling up at the inn.

Paul was now pale with weariness. He had been responsible for the party all day, and now he was done. Miriam understood, and kept close to him, and he left himself in her hands.

They had an hour to wait at Ambergate station. Trains came, crowded with excursionists, returning to Manchester, Birmingham and London.

"We might be going there—folk easily might think we're going that far," said Paul.

They got back rather late. Miriam, walking home with Geoffrey, watched the moon rise big and red and misty. She felt something was fulfilled in her.

She had an elder sister Agatha,* who was a school-teacher. Between the two girls was a feud. Miriam considered Agatha worldly. And she wanted herself to be a school-teacher.

One Saturday afternoon Agatha and Miriam were upstairs dressing. Their bedroom was over the stable. It was a low room, not very large, and bare. Miriam had nailed on the wall a reproduction of Veronese's "St. Catherine."* She loved the woman who sat in the window, dreaming. Her own windows were too small to sit in. But the front one was dripped over with honeysuckle and virginia creeper, and looked upon the tree-tops of the oak-wood across the yard, while the little back window, no bigger than a handkerchief, was a loop-hole to the east, to the dawn beating up against the beloved round hills.

The two sisters did not talk much to each other. Agatha, who was fair and small and determined, had rebelled against the home atmosphere, against the doctrine of "the other cheek." She was out in the world now, in a fair way to be independent. And she insisted on worldly values, on appearance, on manners, on position, which Miriam would fain have ignored.

Both girls liked to be upstairs, out of the way, when Paul came. They preferred to come running down, open the stairfoot door, and see him watching, expectant of them. Miriam stood painfully pulling over her head a rosary he had given her. It caught in the fine mesh of her hair. But at last she had it on, and the red-brown wooden beads looked well against her cool-brown neck. She was a well-developed girl, and very handsome. But in the little looking glass nailed against the white-washed wall, she could only see a fragment of herself at a time. Agatha had bought a little mirror of her own, which she propped up to suit herself. Miriam was near the window. Suddenly she heard the well-known click of the chain, and she saw Paul fling open the gate, push his bicycle into the yard. She saw him look at the house, and she shrank away. He walked in a nonchalant fashion, and his bicycle went with him as if it were a live thing.

"Paul's come!" she exclaimed.

"Aren't you glad?" said Agatha cuttingly.

Miriam stood still in amazement and bewilderment.

"Well, aren't you?" she asked.

"Yes, but I'm not going to let him see it, and think I wanted him."

Miriam was startled. She heard him putting his bicycle in the
5 stable underneath, and talking to Jimmy, who had been a pit-horse,
and who was seedy.

"Well Jimmy my lad, how are ter? Nobbut sick an' sadly, like?
Why then it's a shame, my owd lad!"

She heard the rope run through the hole as the horse lifted its
10 head from the lad's caress. How she loved to listen, when he thought
only the horse could hear. But there was a serpent in her Eden.* She
searched earnestly in herself to see if she wanted Paul Morel. She
felt there would be some disgrace in it. Full of twisted feeling, she
was afraid she did want him. She stood selfconvicted. Then came an
15 agony of new shame. She shrank within herself in a coil of torture.
Did she want Paul Morel, and did he know she wanted him? What a
subtle infamy upon her! She felt as if her whole soul coiled into
knots of shame.

Agatha was dressed first and ran downstairs. Miriam heard her
20 greet the lad gaily, knew exactly how brilliant her grey eyes became
with that tone. She herself would have felt it bold to have greeted
him in such wise. Yet there she stood under the self-accusation of
wanting him, tied to that stake of torture. In bitter perplexity, she
kneeled down and prayed:
25 "Oh Lord, let me not love Paul Morel. Keep me from loving him,
if I ought not to love him."

Something anomalous in the prayer arrested her. She lifted her
head and pondered. How could it be wrong to love him? Love was
God's gift. And yet it caused her shame. That was because of him,
30 Paul Morel. But then, it was not his affair, it was her own, between
herself and God. She was to be a sacrifice. But it was God's
sacrifice, not Paul Morel's or her own. After a few minutes she hid
her face in the pillow again, and said:

"But, Lord, if it is Thy will that I should love him, make me love
35 him—as Christ would, who died for the souls of men. Make me love
him splendidly, because he is Thy son."*

She remained kneeling for some time, quite still, and deeply
moved, her black hair against the red squares, and the lavender
sprigged squares of the patchwork quilt. Prayer was almost essential
40 to her. Then she fell into that rapture of self-sacrifice, identifying

herself with a God who was sacrificed, which gives to so many human souls their deepest bliss.

When she went downstairs, Paul was lying back in an arm-chair, holding forth with much vehemence to Agatha, who was scorning a little painting he had brought to show her. Miriam glanced at the two, and avoided their levity. She went into the parlour, to be alone.

It was tea-time before she was able to speak to Paul, and then her manner was so distant, he thought he had offended her.

Miriam discontinued her practice of going each Thursday evening to the library in Bestwood. After calling for Paul regularly during the whole spring, a number of trifling incidents and tiny insults from his family awakened her to their attitude towards her, and she decided to go no more. So she announced to Paul one evening she would not call at his house again for him on Thursday nights.

"Why?" he asked, very short.

"Nothing. Only I'd rather not."

"Very well."

"But," she faltered, "if you'd care to meet me, we could still go together."

"Meet you where?"

"Somewhere—where you like."

"I shan't meet you anywhere. I don't see why you shouldn't keep calling for me. But if you won't, I don't want to meet you."

So the Thursday evenings, which had been so precious to her, and to him, were dropped. He worked instead. Mrs Morel sniffed with satisfaction at this arrangement.

· He would not have it that they were lovers. The intimacy between them had been kept so abstract, such a matter of the soul, all thought and weary struggle into consciousness, that he saw it only as a Platonic friendship.* He stoutly denied there was anything else between them. Miriam was silent, or else she very quietly agreed. He was a fool who did not know what was happening to himself. By tacit agreement they ignored the remarks and insinuations of their acquaintances.

"We aren't lovers, we are friends," he said to her. "*We* know it. Let them talk. What does it matter, what they say."

Sometimes, as they were walking together, she slipped her arm timidly into his. But he always resented it, and she knew it. It caused a violent conflict in him. With Miriam he was always on the high

plane of abstraction, when his natural fire of love was transmitted into the fine steam of thought. She would have it so. If he were jolly and, as she put it, flippant, she waited till he came back to her, till the change had taken place in him again, and he was wrestling with his
5 own soul, frowning, passionate in his desire for understanding. And in this passion for understanding her soul lay close to his, she had him all to herself. But he must be made abstract first.

Then, if she put her arm in his, it caused him almost torture. His consciousness seemed to split. The place where she was touching
10 him ran hot with friction. He was one internecine battle, and he became cruel to her because of it.*

One evening in midsummer Miriam called at the house, warm from climbing. Paul was alone in the kitchen, his mother could be heard moving about upstairs.
15 "Come and look at the sweet-peas," he said to the girl.

They went into the garden. The sky behind the townlet and the church was orange-red, the flower garden was flooded with a strange warm light that lifted every leaf into significance. Paul passed along a fine row of sweet-peas, gathering a blossom here and there, all cream
20 and pale blue. Miriam followed, breathing the fragrance. To her flowers appealed with such strength she felt she must make them part of herself. When she bent and breathed a flower, it was as if she and the flower were loving each other. Paul hated her for it. There seemed a sort of exposure about the action, something too intimate.
25 When he had got a fair bunch, they returned to the house. He listened for a moment to his mother's quiet movement upstairs, then he said:

"Come here, and let me pin them in for you."

He arranged them two or three at a time in the bosom of her dress,
30 stepping back now and then to see the effect.

"You know," he said, taking the pin out of his mouth, "a woman ought always to arrange her flowers before her glass."

Miriam laughed. She thought flowers ought to be pinned in one's dress without any care. That Paul should take pains to fix her flowers
35 for her was his whim.

He was rather offended at her laughter.

"Some women do—those who look decent," he said.

Miriam laughed again, but mirthlessly, to hear him thus mix her up with women in a general way. From most men she would have
40 ignored it. But from him, it hurt her.

He had nearly finished arranging the flowers when he heard his mother's footstep on the stairs. Hurriedly he pushed in the last pin and turned away.

"Don't let mater know," he said.

Miriam picked up her books and stood in the doorway, looking with chagrin at the beautiful sunset. She would call for Paul no more, she said.

"Goodevening, Mrs Morel," she said, in a deferential way. She sounded as if she felt she had no right to be there.

"Oh is it you Miriam!" replied Mrs Morel coolly.

But Paul insisted on everybody's accepting his friendship with the girl, and Mrs Morel was too wise to have any open rupture.

It was not till he was twenty years old that the family could ever afford to go away for a holiday. Mrs Morel had never been away for a holiday, except to see her sister, since she had been married. Now at last Paul had saved enough money, and they were all going. There was to be a party: some of Annie's friends, one friend of Paul's, a young man in the same office where William had previously been, and Miriam.

It was great excitement writing for rooms. Paul and his mother debated it endlessly between them. They wanted a furnished cottage for two weeks. She thought one week would be enough, but he insisted on two. He went out before the post came in the morning. So, when he came home, his mother's first words to him were:

"Paul, you know that cat at Skegness—she only wants four guineas a week for her measly bungalow."

"Then let her whistle for it," said Paul.

"I should think so," replied his mother, indignantly. Then that evening, he wrote another letter. At last they got an answer from Mablethorpe, a cottage such as they wished for thirty shillings a week. There was immense jubilation. Paul was wild with joy for his mother's sake. She would have a real holiday now. He and she sat at evening picturing what it would be like. Annie came in, and Leonard, and Alice, and Kitty.* There was wild rejoicing and anticipation. Paul told Miriam. She seemed to brood with joy over it. But the Morels' house rang with excitement.

They were to go on Saturday morning by the seven train. Paul suggested that Miriam should sleep at his house, because it was so far for her to walk. She came down for supper. Everybody was so excited that even Miriam was accepted with warmth. But almost as

soon as she entered, the feeling in the family became close and tight. He had discovered a poem by Jean Ingelow which mentioned Mablethorpe,* and so he must read it to Miriam. He would never have got so far in the direction of sentimentality as to read poetry to
5 his own family. But now they condescended to listen. Miriam sat on the sofa, absorbed in him. She always seemed absorbed in him and by him, when he was present. Mrs Morel sat jealously in her own chair. She was going to hear also. And even Annie and the father attended, Morel with his head cocked on one side, like somebody
10 listening to a sermon and feeling conscious of the fact. Paul ducked his head over the book. He had got now all the audience he cared for. And Mrs Morel and Annie almost contested with Miriam who should listen best and win his favour. He was in very high feather.

"But," interrupted Mrs Morel, "what *is* the 'Bride of Enderby',
15 that the bells are supposed to ring."

"It's an old tune they used to play on the bells for a warning against water. I suppose the Bride of Enderby was drowned in a flood," he replied. He had not the faintest knowledge what it really was, but he would never have sunk so low as to confess that to his
20 women-folk. They listened and believed him. He believed himself.

"And the people knew what that tune meant?" said his mother.

"Yes—just like the Scotch when they heard 'The Flowers o' the Forest'*—and when they used to ring the bells backward for alarm."*

"How!" said Annie. "A bell sounds the same whether it's rung
25 backwards or forwards."

"But," he said, "if you start with the deep bell and ring up to the high one—der—der—der—der—der—der—der—der!"

He ran up the scale. Everybody thought it clever. He thought so too. Then, waiting a minute, he continued the poem.

30 "Hm!" said Mrs Morel, curiously, when he finished. "But I wish everything that's written weren't so sad."

"*I* canna see what they want* drownin' theirselves for," said Morel. There was a pause. Annie got up to clear the table.

"I think 'Elizabeth' is a beautiful name," said Miriam, in a low
35 voice. " 'My son's wife Elizabeth—' "

"Yes," said Paul.

"Yes," said his mother. "But I don't like 'Lizzie', and 'Liza' I abominate."

It didn't appear, either to Paul or Miriam, that 'Lizzie' and 'Liza'
40 had anything to do with it.

"But 'Elizabeth'!" murmured Miriam.

"And Queen Elizabeth was awfully fond of being called 'Great Eliza'," said Paul.

"And come again tomorrow!" ejaculated Morel.

Mrs Morel laughed—so did Paul.   5

"I'll bet 'er wor a toe-rag," said Morel, following up his joke.

"Don't you be so cheeky about a queen," said Annie.

"Queens!" said Morel. "Why what's a' on you but queens? You've nowt to do but sit i' your grandeur."

Miriam rose to help with the pots.   10

"Let *me* help to wash up," she said.

"Certainly not," cried Annie. "You sit down again. There aren't many."

And Miriam, who could not be familiar and insist, sat down again to look at the book with Paul.   15

He was master of the party—his father was no good. And great tortures he suffered lest the tin box should be put out at Firsby instead of at Mablethorpe. And he wasn't equal to getting a carriage. His bold little mother did that.

"Here!" she cried to a man, "Here!"   20

Paul and Annie got behind the rest, convulsed with shamed laughter.

"How much will it be to drive to Brook Cottage?" said Mrs Morel.

"Two shillings."

"Why how far is it?"   25

"A good way."

"I don't believe it," she said.

But she scrambled in. There were eight crowded in one old sea-side carriage.

"You see," said Mrs Morel, "it's only threepence each, and if it   30
were a tram car—"

They drove along. Each cottage they came to, Mrs Morel cried:
"Is it this?—now this is it!"

Everybody sat breathless. They drove past. There was a universal sigh.   35

"I'm thankful it wasn't that brute," said Mrs Morel. "I *was* frightened."

They drove on and on.

"That stinking hussy* said ten minutes to the sea—!" exclaimed Mrs Morel.   40

"An' hour if it's a minute," replied Morel.

And everybody fell on him in fury.

"Are we *never* going to get there!" cried Mrs Morel.

"Don't shout so mother," said Annie. "Whatever will he think?"

Mrs Morel looked up quizzically at the driver.

"I'm sure I couldn't say. But not much, from the look of him."

At last they descended at a house that stood alone over the dyke by the high road. There was wild excitement because they had to cross a little bridge to get into the front garden. But they loved the house, that lay so solitary, with a sea-meadow on one side, and immense expanse of land patched in white barley, yellow oats, red wheat, and green root-crops, flat and stretching level to the sky.

Paul kept accounts. He and his mother ran the show. The total expenses, lodging, food everything, was sixteen shillings a week per person. He and Leonard went bathing in the morning. Morel was wandering abroad quite early.

"You Paul," his mother called from the bedroom. "Eat a piece of bread and butter."

"All right," he answered.

And when he got back, he saw his mother presiding in state at the breakfast table. The woman of the house was young. Her husband was blind, and she did laundry work. So Mrs Morel always washed the pots in the kitchen and made the beds.

"But you said you'd have a real holiday," said Paul, "and now you work."

"Work!" she exclaimed. "What are you talking about!"

He loved to go with her across the fields to the village and the sea. She was afraid of the plank bridges, and he abused her for being a baby. On the whole, he stuck to her as if he were *her* man.

Miriam did not get much of him—except, perhaps, when all the others went to the 'Coons.'* Coons were insufferably stupid to Miriam, so he thought they were to himself also, and he preached priggishly to Annie about the fatuity of listening to them. Yet he too knew all their songs, and sang them along the roads, roisterously. And if he found himself listening, the stupidity pleased him very much. Yet to Annie he said:

"Such rot!—there isn't a grain of intelligence in it. Nobody with more gumption than a grasshopper could go and sit and listen." And to Miriam he said, with much scorn, of Annie and the others:

"I suppose they're at the Coons."

It was queer to see Miriam singing Coon songs. She had a straight
chin, that went in a perpendicular line from the lower lip to the turn.
She always reminded Paul of some sad Botticelli angel* when she
sang, even when it was:

> "Come down Lover's Lane   5
> For a walk with me, talk with me—"*

Only when he sketched, or at evening when the others were at the
Coons, she had him to herself. He talked to her endlessly about his
love of horizontals: how they, the great levels of sky and land in
Lincolnshire meant to him the eternality of the will: just as the   10
bowed Norman arches of the church, repeating themselves, meant
the dogged leaping forward of the persistent human soul, on and on,
nobody knows where: in contradiction to the perpendicular lines,
and to the gothic arch,* which, he said, leapt up at heaven and
touched the ecstasy and lost itself in the divine. Himself, he said,   15
was Norman, Miriam was Gothic. She bowed in consent even to
that.

One evening, he and she went up the great, sweeping shore of
sand towards Theddlethorpe. The long breakers plunged and ran in
a hiss of foam along the coast. It was a warm evening. There was not 20
a figure but themselves on the far reaches of sand, no noise but the
sound of the sea. Paul loved to see it clanging at the land. He loved
to feel himself between the noise of it and the silence of the sandy
shore. Miriam was with him. Everything grew very intense. It was
quite dark when they turned again. The way home was through a   25
gap in the sand hills, and then along a raised grass road between two
dykes. The country was black and still. From behind the sandhills
came the whisper of the sea. Paul and Miriam walked in silence.
Suddenly he started. The whole of his blood seemed to burst into
flame, and he could scarcely breathe. An enormous orange moon*   30
was staring at them from the rim of the sand hills. He stood still,
looking at it.

"Ah!" cried Miriam, when she saw it.

He remained perfectly still, staring at the immense and ruddy
moon, the only thing in the far-reaching darkness of the level. His   35
heart beat heavily, the muscles of his arms contracted.

"What is it?" murmured Miriam, waiting for him.

He turned and looked at her. She stood beside him, for ever in
shadow. Her face, covered with the darkness of her hat, was watching him unseen. But she was brooding. She was slightly afraid—   40

deeply moved and religious. That was her best state. He was impotent against it. His blood was concentrated like a flame in his chest. But he could not get across to her. There were flashes in his blood. But somehow she ignored them. She was expecting some
5 religious state in him. Still yearning, she was half aware of his passion, and gazed at him, troubled.

"What is it?" she murmured again.

"It's the moon," he answered, frowning.

"Yes," she assented. "Isn't it wonderful?" She was curious about
10 him. The crisis was past.

He did not know himself what was the matter. He was naturally so young, and their intimacy was so abstract, he did not know he wanted to crush her onto his breast to ease the ache there. He was afraid of her. The fact that he might want her as a man wants a
15 woman had in him been suppressed into a shame.* When she shrank in her convulsed, coiled torture from the thought of such a thing, he had winced to the depths of his soul. And now this 'purity' prevented even their first love kiss. It was as if she could scarcely stand the shock of physical love, even a passionate kiss, and then he was too
20 shrinking and sensitive to give it.

As they walked along the dark fen-meadow, he watched the moon, and did not speak. She plodded beside him. He hated her, for she seemed, in some way, to make him despise himself. Looking ahead, he saw the one light in the darkness, the window of their
25 lamp-lit cottage.

He loved to think of his mother, and the other jolly people.

"Well, everybody else has been in long ago!" said his mother as they entered.

"What does that matter!" he cried irritably. "I can go a walk if I
30 like, can't I?"

"And I should have thought you could get in to supper with the rest," said Mrs Morel.

"I shall please myself," he retorted. "It's not *late*. I shall do as I like."

35 "Very well," said his mother, cuttingly, "then *do* as you like."

And she took no further notice of him that evening. Which he pretended neither to notice nor to care about, but sat reading. Miriam read also, obliterating herself. Mrs Morel hated her for making her son like this. She watched Paul growing irritable,
40 priggish, and melancholic. For this she put the blame on Miriam.

Annie, and all her friends joined against the girl. Miriam had no friend of her own, only Paul. But she did not suffer so much, because she despised the triviality of these other people.

And Paul hated her because, somehow, she spoilt his ease and naturalness. And he writhed himself with a feeling of humiliation.   5

Chapter VIII

Strife in Love

Arthur finished his apprenticeship, and got a job on the electrical plant at Minton pit. He earned very little, but had a good chance of getting on. But he was wild and restless. He did not drink, nor gamble. Yet he somehow contrived to get into endless scrapes, always through some hot-headed thoughtlessness. Either he went rabbiting in the woods, like a poacher, or he stayed in Nottingham all night instead of coming home, or he miscalculated his dive into the canal at Bestwood, and scored his chest into one mass of wounds on the raw stones and tins at the bottom.

He had not been at his work many months, when again he did not come home one night.

"Do you know where Arthur is?" asked Paul at breakfast.

"I do not," replied his mother.

"He is a fool," said Paul. "And if he *did* anything I shouldn't mind! But no, he simply can't come away from a game of whist, or else he must see a girl home from the skating rink—quite proprietously*—and so can't get home. He's a fool."

"I don't know that it would make it any better if he did something to make us all ashamed," said Mrs Morel.

"Well I should respect him more," said Paul.

"I very much doubt it," said his mother coldly.

They went on with breakfast.

"Are you fearfully fond of him?" Paul asked his mother.

"What do you ask that for?"

"Because they say a woman always likes the youngest best."

"She may do—but I don't.—No, he wearies me."

"And you'd actually rather he was good?"

"I'd rather he showed some of a man's common-sense."

Paul was raw and irritable. He also wearied his mother very often. She saw the sunshine going out of him, and she resented it.

As they were finishing breakfast, came the postman with a letter from Derby. Mrs Morel screwed up her eyes to look at the address.

"Give it here, blind eye!" exclaimed her son, snatching it away from her. She started and almost boxed his ears.

"It's from your son Arthur," he said.

"What now—!" cried Mrs Morel.

"'My dearest Mother,'" Paul read. "'I don't know what made me such a fool. I want you to come and fetch me back from here. I came with Jack Bredon yesterday, instead of going to work, and enlisted. He said he was sick of wearing the seat of a stool out, and like the idiot you know I am, I came away with him.

I have taken the King's Shilling,* but perhaps if you came for me they would let me go back with you. I was a fool when I did it. I don't want to be in the army. My dear mother, I am nothing but a trouble to you. But if you get me out of this, I promise I will have more sense and consideration.— —'"

Mrs Morel sat down in her rocking-chair.

"Well *now*," she cried, "let him stop!"

"Yes," said Paul. "Let him stop."

There was silence. The mother sat with her hands folded in her apron, her face set, thinking.

"If I'm not *sick*!" she cried suddenly. "Sick!!"

"Now!" said Paul, beginning to frown, "you're not going to worry your soul out about this, do you hear."

"I suppose I'm to take it as a blessing," she flashed, turning on her son.

"You're not going to mount it up to a tragedy, so there," he retorted.

"The *fool*!—the young fool!" she cried.

"He'll look well in uniform," said Paul, irritatingly.

His mother turned on him like a fury.*

"Oh will he!" she cried. "Not in my eyes—!"

"He should get in a cavalry regiment—he'll have the time of his life, and will look an awful swell."

"Swell!—*swell*!!—a mighty swell indeed!—a common soldier!"

"Well," said Paul, "what am I but a common clerk?"

"A good deal, my boy," cried his mother, stung.

"What?"

"At any rate, a *man*, and not a thing in a red coat."

"I shouldn't mind being in a red coat—or dark blue, that would suit me better—if they didn't boss me about too much."

But his mother had ceased to listen.

"Just as he was getting on, or might have been getting on at his job—a young nuisance—here he goes and ruins himself for life. What good will he be, do you think, after *this*?"

"It may lick him in to shape beautifully," said Paul.

"Lick him into shape!—lick what marrow there *was* out of his bones. A *soldier!*—a common *soldier!!*—nothing but a body that makes movements when it hears a shout! It's a fine thing!"

"I can't understand why it upsets you," said Paul.

"No, perhaps you can't. But *I* understand," and she sat back in her chair, her chin in one hand, holding her elbow with the other, brimmed up with wrath and chagrin.

"And shall you go to Derby?" asked Paul.

"Yes."

"It's no good."

"I'll see for myself."

"And why on earth don't you let him stop. It's just what he wants."

"Of course," cried the mother, "*you* know what he wants."

She got ready and went by the first train to Derby, where she saw her son and the sergeant. It was however no good.

When Morel was having his dinner in the evening, she said suddenly:

"I've had to go to Derby today."

The miner turned up his eyes, showing the whites in his black face.

"Has ter lass—what took thee there?"

"That Arthur!"

"Oh—an' what's agate now?"

"He's only enlisted."

Morel put down his knife and leaned back in his chair.

"Nay," he said, "that he niver 'as!"

"And is going down to Aldershot tomorrow."

"Well!" exclaimed the miner. "That's a winder."

Morel* considered it a moment, said "Hm!", and proceeded with his dinner. Suddenly his face contracted with wrath.

"I hope he may never set foot i' my house again," he said.

"The idea!" cried Mrs Morel. "Saying such a thing!"

"I do," repeated Morel. "A fool as runs away for a soldier—let 'im look after 'issen—I s'll do no more for 'im."

"A fat sight you have done as it is," she said.

And Morel was almost ashamed to go to his public house that evening.

"Well did you go?" said Paul to his mother when he came home.

"I did."

"And could you see him?"

"Yes."

"And what did he say?"

"He blubbered when I came away."

"Hm!"

"And so did I, so you needn't 'hm!'."

Mrs Morel fretted after her son. She knew he would not like the army. He did not. The discipline was intolerable to him.

"But the doctor," she said with some pride, to Paul, "said he was perfectly proportioned—almost exactly, all his measurements were correct. He *is* good-looking, you know."

"He's awfully nice looking. But he doesn't fetch the girls like William, does he?"

"No—it's a different character. He's a good deal like his father, irresponsible."

To console his mother, Paul did not go much to Willey Farm at this time. And in the autumn exhibition of Students' Work in the Castle,* he had two studies, a landscape in water colour and a still-life in oil, both of which had first prize awards. He was highly excited.

"What do you think I've got for my pictures mother?" he asked, coming home one evening. She saw by his eyes he was glad. Her face flushed.

"Now how should I know, my boy!"

"A first prize for those glass jars—"

"Hm!"

"And a first prize for that sketch up at Willey Farm."

"Both first?"

"Yes."

"Hm!"

There was a rosy, bright look about her, though she said nothing.

"It's nice," he said, "isn't it?"

"It is."

"Why don't you praise me up to the skies?"

She laughed.

"I should have the trouble of dragging you down again," she said.

But she was full of joy nevertheless. William had brought her his sporting trophies. She kept them still: and she did not forgive his death. Arthur was handsome, at least a good specimen, and warm and generous, and probably would do well in the end. But Paul was going to distinguish himself. She had a great belief in him, the more because he was unaware of his own powers. There was so much to come out of him. Life for her was rich with promise. She was to see herself fulfilled. Not for nothing had been her struggle.

Several times during the exhibition, Mrs Morel went to the Castle, unknown to Paul. She wandered down the long room looking at the other exhibits. Yes, they were good. But they had not in them a certain something, which she demanded for her satisfaction. Some made her jealous, they were so good. She looked at them a long time trying to find fault with them. Then suddenly she had a shock that made her heart beat. There hung Paul's picture! She knew it as if it were printed on her heart.

"Name—Paul Morel—First Prize."

It looked so strange, there in public, on the walls of the Castle gallery, where in her life-time she had seen so many pictures. And she glanced round to see if anyone had noticed her again in front of the same sketch.

But she felt a proud woman. When she met well-dressed ladies going home to the Park, she thought to herself:

"Yes, you look very well—but I wonder if *your* son has two first prizes in the Castle."

And she walked on, as proud a little woman as any in Nottingham. And Paul felt he had done something for her, if only a trifle. All his work was hers.

One day, as he was going up Castle Gate, he met Miriam. He had seen her on the Sunday, and had not expected to meet her in town. She was walking with a rather striking woman, blonde, with a sullen expression, and a defiant carriage. It was strange how Miriam, in her bowed, meditative bearing, looked dwarfed, beside this woman with the handsome shoulders. Miriam watched Paul searchingly. His gaze was on the stranger, who ignored him. The girl saw his masculine spirit rear its head.

"Hello!" he said. "You didn't tell me you were coming to town."

"No," replied Miriam, half apologetically. "I drove in to Cattle Market with father."

He looked at her companion.

"I've told you about Mrs Dawes,"* said Miriam, huskily. She was
nervous. "Clara, do you know Paul?"

"I think I've seen him before," replied Mrs Dawes indifferently, as
she shook hands with him. She had scornful grey eyes, a skin like
white honey, and a full mouth with a slightly lifted upper lip, that did   5
not know whether it was raised in scorn of all men, or out of eagerness
to be kissed, but which believed the former. She carried her head
back, as if she had drawn away in contempt, perhaps from men also.
She wore a large, dowdy hat of black beaver, and a sort of slightly-
affected simple dress that made her look rather sack-like. She was   10
evidently poor and had not much taste. Miriam usually looked nice.

"Where have you seen me?" Paul asked of the woman.

She looked at him as if she would not trouble to answer. Then:
"Walking with Louie Travers," she said.

Louie was one of the Spiral girls.   15

"Why do you know her?" he asked.

She did not answer. He turned to Miriam.

"Where are you going?" he asked.

"To the Castle."

"What train are you going home by?"   20

"I am driving with father. I wish you could come too. What time
are you free?"

"You know not till eight tonight, damn it."

And directly the two women moved on.

Paul remembered that Clara Dawes was the daughter of an old   25
friend of Mrs Leivers. Miriam had sought her out because she had
once been Spiral overseer at Jordan's, and because her husband,
Baxter Dawes, was smith for the factory, making the irons for
cripple instruments, and so on. Through her, Miriam felt she got
into direct contact with Jordan's, and could estimate better Paul's   30
position. But Mrs Dawes was separated from her husband, and had
taken up women's rights.* She was supposed to be clever. It interested Paul.

Baxter Dawes he knew and disliked. The smith was a man of
thirty one or two. He came occasionally through Paul's corner: a big,   35
well set man, also striking to look at, and handsome. There was a
peculiar similarity between himself and his wife. He had the same
white skin with a clear, golden tinge. His hair was soft brown, his
moustache was golden. And he had a similar defiance in his bearing
and manner. But then came the difference. His eyes, dark brown   40

and quick-shifting, were dissolute. They protruded very slightly, and his eyelids hung over them in a way that was half hate. His mouth too was sensual. His whole manner was of cowed defiance, as if he were ready to knock anybody down who disapproved of
5 him—perhaps because he really disapproved of himself.

From the first day he had hated Paul. Finding the lad's impersonal, deliberate gaze of an artist on his face, he got into a fury.

"What are yer lookin' at?" he sneered, bullying.

The boy glanced away. But the smith used to stand behind the
10 counter and talk to Mr Pappleworth. His speech was dirty, with a kind of rottenness. Again he found the youth with his cool, critical gaze fixed on his face. The smith started round as if he had been stung.

"What'r yer lookin' at, three hap'orth o' pap?"* he snarled.
15 The boy shrugged his shoulders slightly.

"Why yer—!" shouted Dawes.

"Leave him alone," said Mr Pappleworth, in that insinuating voice which means, 'he's only one of your good little sops who can't help it.'
20 Since that time the boy used to look at the man every time he came through, with the same curious criticism, glancing away before he met the smith's eye. It made Dawes furious. They hated each other in silence.

Clara Dawes had no children. When she had left her husband,
25 the home had been broken up, and she had gone to live with her mother. Dawes lodged with his sister. In the same house was a sister-in-law, and somehow Paul knew that this girl, Louie Travers, was now Dawes' woman. She was a handsome, insolent hussy, who mocked at the youth, and yet flushed if he walked along to the station
30 with her as she went home.

The next time he went to see Miriam, it was Saturday evening. She had a fire in the parlour and was waiting for him. The others, except her father and mother and the young children, had gone out so the two had the parlour together. It was a long, low warm room.
35 There were three of Paul's small sketches on the wall, and his photo was on the mantel-piece. On the table, and on the high old rosewood piano were bowls of coloured leaves. He sat in the arm-chair, she crouched on the hearthrug near his feet. The glow was warm on her handsome, pensive face as she kneeled there like a devotee.
40 "What did you think of Mrs Dawes?" she asked, quietly.

"She doesn't look very amiable," he replied.

"No, but don't you think she's a fine woman?" she said, in a deep tone.

"Yes—in stature. But without a grain of taste. I like her for some things. *Is* she disagreeable?"

"I don't think so. I think she's dissatisfied."

"What with?"

"Well—how would *you* like to be tied for life to a man like that?"

"Why did she marry him then, if she was to have revulsions so soon?"

"Ay, why did she!" repeated Miriam bitterly.

"And I should have thought she had enough fight in her to match him," he said.

Miriam bowed her head.

"Ay?" she queried satirically. "What makes you think so?"

"Look at her mouth—made for passion—and the very set-back of her throat—"

He threw his head back in Clara's defiant manner.

Miriam bowed a little lower.

"Yes," she said.

There was a silence for some moments, while he thought of Clara.

"And what were the things you liked about her?" she asked.

"I don't know—her skin and the texture of her—and her—I don't know—there's a sort of fierceness somewhere in her.—I appreciate her as an artist, that's all."

"Yes."

He wondered why Miriam crouched there brooding in that strange way. It irritated him.

"You don't really like her, do you?" he asked the girl.

She looked at him with her great, dazzled dark eyes.

"I do," she said.

"You don't—you can't—not really."

"Then what?" she asked, slowly.

"Eh I don't know—perhaps you like her because she's got a grudge against men."

That was more probably one of his own reasons for liking Mrs Dawes, but this did not occur to him. They were silent. There had come into his forehead a knitting of the brows which was becoming habitual with him, particularly when he was with Miriam. She longed to smooth it away, and she was afraid of it. It seemed the stamp of a man who was not her man in Paul Morel.

There were some crimson berries among the leaves in the bowl. He reached over and pulled out a bunch.

5 "If you put red berries in your hair," he said, "why would you look like some witch or priestess, and never like a reveller."*

She laughed with a naked, painful sound.

"I don't know," she said.

His vigorous, warm hands were playing excitedly with the berries.

10 "Why can't you laugh?" he said. "You never laugh laughter. You only laugh when something is odd or incongruous, and then it almost seems to hurt you."

She bowed her head as if he were scolding her.

"I wish you could laugh at me just for one minute—just for a 15 minute. I feel as if it would set something free."

"But!"—and she looked up at him with eyes frightened and struggling—"I do laugh at you—I *do*."

"Never! There's always a kind of intensity. When you laugh I could always cry, it seems as if it shows up your suffering. Oh, you 20 make me knit the brows of my very soul and cogitate."

Slowly she shook her head, despairingly.

"I'm sure I don't want to," she said.

"I'm so damned spiritual with *you* always," he cried.

She remained silent, thinking 'Then why don't you be otherwise.' 25 But he saw her crouching, brooding figure, and it seemed to tear him in two.

"But there, it's autumn," he said, "and everybody feels like a disembodied spirit then."

There was still another silence. This peculiar sadness between 30 them thrilled her soul. He seemed so beautiful, with his eyes gone dark, and looking as if they were deep as the deepest well.

"You make me so spiritual!" he lamented. "And I don't want to be spiritual."

She took her finger from her mouth with a little pop, and looked 35 up at him almost challenging. But still her soul was naked in her great dark eyes, and there was the same yearning appeal upon her. If he could have kissed her in abstract purity he would have done so. But he could not kiss her thus—and she seemed to leave no other way.* And she yearned to him.

40 He gave a brief laugh.

"Well," he said, "get that French and we'll do some—some Verlaine."*

"Yes," she said, in a deep tone, almost of resignation. And she rose and got the books. And her rather red, nervous hands looked so pitiful, he was mad to comfort her and kiss her. But then he dared not—or could not. There was something prevented him. His kisses were wrong for her.* They continued the reading, till ten o'clock, when they went into the kitchen and Paul was natural and jolly again with the father and mother. His eyes were dark and shining, there was a kind of fascination about him.

When he went into the barn for his bicycle, he found the front wheel punctured.

"Fetch me a drop of water in a bowl," he said to her. "I shall be late, and then I s'll catch it."

He lighted the hurricane lamp, took off his coat, turned up the bicycle and set speedily to work. Miriam came with the bowl of water and stood close to him, watching. She loved to see his hands doing things. He was slim and vigorous, with a kind of easiness even in his most hasty movements. And busy at his work, he seemed to forget her. She loved him absorbedly. She wanted to run her hands down his sides. She always wanted to embrace him, so long as he did not want her.*

"There!" he said, rising suddenly. "Now could you have done it quicker?"

"No!" she laughed.

He straightened himself. His back was towards her. She put her two hands on his sides, and ran them quickly down.

"You are so *fine*!" she said.

He laughed, hating her voice, but his blood roused to a wave of flame by her hands. She did not seem to realise *him* in all this. He might have been an object. She never realised the male he was.*

He lighted his bicycle lamp, bounced the machine on the barn floor to see that the tyres were sound, buttoned his coat.

"That's all right!" he said.

She was trying the brakes, that she knew were broken.

"Did you have them mended?" she asked.

"No!"

"But why didn't you?"

"The back one goes on a bit."

"But it's not safe."

"I can use my toe."

"I wish you'd had them mended," she murmured.

"Don't worry—come to tea tomorrow, with Edgar."

"Shall we?"

5   "Do—about four—I'll come to meet you."

"Very well."

She was pleased. They went across the dark yard to the gate. Looking across, he saw through the uncurtained window of the kitchen, the heads of Mr and Mrs Leivers, in the warm glow. It

10 looked very cosy. The road, with pine-trees, was quite black in front.

"Till tomorrow," he said, jumping on his bicycle.

"You'll take care, won't you?" she pleaded.

"Yes."

His voice already came out of the darkness. She stood a moment

15 watching the light from his lamp race into obscurity along the ground. She turned very slowly indoors. Orion was wheeling up over the wood, his dog twinkling after him, half smothered. For the rest, the world was full of darkness, and silent, save for the breathing of cattle in their stalls. She prayed earnestly for his safety that night.

20 When he left her, she often lay in anxiety, wondering if he had got home safely.

He dropped down the hills on his bicycle. The roads were greasy, so he had to let it go. He felt a pleasure as the machine plunged over the second, steeper drop in the hill. "Here goes!" he said. It was

25 risky, because of the curve in the darkness at the bottom, and because of the brewer's wagons with drunken wagoners asleep. His bicycle seemed to fall beneath him, and he loved it. Recklessness is almost a man's revenge on his woman. He feels he is not valued, so he will risk destroying himself to deprive her altogether.*

30 The stars on the lake seemed to leap like grasshoppers silver upon the blackness, as he spun past. Then there was the long climb home.

"See mother!" he said, as he threw her the berries and leaves onto the table.

"Hm!" she said, glancing at them, then away again. She sat

35 reading, alone, as she always did.

"Aren't they pretty?"

"Yes."

He knew she was cross with him. After a few minutes he said:

"Edgar and Miriam are coming to tea tomorrow."

40 She did not answer.

"You don't mind?"

Still she did not answer.

"Do you?" he asked.

"You know whether I mind or not."

"I don't see why you should—I have plenty of meals there." 5

"You do."

"Then why do you begrudge them tea?"

"I begrudge whom tea?"

"What are you so horrid for?"

"Oh say no more! You've asked her to tea, it's quite sufficient. 10
She'll come."

He was very angry with his mother. He knew it was merely
Miriam she objected to. He flung off his boots and went to bed.

Paul went to meet his friends the next afternoon. He was glad to
see them coming. They arrived home at about four o'clock. Every- 15
where was clean and still for Sunday afternoon. Mrs Morel sat in
her black dress and black apron. She rose to meet the visitors. With
Edgar she was cordial, but with Miriam cold and rather grudging.
Yet Paul thought the girl looked so nice in her brown cashmere
frock. 20

He helped his mother to get tea ready. Miriam would have gladly
proffered, but was afraid. He was rather proud of his home. There
was about it now, he thought, a certain distinction. The chairs were
only wooden, and the sofa was old. But the hearthrug and cushions
were cosy, the pictures were prints in good taste, there was a 25
simplicity in everything, and plenty of books. He was never ashamed
in the least of his home, nor was Miriam of hers, because both were
what they should be and warm. And then, he was proud of the table;
the china was pretty, the cloth was fine: it did not matter that the
spoons were not silver, nor the knives ivory-handled; everything 30
looked nice. Mrs Morel had managed wonderfully, while her children were growing up, so that nothing was out of place.

Miriam talked books a little. That was her unfailing topic. But
Mrs Morel was not cordial, and turned soon to Edgar.

At first Edgar and Miriam used to go into Mrs Morel's pew.* 35
Morel never went to chapel, preferring the public house. Mrs Morel,
like a little champion, sat at the head of her pew, Paul at the other
end; and at first Miriam sat next to him. Then the chapel was like
home. It was a pretty place, with dark pews, and slim, elegant pillars,
and flowers. And the same people had sat in the same places ever 40

since he was a boy. It was wonderfully sweet and soothing to sit there for an hour and a half, next to Miriam, and near to his mother, uniting his two loves under the spell of the place of worship. Then he felt warm and happy and religious at once. And after chapel he
5 walked home with Miriam, whilst Mrs Morel spent the rest of the evening with her old friend Mrs Burns. He was keenly alive on his walks on Sunday nights with Edgar and Miriam. He never went past the pits at night, by the lighted lamp-house, the tall black head-stocks and lines of trucks, past the fans spinning slowly like shadows,
10 without the feeling of Miriam returning to him keen and almost unbearable.

She did not very long occupy the Morels' pew. Her father took one for themselves once more. It was under the little gallery, oppo-site the Morels'. When Paul and his mother came in the chapel, the
15 Leivers' pew was always empty. He was anxious for fear she would not come: it was so far and there were so many rainy Sundays. Then, often very late indeed, she came in with her long stride, her head bowed, her face hidden under her hat of dark green velvet. Her face as she sat opposite was always in shadow. But it gave him a very keen
20 feeling, as if all his soul stirred within him, to see her there. It was not the same glow, happiness and pride, that he felt in having his mother in charge: something more wonderful, less human, and tinged to intensity by a pain, as if there were something he could not get to.

At this time, he was beginning to question the orthodox creed. He
25 was twenty one and she was twenty. She was beginning to dread the spring: he became so wild and hurt her so much. All the way he went cruelly smashing her beliefs. Edgar enjoyed it. He was by nature critical and rather dispassionate. But Miriam suffered exquisite pain, as, with an intellect like a knife, the man she loved examined her
30 religion in which she lived and moved and had her being.* But he did not spare her. He was cruel. And when they went alone he was even more fierce, as if he would kill her soul. He bled her beliefs till she almost lost consciousness.

"She exults—she exults as she carries him off from me," Mrs
35 Morel cried in her heart, when Paul had gone. "She's not like an ordinary woman, who can leave me my share in him. She wants to absorb him. She wants to draw him out and absorb him till there is nothing left of him, even for himself. He will never be a man on his own feet—she will suck him up." So the mother sat and battled and
40 brooded bitterly.

And he, coming home from his walks with Miriam, was wild with torture. He walked biting his lips and with clenched fists, going at a great rate. Then, brought up against a stile, he stood for some minutes and did not move. There was a great hollow of darkness fronting him, and on the black upslopes, patches of tiny lights, and in the lowest trough of the night, a flare of the pit. It was all weird and dreadful. Why was he torn so, almost bewildered and unable to move? Why did his mother sit at home and suffer? He knew she suffered badly. But why should she? And why did he hate Miriam, and feel so cruel towards her, at the thought of his mother? If Miriam caused his mother suffering then he hated her. And he easily hated her. Why did she make him feel as if he were uncertain of himself, insecure, an indefinite thing, as if he had not sufficient sheathing to prevent the night and the space breaking into him? How he hated her! And then, what a rush of tenderness and humility!

Suddenly he plunged on again, running home. His mother saw on him the marks of some agony, and she said nothing. But he had to make her talk to him. Then she was angry with him for going so far with Miriam.

"Why don't you like her, mother?" he cried in despair.

"I don't know, my boy," she replied piteously. "I'm sure I've tried to like her, I've tried and tried—but I can't, I can't—."

And he felt dreary and hopeless, between the two.

Spring was the worst time. He was changeable and intense and cruel. So he decided to stay away from her. Then came the hours when he knew Miriam was expecting him. His mother watched him growing restless. He could not go on with his work. He could do nothing. It was as if something were drawing his soul out, towards Willey Farm. Then he put on his hat and went, saying nothing. And his mother knew he was gone. And as soon as he was on the way, he sighed with relief. And when he was with her, he was cruel again.

One day in March, he lay on the bank of Nethermere, with Miriam sitting beside him. It was a glistening, white and blue day. Big clouds, so brilliant, went by overhead, while shadows stole along on the water. The clear spaces in the sky were of clean, cold blue. Paul lay on his back in the old grass, looking up. He could not bear to look at Miriam. She seemed to want him, and he resisted. He resisted all the time. He wanted now to give her passion and tenderness, and he could not. He felt that she wanted the soul out of his body, and not him. All his strength and energy she drew into herself through some channel which united them. She did not want to meet him, so that there were two of them, man and woman together. She wanted to draw all of him into her. It urged him to an intensity like madness. Which fascinated him, as drug taking might.

He was discussing Michael Angelo.* It felt to her as if she were fingering the very quivering tissue, the very protoplasm of life, as she heard him. It gave her her deepest satisfaction. And in the end it frightened her. There he lay in the white intensity of his search, and his voice gradually filled her with fear, so level it was, almost inhuman as if in a trance.

"Don't talk any more," she pleaded softly, laying her hand on his forehead. He lay quite still, almost unable to move. His body was somewhere discarded.

"Why not—are you tired?"

"Yes, and it wears you out."

He laughed shortly, realising.

"Yet you always make me like it," he said.

"I don't wish to," she said, very low.

"Not when you've gone too far, and you feel you can't bear it. But your unconscious self always asks it of me. And I suppose I want it."

"Then how can I help it?"

"I suppose you can't. Yet you always do it. You switch me off somewhere, and project me out of myself. I am quite ghostish, disembodied."

"Don't!" she pleaded.

"Even now," he continued. "Even now, I look at my hands, and wonder what they are doing there. That water there ripples right through me. I'm sure I am that rippling. It runs right through me, and I through it. There are no barriers between us."

"But—!" she stumbled.

"A sort of disseminated consciousness,* that's all there is of me. I feel as if my body were lying empty, as if I were in the other things—clouds and water—"

She looked at him, and saw in him that strange look, as if he were a thing and not a person, which fascinated her so, and which she feared. Yet, because she feared, she must have more. But now she wanted him to stop.

"You see," he went on, "the individual bodily me is discarded. But if so then I am not alive here. I'm sure it would destroy me.

What you want to do is to make me fat, and normal, not shadowy.
You want to fix my soul well in its sheath. It'll slip out, like the sword
that slipped out of a loose scabbard and fell into the sea,* one of
these days."

Miriam pondered bitterly. Suddenly she lifted her head and
looked at him with shining eyes.

"Then let me be the sheath to you," she said.

Her hands fluttered towards him.

"If you could," he said. "But you are what your unconscious self
makes you,* not so much what you want to be. We're neither of us
quite normal—but now I want to be, and I don't think you do. You
want to be nothing ordinary."

"I don't," she cried. But there was fear again in her voice.

"At any rate," he went on, in his dead fashion, "not now. You
can't take me that way now. Because both you and me are only souls
this minute, bloodless. And it would set up another vibration that
would criss-cross with this like veritable torture.—If only you could
want *me*, and not want what I can reel off for you!"

"I!" she cried bitterly. "I! Why when would you let me take you?"

"Then it's my fault," he said, and gathering himself together, he
got up and began to talk trivialities. He felt insubstantial. In a vague
way, he hated her for it. And he knew he was as much to blame
himself. This however, did not prevent his hating her.

One evening about this time he had walked along the home road
with her. They stood by the pasture leading down to the wood,
unable to part. As the stars came out the clouds closed. They had
glimpses of their own constellation, Orion, towards the west. His
jewels glimmered for a moment, his dog ran low, struggling with
difficulty through the spume of cloud.

Orion was for them chief in significance among the constellations.
They had gazed at him in their strange, surcharged hours of feeling,
until they seemed themselves to live in every one of his stars. This
evening Paul had been moody and perverse. Orion had seemed just
an ordinary constellation to him. He had fought against his glamour
and fascination. Miriam was watching her lover's mood carefully.
But he said nothing that gave him away, till the moment came to
part, when he stood frowning gloomily at the gathered clouds,
behind which the great constellation must be striding still.*

There was to be a little party at his house the next day, at which
she was to attend.

"I shan't come and meet you," he said.

"Oh very well—it's not very nice out," she replied slowly.

"It's not that—only they don't like me to. They say I care more for you than for them. And you understand, don't you?—you know it's only friendship."

Miriam was astonished and hurt for him. It had cost him an effort. She left him, wanting to spare him any further humiliation. A fine rain blew in her face as she walked along the road. She was hurt deep down. And she despised him, for being blown about by any wind of authority. And in her heart of hearts, unconsciously, she felt that he was trying to get away from her. This she would never have acknowledged. She pitied him.

At this time Paul became an important factor in Jordan's warehouse. Mr Pappleworth left to set up a business of his own, and Paul remained with Mr Jordan as Spiral Overseer. His wages were to be raised to thirty shillings at the year end, if things went well.

Still on Friday night Miriam often came down for her French lesson. Paul did not go so frequently to Willey Farm, and she grieved at the thought of her education's coming to an end; moreover they both loved to be together, in spite of discords. So they read Balzac,* and did compositions, and felt highly cultured.

Friday night was reckoning night for the miners. Morel 'reckoned'—shared up the money of the stall—either in the New Inn at Bretty, or in his own house, according as his fellow butties wished. Barker had turned a non-drinker, so now the men reckoned at Morel's house.

Annie, who had been teaching away, was at home again. She was still a tomboy. And she was engaged to be married. Paul was studying design.

Morel was always in good spirits on Friday evening, unless the week's earnings were small. He bustled immediately after his dinner, prepared to get washed. It was decorum for the women to absent themselves while the men reckoned. Women were not supposed to spy into such a masculine privacy as the butties' reckoning—nor were they to know the exact amount of the week's earnings. So, whilst her father was spluttering in the scullery, Annie went out to spend an hour with a neighbour. Mrs Morel attended to her baking.

"Shut that doo-er!" bawled Morel furiously.

Annie banged it behind her and was gone.

"If tha oppens it again while I'm weshin' me, I'll ma'e thy jaw rattle," he threatened, from the midst of his soapsuds. Paul and the mother frowned to hear him.

Presently he came running out of the scullery with the soapy water dripping from him, dithering with cold.

"Oh my sirs!" he said. "Wheer's my towel?"

It was hung on a chair to warm before the fire, otherwise he would have bullied and blustered. He squatted on his heels before the hot baking-fire, to dry himself.

"F-ff-f!" he went, pretending to shudder with cold.

"Goodness man, don't be such a kid!" said Mrs Morel. "It's *not* cold."

"Thee strip thysen stark nak'd to wesh thy flesh i' that scullery," said the miner, as he rubbed his hair; "nowt b'r a h'ice-'ouse!"

"And I shouldn't make that fuss," replied his wife.

"No, tha'd drop down stiff, as dead as a door-knob, wi' thy nesh sides."

"Why is a door-knob deader than anything else?" asked Paul, curious.

"Eh I dunno—that's what they say," replied his father. "But there's that much draught i' yon scullery, as it blows through your ribs like through a five-barred gate."

"It would have some difficulty in blowing through yours," said Mrs Morel.

Morel looked down ruefully at his sides.

"Me!" he exclaimed. "I'm nowt b'r a skinned rabbit. My bones fair juts out on me."

"I should like to know where," retorted his wife.

"Iv'ry-wheer! I'm nobbut a sack o' faggots."

Mrs Morel laughed. He had still a wonderfully young body, muscular, without any fat. His skin was smooth and clear. It might have been the body of a man of twenty eight, except that there were perhaps too many blue scars, like tattoo marks, where the coal-dust remained under the skin, and that his chest was too hairy. But he put his hands on his sides ruefully. It was his fixed belief that, because he did not get fat, he was as thin as a starved rat.

Paul looked at his father's thick, brownish hands, all scarred, with broken nails, rubbing the fine smoothness of his sides, and the incongruity struck him. It seemed strange they were the same flesh.

"I suppose," he said to his father, "you had a good figure once."

"Eh!" exclaimed the miner, glancing round startled and timid, like a child.

"He had," exclaimed Mrs Morel. "If he didn't hurtle himself up as if he was trying to get in the smallest space he could."

"Me!" exclaimed Morel. "Me a good figure! I wor niver much more n'r a skeleton."

"Man!" cried his wife, "don't be such a pulamiter!"

"'Strewth!" he said. "Tha's niver knowed me but what I looked as if I wor goin' off in a rapid decline."

She sat and laughed.

"You've had a constitution like iron," she said. "And never a man had a better start, if it was body that counted. You should have seen him as a young man—" she cried suddenly to Paul, drawing herself up to imitate her husband's once handsome bearing. Morel watched her shyly. He saw again the passion she had had for him. It blazed upon her for a moment. He was shy, rather scared, and humble. Yet again he felt his old glow. And then, immediately, he felt the ruin he had made during these years. He wanted to bustle about, to run away from it.

"Gi'e my back a bit of a wesh," he asked her.

His wife brought a well-soaped flannel and clapped it on his shoulders. He gave a jump.

"Eh tha mucky little 'ussy!" he cried. "Cowd as death!"

"You ought to have been a salamander," she laughed, washing his back. It was very rarely she would do anything so personal for him. The children did those things.

"The next world won't be half hot enough for you," she added.

"No," he said, "tha'lt see as it's draughty for me."

But she had finished. She wiped him in a desultory fashion and went upstairs, returning immediately with his shifting-trousers. When he was dried he struggled into his shirt. Then, ruddy and shiny, with hair on end, and his flannelette shirt hanging over his pit-trousers, he stood warming the garments he was going to put on. He turned them, he pulled them inside out, he scorched them.

"Goodness man," cried Mrs Morel, "get dressed!"

"Should thee like to clap thysen into britches as cowd as a tub o' watter!" he said.

At last he took off his pit trousers and donned decent black. He did all this on the hearthrug, as he would have done if Annie and her familiar friends had been present.

Mrs Morel turned the bread in the oven. Then from the red earthenware panchion of dough that stood in a corner she took another handful of paste, worked it to the proper shape, and dropped it into a tin. As she was doing so Barker knocked and entered. He was a quiet, compact little man who looked as if he 5 would go through a stone wall. His black hair was cropped short, his head was bony. Like most miners, he was pale, but healthy and taut.

"Evenin' Missis," he nodded to Mrs Morel, and he seated himself with a sigh.

"Good evening," she replied cordially. 10

"Tha's made thy heels crack," said Morel.

"I dunno as I have," said Barker.

He sat, as the men always did in Mrs Morel's kitchen, effacing himself rather.

"How's Missis?" she asked of him. 15

He had told her some time back:—

"We're expectin' us third just now, you see—"

"Well," he answered, rubbing his head, "she keeps pretty middlin' I think."

"Let's see, when—?" asked Mrs Morel. 20

"Well—I shouldn't be surprised any time now—"

"Ah! And she's kept fairly?"

"Yes—tidy!"

"That's a blessing, for she's none too strong."

"No.—An' I've done another silly trick." 25

"What's that?"

Mrs Morel knew Barker wouldn't do anything very silly.

"I'n come be-out th' market bag."

"You can have mine."

"Nay, you'll be wantin' that yourself." 30

"I shan't—I take a string bag—always.".

She saw the determined little collier buying in the week's groceries and meat on the Friday nights, and she admired him. 'Barker's little, but he's ten times the man you are,' she said to her husband. 35

Just then Wesson entered. He was thin, rather frail looking, with a boyish ingenuousness and a slightly foolish smile, despite his seven children. But his wife was a passionate woman.

"I see you've kested me," he said, smiling rather vapidly.

"Yes," replied Barker. 40

The newcomer took off his cap and his big woollen muffler. His nose was pointed and red.

"I'm afraid you're cold, Mr Wesson," said Mrs Morel.

"It's a bit nippy," he replied.

5 "Then come to the fire."

"Nay, I s'll do wheer I am."

Both colliers sat away back. They could not be induced to come onto the hearth. The hearth is sacred to the family.

"Go thy ways i' th' armchair," cried Morel, cheerily.

10 "Nay, thank yer, I'm very nicely here."

"Yes, come of course," insisted Mrs Morel.

He rose and went awkwardly. He sat in Morel's armchair awkwardly. It was too great a familiarity. But the fire made him blissfully happy.

15 "And how's that chest of yours?" demanded Mrs Morel.

He smiled again, with his blue eyes rather sunny.

"Oh, it's very middlin'," he said.

"Wi' a rattle in it like a kettle-drum," said Barker shortly.

"T-t-t-t!" went Mrs Morel rapidly with her tongue. "Did you 20 have that flannel singlet made?"

"Not yet," he smiled.

"Then why didn't you?" she cried.

"It'll come," he smiled.

"Ah, an' Doomsday!" exclaimed Barker.

25 Barker and Morel were both impatient of Wesson. But then they were both as hard as nails, physically.

When Morel was nearly ready, he pushed the bag of money to Paul.

"Count it, boy," he asked, humbly.

Paul impatiently turned from his books and pencil, tipped the bag 30 upside down on the table. There was a £5 bag of silver, sovereigns, and loose money. He counted quickly, referred to the checks, the written papers giving amount of coal, put the money in order. Then Barker glanced at the checks.

Mrs Morel went upstairs, and the three men came to table.

35 Morel, as master of the house, sat in his arm-chair with his back to the hot fire. The two butties had cooler seats. None of them counted the money.

"What did we say Simpson's was?" asked Morel, and the butties cavilled for a minute over the day-man's earnings. Then the amount 40 was put aside.

"An' Bill Naylor's?"

This money also was taken from the pack.

Then, because Wesson lived in one of the company's houses, and his rent had been deducted, Morel and Barker took four-and-six each. And because Morel's coals had come, and the leading was stopped,* Barker and Wesson took four shillings each. Then it was plain sailing. Morel gave each of them a sovereign till there were no more sovereigns: each half a crown till there were no more half crowns: each a shilling till there were no more shillings. If there was anything at the end that wouldn't split, Morel took it and stood drinks.

Then the three men rose and went. Morel scuttled out of the house before his wife came down. She heard the door close, and descended. She looked hastily at the bread in the oven. Then, glancing on the table, she saw her money lying. Paul had been working all the time. But now he felt his mother counting the week's money, and her wrath rising.

"T-t-t-t-t!" went her tongue.

He frowned. He could not work when she was cross. She counted again.

"A measly twenty-five shillings!" she exclaimed. "How much was the cheque?"

"Ten pounds eleven," said Paul, irritably. He dreaded what was coming.

"And he gives me a scrattlin' twenty five, an' his club this week! But I know him—he thinks because *you're* earning, he needn't keep the house any longer. No, all he has to do with his money is to guttle it. But I'll show him—"

"Oh mother don't!" cried Paul.

"Don't what, I should like to know?" she exclaimed.

"Don't carry on again—I can't work."

She went very quiet.

"Yes it's all very well," she said. "But how do you think I'm going to manage?"

"Well, it won't make it any better to whittle about it."

"I should like to know what you'd do if you had it to put up with!"

"It won't be long—you can have my money—let him go to Hell."

He went back to his work, and she tied her bonnet strings grimly. When she was fretted he could not bear it. But now he began to insist on her recognising him.

"The two loaves at the top," she said, "will be done in twenty minutes. Don't forget them."

"All right," he answered, and she went to market.

5 He remained alone working. But his usual intense concentration became unsettled. He listened for the yard gate. At a quarter past seven came a low knock, and Miriam entered.

"All alone?" she said.

"Yes."

As if at home, she took off her tam o'shanter and her long coat,
10 hanging them up. It gave him a thrill. This might be their own house, his and hers.

Then she came back and peered over his work.

"What is it?" she asked.

"Still design—for decorating stuffs, and for embroidery."

15 She bent short-sightedly over the drawings.

"And you like it?" she asked.

"I love it. I've got a passion for conventionalising* things just now."

"Yes."

20 She did not care for conventional studies. But she thought he knew best about those things. They were men's things, that did not belong to her. And yet—she would know why he had a passion for conventionalising things. What was there in the conventional to fascinate him?

25 "What makes you like this?" she asked, poring.

He began the old attempt to justify himself. Struggling, he tried to expound to her the theory that the force of gravitation is the great shaper,* and that if it had all its own way, it would have a rose in correct geometrical line and proportion*—and so on. This created in
30 her some sort of feeling for a conventional drawing, which had before seemed a mere lie to her. At last he scooped all the books away.

"Should I—?" he said, balanced, hesitating.

"What?"

35 "Show you?—I meant not to till it was done."

He could not keep from her anything he did.* He went into the parlour and returned with a bundle of brownish linen. Carefully unfolding it, he spread it on the floor. It proved to be a curtain or portière, beautifully stencilled with a design on roses.

40 "Ah, how beautiful!" she cried.

The spread cloth with its wonderful reddish roses and dark green stems, all so simple, and somehow so wicked looking, lay at her feet. She went on her knees before it, her dark curls dropping. He saw her crouched voluptuously before his work, and his heart beat quickly. Suddenly she looked up at him.

"Why does it seem cruel?" she asked.

"What?"

"There seems a feeling of cruelty about it," she said.

"It's jolly good, whether or not," he replied, folding up his work with a lover's hands. She rose slowly, pondering.

"And what will you do with it?" she asked.

"Send it to Liberty's.* I did it for my mother—but I think she'd rather have the money."

"Yes," said Miriam. He had spoken with a touch of bitterness, and Miriam sympathised. Money would mean nothing to *her*.

He took the cloth back into the parlour. When he returned he threw to Miriam a smaller piece. It was a cushion cover with the same design.

"I did that for you," he said.

She fingered the work with trembling hands, and did not speak. He became embarrassed.

"By Jove, the bread!" he cried.

He took the top loaves out, tapped them vigorously. They were done. He put them on the hearth to cool. Then he went to the scullery, wetted his hands, scooped the last white dough out of the panchion, and dropped it in a baking tin. Miriam was still bent over her painted cloth. He stood rubbing the bits of dough from his hands.

"You do like it?" he asked.

She looked up at him with her dark eyes one flame of love. He laughed uncomfortably. Then he began to talk about the design. There was for him the most intense pleasure in talking about his work to Miriam. All his passion, all his wild blood went into this intercourse with her, when he talked and conceived his work. She brought forth to him his imaginations. She did not understand, any more than a woman understands when she conceives a child in her womb. But this was life for her, and for him.

While they were talking, a young woman of about twenty two, small and pale, hollow eyed, yet with a relentless look about her, entered the room. She was a friend at the Morels'.

"Take your things off," said Paul.

"No—I'm not stopping."

She sat down in the arm-chair opposite Paul and Miriam, who were on the sofa. Miriam moved a little further from him. The room
5 was hot, with a scent of new bread. Brown, crisp loaves stood on the hearth.

"I shouldn't have expected to see you here tonight, Miriam Leivers," said Beatrice,* wickedly.

"Why not?" murmured Miriam huskily.

10 "Why let's look at your shoes."

Miriam remained uncomfortably still.

"If tha doesna tha durs'na," laughed Beatrice.

Miriam put her feet from under her dress. Her boots had that queer, irresolute, rather pathetic look about them, which showed
15 how self-conscious and self-mistrustful she was. And they were covered with mud.

"Glory—you're a positive muck-heap!" exclaimed Beatrice. "Who cleans your boots?"

"I clean them myself."

20 "Then you wanted a job," said Beatrice. "It would ha' taken a lot of men to ha' brought me down here tonight.—But love laughs at sludge—doesn't it, 'Postle my duck?"

"Inter alia," he said.

"Oh Lord, are you going to spout foreign languages!—What does
25 it mean, Miriam?"

There was a fine sarcasm in the last question, but Miriam did not see it.

"'Among other things,' I believe," she said, humbly.

Beatrice put her tongue between her teeth, and laughed
30 wickedly.

"'Among other things,' 'Postle?" she repeated. "Do you mean love laughs at mothers and fathers and sisters and brothers and men friends and lady friends, and even at the b'lovèd himself?"

She affected a great innocence.

35 "In fact it's one big smile," he replied.

"Up its sleeve, 'Postle Morel—you believe me," she said.

And she went off into another burst of wicked, silent laughter.

Miriam sat silent, withdrawn into herself. Every one of Paul's friends delighted in taking sides against her, and he left her in the
40 lurch, seemed almost to have a sort of revenge upon her then.

"Are you still at school?" asked Miriam of Beatrice.

"Yes."

"You've not had your notice then?"

"I expect it at Easter."

"Isn't it an awful shame, to turn you off merely because you didn't pass the exam!"

"I don't know," said Beatrice, coldly.

"Agatha says you're as good as any teacher anywhere. It seems to me ridiculous. I wonder why you didn't pass!"

"Short of brains, eh 'Postle?" said Beatrice, briefly.

"Only brains to bite with," replied Paul, laughing.

"Nuisance!" she cried, and springing from her seat, she rushed and boxed his ears. She had beautiful small hands. He held her wrists whilst she wrestled with him. At last she broke free and seized two handfuls of his thick, dark brown hair, which she shook.

"Beat," he said, as he pulled his hair straight with his fingers. "I hate you."

She laughed with glee.

"Mind!" she said. "I want to sit next to you."

"I'd as lief be neighbours with a vixen," he said, nevertheless making place for her between him and Miriam.

"Did it ruffle his pretty hair then!" she cried, and, with her hair comb, she combed him straight.

"And his nice little moustache!" she exclaimed. She tilted his head back, and combed his young moustache.

"It's a wicked moustache, 'Postle," she said. "It's a red for danger.—Have you got any of those cigarettes?"

He pulled his cigarette case from his pocket. Beatrice looked inside it.

"None of those nice little whiffs that Connie gave you?" she asked.

"There's one somewhere—."

Rummaging in his pocket, he found a little box. Beatrice took it.

"Oh yes, just one!" she said. "But Miriam ought to have this. Have Connie's remaining fag, Miriam?"

"No thanks," replied Miriam. "Who is Connie?"

"Hasn't he told you?" cried Beatrice, in great surprise. "Well 'Postle Morel, I don't think it's fair to keep a poor girl in the dark."

"Will you try a smoke?" asked Paul of Miriam.

"You know I won't," she answered.

"And fancy me having Connie's last cig.," said Beatrice, putting the thing between her teeth. He held a lit match to her, and she puffed daintily.

"Thanks so much darling," she said, mockingly.

5 It gave her a wicked delight.

"Don't you think he does it nicely Miriam?" she asked.

"Oh very!" said Miriam.

He took a cigarette for himself.

"Light, old boy?" said Beatrice, tilting her cigarette at him.

10 He bent forward to her to light his cigarette at hers. She was winking at him as he did so. Miriam saw his eyes trembling with mischief, and his full, almost sensual mouth quivering. He was not himself, and she could not bear it. As he was now, she had no connection with him, she might as well not have existed. She saw the

15 cigarette dancing on his full red lips. She hated his thick hair for being tumbled loose on his forehead.

"Sweet boy!" said Beatrice, tipping up his chin and giving him a little kiss on the cheek.

"I s'll kiss thee back, Beat," he said.

20 "Tha wunna!" she giggled, jumping up and going away. "Isn't he shameless, Miriam?"

"Quite!" said Miriam. "By the way, aren't you forgetting the bread?"

"By Jove!" he cried, flinging open the oven door. Out puffed the

25 bluish smoke, and a smell of burned bread.

"Oh Golly!" cried Beatrice, coming to his side. He crouched before the oven, she peered over his shoulder. "This is what comes of the oblivion of love my boy."

Paul was ruefully removing the loaves. One was burnt black on

30 the hot side, another was hard as a brick.

"Poor mater!" said Paul.

"You want to grate it," said Beatrice. "Fetch me the nutmeg grater."

She arranged the bread in the oven. He brought the grater, and

35 she grated the bread onto a newspaper on the table. He set the doors open to blow away the smell of burned bread. Beatrice grated away, puffing her cigarette, knocking the charcoal off the poor loaf.

"My word Miriam, you're in for it this time," said Beatrice.

"I!" exclaimed Miriam in amazement.

40 "You'd better be gone when his mother comes in.—*I* know why

King Alfred burned the cakes.* Now I see it. 'Postle would fix up a tale about his work making him forget, if he thought it would wash. If that old woman had come in a bit sooner, she'd have boxed the brazen thing's ears who made the oblivion, instead of poor Alfred's—"

She giggled as she scraped the loaf. Even Miriam laughed in spite of herself. Paul mended the fire, ruefully.

The garden gate was heard to bang.

"Quick!" cried Beatrice, giving Paul the scraped loaf. "Wrap it up in a damp towel."

Paul disappeared into the scullery. Beatrice hastily blew her scrapings into the fire, and sat down innocently. Annie came bursting in. She was an abrupt, quite smart young woman. She blinked in the strong light.

"Smell of burning!" she exclaimed.

"It's the cigarettes," replied Beatrice demurely.

"Where's Paul?"

Leonard had followed Annie. He had a long, comic face and blue eyes very sad.

"I suppose he's left you to settle it between you," he said.

He nodded sympathetically to Miriam, and became gently sarcastic to Beatrice.

"No," said Beatrice, "he's gone off with number nine."

"I just met number five inquiring for him," said Leonard.

"Yes—we're going to share him up like Solomon's baby,"* said Beatrice.

Annie laughed.

"Oh ay?" said Leonard. "And which bit should you have?"

"I don't know," said Beatrice. "I'll let all the others pick first."

"An' you'd have the leavings, like?" said Leonard, twisting up a comic face.

Annie was looking in the oven. Miriam sat ignored. Paul entered.

"This bread's a fine sight, our Paul," said Annie.

"Then you should stop an' look after it," said Paul.

"You mean *you* should do what you're reckoning to do," replied Annie.

"He should, shouldn't he!" cried Beatrice.

"I s'd think he'd got plenty on hand," said Leonard.

"You had a nasty walk, didn't you Miriam?" said Annie.

"Yes—but I'd been in all week—"

"And you wanted a bit of a change, like," insinuated Leonard kindly.

"Well, you can't be stuck in the house for ever," Annie agreed. She was quite amiable. Beatrice pulled on her coat, and went out with Leonard and Annie. She would meet her own boy.

"Don't forget that bread, our Paul," cried Annie. "Goodnight Miriam, I don't think it will rain."

When they had all gone, Paul fetched the swathed loaf, unwrapped it, and surveyed it sadly.

"It's a mess!" he said.

"But," answered Miriam impatiently, "what is it, after all—twopence ha'penny."

"Yes but—it's the mater's precious baking, and she'll take it to heart.—However, it's no good bothering."

He took the loaf back into the scullery. There was a little distance between him and Miriam. He stood balanced opposite her for some moments, considering, thinking of his behaviour with Beatrice. He felt guilty inside himself, and yet glad. For some inscrutable reason, it served Miriam right. He was not going to repent. She wondered what he was thinking of, as he stood suspended. His thick hair was tumbled over his forehead. Why might she not push it back for him, and remove the marks of Beatrice's comb? Why might she not press his body with her two hands. It looked so firm and every whit living. And he would let other girls, why not her?

Suddenly he started into life. It made her quiver almost with terror as he quickly pushed the hair off his forehead and came towards her.

"Half past eight!" he said. "We'd better buck up. Where's your French?"

Miriam shyly and rather bitterly produced her exercise book. Every week she wrote for him a sort of diary of her inner life, in her own French. He had found this was the only way to get her to do compositions. And her diary was mostly a love-letter. He would read it now; she felt as if her soul's history were going to be desecrated by him in his present mood. He sat beside her. She watched his hand, firm and warm, rigorously scoring her work.

He was reading only the French, ignoring her soul that was there. But gradually his hand forgot its work. He read in silence, motionless. She quivered.

"Ce matin les oiseaux m'ont éveillé," he read. "Il faisait encore un crépuscule. Mais la petite fenêtre de ma chambre était blême, et puis, jaûne, et tous les oiseaux du bois éclatèrent dans un chanson vif et résonnant. Toute l'aûbe tressaillit. J'avais rêvé de vous. Est-ce que vous voyez aussi l'aûbe? Les oiseaux m'éveillent presque tous les matins, et toujours il y a quelque chose de terreur dans le cri des grives. Il est si clair— —"*

Miriam sat tremulous, half ashamed. He remained quite still, trying to understand. He only knew she loved him. He was afraid of her love for him. It was too good for him, and he was inadequate. His own love was at fault, not hers. Ashamed, he corrected her work, humbly writing above her words.

"Look," he said quietly, "the past participle conjugated with 'avoir' agrees with the direct object when it precedes."*

She bent forward, trying to see and to understand. Her free, fine curls tickled his face. He started as if they had been red hot, shuddering. He saw her peering forward at the page, her red lips parted piteously, the black hair springing in fine strands across her tawny ruddy cheek. She was coloured like a pomegranate for richness. His breaths came short as he watched her. Suddenly she looked up at him. Her dark eyes were naked with their love, afraid, and yearning. His eyes too were dark, and they hurt her. They seemed to master her. She lost all her self control, was exposed in fear. And he knew, before he could kiss her, he must drive something out of himself. And a touch of hate for her crept back again into his heart. He returned to her exercise.

Suddenly he flung down the pencil, and was at the oven in a leap, turning the bread. For Miriam he was too quick. She started violently, and it hurt her with real pain. Even the way he crouched before the oven hurt her. There seemed to her something cruel in it, something cruel in the swift way he pitched the bread out of the tins, caught it up again. If only he had been gentle in his movements, she would have felt so rich and warm. As it was, she was hurt.

He returned and finished the exercise.

"You've done well this week," he said.

She saw he was flattered by her diary. It did not repay her entirely.

"You really do blossom out sometimes," he said. "You ought to write poetry."

She lifted her head with joy, then she shook it mistrustfully.

"I don't trust myself," she said.

"You should try!"

Again she shook her head.

"Shall we read, or is it too late?" he asked.

"It is late—but we can read just a little," she pleaded.

She was really getting now the food for her life during the next
5   week. He made her copy Baudelaire's 'Le Balcon.'* Then he read it
for her. His voice was soft and caressing, but growing almost brutal.
He had a way of lifting his lips and showing his teeth, passionately
and bitterly, when he was much moved. This he did now. It made
Miriam feel as if he were trampling on her. She dared not look at
10 him, but sat with her head bowed. She could not understand why he
got into such a tumult and fury. It made her wretched. She did not
like Baudelaire, on the whole—nor Verlaine.

> "Behold her singing in the field
> Yon solitary highland lass—"

15 That nourished her heart—so did 'Fair Ines.' And:

> "It was a beauteous evening, calm and pure,
> And breathing holy quiet like a nun—"*

These were like herself. And there was he, saying in his throat,
bitterly:

20   "Tu te rappelleras la beauté des caresses."

The poem was finished, he took the bread out of the oven,
arranging the burnt loaves at the bottom of the panchion, the good
ones at the top. The desiccated loaf remained swathed up in the
scullery.

25 "Mater needn't know till morning," he said. "It won't upset her
so much then, as at night."

Miriam looked in the book-case, saw what postcards and letters
he had received, saw what books were there. She took one that had
interested him. Then he turned down the gas and they set off. He
30 did not trouble to lock the door.

He was not home again until a quarter to eleven. His mother was
seated in the rocking-chair. Annie, with a rope of hair hanging down
her back, remained sitting on a low stool before the fire, her elbows
on her knees, gloomily. On the table stood the offending loaf,
35 unswathed. Paul entered rather breathless. No one spoke. His
mother was reading the little local newspaper. He took off his coat,
and went to sit down on the sofa. His mother moved curtly aside to
let him pass. No one spoke. He was very uncomfortable. For some

minutes he sat pretending to read a piece of paper he found on the table. Then:

"I forgot that bread mother,"* he said.

There was no answer from either woman.

"Well," he said, "it's only two-pence ha'penny. I can pay you for that."

Being angry, he put three pennies on the table and slid them towards his mother. She turned away her head. Her mouth was shut tightly.

"Yes," said Annie, "you don't know how badly my mother is!"

The girl sat staring glumly into the fire.

"Why is she badly?" asked Paul, in his overbearing way.

"Well!" said Annie. "She could scarcely get home."

He looked closely at his mother. She looked ill.

"*Why* could you scarcely get home?" he asked her, still sharply.

She would not answer.

"I found her as white as a sheet, sitting here," said Annie, with a suggestion of tears in her voice.

"Well *why*?" insisted Paul. His brows were knitting, his eyes dilating passionately.

"It was enough to upset anybody," said Mrs Morel; "hugging those parcels—meat, and green-groceries and a pair of curtains——"

"Well, why *did* you hug them, you needn't have done."

"Then who would?"

"Let Annie fetch the meat."

"Yes, and I *would* fetch the meat, but how was I to know. You were off with Miriam, instead of being in when my mother came."

"And what was the matter with you?" asked Paul of his mother.

"I suppose it's my heart," she replied. Certainly she looked bluish round the mouth.

"And have you felt it before?"

"Yes—often enough."

"Then why haven't you told me, and why haven't you seen a doctor?"

Mrs Morel shifted in her chair, angry with him for his hectoring.

"You'd never notice anything," said Annie. "You're too eager to be off with Miriam."

"Oh am I—and any worse than you with Leonard?"

"*I* was in at a quarter to ten."

There was silence in the room for a time.

"I should have thought," said Mrs Morel bitterly, "that she wouldn't have occupied you so entirely, as to burn a whole ovenful of bread."

5 "Beatrice was here as well as she."

"Very likely. But we know why the bread is spoilt."

"Why?" he flashed.

"Because you were engrossed with Miriam," replied Mrs Morel hotly.

10 "Oh very well—then it was *not!*" he replied angrily.

He was distressed and wretched. Seizing a paper, he began to read. Annie, her blouse unfastened, her long ropes of hair twisted into a plait, went up to bed, bidding him a very curt goodnight.

Paul sat pretending to read. He knew his mother wanted to
15 upbraid him. He also wanted to know what had made her ill, for he was troubled. So, instead of running away to bed, as he would have liked to do, he sat and waited. There was a tense silence. The clock ticked loudly.

"You'd better go to bed before your father comes in," said the
20 mother, harshly. "And if you're going to have anything to eat, you'd better get it."

"I don't want anything."

It was his mother's custom to bring him some trifle for supper on Friday night, the night of luxury for the colliers. He was too angry
25 now to go and find it in the pantry this night. This insulted her.

"If I *wanted* you to go to Selby on Friday night, I can imagine the scene," said Mrs Morel. "But you're never too tired to go if *she* will come for you. Nay, you neither want to eat nor drink then."

"I can't let her go alone."

30 "Can't you—and why does she come?"

"Not because I ask her."

"She doesn't come without you want her—"

"Well, what if I *do* want her—!" he replied.

"Why, nothing, if it was sensible or reasonable. But to go trapse-
35 ing* up there miles and miles in the mud, coming home at midnight, and got to go to Nottingham in the morning—"

"If I hadn't, you'd be just the same."

"Yes I should, because there's no sense in it. Is she *so* fascinating, that you must follow her all that way—?" Mrs Morel was bitterly
40 sarcastic. She sat still, with averted face, stroking with a rhythmic,

jerked movement, the black sateen of her apron. It was a movement that hurt Paul to see.

"I do like her," he said, "but—."

"*Like* her!" said Mrs Morel, in the same biting tones. "It seems to me you like nothing and nobody else. There's neither Annie, nor me, nor anyone now for you."

"What nonsense, mother—you know I don't love her—I—I tell you I *don't* love her—she doesn't even walk with my arm, because I don't want her to."

"Then why do you fly to her so often?"

"I *do* like to talk to her—I never said I didn't. But I *don't* love her."

"Is there nobody else to talk to?"

"Not about the things we talk of. There's lots of things that you're not interested in, that—"

"What things—?"

Mrs Morel was so intense that Paul began to pant.

"Why—painting—and books. *You* don't care about Herbert Spencer."*

"No," was the sad reply. "And *you* won't at my age."

"Well, but I do now—and Miriam does—"

"And how do you know," Mrs Morel flashed defiantly, "that *I* shouldn't. Do you ever try me—!"

"But you don't, mother, you know you don't care whether a picture's decorative or not—you don't care what *manner** it is in."

"How do you know I don't care—do you ever try me? Do you ever talk to me about these things, to try?"

"But it's not that that matters to you mother, you know it's not."

"What is it then—what is it then that matters to me," she flashed. He knitted his brows with pain.

"You're old, mother, and we're young."

He only meant that the interests of *her* age, were not the interests of his. But he realised the moment he had spoken, that he had said the wrong thing.

"Yes, I know it well—I am old! And therefore I may stand aside, I have nothing more to do with you. You only want me to wait on you—the rest is for Miriam."

He could not bear it. Instinctively, he realised that he was life to her. And after all she was the chief thing to him, the only supreme thing.

"You know it isn't, mother, you know it isn't."

She was moved to pity by his cry.

"It looks a great deal like it," she said, half putting aside her despair.

"No mother—I really *don't* love her. I talk to her—but I want to come home to you."

5 He had taken off his collar and tie, and rose, bare-throated, to go to bed. As he stooped to kiss his mother, she threw her arms round his neck, hid her face on his shoulder, and cried, in a whimpering voice, so unlike her own that he writhed in agony:

"I can't bear it. I could let another woman—but not her—she'd 10 leave me no room, not a bit of room—"

And immediately he hated Miriam bitterly.

"And I've never—you know, Paul—I've never had a husband—not really—"

He stroked his mother's hair, and his mouth was on her throat.

15 "And she exults so in taking you from me—she's not like ordinary girls."

"Well, I don't love her, mother," he murmured, bowing his head and hiding his eyes on her shoulder in misery. His mother kissed him a long, fervent kiss:

20 "My boy!" she said, in a voice trembling with passionate love. Without knowing, he gently stroked her face.

"There," said his mother, "now go to bed. You'll be *so* tired in the morning."

As she was speaking, she heard her husband coming.

25 "There's your father—now go.—" Suddenly she looked at him almost as if in fear. "Perhaps I'm selfish. If you want her, take her, my boy."

His mother looked so strange, Paul kissed her, trembling.

"Ha—mother!" he said softly.

30 Morel came in, walking unevenly. His hat was over one corner of his eye. He balanced in the doorway.

"At your mischief again?" he said, venomously.

Mrs Morel's emotion turned into sudden hate of the drunkard who had come in thus upon her.

35 "At any rate, it is sober," she said.

"Hm—hm! hm—hm!" he sneered.

He went into the passage, hung up his hat and coat. Then they heard him go down three steps to the pantry. He returned with a piece of pork-pie in his fist. It was what Mrs Morel had bought for her son.

40 "Nor was that bought for you. If you can give me no more than

twenty five shillings, I'm sure I'm not going to buy you pork-pie to stuff, after you've swilled a belly-ful of beer."

"Wha-at—wha-at!" snarled Morel, toppling in his balance. "Wha-at—not for me?" He looked at the piece of meat and crust, and suddenly, in a vicious spurt of temper, flung it into the fire. 5

Paul started to his feet.

"Waste your own stuff," he cried.

"What—what!!" suddenly shouted Morel, jumping up and clenching his fist. "I'll show yer yer young jockey—!"

"All right!" said Paul viciously, putting his head on one side. 10 "Show me—!"

He would at that moment dearly have loved to have a smack at something. Morel was half crouching, fists up, ready to spring.

The young man stood, smiling with his lips.

"—Ussha!" hissed the father, swiping round with a great stroke, 15 just past his son's face. He dared not, even though so close, really touch the young man, but swerved an inch away.

"Right!" said Paul, his eyes upon the side of his father's mouth, where in another instant his fist would have hit. He ached for that stroke. But he heard a faint moan from behind. His mother was 20 deadly pale, and dark at the mouth. Morel was dancing up to deliver another blow.

"Father!" said Paul, so that the word rang.

Morel started, and stood at attention.

"Mother!" moaned the boy. "Mother!" 25

She began to struggle with herself. Her open eyes watched him, although she could not move. Gradually she was coming to herself. He laid her down on the sofa, ran upstairs for a little whiskey, which at last she could sip. The tears were hopping down his face. As he kneeled in front of her, he did not cry, but the tears ran down his 30 face quickly. Morel, on the opposite side of the room, sat with his elbows on his knees, glaring across.

"What's a-matter with 'er?" he asked.

"Faint!" replied Paul.

"Hm!" 35

The elderly man began to unlace his boots. He stumbled off to bed. His last fight was fought in that home.

Paul kneeled there, stroking his mother's hand.

"Don't be poorly, mother—don't be poorly!" he said, time after time. 40

"It's nothing, my boy," she murmured.

At last he rose, fetched in a large piece of coal, and raked the fire. Then he cleared the room, put everything straight, laid the things for breakfast, and brought his mother's candle.

5   "Can you go to bed, mother?"

"Yes, I'll come."

"Sleep with Annie, mother, not with him."

"No, I'll sleep in my own bed."

"Don't sleep with him, mother."

10   "I'll sleep in my own bed."

She rose, and he turned out the gas, then followed her closely up stairs, carrying her candle. On the landing he kissed her close.

"Goodnight mother."

"Goodnight!" she said.

15   He pressed his face upon the pillow in a fury of misery. And yet, somewhere in his soul, he was at peace because still he loved his mother best. It was the bitter peace of resignation.

The efforts of his father to conciliate him next day were a great humiliation to him.

20   Everybody tried to forget the scene.

Chapter IX

Defeat of Miriam

Paul was dissatisfied with himself and with everything. The deepest of his love belonged to his mother. When he felt he had hurt her, or wounded his love for her, he could not bear it. Now it was spring and there was battle between him and Miriam. This year he had a good deal against her. She was vaguely aware of it. The old feeling that she was to be a sacrifice to this love, which she had had when she prayed, was mingled in all her emotions. She did not at the bottom believe she ever would have him. She did not believe in herself, primarily: doubted whether she could ever be what he would demand of her. Certainly she never saw herself living happily through a life-time with him. She saw tragedy, sorrow, and sacrifice ahead. And in sacrifice she was proud, in renunciation she was strong; for she did not trust herself to support everyday life. She was prepared for the big things and the deep things, like tragedy. It was the sufficiency of the small day-life she could not trust.*

The Easter holidays began happily. Paul was his own frank self. Yet she felt it would go wrong. On the Sunday afternoon she stood at her bedroom window, looking across at the oak-trees of the wood, in whose branches a twilight was tangled, below the bright sky of the afternoon. Grey-green rosettes of honeysuckle leaves hung before the window, some already, she fancied, showing bud. It was spring, which she loved and dreaded.

Hearing the clack of the gate, she stood in suspense. It was a bright grey day. Paul came into the yard with his bicycle, which glittered as he walked. Usually he rang his bell and laughed towards the house. Today he walked with shut lips, and cold, cruel bearing, that had something of a slouch and a sneer in it. She knew him well by now, and could tell from that keen-looking, aloof young body of his what was happening inside him. There was a cold correctness in the way he put his bicycle in its place, that made her heart sink.

She came downstairs nervously. She was wearing a new net blouse, that she thought became her. It had a high collar with a tiny ruff, reminding her of Mary Queen of Scots, and making her, she thought, look wonderfully a woman, and dignified. At twenty, she was full-breasted and luxuriously formed. Her face was still like a soft rich mask, unchangeable. But her eyes, once lifted, were wonderful. She was afraid of him. He would notice her new blouse.

5　He, being in a hard, ironical mood, was entertaining the family to a description of a service given in the Primitive Methodist Chapel,* conducted by one of the well-known preachers of the sect. He sat at the head of the table, his mobile face, with the eyes that could be so beautiful, shining with tenderness or dancing with laughter, now
10　taking on one expression and then another, in imitation of various people he was mocking. His mockery always hurt her—it was too near the reality. He was too clever and cruel. She felt that when his eyes were like this, hard with mocking hate, he would spare neither himself nor anybody else. But Mrs Leivers was wiping her eyes with
15　laughter, and Mr Leivers, just awake from his Sunday nap, was rubbing his head in amusement. The three brothers sat with ruffled, sleepy appearance, in their shirt sleeves, giving a guffaw from time to time. The whole family loved a "take-off" more than anything.

He took no notice of Miriam. Later, she saw him remark her new
20　blouse, saw that the artist approved, but it won from him not a spark of warmth. She was nervous, could hardly reach the tea-cups from the shelves.

When the men went out to milk, she ventured to address him personally.
25　"You were late," she said.

"Was I?" he answered.

There was silence for awhile.

"Was it rough riding?" she asked.

"I didn't notice it."
30　She continued quickly to lay the table. When she had finished,

"Tea won't be for a few minutes. Will you come and look at the daffodils?" she said.

He rose without answering. They went out into the back garden, under the budding damson trees. The hills and the sky were clean
35　and cold. Everything looked washed, rather hard. Miriam glanced at Paul. He was pale and impassive. It seemed cruel to her that his eyes and brows, which she loved, could look so hurting.

"Has the wind made you tired?" she asked.

She detected an underneath feeling of weariness about him.
40　"No, I think not," he answered.

"It must be rough on the road—the wood moans so."

"You can see by the clouds it's a south-west wind: that helps me here."

"You see I don't cycle, so I don't understand," she murmured.

"Is there need to cycle to know that?" he said. 5

She thought his sarcasms were unnecessary. They went forward in silence. Round the wild, tussocky lawn at the back of the house was a thorn hedge, under which daffodils were craning forward from among their sheaves of grey-green blades. The cheeks of the flowers were greenish with cold. But still some had burst, and their 10 gold ruffled and glowed. Miriam went on her knees before one cluster, took a wild looking daffodil between her hands, turned up its face of gold to her, and bowed down, caressing it with her mouth and cheeks and brow. He stood aside with his hands in his pockets, watching her. One after another she turned up to him the faces of 15 the yellow, bursten flowers, appealingly, fondling them lavishly all the while.

"Aren't they magnificent?" she murmured.

"Magnificent!—it's a bit thick!—they're pretty!"

She bowed again to her flowers at his censure of her praise. He 20 watched her crouching, sipping the flowers with fervid kisses.

"Why must you always be fondling things!" he said, irritably.

"But I love to touch them," she replied, hurt.

"Can you never like things without clutching them as if you wanted to pull the heart out of them? Why don't you have a bit more 25 restraint or reserve or something?"

She looked up at him, full of pain, then continued slowly to stroke her lips against a ruffled flower. Their scent, as she smelled it, was so much kinder than he, it almost made her cry.

"You wheedle the soul out of things," he said. "I would never 30 wheedle—at any rate I'd go straight."

He scarcely knew what he was saying. These things came from him mechanically. She looked at him. His body seemed one weapon, firm and hard against her.

"You're always begging things to love you," he said, "as if you 35 were a beggar for love. Even the flowers, you have to fawn on them—"

Rhythmically, Miriam was swaying and stroking the flower with her mouth, inhaling the scent which ever after made her shudder as it came to her nostrils. 40

"You don't want to love—your eternal and abnormal craving is to be loved. You aren't positive, you're negative. You absorb, absorb, as if you must fill yourself up with love, because you've got a shortage somewhere."

5   She was stunned by his cruelty, and did not hear. He had not the faintest notion of what he was saying. It was as if his fretted, tortured soul, run hot by thwarted passion, jetted off these sayings like sparks from electricity. She did not grasp anything he said. She only sat crouched beneath his cruelty and his hatred of her. She never
10   realised in a flash. Over everything she brooded and brooded.

After tea he stayed with Edgar and the brothers, taking no notice of Miriam. She, extremely unhappy on this looked-for holiday, waited for him. And at last he yielded and came to her. She was determined to track this mood of his to its origin. She counted it not
15   much more than a mood.

"Shall we go through the wood a little way?" she asked him, knowing he never refused a direct request.

They went down to the warren. On the middle path they passed a trap, a narrow horse-shoe hedge of small fir-boughs, baited with the
20   guts of a rabbit. Paul glanced at it frowning. She caught his eye.

"Isn't it dreadful?" she asked.

"I don't know! Is it worse than a weasel with its teeth in a rabbit's throat?—One weasel or many rabbits?—One or the other must go—!"

25   He was taking the bitterness of life badly. She was rather sorry for him.

"We will go back to the house," he said. "I don't want to walk out."

They went past the lilac-tree, whose bronze leaf-buds were
30   coming unfastened. Just a fragment remained of the haystack, a monument squared and brown, like a pillar of stone. There was a little bed of hay from the last cutting.

"Let us sit here a minute," said Miriam.

He sat down, against his will, resting his back against the hard
35   wall of hay. They faced the amphitheatre of round hills, that glowed with sunset, tiny white farms standing out, the meadows golden, the woods dark and yet luminous, tree-tops folded over tree-tops, distinct in the distance. The evening had cleared, and the east was tender with a magenta flush, under which the land lay still and rich.
40   "Isn't it beautiful?" she pleaded.

But he only scowled. He would rather have had it ugly just then.

At that moment a big bull terrier came rushing up, open mouthed, pranced his two paws on the youth's shoulders, licking his face. Paul drew back, laughing. Bill was a great relief to him. He pushed the dog aside, but it came leaping back.

"Get out," said the lad, "or I'll dot thee one."

But the dog was not to be pushed away. So Paul had a little battle with the creature, pitching poor Bill away from him, who however only floundered tumultuously back again, wild with joy. The two fought together, the man laughing grudgingly, the dog grinning all over. Miriam watched them. There was something pathetic about the man. He wanted so badly to love, to be tender. The rough way he bowled the dog over was really loving. Bill got up, panting with happiness, his brown eyes rolling in his white face, and lumbered back again. He adored Paul. The lad frowned.

"Bill, I've had enough o' thee," he said.

But the dog only stood with two heavy paws, that quivered with love, upon his thigh, and flickered a red tongue at him. He drew back.

"No," he said. "No—I've had enough."

And in a minute the dog trotted off, happily, to vary the fun.

He remained staring miserably across at the hills, whose still beauty he begrudged. He wanted to go and cycle with Edgar. Yet he had not the courage to leave Miriam.

"Why are you sad?" she asked, humbly.

"I'm not sad, why should I be," he answered. "I'm only normal."

She wondered why he always claimed to be normal when he was disagreeable.

"But what is the matter?" she pleaded, coaxing him soothingly.

"Nothing!"

"Nay!" she murmured.

He picked up a stick and began to stab the earth with it.

"You'd far better not talk," he said.

"But I wish to know—" she replied.

He laughed resentfully.

"You always do," he said.

"It's not fair to me," she murmured.

He thrust, thrust, thrust at the ground with the pointed stick, digging up little clods of earth, as if he were in a fever of irritation. She gently and firmly laid her hand on his wrist.

"Don't!" she said. "Put it away."

He flung the stick into the currant bushes, and leaned back. Now he was bottled up.

"What is it?" she pleaded softly.

5 He lay perfectly still, only his eyes alive, and they full of torment.

"You know," he said at length, rather wearily, "you know—we'd better break off."

It was what she dreaded. Swiftly, everything seemed to darken before her eyes.

10 "Why!" she murmured. "What has happened?"

"Nothing has happened.—We only realise where we are.—It's no good—."

She waited in silence, sadly, patiently. It was no good being impatient with him. At any rate he would tell her now what ailed

15 him.

"We agreed on friendship," he went on, in a dull, monotonous voice, "How often *have* we agreed for friendship!—And yet—it neither stops there, nor gets anywhere else."

He was silent again. She brooded. What did he mean? He was so

20 wearying. There was something he would not yield. Yet she must be patient with him.

"I can only give friendship—it's all I'm capable of—it's a flaw in my make-up.—The thing overbalances to one side—I hate a toppling balance*—let us have done."

25 There was warmth of fury in his last phrases. He meant she loved him more than he her. Perhaps he could not love her. Perhaps she had not in herself that which he wanted. It was the deepest motive of her soul, this self-mistrust. It was so deep she dared neither realise nor acknowledge it. Perhaps she was deficient. Like an infinitely

30 subtle shame, it kept her always back. If it were so, she would do without him. She would never let herself want him. She would merely see.

"But what has happened?" she said.

"Nothing—it's all in myself—it only comes out just now.—We're

35 always like this towards Easter time."

He grovelled so helplessly, she pitied him. At least she never floundered in such a pitiable way. After all, it was he who was chiefly humiliated.

"What do you want?" she asked him.

40 "Why—I mustn't come often—that's all. Why should I monopo-

lise you, when I'm not—. You see, I'm deficient in something with
regard to you—."

He was telling her he did not love her, and so ought to leave her a
chance with another man. How foolish and blind and shamefully
clumsy he was! What were other men to her! What were men to her   5
at all! But he, ah, she loved his soul. Was *he* deficient in something?
Perhaps he was.

"But I don't understand," she said huskily. "Yesterday—."

The night was turning jangled and hateful to him as the twilight
faded. And she bowed under her suffering.   10

"I know," he cried, "you never will. You'll never believe that I
can't—can't physically, any more than I can fly up like a skylark—"

"What?" she murmured. Now she dreaded.

"Love you."

He hated her bitterly at that moment, because he made her suffer.   15
Love her! She knew he loved her. He really belonged to her. This
about not loving her, physically, bodily, was a mere perversity on his
part, because he knew she loved him. He was stupid like a child. He
belonged to her.* His soul wanted her. She guessed somebody had
been influencing him. She felt upon him the hardness, the foreign-   20
ness of another influence.

"What have they been saying at home?" she asked.

"It's not that," he answered.

And then she knew it was. She despised them for their common-
ness, his people. They did not know what things were really worth.   25

He and she talked very little more that night. After all he left her
to cycle with Edgar.

He had come back to his mother. Hers was the strongest tie in his
life. When he thought round, Miriam shrank away. There was a
vague, unreal feel about her. And nobody else mattered. There was   30
one place in the world that stood solid and did not melt into unreality:
the place where his mother was. Everybody else could grow shadowy,
almost non-existent to him, but she could not. It was as if the pivot
and pole of his life, from which he could not escape, was his mother.

And in the same way, she waited for him. In him was established   35
her life now. After all, the life beyond offered very little to Mrs
Morel. She saw that our chance for *doing* is here, and doing counted
with her. Paul was going to prove that she had been right: he was
going to make a man whom nothing should shift off his feet, he was
going to alter the face of the earth, in some way which mattered.   40

Wherever he went, she felt her soul went with him. Whatever he did, she felt her soul stood by him, ready, as it were, to hand him his tools. She could not bear it when he was with Miriam. William was dead. She would fight to keep Paul.

5   And he came back to her. And in his soul was a feeling of the satisfaction of self-sacrifice because he was faithful to her. She loved him first, he loved her first. And yet it was not enough. His new, young life, so strong and imperious, was urged towards something else. It made him mad with restlessness. She saw this, and wished

10   bitterly that Miriam had been a woman who could take this new life of his, and leave her the roots. He fought against his mother almost as he fought against Miriam.

It was a week before he went again to Willey Farm. Miriam had suffered a great deal, and was afraid to see him again. Was she now

15   to endure the ignominy of his abandoning her? That would only be superficial and temporary. He would come back. She held the keys to his soul. But meanwhile, how he would torture her with his battle against her. She shrank from it.*

However, the Sunday after Easter he came to tea. Mrs Leivers was

20   glad to see him. She gathered something was fretting him, that he found things hard. He seemed to drift to her for comfort. And she was good to him. She did him that great kindness of treating him almost with reverence.

He met her with the young children in the front garden.

25   "I'm glad you've come," said the mother, looking at him with her great, appealing brown eyes. "It is such a sunny day.—I was just going down the fields, for the first time this year."

He felt she would like him to come. That soothed him. They went, talking simply, he gentle and humble. He could have wept

30   with gratitude that she was deferential to him. He was feeling humiliated.

At the bottom of the mow close they found a thrush's nest.

"Shall I show you the eggs?" he said.

"Do!" replied Mrs Leivers. "They seem *such* a sign of spring, and

35   so hopeful."

He put aside the thorns and took out the eggs, holding them in the palm of his hand.

"They are quite hot—I think we frightened her off them," he said.

40   "Ay, poor thing," said Mrs Leivers.

Miriam could not help touching the eggs, and his hand, which, it seemed to her, cradled them so well.

"Isn't it a strange warmth!" she murmured, to get near him.

"Blood heat," he answered.

She watched him putting them back, his body pressed against the 5 hedge, his arm reaching slowly through the thorns, his hand folded carefully over the eggs. He was concentrated on the act. Seeing him so, she loved him, he seemed so simple and sufficient to himself. And she could not get to him.

Over tea he discussed with Mrs Leivers the Good Friday sermon. 10 It was too far for the mother to get to Chapel now: and she liked almost better to have the sermon through Paul, with his comments and arguments. The others listened. Even the big, rough lads were attentive, interested, gathering food from the discourse.

"He took," said Paul, "that Chapter—'Who hath believed our 15 report'*—I like it."

Mrs Leivers' large brown eyes flushed with light at the thought of it.

"And he spoilt it altogether—he spoilt it."

He glanced suddenly at Miriam, for her to be with him now.

"He said—." 20

Paul, earnest and wrathful, gave the sermon over again. It was thus Miriam loved him. She watched him, and was filled with deep satisfaction. She loved him in the same way that Mary loved at Bethany.* Only when the man came up in him was there war between them. And which was stronger in him, the Disciple or the 25 man. She believed the former, and by the former she held him.

When she was clearing the tea-table he said, in rather a forced tone:

"We'll go out when you've done."

And he helped her to wipe the pots in the scullery. She quivered 30 slightly in apprehension. But she knew she had no cause for fear from his resentment that night.

"Shall we take a book?" she said, laying her fingers on her favourite Palgrave's *Golden Treasury*.* He was his best with her when they read poetry. 35

"Not that," he said.

Her heart sank. She stood hesitating at the book-shelf. He took *Tartarin de Tarascon*.* Again they sat on the bank of hay at the foot of the stack. He read a couple of pages, but without any heart for it. Again the dog came racing up, to repeat the fun of the other day. He 40 shoved his muzzle in the man's chest. Paul fingered his ear for a moment. Then he pushed him away.

"Go away, Bill," he said. "I don't want you."

Bill slunk off, and Miriam wondered, and dreaded what was
5 coming. There was a silence about the youth that made her still with apprehension. It was not his furies, but his quiet resolutions that she feared.

Turning his face a little to one side, so that she could not see him, he began, speaking slowly and painfully:
10 "Do you think—if I didn't come up so much—you might get to like somebody else—another man—?"

So this was what he was still harping on.

"But I don't know any other men—why do you ask?" she replied, in a low tone that should have been a reproach on him.
15 "Why," he blurted, "because they say I've no right to come up like this—without we mean to marry—"

Miriam was indignant at anybody's forcing the issues between them. She had been furious with her own father for suggesting to Paul, laughingly, that he knew why he came so much.
20 "Who says?" she asked, wondering if her people had anything to do with it. They had not.

"Mother—and the others. They say, at this rate, everybody will consider me engaged, and I ought to consider myself so, because it's not fair to you.—And I've tried to find out—and I don't think I love
25 you as a man ought to love his wife.—What do *you* think about it?"

Miriam bowed her head moodily. She was angry at having this struggle. People should leave him and her alone.

"I don't know," she murmured.

"Do you think we love each other enough to marry?" he asked,
30 definitely. It made her tremble.

"No," she answered, truthfully. "I don't think so—we're too young."

"I thought perhaps," he went on miserably, "that you, with your intensity in things, might have given me more—than I could ever
35 make up to you.—And even now—if you think it better—we'll be engaged."

Now Miriam wanted to cry. And she was angry too. He was always such a child, for people to do as they liked with.*

"No, I don't think so," she said firmly.
40 He pondered a minute.

"You see," he said, "with me—I don't think one person would ever monopolise me—be everything to me—I think never."
This she did not consider.
"No," she murmured. Then after a pause, she looked at him and her dark eyes flashed: 5
"This is your mother," she said. "I know she never liked me."
"No no, it isn't," he said hastily. "It was for your sake she spoke this time. She only said, if I was going on, I ought to consider myself engaged." There was a silence.—"And if I ask you to come down any time, you won't stop away, will you?"   10
She did not answer. By this time she was very angry.
"Well, what shall we do?" she said shortly. "I suppose I'd better drop French. I was just beginning to get on with it.—But I suppose I can go on alone."
"I don't see that we need," he said. "I can give you a French   15
lesson, surely."
"Well—and there are Sunday nights. I shan't stop coming to chapel, because I enjoy it, and it's all the social life I get. But you've no need to come home with me. I can go alone."
"All right," he answered, rather taken aback. "But if I ask Edgar, 20
he'll always come with us, and then they can say nothing."
There was silence. After all then, she would not lose much. For all their talk down at his home, there would not be much difference. She wished they would mind their own business.
"And you won't think about it, and let it trouble you, will you?" he 25
asked.
"Oh no," replied Miriam, without looking at him.
He was silent. She thought him unstable. He had no fixity of purpose, no anchor of righteousness* that held him.
"Because," he continued, "a man gets across his bicycle—and   30
goes to work—and does all sorts of things. But a woman broods."*
"No, I shan't bother," said Miriam. And she meant it.
It had gone rather chilly. They went indoors.
"How white Paul looks!" Mrs Leivers exclaimed. "Miriam, you shouldn't have let him sit out of doors.—Do you think you've taken 35
cold Paul?"
"Oh no!" he laughed.
But he felt done up. It wore him out, the conflict in himself. Miriam pitied him now. But quite early, before nine o'clock, he rose to go.   40

"You're not going home, are you?" asked Mrs Leivers anxiously.

"Yes," he replied. "I said I'd be early."

He was very awkward.

"But this *is* early," said Mr Leivers.

5   Miriam sat in the rocking-chair, and did not speak. He hesitated, expecting her to rise and go with him to the barn as usual for his bicycle. She remained as she was. He was at a loss.

"Well—goodnight all!" he faltered.

She spoke her goodnight along with all the others. But as he went
10   past the window, he looked in. She saw him pale, his brows knit slightly in a way that had become constant with him, his eyes dark with pain.

She rose and went to the doorway to wave goodbye to him as he passed through the gate. He rode slowly under the pine trees,
15   feeling a cur and a miserable wretch. His bicycle went tilting down the hills at random. He thought it would be a relief to break one's neck.

Two days later he sent her up a book* and a little note, urging her to read and be busy.

20   And yet, he was different afterwards. He had seen the position. He knew he did *not* want to marry her. The reasons why he loved her were not reasons why he should want to marry her; that he had decided upon. And his mother had dinned it into him that this present situation could not go on for ever, and was grossly unfair to
25   the girl. So he tried to put as much distance between him and her, as he could. He was cold and hard to her. She felt it all bitterly, ascribed it to his mother, and waited. She knew he could not leave her alone. But he seemed to be trying to throw up barriers between them, him and her, behind which he could retreat, away from her.
30   She suffered rather badly.

At this time, he gave all his friendship to Edgar. He loved the family so much, he loved the farm so much, it was the dearest place on earth to him. His home was not so lovable. It was his mother. But then he would have been just as happy with his mother anywhere.
35   Whereas Willey Farm he loved passionately. He loved the little, pokey kitchen, where men's boots tramped and the dog slept with one eye open, for fear of being trodden on: where the lamp hung over the table at night, and everything was so silent. He loved Miriam's long, low parlour, with its atmosphere of romance, its
40   flowers, its books, its high rosewood piano. He loved the gardens

and the buildings, that stood with their scarlet roofs on the naked
edges of the fields, crept towards the wood as if for cosiness, the wild
country scooping down a valley and up the uncultured hills of the
other side. Only to be there was an exhilaration and a joy to him. He
loved Mrs Leivers, with her unworldliness and her quaint cynicism;
he loved Mr Leivers, so warm and young and lovable; he loved
Edgar, who lit up when he came, and the boys and the children and
Bill—even the sow Circe and the Indian game cock called Tippoo.*
All this besides Miriam. He could not give it up.

So he went as often, but he was usually with Edgar. Only, all the
family, including the father, joined in charades and games at
evening. And later, Miriam drew them together, and they read
Macbeth out of penny books,* taking parts. It was great excitement.
Miriam was glad, and Mrs Leivers was glad, and Mr Leivers
enjoyed it. Then they all learned songs together, from tonic solfa,
singing in a circle round the fire. But now, Paul was very rarely alone
with Miriam. She waited. When she and Edgar and he walked home
together from Chapel or from the literary society in Bestwood, she
knew his talk, so passionate and so unorthodox nowadays, was for
her. She did envy Edgar, however, his cycling with Paul, his Friday
nights, his days working in the fields. For her Friday nights and her
French lessons were gone. She was nearly always alone, walking
pondering in the wood, reading, studying, dreaming, waiting. And
he wrote to her frequently.

One Sunday evening they attained to their old, rare harmony.
Edgar had stayed to Communion—he wondered what it was like—
with Mrs Morel. So Paul came on alone with Miriam to his home.
He was more or less under her spell again. As usual, they were
discussing the sermon. He was setting now full sail towards Agnosticism, but such a religious Agnosticism that Miriam did not suffer
so badly. They were at the Renan *Vie de Jésus* stage.* Miriam was the
threshing floor on which he threshed out all his beliefs. While he
trampled his ideas upon her soul, the truth came out for him. She
alone was his threshing floor. She alone helped him towards real-
isation. Almost impassive, she submitted to his argument and
expounding. And somehow, because of her, he gradually realised
where he was wrong. And what he realised, she realised. She felt he
could not do without her.

They came to the silent house. He took the key out of the scullery
window, and they entered. All the time, he went on with his

discussion. He lit the gas, mended the fire, and brought her some cakes from the pantry. She sat on the sofa, quietly, with a plate on her knee. She wore a large white hat with some pinkish flowers. It was a cheap hat, but he liked it. Her face beneath was still and 5 pensive, golden brown and ruddy. Always her ears were hid in her short curls. She watched him.

She liked him on Sundays. Then he wore a dark suit that showed the lithe movement of his body. There was a clean, clear-cut look about him. He went on with his thinking to her. Suddenly he 10 reached for a bible. Miriam liked the way he reached up, so sharp, straight to the mark. He turned the pages quickly, and read her a chapter of St. John. As he sat in the arm-chair, reading, intent, his voice only thinking, she felt as if he were using her unconsciously, as a man uses his tools at some work he is bent on. She loved it. And 15 the wistfulness of his voice was like a reaching to something, and it was as if she were what he reached with. She sat back on the sofa, away from him, and yet feeling herself the very instrument his hand grasped. It gave her great pleasure.

Then he began to falter, and to get self-conscious. And when he 20 came to the verse:* "A woman, when she is in travail, hath sorrow because her hour is come," he missed it out. Miriam had felt him growing uncomfortable. She shrank when the well-known words did not follow. He went on reading, but she did not hear. A grief and shame made her bend her head.* Six months ago, he would have 25 read it simply. Now there was a scotch in his running with her. Now she felt there was really something hostile between them, something of which they were ashamed.

She ate her cake mechanically. He tried to go on with his argument, but could not get back the right note. Soon Edgar came 30 in. Mrs Morel had gone to her friend's. The three set off to Willey Farm.

Miriam brooded over his split with her. There was something else he wanted. He could not be satisfied, he could give her no peace. There was between them now always a ground for strife. She 35 wanted to prove him. She believed that his chief need in life was herself. If she could prove it, both to herself and to him, the rest might go, she could simply trust to the future.

So, in May, she asked him to come to Willey Farm and meet Mrs Dawes. There was something he hankered after. She saw him, 40 whenever they spoke of Clara Dawes, rouse and get slightly angry.

He said he did not like her. Yet he was keen to know about her. Well, he should put himself to the test. She believed that there were in him desires for higher things, and desires for lower, and that the desire for the higher would conquer. At any rate, he should try. She forgot that her 'higher' and 'lower' were arbitrary.   5

He was rather excited at the idea of meeting Clara at Willey Farm. Mrs Dawes came for the day. Her heavy, dun-coloured hair was coiled on top of her head. She wore a white blouse and navy skirt, and somehow, wherever she was, seemed to make things look paltry and insignificant. When she was in the room, the kitchen seemed too   10 small and mean altogether. Miriam's beautiful twilighty parlour looked stiff and stupid. All the Leivers were eclipsed like candles. They found her rather hard to put up with. Yet she was perfectly amiable, but indifferent, and rather hard.

Paul did not come till afternoon. He was early. As he swung off   15 his bicycle, Miriam saw him look round at the house, eagerly. He would be disappointed if the visitor had not come. Miriam went out to meet him, bowing her head because of the sunshine. Nasturtiums were coming out crimson under the cool green shadow of their leaves. The girl stood dark haired, glad to see him.   20

"Hasn't Clara come?" he asked.

"Yes," replied Miriam, in her musical tone. "She's reading."

He wheeled his bicycle into the barn. He had put on a handsome tie, of which he was rather proud, and socks to match.

"She came this morning?" he asked.   25

"Yes," replied Miriam, as she walked at his side. "You said you'd bring me that letter from the man at Liberty's. Have you remembered?"

"Oh dash, no!" he said. "But nag at me till you get it."

"I don't like to nag at you."   30

"Do it whether or not. And is she any more agreeable?" he continued.

"You know I always think she is quite agreeable."

He was silent. Evidently his eagerness to be early today had been the new-comer. Miriam already began to suffer. They went together 35 towards the house. He took the clips off his trousers, but was too lazy to brush the dust from his shoes, in spite of the socks and tie.

Clara sat in the cool parlour, reading. He saw the nape of her white neck, and the fine hair lifted from it. She rose, looking at him indifferently. To shake hands, she lifted her arm straight in a   40 manner that seemed at once to keep him at a distance, and yet to fling something to him. He noticed how her breasts swelled inside her blouse, and how her shoulder curved handsomely under the thin muslin at the top of her arm.

5   "You have chosen a fine day," he said.

"It happens so," she said.

"Yes," he said, "I am glad."

She sat down, not thanking him for his politeness.

"What have you been doing all morning?" asked Paul of Miriam.

10   "Well you see," said Miriam, coughing huskily, "Clara only came with father—and so—she's not been here very long."

Clara sat leaning on the table, holding aloof. He noticed her hands were large but well kept. And the skin on them seemed almost coarse, opaque and white, with fine golden hairs. She did not mind

15 if he observed her hands. She intended to scorn him. Her heavy arm lay negligently on the table. Her mouth was closed as if she were offended, and she kept her face slightly averted.

"You were at Margaret Bonford's meeting* the other evening," he said to her. Miriam did not know this courteous Paul. Clara

20 glanced at him:

"Yes," she said.

"Why," asked Miriam, "how do you know?"

"I went in for a few minutes before the train came," he answered.

Clara turned away again rather disdainfully.

25   "I think she's a lovable little woman," said Paul.

"Margaret Bonford!" exclaimed Clara. "She's a great deal cleverer than most men."

"Well, I didn't say she wasn't," he said, deprecating. "She's lovable for all that."

30   "And of course that is all that matters," said Clara witheringly.

He rubbed his head, rather perplexed, rather annoyed.

"I suppose it matters more than her cleverness," he said; "—which after all would never get her to heaven."

"It's not heaven she wants to get—it's her fair share on earth,"

35 retorted Clara. She spoke as if he were responsible for some deprivation which Miss Bonford suffered.

"Well," he said, "I thought she was warm, and awfully nice—only too frail. I wished she was sitting comfortably in peace—"

"'Darning her husband's stockings',"* said Clara, scathingly.

40   "I'm sure she wouldn't mind darning even my stockings," he said.

"And I'm sure she'd do them well.—Just as I wouldn't mind blacking her boots, if she wanted me to."

But Clara refused to answer this sally of his. He talked to Miriam for a little while. The other woman held aloof.

"Well," he said, "I think I'll go and see Edgar. Is he on the land?" "I believe," said Miriam, "he's gone for a load of coal. He should be back directly."

"Then," he said, "I'll go and meet him."

Miriam dared not propose anything for the three of them. He rose and left them.

On the top road, where the gorse was out, he saw Edgar walking lazily beside the mare, who nodded her white-starred forehead as she dragged the clanking load of coal. The young farmer's face lighted up as he saw his friend. Edgar was good-looking, with dark warm eyes. His clothes were old and rather disreputable, and he walked with considerable pride.

"Hello!" he said, seeing Paul bareheaded. "Where are you going?"

"Came to meet you. Can't stand 'Nevermore'."

Edgar's teeth flashed in a laugh of amusement.

"Who is 'Nevermore'?" he asked.

"The lady—Mrs Dawes—it ought to be Mrs the Raven that quothed 'Nevermore'."*

Edgar laughed with glee.

"Don't you like her?" he asked.

"Not a fat lot," said Paul. "Why, do you?"

"No!" The answer came with a deep ring of conviction. "No!" Edgar pursed up his lips. "I can't say she's much in my line." He mused a little. Then: "But why do you call her 'Nevermore'?" he asked.

"Well," said Paul. "If she looks at a man, she says haughtily 'Nevermore,' and if she looks at herself in the looking-glass she says disdainfully 'Nevermore,' and if she thinks back she says it in disgust, and if she looks forward she says it cynically—"

Edgar considered this speech, failed to make much out of it, and said, laughing:

"You think she's a man-hater?"

"*She* thinks she is," replied Paul.

"But you don't think so?"

"No," replied Paul.

"Wasn't she nice with you then?"

"Could you imagine her *nice* with anybody?" asked the young man.

Edgar laughed. Together they unloaded the coal in the yard. Paul was rather self-conscious because he knew Clara could see if she looked out of the window. She didn't look.

On Saturday afternoons the horses were brushed down, and groomed. Paul and Edgar worked together, sneezing with the dust that came from the pelts of Jimmy and Flower.

"Do you know a new song to teach me?" said Edgar.

He continued to work all the time. The back of his neck was sun-red, when he bent down, and his fingers that held the brush were thick. Paul watched him sometimes.

"'Mary Morrison'?"* suggested the younger.

Edgar agreed. He had a good tenor voice, and he loved to learn all the songs his friend could teach him, so that he could sing whilst he was carting. Paul had a very indifferent baritone voice, but a good ear. However, he sang softly, for fear of Clara. Edgar repeated the line in a clear tenor. At times they both broke off to sneeze, and first one, then the other, abused his horse.

Miriam was impatient of men. It took so little to amuse them—even Paul. She thought it anomalous in him that he could be so thoroughly absorbed in a triviality.

It was tea-time when they had finished.

"What song was that?" asked Miriam.

Edgar told her. The conversation turned to singing.

"We have such jolly times," Miriam said to Clara.

Mrs Dawes ate her meal in a slow, dignified way. Whenever the men were present, she grew distant.

"Do you like singing?" Miriam asked her.

"If it is good," she said.

Paul, of course, coloured.

"You mean if it is high-class, and trained?" he said.

"I think a voice needs training before the singing is anything," she said.

"You might as well insist on having people's voices trained before you allowed them to talk," he replied. "Really, people sing for their own pleasure, as a rule."

"And it may be for other people's discomfort."

"Then the other people should have flaps to their ears," he replied.

The boys laughed. There was a silence. He flushed deeply and ate in silence.

The conversation turned again on the point whether women's wages should be equal with those of men. Mrs Leivers upheld that men had families to keep; Clara said, so much work should have so much pay, man or woman. Mr Leivers was inclined to agree with her. Whatever Mrs Dawes had said, Paul would have taken sides against her. He argued that a woman was only an accessory in the labour market, and that, in the majority of cases she was a transitory thing, supporting herself alone for a year or two. Clara quoted the number of women who supported father, mother, sisters etc.

"And almost every man in the world, over thirty, supports a wife and family—and as a *rule*, the said wives are not wage-earners," he replied.

"I think my friend," said Clara very coldly, "that I have met your sort before: the young man who thinks he knows everything—."

"And you are the young woman who thinks I know nothing," he retorted.

"Oh yes—you know how to make yourself heard," she said.

He was furious. Then he burst into a laugh.

"Sounds like a suffragette meeting," he said, "you on the platform."

And then Clara coloured to the roots of her hair.

"Why should I be called 'Men'* when I'm only myself," he continued.

"As if that weren't enough," laughed Edgar.

"And then," Paul resumed, "I'm made responsible for every sin in English history, from Queen Boadisca down to the Song of the Shirt.* It's not fair.—I wish Man had a right to exist in modern society—any corner in which to lay his head."*

"Why," jested Mrs Leivers, "when all comes to all, his place remains very much the same, while we're made as we are."

But this joke was too subtle for all but Clara. She was indignant.

After tea, when all the men had gone but Paul, Mrs Leivers said to Clara:

"And you find life happier now?"

"Infinitely."

"And you are satisfied?"

"So long as I can be free and independent."

"And you don't *miss* anything in your life?" asked Mrs Leivers gently.

"I've put all that behind me."

Paul had been feeling uncomfortable during this discourse. He got up:

"You'll find you're always tumbling over the things you've put behind you,"* he said. Then he took his departure to the cowsheds. He felt he had been witty, and his manly pride was high. He whistled as he went down the brick track.

Miriam came for him a little later to know if he would go with Clara and her for a walk. They set off down to Strelley Mill farm. As they were going beside the brook, on the Willey Water side, looking through the brake at the edge of the wood, where pink campions glowed under a few sunbeams, they saw, beyond the tree trunks and the thin hazel-bushes, a man leading a great bay horse through the gullies. The big, red beast seemed to dance romantically through that dimness of green hazel-drift, away there where the air was shadowy as if it were in the past, among the fading bluebells that might have bloomed for Deirdre or Iseult.*

The three stood charmed.

"What a treat to be a knight," he said, "and to have a pavilion here."

"And to have us shut up safely?" replied Clara.

"Yes," he answered, "singing with your maids at your broidery.* I would carry your banner of white and green and heliotrope. I would have W.S.P.U.* emblazoned on my shield, beneath a woman rampant—."

"I have no doubt," said Clara, "that you would much rather fight for a woman than let her fight for herself."*

"I would! When she fights for herself she seems like a dog before a looking glass, gone into a mad fury with its own shadow."*

"And *you* are the looking-glass?" she asked, with a curl of the lip.

"Or the shadow," he replied.

"I am afraid," she said, "that you are too clever."

"Well, I leave it to you to be *good*," he retorted, laughing. "Be good, sweet maid, and just let *me* be clever."*

But Clara wearied of his flippancy. Suddenly, looking at her, he saw that the upward lifting of her face was misery and not scorn. His heart grew tender for everybody. He turned and was gentle with Miriam, whom he had neglected till then.

At the wood's edge, they met Limb, a thin, swarthy man of forty, tenant of Strelley Mill, which he ran as a cattle raising farm. He held the halter of the powerful stallion indifferently, as if he were tired. The three stood to let him pass over the stepping stones of the first brook. Paul admired that so large an animal should walk on such springy toes, with an endless excess of vigour. Limb pulled up before them.

"Tell your father, Miss Leivers," he said, in a peculiar piping voice, "that his young beas'es 'as broke that bottom fence three days an' runnin'."

"Which?" asked Miriam, tremulous.

The great horse breathed heavily, shifting round its red flanks, and looking suspiciously with its wonderful big eyes, upwards from under its lowered head and falling mane.

"Come along a bit," replied Limb, "an' I'll show you."

The man and the stallion went forward. It danced sideways, shaking its white fetlocks, and looking frightened as it felt itself in the brook.

"No hanky-pankyin'," said the man affectionately to the beast.

It went up the bank in little leaps, then splashed finely through the second brook. Clara, walking with a kind of sulky abandon, watched it half fascinated, half contemptuous. Limb stopped and pointed to the fence under some willows.

"There, you see where they got through," he said. "My man's druv 'em back three times."

"Yes," answered Miriam, colouring as if she were at fault.

"Are you comin' in?" asked the man.

"No thanks—but we should like to go by the pond."

"Well just as you've a mind," he said.

The horse gave little whinneys of pleasure at being so near home.

"He is glad to be back," said Clara, who was interested in the creature.

"Yes—'e's been a tidy step today."

They went through the gate, and saw approaching them from the big farm-house a smallish dark, excitable-looking woman of about thirty five. Her hair was touched with grey, her dark eyes looked wild. She walked with her hands behind her back. Her brother went forward. As it saw her, the big bay stallion whinneyed again. She came up excitedly.

"Are you home again, my boy!" she said tenderly, to the horse,

not to the man. The great beast shifted round to her, ducking his head. She smuggled into his mouth the wrinkled yellow apple she had been hiding behind her back, then she kissed him near the eyes. He gave a big sigh of pleasure. She held his head in her arms,
5 against her breast.

"Isn't he splendid!" said Miriam to her.

Miss Limb looked up. Her dark eyes glanced straight at Paul.

"Oh good evening, Miss Leivers," she said. "It's ages since you've been down."

10 Miriam introduced her friends.

"Your horse *is* a fine fellow!" said Clara.

"Isn't he!" Again she kissed him. "As loving as any man!"

"More loving than most men, I should think," replied Clara.

"He's a nice boy!" cried the woman, again embracing the horse.

15 Clara, fascinated by the big beast, went up to stroke his neck.

"He's quite gentle," said Miss Limb. "Don't you think big fellows are?"

"He's a beauty!" replied Clara.

She wanted to look in his eyes. She wanted him to look at her.

20 "It's a pity he can't talk," she said.

"Oh but he can, all but," replied the other woman.

Then her brother moved on with the horse.

"Are you coming in?—*do* come in Mr—I didn't catch it—"

"Morel!" said Miriam. "No—we won't come in, but we should
25 like to go by the mill-pond."

"Yes—yes do. Do you fish Mr Morel?"

"No," said Paul.

"Because if you do you might come and fish any time," said Miss Limb. "We scarcely see a soul from week's end to week's end. I
30 should be thankful."

"What fish are there in the pond?" he asked.

They went through the front garden, over the sluice, and up the steep bank to the pond, which lay in shadow, with its two wooded islets. Paul walked with Miss Limb.

35 "I shouldn't mind swimming here," he said.

"Do," she replied. "Come when you like. My brother will be awfully pleased to talk with you. He is so quiet, because there is no one to talk to. Do come and swim."

Clara came up.

40 "It's a fine depth," she said, "and so clear."

"Yes," said Miss Limb.

"Do you swim?" said Paul. "Miss Limb was just saying we could come when we liked."

"Of course there's the farm-hands," said Miss Limb.

They talked a few moments, then went on up the wild hill, leaving the lonely, haggard-eyed woman on the bank.

The hillside was all ripe with sunshine. It was wild and tussocky, given over to rabbits. The three walked in silence. Then:

"She makes me feel uncomfortable," said Paul.

"You mean Miss Limb?" asked Miriam. "Yes!"

"What's a matter with her? Is she going dotty with being too lonely?"

"Yes," said Miriam. "It's not the right sort of life for her. I think it's cruel to bury her there. *I* really ought to go and see her more. But—she upsets me."

"She makes me feel sorry for her—yes and she bothers me—" he said.

"I suppose," blurted Clara suddenly, "she wants a man."

The other two were silent for a few moments.

"But it's the loneliness sends her cracked," said Paul.

Clara did not answer, but strode on uphill. She was walking with her head hanging, her legs swinging as she kicked through the dead thistles and the tussocky grass, her arms hanging loose. Rather than walking, her handsome body seemed to be blundering up the hill. A hot wave went over Paul. He was curious about her. Perhaps life had been cruel to her. He forgot Miriam, who was walking beside him talking to him. She glanced at him, finding he did not answer her. His eyes were fixed ahead on Clara.

"Do you still think she is disagreeable?" she asked.

He did not notice that the question was sudden. It ran with his thoughts.

"Something's the matter with her," he said.

"Yes," answered Miriam.

They found at the top of the hill a hidden wild field, two sides of which were backed by the wood, the other sides by high loose hedges of hawthorn and elder-bushes. Between these overgrown bushes were gaps that the cattle might have walked through, had there been any cattle now. There the turf was smooth as velveteen, padded and holed by the rabbits. The field itself was coarse, and crowded with tall big cowslips, that had never been cut. Clusters of

strong flowers rose everywhere above the coarse tussocks of bent. It
was like a roadstead crowded with tall fairy-shipping.

"Ah!" cried Miriam, and she looked at Paul, her dark eyes dilating. He smiled. Together they enjoyed the field of flowers. Clara, a
5 little way off, was looking at the cowslips, disconsolately. Paul and
Miriam stayed close together, talking in subdued tones. He kneeled
on one knee, quickly gathering the best blossoms, moving from tuft
to tuft restlessly, talking softly all the time. Miriam plucked the
flowers lovingly, lingering over them. He always seemed to her too
10 quick and almost scientific. Yet his bunches had a natural beauty
more than hers. He loved them, but as if they were his and he had a
right to them. She had more reverence for them: they held something she had not.

The flowers were very fresh and sweet. He wanted to drink
15 them. As he gathered them, he ate the little yellow trumpets. Clara
was still wandering about disconsolately. Going towards her, he
said:

"Why don't you get some?"

"I don't believe in it. They look better growing."

20 "But you'd like some?"

"They want to be left."

"I don't believe they do."

"I don't want the corpses of flowers about me," she said.

"That's a stiff artificial notion," he said. "They don't die any
25 quicker in water than on their roots.—And besides, they *look* nice
in a bowl, they look jolly. And you only call a thing a corpse because
it looks corpse-like."

"Whether it is one or not?" she argued.

"It isn't one to me. A dead flower isn't a corpse of a flower."
30 Clara now ignored him.

"And even so—what right have you to pull them?" she asked.

"Because I like them, and want them—and there's plenty of
them."

"And that is sufficient?"

35 "Yes—why not. I'm sure they'd smell nice in your room in Nottingham."

"And I should have the pleasure of watching them die."

"But then—it does not matter if they do die."

Whereupon he left her, and went stooping over the clumps of
40 tangled flowers, which thickly sprinkled the field like pale, lumin-

ous foam-clots. Miriam had come close. Clara was kneeling breathing some scent from the cowslips.

"I think," said Miriam, "if you treat them with reverence—you don't do them any harm—it is the spirit you pluck them in that matters." 5

"Yes," he said. "But no, you get 'em because you want 'em, and that's all." He held out his bunch.

Miriam was silent. He picked some more.

"Look at these!" he continued; "sturdy and lusty like little trees and like boys with fat legs—" 10

Clara's hat lay on the grass not far off. She was kneeling, bending forward still to smell the flowers. Her neck gave him a sharp pang, such a beautiful thing, yet not proud of itself just now. Her breasts swung slightly in her blouse. The arching curve of her back was beautiful and strong: she wore no stays. Suddenly, without knowing, 15 he was scattering a handful of cowslips over her hair and neck, saying:

> "Ashes to ashes and dust to dust
> If the Lord won't have you the devil must."*

The chill flowers fell on her neck. She looked up at him, with 20 almost pitiful, scared grey eyes, wondering what he was doing. Flowers fell on her face and she shut her eyes.

Suddenly, standing there above her, he felt awkward.

"I thought you wanted a funeral," he said, ill at ease.

Clara laughed strangely, and rose, picking the cowslips from her 25 hair. She took up her hat and pinned it on. One flower had remained tangled in her hair. He saw, but would not tell her. He gathered up the flowers he had sprinkled over her.

At the edge of the wood the bluebells had flowed over into the field and stood there like flood-water. But they were fading now. 30 Clara strayed up to them. He wandered after her. The bluebells pleased him.

"Look how they've come out of the wood!" he said.

Then she turned with a flash of warmth and of gratitude.

"Yes!" she smiled. 35

His blood beat up.*

"It makes me think of the wild men of the woods, how terrified they would be when they got breast to breast with the open space."

"Do you think they were?" she asked.

"I wonder which was more frightened, among old tribes: those bursting out of their darkness of woods upon all the space of light, or those from the open tip-toeing into the forests."*

"I should think the second," she answered.

5 "Yes, you *do* feel like one of the open space sort—trying to force yourself into the dark—don't you?"

"How should I know?" she answered, queerly.

The conversation ended there.

The evening was deepening over the earth. Already the valley was
10 full of shadow. One tiny square of light stood opposite at Crossleigh Bank Farm. Brightness was swimming on the tops of the hills. Miriam came up slowly, her face in her big, loose bunch of flowers, walking ankle deep through the scattered froth of the cowslips. Beyond her, the trees were coming into shape, all shadow.*

15 "Shall we go?" she asked.

And the three turned away. They were all silent. Going down the path, they could see the light of home right across, and on the ridge of the hill, a thin dark outline with little lights, where the colliery village touched the sky.

20 "It has been nice, hasn't it?" he asked.

Miriam murmured assent. Clara was silent.

"Don't you think so?" he persisted.

But she walked with her head up, and still did not answer. He could tell by the way she moved, as if she didn't care, that she
25 suffered.

At this time Paul took his mother to Lincoln. She was bright and enthusiastic as ever, but as he sat opposite her in the railway carriage, she seemed to look frail. He had a momentary sensation as if she were slipping away from him. Then he wanted to get hold of
30 her, to fasten her, almost to chain her. He felt he must keep hold of her with his hand.

They drew near to the city. Both were at the window looking for the cathedral.

"There she is, mother!" he cried.

35 They saw the great cathedral lying couchant* above the plain.

"Ah!" she exclaimed. "So she is!"

He looked at his mother. Her blue eyes were watching the cathedral quietly. She seemed again to be beyond him. Something in the eternal repose of the uplifted cathedral, blue and noble
40 against the sky, was reflected in her, something of the fatality. What

was, *was!*—with all his young will he could not alter it. He saw her face, the skin still fresh and pink and downy, but crow's-feet near her eyes, her eyelids steady, sinking a little, her mouth always closed with disillusion; and there was on her the same eternal look, as if she knew fate at last. He beat against it with all the strength of his soul.

"Look mother how big she is above the town! Think, there are streets and streets below her: she looks bigger than the city altogether."

"So she does!" exclaimed his mother, breaking bright into life again. But he had seen her sitting, looking steady out of the window at the cathedral, her face and eyes fixed, reflecting the relentlessness of life. And the crow's-feet near her eyes, and her mouth shut so hard, made him feel he would go mad.

They ate a meal that she considered wildly extravagant.

"Don't imagine I like it," she said, as she ate her cutlet. "I *don't* like it, I really don't! Just *think* of your money wasted!"

"You never mind my money," he said. "You forget I'm a fellow taking his girl for an outing."

And he bought her some blue violets.

"Stop it at once, Sir!" she commanded. "How can I do it?"

"You've got nothing to do! Stand still."

And in the middle of the High Street, he stuck the flowers in her coat.

"An old thing like me!" she said, sniffing.

"You see," he said, "I want people to think we're awful swells. So look ikey."*

"I'll jowl your head," she laughed.

"Strut," he commanded. "Be a fantail pigeon."

It took him an hour to get her through the street. She stood above Glory Hole, she stood before Stone Bow, she stood everywhere, and exclaimed. A man came up, took off his hat and bowed to her:

"Can I show you the town, Madam?"

"No thank you," she answered. "I've got my son."

Then Paul was cross with her for not answering with more dignity.

"You go away with you," she exclaimed. "Ha—that's the Jew's House! Now do you remember that lecture,* Paul———"

But she could scarcely climb the Cathedral hill. He did not notice. Then suddenly he found her unable to speak. He took her into a little public house, where she rested.

"It's nothing!" she said. "My heart is only a bit old; one must expect it."

He did not answer, but looked at her. Again his heart was crushed in a hot grip. He wanted to cry, he wanted to smash things in fury.

5 They set off again, pace by pace, so slowly. And every step seemed like a weight on his chest. He felt as if his heart would burst. At last they came to the top. She stood enchanted, looking at the castle gate, looking at the Cathedral front. She had quite forgotten herself.

10 "Now *this* is better than I thought it could be!" she cried.

But he hated it. Everywhere he followed her, brooding. They sat together in the Cathedral. They attended a little service in the choir. She was timid.

"I suppose it is open to anybody?" she asked him.

15 "Yes," he replied. "Do you think they'd have the damned cheek to send us away."

"Well I'm, sure!" she exclaimed; "they would if they heard your language."

Her face seemed to shine again with joy and peace, during the 20 service. And all the time he was wanting to rage and smash things and cry.

Afterwards, when they were leaning over the wall, looking at the town below, he blurted suddenly:

"Why can't a man have a *young* mother? What is she old for?"

25 "Well," his mother laughed, "she can scarcely help it."

"And why wasn't I the oldest son! Look—they say the young ones have the advantage—but look, *they* had the young mother. You should have had me for your eldest son."

"*I* didn't arrange it," she remonstrated. "Come to consider, 30 you're as much to blame as me."

He turned on her, white, his eyes furious.

"What are you old for!" he said, mad with his impotence. "*Why* can't you walk? *Why* can't you come with me to places?"

"At one time," she replied, "I could have run up that hill a good 35 deal better than you."

"What's the good of that to *me*?" he cried, hitting his fist on the wall. Then he became plaintive. "It's too bad of you to be ill, Little, it is—."

"Ill!" she cried. "I'm a bit old, and you'll have to put up with it, 40 that's all."

They were quiet. But it was as much as they could bear. They got jolly again over tea. As they sat by Brayford, watching the boats, he told her about Clara. His mother asked him innumerable questions.

"Then who does she live with?"

"With her mother, on Bluebell Hill." 5

"And have they enough to keep them?"

"I don't think so: I think they do lace work."

"And wherein lies her charm, my boy?"

"I don't know that she's charming, mother. But she's nice. And she seems straight, you know—not a bit deep, not a bit." 10

"But she's a good deal older than you."

"She's thirty, I'm going of twenty-three."

"You haven't told me what you like her for."

"Because I don't know—a sort of defiant way she's got—a sort of angry way—" 15

Mrs Morel considered. She would have been glad now for her son to fall in love with some woman who would—she did not know what. But he fretted so, got so furious suddenly, and again was melancholic. She wished he knew some nice woman—. She did not know what she wished, but left it vague. At any rate she was not 20 hostile to the idea of Clara.

Annie too was getting married. Leonard had gone away to work in Birmingham. One week-end when he was home, she had said to him:

"You don't look very well, my lad." 25

"I dunno," he said. "I feel anyhow or nohow, Ma."

He called her Ma already, in his boyish fashion.

"Are you sure they're good lodgings?" she asked.

"Yes—yes. Only—it's a winder when you have to pour your own tea out—an' nobody to grouse if you team it in your saucer and sup it 30 up. It somehow takes a' th' taste out of it."

Mrs Morel laughed.

"And so it knocks you up?" she said.

"I dunno.—I want to get married," he blurted, twisting his fingers, and looking down at his boots. There was a silence. 35

"But," she exclaimed, "I thought you said you'd wait another year."

"Yes, I did say so," he replied stubbornly.

Again she considered.

"And you know," she said, "Annie's a bit of a spendthrift. She's 40 saved no more than eleven pounds—and I know, lad, you haven't had much chance."

He coloured up to the ears.

"I've got twenty three quid," he said.

5   "It doesn't go far," she answered.

He said nothing, but twisted his fingers.

"And you know," she said, "I've nothing—."

"I didn't want, Ma—!" he cried, very red, suffering, and remonstrating.

10   "No my lad, I know.—I was only wishing I had.—And take away five pounds for the wedding and things—it leaves twenty nine pounds—you won't do much on that—"

He twisted still, impotent, stubborn, not looking up.

"But do you really want to get married?" she asked. "Do you feel

15   as if you ought?"

He gave her one straight look from his blue eyes.

"Yes!" he said.

"Then," she replied, "we must all do the best we can for it, lad."

The next time he looked up there were tears in his eyes.

20   "I don't want Annie to feel handicapped—!" he said, struggling.

"My lad," she said, "you're steady—you've got a decent place. If a man had *needed* me, I'd have married him on his last week's wages. She may find it a bit hard, to start humbly. Young girls *are* like that. They look forward to the fine home they think they'll

25   have. But *I* had expensive furniture! It's not everything."

So the wedding took place almost immediately. Arthur came home, and was splendid in uniform. Annie looked nice in a dove-grey dress that she could take for Sundays. Morel called her a fool for getting married, and was cool with his son-in-law. Mrs Morel

30   had white tips in her bonnet, and some white on her blouse, and was teased by both her sons for fancying herself so grand. Leonard was jolly and cordial, and felt a fearful fool. Paul could not quite see what Annie wanted to get married for. He was fond of her, and she of him. Still, he hoped rather lugubriously that it would turn

35   out all right. Arthur was astonishingly handsome in his scarlet and yellow, and he knew it well, but was secretly ashamed of the uniform. Annie cried her eyes up in the kitchen, on leaving her mother. Mrs Morel cried a little, then patted her on the back and said:

40   "But don't cry, child, he'll be good to you."

Morel stamped and said she was a fool to go and tie herself up.
Leonard looked white and overwrought. Mrs Morel said to him:

"I s'll trust her to you, my lad, and hold you responsible for her."

"You can," he said, nearly dead with the ordeal. And it was all
over.

When Morel and Arthur were in bed, Paul sat talking, as he often
did, with his mother.

"You're not sorry she's married, mother, are you?" he asked.

"I'm not sorry she's married—but—it seems strange that she
should go from me. It even seems to me hard that she can prefer to
go with her Leonard. That's how mothers are—I know it's silly."

"And shall you be miserable about her?"

"When I think of my own wedding day," his mother answered, "I
can only hope her life will be different."*

"But you can trust him to be good to her?"

"Yes. Yes! They say he's not good enough for her. But I say if a
man is *genuine*, as he is, and a girl is fond of him—then—it should be
all right—he's as good as she."

"So you don't mind?"

"I would *never* have let a daughter of mine marry a man I didn't
feel to be genuine through and through.—And yet, there's the gap
now she's gone—"

They were both miserable, and wanted her back again. It seemed
to Paul, his mother looked lonely, in her new black silk blouse with
its bit of white trimming.

"At any rate, mother, I s'll never marry," he said.

"Ay, they all say that, my lad. You've not met the one yet. Only
wait a year or two."

"But I shan't marry mother—I shall live with you, and we'll have a
servant."

"Ay my lad—it's easy to talk. We'll see when the time comes."

"What time? I'm nearly twenty three."

"Yes—you're not one that would marry young. But in three years'
time—"

"I shall be with you just the same."

"We'll see, my boy, we'll see."

"But you don't want me to marry?"

"I shouldn't like to think of you going through your life without
anybody to care for you and do—no—."

"And you think I ought to marry?"

"Sooner or later, every man ought."

"But you'd rather it were later."

"It would be hard—and very hard. It's as they say:

'A son's my son till he takes him a wife,
5   But my daughter's my daughter the whole of my life.'"*

"And you think I'd let a wife take me from you?"

"Well, you wouldn't ask her to marry your mother as well as you," Mrs Morel smiled.

"She could do what she liked—she wouldn't have to interfere."

10   "She wouldn't—till she'd got you—and then you'd see."

"I never will see. I'll never marry while I've got you—I won't."

"But I shouldn't like to leave you with nobody, my boy," she cried.

"You're not going to leave me. What are you—fifty three! I'll
15 give you till seventy five. There you are, I'm fat and forty four. Then I'll marry a staid body. See—!"

His mother sat and laughed.

"Go to bed," she said, "go to bed."

"And we'll have a pretty house, you and me, and a servant, and
20 it'll be just all right.—I s'll perhaps be rich with my painting."

"Will you go to bed!"

"And then you s'll have a pony carriage. See yourself, a little Queen Victoria trotting round."

"I tell you to go to bed," she laughed.

25   He kissed her, and went. His plans for the future were always the same.

Mrs Morel sat brooding, about her daughter, about Paul, about Arthur. She fretted at losing Annie. The family was very closely bound. And she felt she *must* live now, to be with her children. Life
30 was so rich for her. Paul wanted her, and so did Arthur. Arthur never knew how deeply he loved her. He was a creature of the moment. Never yet had he been forced to realise himself. The army had disciplined his body, but not his soul. He was in perfect health, and very handsome. His dark, vigorous hair sat close to his
35 smallish head. There was something childish about his nose, something almost girlish about his dark blue eyes. But he had the full, red mouth of a man under his brown moustache, and his jaw was strong. It was his father's mouth, it was the nose and eyes of her own mother's people, good-looking, weak-principled folk. Mrs

Morel was anxious about him. Once he had really run the rig* he was safe. But how far would he go?

The army had not really done him any good. He resented bitterly the authority of the petty officers. He hated having to obey as if he were an animal. But he had too much sense to kick. So he turned his attention to getting the best out of it. He could sing, he was a boon-companion. Often he got into scrapes, but they were the manly scrapes that are easily condoned. So he made a good time out of it, whilst his self-respect was in suppression. He trusted to his good looks and handsome figure, his refinement, his decent education, to get him most of what he wanted, and he was not disappointed. Yet he was restless. Something seemed to gnaw him inside. He was never still, he was never alone. With his mother he was rather humble. Paul he admired and loved and despised slightly. And Paul admired and loved and despised him slightly.

Mrs Morel had had a few pounds left to her by her father, and she decided to buy her son out of the army.* He was wild with joy. Now he was like a lad taking a holiday.

He had always been fond of Beatrice Wyld, and during his furlough he picked up with her again. She was stronger and better in health. The two often went long walks together, Arthur taking her arm in soldier's fashion, rather stiffly. And she came to play the piano whilst he sang. Then Arthur would unhook his tunic collar. He grew flushed, his eyes were bright, he sang in a manly tenor. Afterwards they sat together on the sofa. He seemed to flaunt his body: she was aware of him so, the strong chest, the sides, the thighs in their close-fitting trousers.

He liked to lapse into the dialect when he talked to her. She would sometimes smoke with him. Occasionally she would only take a few whiffs at his cigarette.

"Nay," he said to her one evening, when she reached for his cigarette: "Nay tha doesna. I'll gi'e thee a smoke kiss if ter's a mind."

"I wanted a whiff, no kiss at all," she answered.

"Well—an' tha s'lt ha'e a whiff," he said, "along wi' t' kiss."

"I want a draw at thy fag," she cried, snatching for the cigarette between his lips.

He was sitting with his shoulder touching her. She was small and quick as lightning. He just escaped.

"I'll gi'e thee a smoke kiss," he said.

"Tha'rt a knivey nuisance, Arty Morel," she said, sitting back.
"Ha'e a smoke kiss!"

The soldier leaned forward to her, smiling. His face was near
hers.

5   "Shonna!" she replied, turning away her head.

He took a draw at his cigarette, and pursed up his mouth, and put
his lips close to her. His dark-brown, cropped moustache stood out
like a brush. She looked at the puckered crimson lips, then suddenly
snatched the cigarette from his fingers and darted away. He, leaping

10   after her, seized the comb from her back hair. She turned, threw the
cigarette at him. He picked it up, put it in his mouth, and sat down.

"Nuisance!" she cried. "Give me my comb!"

She was afraid that her hair, specially done for him, would come
down. She stood with her hands to her head. He hid the comb

15   between his knees.

"I'n non got it,' he said.

The cigarette trembled between his lips with laughter, as he
spoke.

"Liar!" she said.

20   "'S true as I'm here!" he laughed, showing his hands.*

"You brazen imp!" she exclaimed, rushing and scuffling for the
comb, which he had under his knees. As she wrestled with him,
pulling at his smooth, tight-covered thighs, he laughed till he lay
back on the sofa shaking with laughter. The cigarette fell from his

25   mouth, almost singeing his throat. Under his delicate tan, the blood
flushed up, and he laughed till his blue eyes were blinded, his throat
swollen almost to choking. Then he sat up. Beatrice was putting in
her comb.

"Tha tickled me,* Beat," he said thickly.

30   Like a flash, her small white hand went out and smacked his face.
He started up, glaring at her. They stared at each other. Slowly the
flush mounted her cheek, she dropped her eyes, then her head. He
sat down sulkily. She went into the scullery to adjust her hair. In
private there she shed a few tears, she did not know what for.

35   When she returned, she was pursed up close. But it was only a
film over her fire. He, with ruffled hair, was sulking upon the sofa.
She sat down opposite, in the arm-chair, and neither spoke. The
clock ticked in the silence, like blows.

"You are a little cat, Beat," he said at length, half apologetically.

40   "Well, you shouldn't be brazen," she replied.

There was again a long silence. He whistled to himself, like a man much agitated, but defiant. Suddenly she went across to him and kissed him.

"Did it, pore fing?" she mocked.

He lifted his face, smiling curiously.

"Kiss?" he invited her.

"Daren't I?" she asked.

"Go on!" he challenged, his mouth lifted to her.

Deliberately, and with a peculiar quivering smile, that seemed to overspread her whole body, she put her mouth on his. Immediately his arms folded round her. As soon as the long kiss was finished, she drew back her head from him, put her delicate fingers on his neck, through the open collar. Then she closed* her eyes, giving herself up again in a kiss.

She acted of her own free will. What she would do, she did, and made nobody responsible.

Paul felt life changing around him. The conditions of youth were gone. Now, it was a home of grown-up people. Annie was a married woman, Arthur was following his own pleasure, in a way unknown to his folk. For so long, they had all lived at home, and gone out to pass their time. But now, for Annie and Arthur, life lay outside their mother's house. They came home for holiday and for rest. So there was that strange, half empty feeling about the house, as if the birds had flown. Paul became more and more unsettled. Annie and Arthur had gone. He was restless to follow. Yet home was for him beside his mother. And still, there was something else, something outside, something he wanted.

He grew more and more restless. Miriam did not satisfy him. His old mad desire to be with her grew weaker. Sometimes he met Clara in Nottingham, sometimes he went to meetings with her, sometimes he saw her at Willey Farm. But on these last occasions, the situation became strained. There was a triangle of antagonism between Paul and Clara and Miriam. With Clara, he took on a smart, worldly, mocking tone very antagonistic to Miriam. It did not matter what went before. She might be intimate and sad with him. Then as soon as Clara appeared, it all vanished, and he played to the newcomer.

Miriam had one beautiful evening with him in the hay. He had been on the horse-rake, and, having finished, came to help her to put the hay in cocks. Then he talked to her of his hopes and despairs, and his whole soul seemed to lie bare before her. She felt

as if she watched the very quivering stuff of life in him. The moon
came out: they walked home together: he seemed to have come to
her because he needed her so badly, and she listened to him, gave
him all her love and her faith. It seemed to her, he brought her the
5 best of himself to keep, and that she would guard it all her life. Nay,
the sky did not cherish the stars more surely and eternally than she
would guard the good in the soul of Paul Morel. She went on home
alone feeling exalted, glad in her faith.

And then, the next day, Clara came. They were to have tea in the
10 hayfield. Miriam watched the evening drawing to gold and shadow.
And all the time, Paul was sporting with Clara. He made higher and
higher heaps of hay, that they were jumping over. Miriam did not
care for the game, and stood aside. Edgar and Geoffrey and
Maurice and Clara and Paul jumped. Paul won, because he was
15 light. Clara's blood was roused. She could run like an Amazon. Paul
loved the determined way she rushed at the hay-cock and leaped,
landed on the other side, her breasts shaken, her thick hair coming
undone.

"You touched!" he cried, "you touched."

20 "No!" she flashed, turning to Edgar. "I didn't touch, did I?
Wasn't I clear?"

"I couldn't say," laughed Edgar.

None of them could say.

"But you touched," said Paul, "you're beaten."

25 "I did *not* touch," she cried.

"As plain as anything," said Paul.

"Box his ears for me," she cried to Edgar.

"Nay," Edgar laughed, "I daren't. You must do it yourself."

"And nothing can alter the fact that you touched," laughed Paul.

30 She was furious with him. Her little triumph before these lads
and men was gone. She had forgotten herself in the game. Now he
was to humble her.

"I think you are despicable!" she said.

And again he laughed, in a way that tortured Miriam.

35 "And I *knew* you couldn't jump that heap," he teased.

She turned her back on him. Yet, everybody could see, that the
only person she listened to, or was conscious of, was he, and he of
her. It pleased the men to see this battle between them. But Miriam
was tortured.

40 Paul could choose the lesser in place of the higher, she saw. He

could be unfaithful to himself, unfaithful to the real, deep Paul Morel. There was a danger of his becoming frivolous, of his running after his satisfactions like any Arthur, or like his father. It made Miriam bitter, to think that he should throw away his soul for this flippant traffic of triviality with Clara. She walked in bitterness and silence, while the other two rallied each other, and Paul sported.

And afterwards, he would not own it, but he was rather ashamed of himself, and prostrated himself before Miriam. Then again he rebelled.

"It's not religious to be religious," he said. "I reckon a crow is religious when it sails across the sky. But it only does it because it feels itself carried to where it's going, not because it thinks it is being eternal."

But Miriam knew that one should be religious in everything, have God, whatever God He might be, present in everything.

"I don't believe God knows such a lot about himself," he cried. "God doesn't *know* things, he *is* things—and I'm sure he's not soulful."

And then it seemed to her that Paul was arguing God onto his own side, because he wanted his own way, and his own pleasure. There was a long battle between him and her. He was utterly unfaithful to her even in her own presence; then he was ashamed, then repentant; then he hated her and went off again. Those were the ever-recurring conditions.

She fretted him to the bottom of his soul. There she remained, sad, pensive, a worshipper. And he caused her sorrow. Half the time he grieved for her, half the time he hated her. She was his conscience; and he felt, somehow, he had got a conscience that was too much for him. He could not leave her, because in one way she did hold the best of him. He could not stay with her because she did not take the rest of him, which was three quarters. So he chafed himself into rawness over her.

When she was twenty-one, he wrote her a letter which could only have been written to her.

"Must I write you a birthday letter?—It seems a pernicious thing to do deliberately, don't you think? Because I'm sure to get flatulent and sententious." Then followed a certain amount of flatulence.

"My last letter prepared you, did it not, to rejoice over your coming of age. Do you not feel like an heiress being installed into her heritage? For now you come publicly into full possession of yourself. Would you have more than yourself?—Impossible!"

Now he began to feel the torture of self-consciousness. He seemed cut away underneath, as if he could not stand on his feet, but must flounder and flounder.

"—May I speak of our old, worn love, this last time. It too is
5   changing, is it not? Say, has not the body of that love died, and left you its invulnerable soul! You see, I can give you a spirit love, I have given it you this long, long time: but not embodied passion. See, you are a nun. I have given you what I would give a holy nun—as a mystic monk to a mystic nun: surely you esteem it best. Yet you
10 regret—no, have regretted—the other. In all our relations, no body enters. I do not talk to you through the senses—rather through the spirit. That is why we cannot love in the common sense. When I talk to you, I do not look at you, often, for, can you understand, I do not talk to your eyes, though they are dark and fine, nor to your ears,
15 hidden under a graceful toss of silky hair—but to you away inside, beyond. So I shall continue to do a whole life-time, if fate does not intervene. Do you see? And do you understand now why I only kiss you under the mistletoe. Do you understand?—and do I?—and is it better, think you? I think I am too refined, too civilised. I think many
20 folk are.

You have a place in my nature which no one else could fill. You have played a fundamental part in my development. And this grief, which has been like a cloud between our two souls, does it not begin to dissipate? Ours is not an everyday affection. As yet, we are mortal,
25 and to live side by side with one another would be dreadful, for somehow, with you I cannot long be trivial, and, you know, to be always beyond this mortal state would be to lose it. If people marry, they must live together as affectionate humans who may be commonplace with each other without feeling awkward—not as two
30 souls. So I feel it.

I might marry in the years to come. It would be a woman I could kiss and embrace, whom I could make the mother of my children, whom I could talk to playfully, trivially, earnestly, but never with this dreadful seriousness. See how fate has disposed things. You, you
35 might marry, a man who would not pour himself out like fire before you. I wonder if you understand—I wonder if I understand myself. But you do know that these things make me sick, and now here is an end of our talk on the matter. Forgive me for all this—it is unnatural, I know—and burn this letter, and do not think of it, or make me
40 think of it, and so help us to bear the burden of ourselves.

How will you like a *Manual of Ethics?** You will like it, and we can talk about that, and learn—oh yes. And you will be richer. Is it not so?—You see our intimacy would have been all beautiful, but for one little mistake.

And you are twenty one. I am so glad you are an independent woman now. You are as strong as I, are you not?—yes stronger. Oh, if we are to live, we must be wise, and not drive ourselves too far. We must be trivial, and we must seek beauty, and not pain, or else we are in a quandary. Mind, mind, not a word on the sensitive places yet.

Oh we will be gay at your party on Saturday. I am not sad, not a bit sad, now, in my heart.

Ought I to send this letter—I doubt it. But there—it is best to understand.—Au revoir—"

Miriam read this letter twice, after which she sealed it up. A year later she broke the seal to show her mother the letter.*

"You are a nun—you are a nun"—the words went into her heart again and again. Nothing he ever had said, had gone into her so deeply, fixedly, like a mortal wound.

She answered him two days after the party. "'Our intimacy would have been all beautiful, but for one little mistake,'" she quoted. "Was the mistake mine?"

Almost immediately, he replied to her from Nottingham, sending her at the same time a little *Omar Khayyam.**

"—You will find a good deal between the flimsy covers of this little book, but the lesson that we should drink the red wine of life and let it make us glad awhile is the reason why I got it. Also I want to bring you *The Blessed Damosel*, to spend an evening with you and Rossetti.*

'The little mistake was yours?' you ask? Why, whoever erred alone! Your share of the mistake was glorious, making for immortality. But mine was an unflagging recognition of the clay of the pot—brittle—rigid—confining. And I alternately hated and loved the earthy stuff of myself. When I loved it I was cruel to you, when I hated it I was cruel to myself, and everything. Have I not a faculty for being very cruel?

If on your birthday I was still somewhat stormy, it was because I recognised in your sun of Wednesday the washed brightness of your long day of sleet on Tuesday. I do not sit down and fight my battles out as you do. I shake my enemy by the throat and tell him he's a villain and a dog. With that I bid him go, and for a while, I am free.

Then I say he was a weakling farce, and I laugh. After awhile, I am
plunged again into blackness on finding he is not gone or dead—
when this is unbearable I have another wild fling at him. By such
guerilla warfares I succeed, or I do not succeed. No triumphs, no
5 Waterloos. Thus I do not suffer so keenly, and am less stable. After
all, it is a joke, this of 'us', is it not?

I am glad you answered—you are so calm and natural you put me
to shame. What a ranter I am! I must play though—. You do not
understand how I must dance round my enemies, howling at them
10 and spying them out, playing with anything that comes my way,
having occasional tussles. If I closed with everything, and kept my
sorrow hugged in my breast as you do, I should die of exhaustion. In
these things our natures are radically different.

So we are often out of sympathy. But in fundamentals, we may
15 always be together, I think.

I must thank you for your sympathy with my painting and
drawing. Many a sketch is dedicated to you. I do look forward to
your criticisms, which, to my shame and glory, are always grand
appreciations. It is a lovely joke that.

20 Au revoir. Now I must balance up a damned dry account. I hope
you burn these letters. It is my rule to burn all—for none are so nice
but what I can recall the pleasure they refer to, and most are full of
lurking tears which I must run away from— —"

This was the end of the first phase of Paul's love affair. He was
25 now about twenty-three years old, and, though still virgin, the sex
instinct that Miriam had over refined for so long now grew particularly strong. Often, as he talked to Clara Dawes, came that
thickening and quickening of his blood, that peculiar concentration
in the breast, as if something were alive there, a new self or a new
30 centre of consciousness, warning him that sooner or later he would
have to ask one woman or another. But he belonged to Miriam. Of
that she was so fixedly sure, that he allowed her right.*

9 780521 013062